LIFE AFTER HUMANITY

Thorns and Fangs, Book Three

Gillian St. Kevern

Ben is a recovering vampire determined to pick up the pieces of the life that came to a halt when he was murdered over a year ago—even if that means distancing himself from his few remaining friends. Nate, struggling to navigate his new identity as a Class 3 Unknown paranormal, knows it will take more than mastery of his affinity with plants to convince Ben they belong together.

When Ben's application for human status is denied, he must fight to leave the paranormal world behind him while Nate's generous impulses drag him into conflict with a werewolf pack with designs on ruling New Camden. As Ben's vampire family draws closer to finding him, his vampire instinct awakens—throwing his continued existence into jeopardy. The hunt for the missing werewolf continues, and Nate and Ben become pawns in Councilor Wisner's plans to take control of the city. Their only hope is each other—if they can see that before all is lost.

A NineStar Press Publication

Published by NineStar Press
P.O. Box 91792,
Albuquerque, New Mexico, 87199 USA.
www.ninestarpress.com

Life After Humanity

ISBN: 978-1-947904-87-3

Printed in the USA
First Edition
January, 2018

Also available in eBook, ISBN: 978-1-947904-80-4

To Sarah, Stuart, Rose, and Mac, for giving me a place to stay while I was writing.

Acknowledgements

As always, this story wouldn't have been possible without support from Sera, Julia, Zenia, Melissa, and Claire. Thank you so much for your friendship, your encouragement and your patience.

Chapter One

SOMEONE HAD BROKEN in.

Ben stood in the doorway of his New Camden apartment. The door swung open at his touch, even before he'd fished his key out of his pocket. Beneath his feet, the protective wards laid around the apartment throbbed like an open wound. Someone had forced their way past Ben's carefully laid defenses—someone who was still there.

Damnit. Ben set his briefcase down noiselessly beside the door. *Just one day. One day without anything supernatural happening. Is that too much to ask?*

He didn't move, using his senses to probe the darkness beyond the door. *Vampire—or werewolf?* He hadn't felt any interference with his wards until he'd reached his apartment. That ruled out a magical practitioner or any lesser supernatural being that would have needed to unpick the spell piece by piece. *Please, not another demon.* None of the boxes dotted around the living room were big enough to hide an intruder. Unless they crouched behind the sofa or pressed against the wall in the shadows, they weren't in the living room.

Keeping his attention focused on the apartment, Ben fished for his umbrella stand and the cane leaning against its back. It looked benign, as if it had been forgotten by an elderly visitor, but when Ben twisted the handle, he released the long blade hidden within.

Not Ben's first choice of weapon—the blade was too long and too dainty—but it was a weapon, able to stand up to vampire or demon. *If this is a werewolf, I am in serious trouble.* The stale air of his apartment lacked the distinctive ripe odor of werewolf. Still, Ben couldn't rule it out.

Why would a werewolf break into my apartment? True, Ben had a past as a supernatural investigator for ARX and had killed a few werewolves in his time—but that was the past. There was nothing linking his life now to ARX—was there?

Ben slipped noiselessly into the dimly lit living room, heading for the sofa. Nothing there—or in the shadows. He scanned the room, but everything looked as it had that afternoon when he'd stepped out to meet his accountant. *All I did was my taxes! Where's the harm in that?*

But bringing his financial records up-to-date for the year he'd been dead had taken all of the afternoon. Ample time for whoever it was to find a hiding place. Ben stood motionless in the living room, straining with his senses for any clue to the intruder.

The open doors of his apartment were in deeper shadow than the rest of the living room. Reaching for the light switch was tempting, but Ben's eyes were now accustomed to the dark. Readjusting would cost seconds he wasn't sure he had. His eyes fell on the stacks of paper on his living room table.

At first glance they seemed undisturbed, but a closer look revealed a few papers had drifted to the side. *Disturbed by a breeze?* Ben turned to the kitchen door. A sliver of light was just visible through the crack beneath.

A trap. There was nothing of interest to any supernatural being in the kitchen, so it would be the last place he searched. His guard down, his senses dull, he'd be unprepared for whatever waited beyond. Or—Ben frowned as he approached the door—was there another explanation?

A faint sizzling sound emanated from beyond the door, followed by the heavy smell of garlic.

Ben's nose twitched. A werewolf would not cook an enemy dinner. A demon wouldn't know how. A vampire might—but a vampire would not use garlic.

I've got a bad feeling about this. Taking a deep breath, Ben slowly levered the handle down and let the door drift open. His fear was confirmed.

Nate stood at the counter, his back to the door. The strength implicit in his broad shoulders and muscular arms was softened—but not disguised—by the domesticity of his actions. As Ben watched, Nate lay down the knife and used the chopping board to slide his neatly diced peppers into the frying pan. At his elbow a pot boiled merrily.

Far more dangerous than any werewolf. Ben swallowed, finding it hard to speak. He felt as if he were caught in a spell, unable to do anything but watch.

Absorbed in his task, Nate seemed unaware of Ben's presence. He was dressed down, wearing a faded T-shirt that hugged his torso. The edges of his jeans were frayed, hanging down over his bare feet. His hair hadn't been styled, and it curled up at the base of his neck. Finished adding the mushrooms to the pan, he stirred its contents and then stretched out a hand to the basil growing in a pot on the windowsill. The window reflected his smile, inward and alarmingly personal.

Ben swallowed. Nate had broken in—so why did he feel like the intruder?

Dangerous. Ben dug his fingers into his arm. *Focus!* Casual worked annoyingly well for Nate, made more effective by the knowledge that Nate made a point of looking good. There were few people who got to see Nate dressed down. But Ben couldn't think about that, or how right Nate looked in his kitchen. He had to get Nate out of his apartment before it was too late.

"What happened to seeing less of each other?"

Nate started, snatching his hand back from the basil. He turned, and Ben's initial flash of triumph gave way to alarm. Nate's eyes were a great weapon. Hazel and framed by dark, almost decadently soft lashes, they radiated whatever Nate felt with an immediacy that was hard to resist.

"Jesus, Ben! You scared the shit out of me—" He came to a halt. "Is that a sword?"

Ben looked down at the blade in his hand. It wouldn't help him now. "It's a family heirloom. Used to be my grandfather's." He turned back toward the front door.

"And you just keep it there by the door?" Nate followed Ben to the kitchen door to watch.

"In case of intruders." Ben sheathed the sword and dropped the cane back in the stand. He shut the door. His heart raced. Ben took a moment to summon all his anger. *I was this close to a day without anything supernatural happening!* "You'd better have a good reason for breaking into my apartment."

"I do." Nate stood in the kitchen doorway, one hand resting against the frame.

"Let's hear it then."

"I had a bad feeling this afternoon. A premonition."

Not this again! "It wasn't a premonition."

"It felt really real. I was just watching TV and all of a sudden, these words popped into my mind. You were gone and I wasn't going to see you again. It really freaked me out."

"Enough to add breaking and entering to your criminal file?"

Nate radiated hurt. He wrapped his arms around himself. "I had to see you. No one answered the door, so I tried calling. When it had been a couple of hours and you hadn't answered your phone, I—well, I got worried."

"And that's when you broke in?" Ben pulled his phone out of his pocket, tapping in his pin.

"That was an accident. I had my hand on the door, and I was thinking about how much I wanted to be on the other side, and the door just...relaxed."

Eight missed calls... Ben jerked his head up. "Relaxed?"

"I tried the handle and it opened." Nate's eyes settled anxiously on Ben's. "Did I break anything?"

Ben looked down at the welcome mat beneath his feet. He didn't need to lift it to know what he would find. His runes, intact but faintly smudged. "Only the natural laws regarding the magical properties of runes."

Nate scratched the back of his neck. He dropped his gaze, shuffling his feet, but was unable to keep from looking up to check Ben's expression. "Are you mad?"

Embarrassment looked wrong on Nate. Ben was reminded of a dog caught doing something he knew he shouldn't be—and felt the tight knot of anger in his stomach undo. *Curse him!* If Ben was going to get out of this encounter unscathed he needed his anger. "Of course I'm mad. My apartment is *my* place. Coming home to find someone's forced their way in is...not good." Not good? That wasn't going to convince anyone—least of all anyone with Nate's perceptive nature.

It was hard to read Nate's expression. "I made dinner. As an apology."

At least he realized he needed to apologize— *No! I have to be firm.* "I think your apology is burning."

"Shit!" Nate ducked back through the doorway to attend to the frying pan.

Ben took the opportunity to escape.

WHAT IS WRONG with me? Ben leaned against his bathroom counter, letting the cold marble soothe his racing thoughts. The locked bathroom door wasn't much of a defense—not if what Nate had said about the door opening for him was true. *How does that even work? His powers are related to plants...* Ben's eyes widened. *The wooden door?* He hadn't thought about it, but if Nate could command dead wood as well as living—

I'm not thinking about this. Ben pulled his attention firmly back to the present. He took a deep breath, letting it out slowly, purposefully calming his racing thoughts. *Think ordinary thoughts. Human thoughts.*

His cheeks felt hot. Ben glanced in the mirror and discovered he had color in his face. For once, he looked normal.

Damnit, Nate! Ben splashed water on his cheeks.

It wasn't fair. He could go days without feeling anything—not anger, not joy, not even hunger. But five minutes with Nate and his body raced with conflicting emotions. *This is the most human I've felt all week—and it's because of Nate.*

Ben caught his lip between his teeth. It would be easy—very easy—to lean on Nate's strength, let himself be caught up in the maelstrom of feeling Nate produced.

No. I have to do this myself. Ben roughly toweled his face dry.

"Hey, Ben?" Nate's voice sounded outside the door. "You want to eat in the dining room or the kitchen?"

The thought of the long living room table surrounded by unpacked boxes did not appeal, but the intimacy of the tiny kitchen table was too great a risk coupled with Nate's familiarity. "The dining room."

Nate still hesitated. "The table's got all your papers on it."

"Leave them," Ben said immediately. "I'll clear a space."

Not until he heard Nate's footsteps depart did Ben realize what a mistake he'd made. *Stupid!* He'd agreed to dinner—accepting Nate's apology at the same time.

Every time I give in, it gets harder to say no. Ben gave his reflection a critical glance. He was still more flushed than he was comfortable with, but it would have to do. He couldn't risk Nate making himself any more at home.

His briefcase was still by the door. Ben set it on the table, quickly stacking the papers on the table and placing them out of sight within the case. Luckily, anticipating a long wait in his accountant's office, he'd taken his application for humanity with him. If Nate had seen it...

Hold on to that thought. Ben snapped the briefcase shut. *This is an intrusion.*

"Sorry about that. I didn't want to put you out." Nate reappeared. He had a steaming plate in either hand.

"Then maybe you shouldn't have broken into my apartment." Ben kept his voice firm. He'd given way enough for one evening. He deliberately set down two place mats on opposite sides of the wide table.

"I haven't told you the whole story." Nate set the plates down and went back for cutlery. "Right after the premonition—"

"It wasn't a premonition." Ben sat.

"Weird feeling then." Nate handed him a knife and fork, before walking back the length of the table to his own place. "Ethan called."

Ben raised an eyebrow. "I can see why that would be unsettling." Ethan was Nate's notoriously antisocial twin brother.

"Hey." Nate frowned at Ben even as his mouth twisted in amusement. "Ethan can use a phone when he wants."

"He just doesn't want to very often?" Unlike Nate, a confirmed people person, Ethan could go hours without saying more than a couple of words. He was happiest working in his orchard alone with his plants.

"Yeah." Nate's grin faded. "He had news. Someone came to the farm last night. Someone—off." Nate glanced at Ben. "I think it was Hunter."

A cold jolt shot through Ben's entire body. His heart began to thump again, not with the heat of awareness of Nate's presence, but a cold stab of fear. He couldn't be found by his vampire family. Not now. "What makes you think that?"

"The description matches. The guy had a nice car and clothes, and black hair. He asked about you."

Ben forced his throat muscles to relax. "What did Ethan tell him?"

"Nothing." Nate raised a hand, his fingers grasping for the right word. "He said the guy felt—rotten. He didn't like him. He told him to leave."

"Your brother always did have a talent for hospitality." Ben pinched the bridge of his nose. "How did he trace me? Did you—"

"The only one who knows where we were is Aki," Nate said. "And he doesn't know exactly where. I don't give my address out to anyone."

At least Nate had that much sense. Aki was not Nate's best friend based on his ability to keep his mouth shut. "The police. The sheriff's department in Little River had my ARX record. So did the team from

Chinquapin. If they'd requested confirmation from ARX, that would be logged. Hunter must have seen my name in the records and decided to look into it."

"You think that's all it is?" Nate pushed the pasta around on his plate. "You don't think he's investigating us?"

Ben couldn't blame Nate for being alarmed. His family farm in Little River hid a big secret. "His main priority will be finding me. He knows you're not what you seem, but currently he'll be more concerned with locating us than spending time uncovering your secrets—and it would take more than one night to work out you and Ethan."

Nate's smile was faint. "I don't like this. What's to say he won't come back? Or worse—come here?"

"That's a possibility I'm prepared for." Ben glanced toward the front door. "I've been working on a systematic upgrade of my wards. No way Hunter is getting past them."

Nate turned his head to look. "I haven't—screwed that up?"

"If anything, you've alerted me to a possible security issue." Figuring out how Nate had breached his wards would help Ben make them stronger. "Not that I want you to make a habit of breaking in."

Nate shook his head. "It was just Ethan's call coming straight after my—weird feeling." He looked at Ben. "You're sure what I felt wasn't...anything more?"

"Positive," Ben said promptly. Better to nip this in the bud. "Real premonitions are incredibly rare, even among people with a proven record of psychic sensitivity. You have the magical sensitivity of a log."

"Hey!"

Ben nudged Nate's leg beneath the table. "You spent three days living in Gunn's bathtub without any idea the guy was a *lemur*."

"To be fair, I was more concerned by the guy's complete lack of any housekeeping skills." Nate paused. "You're sure—what am I saying? Of course you're sure." He picked up his knife and fork, digging into his meal.

Ben watched him eat. Nate's complete confidence in his statements was unnerving—but at the same time, it eased some of the disquiet he felt. He picked up his own fork.

The silence between them grew. *Good.* The added distance would help. Ben applied himself to his meal. Nate had made spaghetti with a meat sauce. Ben carefully separated his noodles from the sauce before eating the pasta one at a time.

Nate finished his meal well before Ben. He looked around the apartment. "You still haven't unpacked?"

"I'm working on it." The remark was defensive, and Ben immediately regretted it. "I'm taking my time, making up a list of everything. For the insurance."

"That makes sense, I guess." Nate continued to look around. "What about that painting? You going to put it up?"

Ben felt heat rush to his cheeks. *How does Nate always know?* He'd unpacked the painting, determined to hang it up and make his apartment look more like someone lived there. Instead, he'd been paralyzed, unable to make the decision of where to place it. After two hours second-guessing himself, he'd left the painting leaning against the wall. "When I decide where to put it. I don't want to leave a bunch of holes in the wall."

Nate glanced at him. "I wondered if maybe you were having trouble adjusting to living here."

Ben felt his heart start to beat with an awareness of danger. "Trouble?"

"The same way you're having trouble adjusting to not being a vampire anymore."

Ben put down his fork. "I'm not having trouble." The words were harsher than he'd intended, but it was too late to take them back. "I hated being a vampire. Loathed every second of it. I don't miss it!" He caught his breath.

Nate's gaze was steady, and he met Ben's eyes with concern. "I never said you did. It's just... It's been weeks and you're still living out of boxes. You don't go out, except on business, and a lot of the time...you don't go out at all."

Ben swallowed. "You've been watching me?"

"Not like that. But Aki and I... Well, we're worried about you, right? So we notice things."

"You don't need to worry. I'm doing fine." Ben kept his tone firm. "You've got to remember you and Aki might be extroverts, but I'm not. I like being on my own—living my new life the way I want to."

"You sure living's the right word?"

Ben narrowed his eyes. "What do you mean?"

Nate nodded toward the kitchen door. "Your cupboards."

"What's wrong with my cupboards?"

"You tell me."

Ben shot Nate a glance, but it was impossible to read his thoughts. "All right." He went to the kitchen, opening the pantry. The shelves held a neat stack of packets of candles, bulbs of garlic in a net, and a bulk bag of salt. "It looks fine. Everything's tidy. A bit empty perhaps, but I am the only person living in this apartment."

"Nothing's missing?" Nate had followed him as far as the kitchen doorway.

Ben shook his head. "I've got all the basics of spell craft covered."

"And the basics of living? You know, like food?" Nate waved toward the pantry. "Unless you plan to subsist entirely on garlic, in which case we're gonna need to talk about that."

Ben snapped his head back to stare at his pantry. He felt his cheeks heat. *I never even thought of that.* "I—"

"While I was waiting for you to come back, I took a look at your fridge." Nate waved his hand toward it. "Looked like you were getting low on supplies. So I went out and got you a few things."

Ben opened the fridge. He saw a loaf of bread, a carton of eggs, a carton of milk, and a plastic container holding what remained of their dinner.

"I know your tastes are pretty simple, so I didn't want to get too much." Nate scratched the back of his neck. "I figured I'd stick with toast and things you could have with it."

Ben stared wordlessly at the loaf of bread. It was a little alarming to discover just how well Nate knew him. "Thanks. I—appreciate this." He turned his head back to look at Nate. "Did you break into my apartment, go out for groceries, and come back?"

Nate squirmed. "Maybe?"

Ben shut the fridge door and leaned against it. "You realize that's not exactly ordinary behavior either."

"Yeah, well." Nate scowled. "I'm not trying to be ordinary, am I?"

Have I touched a nerve? Ben fought the impulse to apologize. *This is good.* Even if it felt wrong. "You're finally working on your supernatural abilities?"

"Yeah. Matter of fact, I've got something to show you. Come see." Nate led the way through the apartment to Ben's bedroom.

Bad idea. Ben couldn't help the jolt of interest that went through him at the memory of lying tangled with Nate in the sheets of his bed. He quickened his pace. "We're not—"

Nate had pulled the window up and sat perched on the windowsill, his legs resting on the fire escape outside. "We're not?" he prompted, voice deliberately innocent.

As if he doesn't know. Ben narrowed his eyes. He was not going to play those games. Nate always won. "What is this 'something' you want to show me?"

The fire escape creaked as Nate slid onto it. "Out here."

Ben leaned out the open window. He breathed in the New Camden night. The familiar smell of burnt rubber and rust met his nose. In the street beneath them, a steady stream of cars passed despite the lateness of the hour.

Ben frowned as his nose caught a smell he associated with Nate—the earthy smell of growing things. His eyes picked out dark shapes that rustled in the slight breeze. "Plants on the fire escape? I'm pretty sure that's a hazard."

"Relax, Mr. Landlord." Nate had descended the stairs to the platform halfway between his room and Ben's. "They're not in anyone's way. Turn the light on?"

Ben did as he was told. The light illuminated a collection of house plants. Hanging out with Nate had done wonders for Ben's plant knowledge. He thought he recognized a few of them. "You'll have to move these before the next safety inspection."

"Don't worry about that now." Nate put his hands in the pocket of his jeans. "Watch the morning glory."

Which was the morning glory? Ben frowned at the pots, and then he realized—one of the vines was moving. It was twined around the railing, with broad leaves and tightly wound dark-blue buds. As Ben watched, the buds unfolded into rich blue flowers, their perfume adding a sweet note to the night air. "You're doing that?"

"Cool, right?" Nate grinned. "And no hands."

Ben's head jerked up, and quickly back to the plants. Nate's eyes were flushed with pleasure, and his grin said only too clearly how pleased he was with himself. Ben's heart lurched. "Impressive." He hesitated. From being entirely ignorant of his powers, to refining his use of them in less than a month... It was an achievement for anyone, especially for Nate, who had resisted his supernatural abilities for most of his life. "You've come a long way, Nate."

"Not bad for a guy who doesn't even know what he is." The fire escape creaked again as Nate shuffled. "Actually... I was thinking of celebrating my progress by going out for dinner. You want to come?"

Ben drew a deep breath. *There it is.* The moment he'd been dreading. "A date?"

"Not necessarily." Nate's shoulders hunched. The shadows hid his face, but Ben had too good an idea of his expression. "I mean, we're friends, right? And friends do things together."

Ben clenched the windowsill. "I don't think it's a good idea."

"Why not? We're important to each other, so why pretend otherwise? Not seeing each other is—well, it's stupid. What are you afraid of? Getting involved? We're already involved."

Ben's mouth twisted. That boat had long sailed. "It's not that."

"So what is it?" Nate ran a hand through his hair. "We decided we needed time to get ourselves together, right? And in that time, I haven't seen you at all."

"I'm working on things."

"Are you? Because it feels like—" Nate caught himself with a rapid intake of breath.

Ben's hands tightened on the railing. "Like I'm avoiding you?"

The railing creaked as Nate leaned heavily against it. "I wasn't going to say that. I don't want to pressure you. But at the same time—"

"You can't help feeling what you feel." Ben breathed out. He'd been so focused on the end goal of their separation that he hadn't stopped to think how Nate might take it.

"When I don't hear anything from you, it's really easy to worry. I'm not asking much. Just—an update every now and then."

"An update." Ben wrapped his arms around himself.

"So I know you haven't forgotten me."

It was impossible to think of forgetting Nate. Might as well talk about forgetting a hurricane! He'd waltzed into Ben's life, turning it upside down, leaving Ben reeling from the sheer force of his personality. "I'm not going to forget you. As a matter of fact, I've been thinking a lot about us." He took a deep breath, gripping the windowsill. "I'm lodging an application for humanity."

Anyone else would have laughed. Nate climbed the stairs to get a better view of Ben's expression. "For humanity? You mean—being human?"

Ben's heart thumped again as he nodded. "I want my supernatural status overturned and to be recognized as human."

"Seriously?" Nate frowned at him. "Why is there even an application for that? You're the most human person I know."

It was patently untrue. Only Nate would have the nerve to lie so badly. Looking up, Ben caught Nate's gaze and swallowed. *He can't—he doesn't believe that?* "Vampires don't stop being vampires. This isn't supposed to happen. I should be dead. Not moving back into my childhood home."

"So they still want to treat you like a vampire? That's ridiculous! What do they think you're going to do—drink blood?" Nate thumped his hand against the railing. "Department Seven cleared you. Pulse, no aversion to crosses, garlic—hell, you walk around in daylight—"

Ben smiled faintly. Nate's belief was somehow welcome. "I'm still on the supernatural register as a vampire."

"But you're obviously not a vampire."

"Right. But the supernatural listing means I'm subject to ARX attention. As long as Saltaire thought I was dead, I was safe. But now Hunter's looking for me, I need to get declassified as soon as possible."

"Shit." Nate straightened. "I didn't even think of that."

Ben smiled thinly. "I've got some time. Saltaire's out of the country. I just have to make sure my application's approved before he comes back—or before Hunter finds me."

"But will your legal status really deter Saltaire? I mean—well, he is a megavampire, right? And he's already tried to kill you once. Will a bit of red tape really stop him?"

Megavampire? Ben decided it was better to leave Nate's appalling ignorance of the supernatural for another time. "This particular red tape, yes. Saltaire might be a law unto himself, but he's got a code that he sticks to. Supernatural creatures, other vampires, magic-users, they're all fair game. But he will never kill a human. That's where he draws the line."

"And vampires don't change." Nate twisted one of the morning glory's leaves in his fingers. "What does getting classified as human entail?"

Ben shrugged. "It's hard to say. There's a precedent for getting declassified as a magic-user or occult specialist, but going from something like vampire... As far as I know, I'm the first to apply. I've got all the information they could possibly need. The results of the

Department Seven examination, a medical exam, a letter confirming my identity from my father's lawyer, but I don't know if it'll be enough."

"What more could they ask for?"

Ben took a deep breath. "There's a good chance they'll look into my lifestyle. Including my acquaintances."

Nate went very still. "Meaning me."

"Whether you're Class Three Unknown or Class Five At Risk doesn't make a single bit of difference to me. You're more important to me than anyone else I know," Ben said immediately. "This won't be forever. Just until my application is approved."

"You should have said something. What if I'd bungled in while—I don't know—you were being interviewed or something? I could have ruined everything."

"I was afraid to tell you." Ben leaned against the windowsill. "I didn't want you to be upset. You—being human was such a big part of your identity. Watching me pursue this, knowing you can't—"

"It's a good thing, Ben." Nate's hands were warm on Ben's shoulders. "If it gets Saltaire off your back, a very good thing."

Holding himself apart from that warmth was too hard. Ben gave in, leaning against Nate's chest. "You're sure?"

"Totally." Nate's arms settled around him. "No one deserves a break more than you, Ben. After all the crap you've been through, there's no way I'd hold this against you."

Ben breathed out. Hearing Nate say the words made him realize just how much he'd feared his reaction. "That means a lot."

"Hang on a second." Nate turned down the fire escape. "I've got something for you."

"For me?" Ben stayed where he was. He heard the scrape as Nate opened his own window and climbed through it.

Nate's voice floated back to him. "It's not much. Sort of a—good luck charm."

"I wasn't aware your talents extended to luck. Or is this like your premonitions?"

"Careful, or I might decide to keep it." The fire escape announced Nate's return. He held out his hand to Ben. "Here. I was planning to put it on a piece of leather, so you could wear it if you wanted."

It was an acorn, plump and glossy in Nate's hand. Ben took it, relishing the smoothness of the seed. "An acorn?"

"It's small, but it's strong—strong enough to become an oak." Nate glanced at him. "It's from the tree in Mason's Park."

Ben's head snapped up. "Where you got murdered?" He didn't think he'd ever forget the horror of finding Nate's dead body beneath the oak. "You went back there? Why?" That was the last place Ben wanted to go.

"That tree kept us safe from the revenants. And it's where I figured out how to find you again and where you found me. It reminds me, even when the worst happens, we can—and have—overcome it."

Finding strength in his own death? Ben caught his breath. Once again, Nate had taken him entirely unaware. "I'd never thought of it like that."

"I usually keep it in my pocket. If I'm having a bad day, or something happens, it's a good reminder of my own strength."

"This is yours? Nate, I can't take this—"

"I want you to have it. If I can't be around to remind you how strong you are, then this is a good reminder."

Ben's hand tightened around the acorn. "It won't be forever. Just until I get declassified."

"I know." Nate placed his hand over Ben's. "Until then." He leaned in.

I shouldn't do this. Ben's body tugged toward Nate, as if they were magnetically charged. He braced himself, but the touch of Nate's mouth on his was still a shock. Nate was electric, the contact between them sending a buzz through Ben's entire body. And weakened by days without any contact at all, Ben responded to it greedily. He tangled his fingers into the cloth of Nate's T-shirt, holding him close as he sank into the kiss.

Nate hummed, a satisfied sound that rippled through Ben. How dare he sound so pleased with himself? Ben squeezed Nate's arm in warning, as he fought for control of the kiss. It didn't matter what he did. Nate was a master at this, and Ben's heart pounded with awareness of how neatly he was trapped. And with Nate's smooth lips trapping his tongue, his earthy scent mingling with the morning glory in every breath Ben took, he didn't care—

He surged toward Nate, needing to feel more of him and collided with the edge of the ledge. Ben jerked back in pain. The arm not holding the acorn was still tangled around Nate's shoulders—*I don't even remember when that happened*—and Nate's arms wrapped around his back. Ben took a deep breath.

And stepped back.

Nate let go as he did, straightening. The light from Ben's bedroom caught his lips, made them shine. His eyes were almost completely dark. His cheeks were flushed, and it took him a moment to get his breathing under control.

Ben's own chest rose and fell rapidly. He sucked in a breath, aware of just how close he'd come to succumbing to Nate's charm. A part of him cried out to be trapped again. "Good night, Nate." Oh fuck. He sounded shaky—far too breathless.

Nate's mouth curved in amusement. "Night, Ben." He turned, making his way down the fire escape. As he reached the platform beside his window, his voice floated back to Ben. "Don't be a stranger." His window clicked shut behind him.

Ben breathed out. He pulled the window of his room down. "Dangerous." Every second he spent around Nate, the man got further beneath his skin.

And is that so bad? Ben tried to stamp down on the thought, but it persisted. *He saved your life. Really cares about you. Wants what's best for you—*

But that was the problem. Ben took a deep breath. He didn't know who he was. He had to figure that out first. Otherwise, he'd end up influenced by Nate."

Is that such a bad thing?

Ben's grip on the acorn tightened. Their relationship was too important to end up tainted, like... He swallowed. Thinking of his vampire family was always hard. He'd trusted them. Believed them. Really thought he was doing what he wanted... And now, he could never be sure just how far he'd been influenced.

Nate's not Saltaire—or Hunter. He's not even a vampire.

He was unknown. Ben put the acorn in his pocket and pulled the curtains firmly shut. No. It had to be this way.

Chapter Two

"So. Did breaking into his apartment impress Ben with your strength of character or are you looking at a restraining order?"

Nate jolted back to his surroundings. He was standing in the center of the jogging track that looped around Mason's Park, and judging from the dirty looks passing joggers sent him, he'd been there some time. In front of him stood Aki, Nate's best friend and roommate, his hands on hips, drumming one foot against the path.

"I wasn't doing it to impress him." Nate resumed their jog.

Aki easily fell into pace beside him. "Didn't work then. Why am I not surprised?"

"I had to talk to him about something serious."

"Uh-huh." Aki darted ahead, turning around to jog backward, so he could watch Nate's expression. "Talk me through this. I want to know all about last night."

"You're going to collide with someone. Or fall."

"Come on, Nate. Give me the play-by-play. You forced your way into his apartment and somehow he didn't call the cops." Aki was unrelenting. "I don't know which one of you is more at fault here."

"I needed to see him. And I did have news he needed to hear." Nate grabbed Aki's arm. "Corner."

Aki slowed to a halt. "I can't tell if this is a new level of desperation, or you've chosen the worst possible way to finally develop a spine."

Nate squeezed Aki's arm. "I'm not spineless. You remember when I took on a necromancer?"

"Accidentally. And you weren't trying to date the necromancer."

"Still."

Aki shook his head. "Doesn't count. Or do I have to remind you how long you held a torch for the demon who tried to kill you?"

Nate winced. He didn't bother pointing out that it hadn't been the demon he'd had feelings for, but the demon's agent. It made no difference. Since their very first meeting, the guy had been bad for Nate. *And everyone saw it but me.*

The jogging track turned onto the square at the main entrance to Founder's Park. Even midmorning on a weekday, the square was busy with people sitting on benches around the ornamental fountain. A food truck parked beside the entrance was in the process of setting up.

Aki headed toward a clear patch of the square, starting his post-run routine of stretches. "When it comes to Ben, you're a complete pushover. The guy is obviously avoiding you, and instead of calling him on it or accepting his disinterest and getting a new hook-up, you pine."

"Geez, Aki. You make it sound like I've done nothing but mope." Nate copied Aki's movements, standing one-legged to pull his foot toward his back.

Aki rolled his eyes. "Right. I forgot. You've been taking your plant obsession to new levels."

Nate switched legs. "Exploring my powers is an important part of accepting who I am as a supernatural. If I want to get stronger and protect myself against supernatural threats, I need to know how to use what I've got."

Aki paused, rotating his shoulders to tilt his head at Nate. "Protecting yourself against supernatural threat—or protecting Ben?"

Nate stiffened. "Not everything I do revolves around other people."

"You really expect me to believe that your sudden willingness to embrace the supernatural aspects you've spent your entire life denying has nothing to do with the vampire upstairs?"

"He's not a vampire. And—well, what happened with Sandy was a huge wake-up call." Nate rubbed his shoulder. "I realized that ignorance isn't any protection against the supernatural. I know I'm not going to please everyone—and I'm cool with that."

"Uh-huh." Aki narrowed his eyes. "If you're so down with your supernatural self, you'll have no problems telling me what you are."

Damnit. "Aki. We've been over this. It's not that I don't want to tell you—it's that I don't know. There's not exactly a dictionary definition of it."

"Dryad?"

"Dryads are girls." Nate ran his hand through his hair. "Look. You know about my powers and that I'm unknown. If I could tell you more, I would."

"When you're ready to admit that you're a dryad, I'll be right here. Until then, you're proving my point."

"I'm proving nothing. It's not my secret to tell, Aki. If it was, you'd be the first to know." Nate made his way toward the drinking fountain.

Aki followed. "Okay. Even accepting that you *can't* tell me the truth about being a dryad, when was the last time you did something purely because you wanted to?"

Nate raised his head from the fountain. "Right now. I'm going jogging with my friend."

"Going for the brownie points, huh? But tell me honestly—you ever go jogging without me?" Aki folded his arms and waited.

"I—" Nate's brain stalled. The stream of water from the drinking fountain hit him on the chin. Nate stepped back, wiping water off himself.

"Point proved." Aki smirked, stepping forward to use the fountain.

"It's more fun jogging with you," Nate protested.

"Despite the fact that as soon as I finish my warm-up, we're travelling at two different speeds?"

"Yeah." Nate wrung his T-shirt out and smoothed it down. "I enjoy talking with you. Like this."

Aki snorted but didn't quite manage to hide his smile. "Clumsy—but flattery will get you everywhere."

The smell of cooking meat floated across the square. Nate looked to where the sausages were frying on the food truck grill. "Will it get me a hot dog? 'Cause I am starving."

Aki turned to consider the truck. "You can't pretend you forgot your wallet. Not when our wristbands come with a payment system."

"I kind of used the last of my money on groceries yesterday."

"But you went shopping on Saturday."

Nate scratched the back of his neck. "Groceries for Ben."

There was a long silence.

Aki sighed. "This is exactly what I'm talking about. Mustard or ketchup?"

"Sauerkraut and cheese."

"At least your choice in hot dog condiments isn't intended to impress anyone. Gross."

Nate claimed an empty bench in the sun. A breeze lifted the hair at the back of his neck, and he shut his eyes. He'd always liked the sun. As a kid, he'd loved finding a sun-speckled patch beneath the apple trees in the orchard to sit and pretend the rustling he heard was the wind rustling through his own leaves. Now, he didn't have to imagine how sunlight felt to a tree. He knew.

"Here." Aki had returned holding two cardboard containers. "One disgusting travesty of a hot dog for you, and a delicious chili dog with extra cheese for me. You can beg all you want, but you're not getting a bite of mine."

"Thanks, Aki." Nate took the hot dog, immediately taking a big bite.

Aki shook his head as he sat on the bench. "I don't know why I bother."

"Rye et." Nate swallowed and made a second attempt. "Try it. It's really good—"

"I was talking about you spending your last dime on shopping for a guy who hasn't called you in over a week." Aki took a neat bite out of his hot dog. "I hope I don't need to tell you how dumb that is."

"It's not dumb. He needed groceries."

"Ben needs a lot of things, but I wouldn't put groceries at the top of the list." Aki pursed his lips. "You're going about this all wrong."

"So what do you suggest I do? I can't drag him out of his apartment and make him have fun."

"Sure about that? The guy's been surrounded by alpha werewolves, master vampires, and supernatural hunters. Strength. He doesn't need a personal shopper. He needs someone who is going to take charge. Not someone whose impulsive need to take care of people continually gets him in trouble."

Nate hunched his shoulders. "There's nothing wrong with being generous."

"There's a fine line between generous and pushover." Aki paused to pick an onion out of his hot dog and flick it to the ground. "You've got to put your foot down somewhere."

His action caught the attention of a dog. It slunk up to them, a shaggy dog, dirty with tangled gray fur. It gobbled up the onion and looked up at the two of them. It wagged its tail hopefully.

"Go away." Aki stood, waving his hand at the dog. "Scram—Nate! Don't encourage it!"

Nate threw the dog a chunk of hot dog. It gobbled it up at once. "Look how skinny it is. Poor thing's probably starving."

"It's a walking flea factory. Ignore it." Aki sat down, taking another bite of his hot dog. "What you want to do is take a leaf out of my book. Be more selfish."

Nate raised an eyebrow. "That really a good thing?"

"Where you're concerned? Yeah." Aki nodded. "I'm up front about what I want—and I generally get it."

Nate made a noncommittal noise around another bite of hot dog. Aki's opinionated statements did not get him a huge amount of fans, and his dating history consisted of a string of one-night stands that never turned into anything more. He looked up—and met the pleading eyes of the dog.

"If you don't put yourself first, who will? New Camden is no place for the weak."

Nate jerked his gaze away from the dog to frown at Aki. "Being strong isn't the same as being selfish."

Aki delicately sucked a dash of sauce off his finger. "Yeah? How strong can you be when you've stretched yourself thin worrying about everyone except yourself?"

Nate looked down. "If you're strong enough, you can handle that."

The tawny eyes of the dog intruded into his vision. He tossed it the rest of the hot dog.

"That's not strong. That's—Nate! Seriously, what did I tell you?"

The dog gulped down the remainder of Nate's hot dog in one bite. He nosed the ground, checking that he hadn't missed anything, before looking up, his tail wagging.

"Hope you're not expecting a second hot dog because if this is what you do with them…"

"Look how happy he is." Nate stretched out his hand to the dog. "Here, boy."

"He's happy all right. He's found the easiest mark in New Camden." Aki glared at the dog. "Don't look at me. I'm not a bleeding heart."

"Don't listen to him." Nate stroked the dog's ears. "He's just mad because his last serious boyfriend dumped him over a beagle."

"Shut the fuck up, Nate! That is not what happened."

"Isn't it?" Nate continued to stroke the dog. His fingers encountered something rough. "Look—it's got a collar."

"More fool you, then, for feeding someone else's dog."

"Do you see anyone who looks like its owner?" The dog tried to pull away, but Nate hooked his finger through the collar and held it in place. "Look. It's got weird symbols on it instead of a number."

Aki leaned forward to get a closer look. "You're right. They look almost like runes—fuck!"

The dog made a sudden lunge. Aki jumped back—dropping his hot dog. In an instant it was gone, and the dog was licking its lips with noisy satisfaction.

"You see what comes of being nice?" Aki folded his arms.

Nate released the dog. "He's just a hungry dog. He probably thought you were going to feed him."

"And whose fault is that?" Aki dusted his hands off on his T-shirt. "If you don't learn when to put your foot down, your impulsive generosity is going to get you in big trouble."

"Will you chill? It's just a hot dog." Nate draped an arm around Aki's shoulder. "Soon as I get my next pay check, I'll treat you to another one."

Aki sighed, letting Nate steer him toward the gates. "Will you at least think about what I'm saying?"

"I am thinking about it."

"And?"

"Being generous is just who I am. I can't change that—and if I do, aren't I just doing what you say I shouldn't be doing? Changing to try to make Ben happy?"

Aki frowned, leaning back against Nate. "How do you figure that?"

"If I'm trying to be someone I'm not, I'm not really changing. Just putting on an act. Like you being nice when you meet a hot guy for the first time."

Aki elbowed him. "We're not talking about my love life."

"I'm just saying. When you meet someone new, you pull out all the stops. I've even heard you faking an interest in *Top Gear* for a guy."

"That's just what you do when you meet someone new. You go after them. And then as you get to know them, you care less about impressing them, and the real you comes through. And if you're compatible, they stick around." Aki shrugged. "It's just bad luck that none of the guys I fall for click with me."

"You don't think that maybe they fall for the persona you present and not you?"

"Nate, you're my best friend. You really think anyone would date me knowing my true personality?"

"Why not? I like you."

Aki narrowed his eyes at him. "Yeah. But you're—" He paused. "On second thought, Nate, you're right. Don't change."

ACCEPTING HIS SUPERNATURAL self was one thing, walking into Department Seven was another. The police department dealing with New Camden's supernatural crime was not part of the city police headquarters, or even City Hall. It was tucked down a bystreet, occupying a building that had seen better days as a dental clinic.

Nate hesitated at the door with a feeling of dread very similar to the fear of needing to get a tooth pulled. *What am I afraid of? I've been arrested by them once. What is the worst that could happen?*

The theme of the waiting room was "linoleum of the 1970s." Being uncomfortable and ergonomically impossible did not prevent the rows of plastic chairs from being full. In fact, Department Seven appeared to be standing room only. To reach the front desk, Nate squeezed past a heavyset man with a beard straight out of *Exodus*.

A frazzled-looking woman answered the bell. "The briefing will start once our agents have finished interviewing a witness with knowledge of the missing wolf. I can't say when that will be."

"Uh—what?"

"The rogue werewolf," the woman said. "If you're after information, you'll have to wait like all the rest."

Nate glanced at the crowd. "I'm not here for a briefing."

"You're not?" The woman gave Nate a closer look, her gaze lingering on his chest. She patted her hair absently. "Here to report a supernatural crime?"

"Not that either." Nate stood a little taller.

"I'm afraid that with the missing werewolf being a priority now, all nonessential work like hunting licenses or assessments are on hold."

"I've got an appointment. With a counselor."

The woman looked down at a paper in front of her. "Nathan Granger?"

"Yes, ma'am."

"Take a seat. Well—find somewhere to wait. I'll let Officer Kenzies know you're here."

"Kenzies is my counselor?" But the woman had already stepped through an internal door and vanished into the department.

Nate turned his attention back to the rest of the room. *Is everyone here a supernatural hunter?* It was a very mixed crowd. Predominantly male and indiscriminately fond of khaki, but there was a range of ages, experience, and style. Some, like the man blocking the entrance, Nate could have picked as a hunter—if not necessarily a werewolf hunter—immediately. Others, like the woman in a crisp business suit, he'd never have guessed. And others—

Others he knew very well.

"George? What are you doing here?"

George grinned at him. "I could ask you the same question. Considering a career change?" She wore a headscarf wound tightly around her skull, but a bandage protruding out from under it revealed the burns that she had been lucky to survive.

"Are you even well enough to hunt? Seriously, you only got discharged from hospital—what?" Nate did some mental calculations. "Three days ago?"

"Four. And before you tell me I should wait at least a month before going after a potentially fatal target, I'm here with an ulterior motive." George motioned around her. "These guys don't know it, but I'm auditioning them for the role of being my partner."

Nate followed her gaze. "Makes sense." George's former partner in supernatural bounty hunting had been murdered a few weeks earlier—on Nate's family farm. He cast around for something sympathetic to say.

"You interested? 'Cause for you I might consider a sixty-forty split of the profits."

Nate snorted. "Thanks, but no. I had enough of supernatural investigations being on the receiving end of one."

"Had to try." George shrugged. "And the bounty offered for this wolf is really tempting. Too bad a werewolf's the one thing you never hunt alone."

"Even worse than a vampire?"

"Depends on the vampire." George turned her head toward the door linking the waiting room to the department's inner corridors. "Finally."

The door swung open, and a powerfully built man in a suit emerged, speaking loudly. "—not impressed with the efforts of the investigation so far." His voice was automatically pitched for podiums and his eyes ranged across the room professionally.

"You said. Repeatedly." Even without being close enough to catch the air of stale tobacco and sulfur that hung around Gunn, Nate recognized his voice. No one else could inject three ordinary words with such venom. As he watched, a man with messy brown hair and an air of being a professional loiterer sauntered after the business-suited man. "Kind of hard to investigate a case without being allowed to release any information, Councilor Wisner. The media's perfectly willing to run the story, but if we want the public to help us, they're gonna need a bit more information. The guy's name, for a start."

Wisner frowned, tugging a handkerchief from his pocket. He held it over his nose. "I've made my wishes on that matter perfectly clear. It's up to you to do the rest." He eyed the room with distaste. "The operatives you mentioned?"

"You've barred us enlisting the help of the Magic-Users Guild."

"I will not have them called in for what is pack business."

"But you've got no problems using taxpayers' money to run down your missing puppy."

Wisner's eyes flashed. "The rogue wolf is a danger to the city. His immediate capture is in the best interest of everyone concerned."

"So you say." Gunn raised his voice. "Ladies and, since I'm not allowed to use a more accurate appellation, gentlemen, you can stop cluttering up the waiting room and avail yourself of the briefing room. Form a line. Officer Simeon will take your names and check your license is current."

"That's me." George joined the line of hunters. "Catch you later."

As the hunters filed through the door, Nate made his way toward Gunn. The officer lit a cigarette, pointedly ignoring the ashtray the receptionist thrust at him.

Wisner stood next to him. "I'll be taking the matter of your insubordination up before City Hall. Do you want to have another case of the necromancer on your hands?"

Gunn blew smoke out lazily. "Go ahead. Let's find out what City Hall thinks about your refusal to allow us to take any action that might actually find the wolf."

Wisner growled. The sound was low, fierce—and not at all human. Nate stumbled to a halt.

His clumsy movement caught Wisner's attention. The man jerked his head back. As his eyes fell on Nate, he stiffened. His nostrils flared, and he stared at Nate. His eyes were yellow.

"What are you doing here?" Gunn tapped his cigarette against the front desk. "Please don't tell me you want in on the werewolf."

"I'm here for counseling." Nate was conscious of Wisner's hard stare. "It's one of the conditions of my—"

"Class three status. Gotcha." Gunn motioned toward the door. "In the interrogation room. You remember how to find your way there?"

"I'll work it out." Nate hunched his shoulders. Gunn didn't need to make it sound like he spent regular periods of time being interviewed by the police! Even if he had spent an inordinate amount of time in police company over the last two months...

Officer Simeon, a pale man with a moon-shaped face, gulped as Nate passed, ushering the last of the hunters into the briefing room. The interrogation room was farther down the hall. Even if Nate hadn't remembered where to find it, the notice taped to the door would have given it away: *Counseling Group-At Risk Supernaturals.*

This can't be right. Nate pushed the door open. *I'm not at risk—and no one said anything about a group!*

The room was just as it had been the last time Nate saw it. Table in the center of the room with a water cooler in one corner. Two of the plastic chairs were already occupied. A girl slouched in her seat. Her long brown hair was styled like something from *The Lord of the Rings*. She wore a long-sleeved cardigan and a patchwork skirt and was talking to a scowling guy wearing a fedora. He had his elbows on the table and leaned forward, energetically arguing his point. Nate's confusion increased. Neither of his companions looked like at-risk supernaturals. As he entered the room, they fell silent.

"Hey." Nate fought the urge to wipe his hands on his jeans. "I'm supposedly here for counseling. Am I interrupting?"

"We haven't started yet." The girl motioned to the seat beside her. She sat up straight, and Nate realized she was easily as tall as he was. "Um—"

"Fresh blood." The guy looked at Nate with undisguised interest. "Well, well. What are you then?"

Nate gulped. He'd known he'd have to face these sorts of questions, but he hadn't expected it to be so soon! He took the seat offered, conscious that they were both watching him. "Actually—"

"He's a witch," the girl said. Her face was flushed. "I can sense it. You have a very strong connection to the earth." She wound a thin plait of hair around her finger. "Me, too. Air. I mean—I'm a witch but my strongest connection is to air."

What on earth have I gotten myself into? "I'm a Class Three Unknown, actually."

"Unknown," the guy repeated. "Interesting." His face still wore a scowl, but Nate was beginning to think that was his habitual expression—he didn't sound annoyed. "I too, prefer to remain an enigma. No labels for me."

"Funny." The door had swung open without them noticing, and Kenzies stood in the doorway. She was a short but powerfully built woman with rust-colored red hair and sharp, tawny eyes. She moved extremely lightly for her heavy build. Setting a pile of files down on the table in front of her, she took a seat at the head of the table. "I can think of plenty." She looked across the table. "Pleased you could join us, Nate."

"Happy to be here," Nate mumbled. "But I thought these sessions were one-on-one?"

"Usually they are." Kenzies settled back in her chair with the ease of someone long inured to their discomfort. "But due to a lack of resources, we had to combine them. Hopefully, we'll be back to normal in a few weeks. Until then, it's our hope that the three of you might be able to support each other." She looked at the other two. "You introduced yourselves?"

"Just getting to that," the guy said stiffly. "Greetings, Nate. I am Vazul." He raised his hat.

"And I'm Charlotte." She smiled at him. "It's great to have you here."

Nate ducked his head awkwardly. "It's cool to meet you."

"Now that's done..." Kenzies opened the file in front of her. "Business."

Nate held up his hand. "I've got a question."

"Go for it, blossom." Kenzies grinned at him. There was a disconcerting amount of teeth in her smile.

Werewolf. Right. Nate didn't know why the reminder of Kenzies's animal nature was such a surprise to him. He'd seen her as a wolf. "The sign on the door said 'at risk'?"

"It's a new initiative. Started by Councilor 'Department Seven isn't overworked enough' Wisner." Kenzies rolled her eyes. "Younger supernaturals considered to be at risk of developing dangerous tendencies are closely monitored, introduced to appropriate support networks, and a range of community-focused tasks designed to engender positive self-worth."

Vazul sneered. "In other words, we're to be subjected to arbitrary checkups, forced to account for our time, and made to work as unpaid labor for the good of the city."

Nate studied him. Suddenly the "at risk" part made sense.

"We caught Vazul spray-painting anti-human sentiment onto walls in the city," Kenzies said, answering Nate's unasked question.

"I protest! I was framed—you have no evidence that I was responsible!"

Kenzies ignored him. "Charlotte's here for the indiscriminate use of magic in a public place."

Charlotte frowned. "It wasn't indiscriminate! There was this pigeon with an injured wing. I wanted to help it, but it kept running away. So I—called on a wind to gently lift it to me."

"You need a Class-Five license for any sort of magic in a public place," Kenzies reminded her. "And Nate. You've added to your file since our last meeting."

Nate squirmed. "I don't think we need to go into that."

"You sure? Because I'd really like to know about some of these charges." Kenzies opened a file. Nate could see his name on the cover. "But hey, as long as you haven't put any more trees through any walls, we're moving in the right direction."

"Trees?" Vazul frowned.

"I'm good with plants," Nate said. "Um. Very good, actually."

"Why don't we start with our plant whisperer then. How are things going, Nate?"

Nate tugged at the collar of his T-shirt. "Good? I mean—I'm back at work."

"Participating in social activities with your peers?"

"Uh—I went jogging with Aki this morning if that's what you mean."

Kenzies checked off a box. "Threatened anyone with intentional harm or caused or nearly caused injury, inadvertently or otherwise, to anyone this week?"

Nate stared at her. "No!" Breaking in did not count, right? Because he'd left Ben's apartment in better condition—

"Great." Kenzies closed his file. "Now, Vazul—"

"My affairs are in order, though I would like to register that I resent being forced to report like a common miscreant." Vazul leaned forward.

"Socialized with your peers? Playing World of Warcraft doesn't count."

Vazul scowled. "I don't see why not. No—unless you count attending tutoring sessions with my so-called 'peers.'"

"Caused harm?"

Vazul rolled his eyes. "No—but I have to protest the underlying assumption of your question—"

There was a knock at the door. Officer Simeon stuck his head around the door and gulped.

Kenzies swiveled in her chair to face him. "Kind of in the middle of something. It can't wait?"

Simeon shook his head. His eyes were pale and prominent. As he gazed across the room, he refused to meet anyone's eyes. "The hunters want a werewolf perspective."

Nate stared. It was the first time he'd ever heard Simeon speak, and the sibilant lisp gave him a distinctly uneasy feeling.

"What do they think I am, a performing dog?" Kenzies picked up the files. "Talk among yourselves. You can get started on that group bonding."

As soon as the door closed behind her, Vazul looked at Nate. "How do you put a tree through a wall?"

"There were circumstances, okay?" Nate poked at the surface of the table. He hunched his shoulders, avoiding looking at either of his companions.

"There would have to be. An entire tree?"

"Just the top half." Nate bit his lip. He really didn't want to talk about this. "This werewolf situation's really serious, huh? I heard a bit about it on the news, but turning up, seeing all those hunters... This is a really big deal."

"Don't you believe it." Vazul leaned back in his chair. He folded his arms across his chest. "It's all a contrived spectacle."

"But the werewolf—are you saying there isn't one?"

Charlotte tucked her plait of hair behind her ear. "He's out there all right. But he isn't dangerous." Her eyes darted across the table. "As a matter of fact, he's the third member of this group."

"No way." Nate followed her gaze to the empty chair. "And he's gone rogue?"

Vazul snorted. "Grant's not the type to do something like that. He's the responsible member of the group."

Charlotte nodded. "I think being around Kenzies was hard for him—wolves tend to rub each other the wrong way—but they also got each other in a way the rest of us didn't. He was pretty much the poster child for the success of this program."

"Huh." Nate frowned. "So what happened?"

"Nothing." Vazul slapped the table. "This entire thing is a farce."

Nate remembered the reception area crowded with hunters. "It can't be nothing. Every hunter in the city is out there looking for him!"

"All that happened is that the guy left his house one day and didn't come back. Ludicrous! The guy is a young man in his prime. Of course he is going to go out—"

"He didn't come back? But that's a big deal, isn't it?" Nate was still in trouble for going home after the necromancer attacks and not giving the department his address.

"He didn't get the chance," Charlotte said. "His pack freaked out and the city launched a manhunt—"

"So even if he was planning on coming home, he couldn't—not without being arrested," Vazul finished. "The entire situation is preposterous."

Charlotte nodded eagerly. "Grant suspects it was planned—"

Nate sat up. "Wait. You've talked to him?"

Charlotte and Vazul shared a glance. "At the start," Charlotte said. "Before things spiraled into the mess they are now."

"And we have no idea where he is now." Vazul scowled. "So it's no good getting on your high horse and telling us to come clean. We know nothing that can help the department—not that they're going to be deterred from this counseling farce."

"Are you saying that the counseling is a—" Nate hesitated.

"A front to keep us under observation?" Charlotte picked a piece of fluff off her sleeve. "I thought so—until you showed up."

"The city's on edge since the necromancer attacks," Vazul agreed. "Individual supernatural rights are getting trampled just to make the public feel safe." He slung his satchel onto the table and started digging through it. "I produce a pro-supernatural rights newsletter. My latest editorial—"

Kenzies opened the door. "Sorry, kids. We're going to have to cut this short. My colleagues are apparently unable to deal with such high technology as PowerPoint without me."

Charlotte and Vazul stood, and Nate hastily followed. From their attitudes, he gathered this wasn't an uncommon occurrence.

Kenzies stepped back so they could file out of the doorway past her. "Any news of our mutual friend?"

"None," said Vazul loftily. "And I resent your use of 'our.' You're not Grant's friend."

"Why aren't you looking for him?" Charlotte asked. "As a werewolf, wouldn't that give you an advantage?"

Kenzies smiled grimly. "You'd think so. But Wisner isn't thrilled with the idea of a wolf that is outside his jurisdiction entering his pack's territory."

"Strange," Vazul said. "It's almost like he doesn't want Grant found." He walked away, Charlotte hurrying after him.

Nate hesitated.

Kenzies gave him a brief smile. "That wasn't that bad, was it, petal?"

And I thought it couldn't get any worse than 'blossom.' "I guess not. It wasn't entirely what I was expecting."

"It never is." Kenzies glanced at the files she held. "Next session is the same time next week. See you then—providing you can go a week without incident."

Nate snorted. "You make it sound like I'm some sort of trouble magnet."

Kenzies raised an eyebrow. "Aren't you?"

IT WAS A long walk back to the apartment from Department Seven, but without bus fare, Nate had no other choice. As he approached their building, Nate was still turning over the events of that morning. *Trouble magnet? What is with everyone giving me a hard time today? First Aki, then Kenzies...* "It's not like I actively go looking to endanger myself."

A sudden sound to his right made him jump. Something in the alley beside the apartment block had moved. Nate looked around, but he was the only person in sight.

That's definitely suspicious. Nate climbed back down the stairs. *Smoking's not against the law, so why hide? And if they're not smoking, why would anyone be lurking in an alley next to an apartment block unless they were up to something?*

At first glance, the alley was empty. The dumpster was full and residents had stacked their excess rubbish bags beside it ready for collection. One of the bags had been torn open, its contents strewn across the concrete.

An animal? New Camden's crows were notorious for getting into things. Nate peered down the alley and caught movement in the shadows beyond the sofa that had been sitting there ever since 5-A moved out. "Hey. You again."

The dog from the park raised its ears. He stepped cautiously into the alley, his tail beginning to wag. Evidently, he recognized Nate.

"Looking for a meal, huh? I guess those hot dogs wouldn't feed a dog for long." Nate held out his hand. "Well, I won't tell if you don't."

The dog padded up to him, happily accepting the petting.

Totally someone's pet. Nate bit his lip. His owner clearly cared for the dog—he was too well socialized not to have come from a caring home—but something must have happened for the dog to end up on the street.

Nate remembered Aki's words and straightened. *Not your problem.* Wherever the dog's owner was, they could find him themselves. "Good dog. Hope you find something more appealing than trash."

The dog sat back on his hind legs and looked up at Nate. His tail beat the ground.

Nate shook his head. "Sorry. I'm all out of hot dogs." He turned, climbing the stairs to the automatic doors.

As he keyed in the entry code, Nate became aware of a pressure between his shoulder blades, as if he was being closely observed. He turned.

The dog stood behind him on the stairs. His tail began to work again.

"Oh no." Nate shook his head. "No way. You wouldn't believe the fit Aki would throw—and I'm pretty sure there was a no-pet clause in our lease."

The dog took a step toward him. His yellow eyes, turned pleadingly upon Nate, shone in the dim light.

"I said no, and I meant it." Nate turned, stepping quickly through the door. He pulled it shut behind him before the dog could dart in.

Success!

Nate hit the button for the elevator. *Not quite such a pushover, after all.* Aki would have to eat his words.

The elevator doors opened. Nate stepped in, turning to hit the button for the seventh floor. His eyes met those of the dog, watching him mournfully through the glass door. His tail, his ears—everything about the dog—drooped.

Nate wavered.

Chapter Three

THE REGISTRY WAS located in a stone building, built in Neo-Gothic style. Dwarfed by surrounding skyscrapers, the building was in deep shadow, even this late in the morning. There was something distinctly sepulchral in the columns and arches of the building, something that reminded Ben way too closely of a crypt. He hesitated before the main door, clutching his application in his hands.

"For what it's worth, I think you're making a big mistake." George stuck her hands in her jean pockets.

Ben shot her a look. "If you think it's a mistake, why did you come?"

George shrugged. "It's a mistake that's important to you. Though I got to ask, you're serious about this whole declassification thing?"

He looked down at the papers he held. "Absolutely."

"Think of what you're giving up." George motioned extravagantly. The two guys slouched against the building's wall gave her a strange look. "A life of excitement, of danger, of high risk—and even higher rewards!"

"I was never in hunting for the money."

"That's only part of it! Admit it—you liked knowing that at the end of the day, New Camden was a safer place because of you."

Ben winced. As a vampire, he'd known that at any moment, if he lowered his guard he stood the risk of losing control, killing innocents or—worst of all—dooming other people to share his fate. "I'm okay with being ordinary."

"But the freedom of it all, the knowledge you're breaking new ground every time you go to work? You're really going to give that up for"—George cast a look at the surrounding streets—"boredom central?"

Ben grinned. "Yeah. It's going to be *great*."

George shook her head. "One week of ordinary and you're going to be wishing for a ghoul or a phantom, anything to break the monotony. Trust me, I know. You don't know how many hours I spent in that hospital, praying for a revenant to leap into that ward." She stepped up to the door and pushed it open. "Ladies first." She stepped through.

"If you were that bored, you should have said." Ben followed George into the reception area.

The Registry was arranged more like the foyer of a stately home than the office building it was. An array of wooden chairs formed a line against one wall. A woman wearing pince-nez glasses sat upright behind the reception desk. Ben stepped toward her.

A man loomed out of the shadows beside the door. "What's your business here?"

Ben jerked to a halt. "Excuse me?"

The man's eyes flashed. He wore a suit, but it didn't sit right on him, giving the impression of a hand-me-down from a bigger man. "State your business."

"That's a personal matter—hey!" Ben was too slow to stop the man snatching his application, and he didn't dare risk tearing the papers by grabbing them back. "Are you Registry staff? I want to see some ID!"

The man ignored his protests. He thumbed through the papers and then shoved them back at Ben.

"What the hell is that about?" George placed her hands on her hips. "You owe us an explanation."

The man growled. "I don't owe you anything." He stalked out the door.

Ben and George stared after him.

"That part of the application process?"

Ben shook his head. "I didn't see anything online about it—"

The lady with the pince-nez cleared her throat. "If I can help?"

Ben handed over his application. She looked at it and then cast a sharp look at him. "An unprecedented request."

"I know." Ben grimaced. "I've included everything I could think of."

She flipped through the pages. "You certainly appear to have made a thorough job of it. You've included your address? Good."

George leaned on the desk. "What's the deal with Mr. Personality at the door? I thought the Registry was just an office."

"The Registry is where all the official records of New Camden's supernatural population are kept," the woman corrected her. "Department Seven enforces the classifications, while the Register makes the rulings on them. We're usually quiet, but lately the council thought we should have more in the way of security." Her expression was disapproving. "I'm afraid that this is an interim measure until the council can vote on the matter. I don't wish to criticize volunteers but a more personable approach would not go amiss." She stamped Ben's papers. "I'll take these through to the office. One moment."

The echoes of her footsteps died away, leaving only silence. Ben became aware of just how quiet the building was. The air weighed down on them. "You feel that?"

George looked around. "Magic?"

"It makes sense. There'd have to be pretty powerful wards on the place, given what it contains." Ben resisted the urge to shiver. The atmosphere of the building was getting to him. *It feels like a grave in here—and I should know.*

The woman returned with a piece of paper acknowledging receipt of Ben's papers. "You'll hear from us soon."

The air was warmer outside the building, but Ben couldn't shake off the feeling of cold that followed him. He put his hands in the pockets of his jacket, setting off down the street at a fast pace.

The man in the suit was in conversation with the two men loitering outside the Registry. He didn't so much as glance at Ben and George as they passed.

"Someone's in a hurry." George jogged to keep up with Ben. She glanced as his face. "Don't tell me you're having second thoughts already? I figured it'd be fast, but not this fast!"

Ben shook his head. "It's not that." He came to a halt. "The altercation with that guy in the suit. I felt pretty confident about my application before, but now... I guess he's thrown me."

"How sadly the former hunter declines. Once taking werewolves and vampires in stride, now he shakes before a minor official with a jacked-up sense of self-importance."

Ben snorted. "Thanks for the understanding." He bit his lip. "Actually, George, you busy? There's something I wanted to show you."

A taxi-ride later, they stood in Ben's father's office. George looked around the room, taking in the stately desk, business-like armchair, metal filing cabinet and ample bookcase. "I take back everything I said about you being bored. I didn't realize you were the kind of person to have an *office*."

Ben leaned against the door. "So it's your opinion that there's nothing in here of interest to a hunter? That's too bad. I was going to offer you the loan of my dad's collection."

George eyed him skeptically. "Your dad's collection of what, paper clips? Fountain pens?"

"Watch." Ben took a key from his pocket and inserted it into a hidden lock above the center filing cabinet. It clicked open, sliding noiselessly back on seamless metal coasters.

"What the hell?" George squinted at the open door.

"I told you my dad was in the business." Ben couldn't help a surge of pride. He'd glimpsed the room once as a child, but his father had quickly sent him out of the room. He'd spent fruitless hours searching for the secret to unlocking the room. Even as an adult, it had taken him days of careful searching to find the lock. "This was his armory."

It was little more than a cupboard. George and Ben had to duck to climb in, and there was barely room for both of them to stand in the small space. The bulk of the room was taken up with two long wooden bars on which hung axes, firearms and swords of all description.

George raised her hand reverently to the biggest axe. "An actual, useable, double-headed axe. You know how hard it is to find these? They go for hundreds on eBay."

"This one's worth thousands." Ben leaned back. "Lift it."

She did. "Feel that balance! That's an expert's work." She adjusted her grip, clearly reluctant to put it back on the stand. "It's such a waste, having these and retiring from hunting!"

"I know," Ben said. "Which is why I want you to use them."

She swung her head up to him. "Excuse me?"

Ben stretched out his hand to the hilt of a pistol he'd always coveted. "Dad didn't collect these because he liked collecting them. He worked for ARX as a field agent, keeping people safe. He'd want them used, not admired." Ben looked down. "I'd like the collection kept here. It's safe—and it means I've still got something of his here. But you can borrow them at any time."

George put her hand on his shoulder. "I'll take good care of them. I promise."

"Just as long as you take good care of you." Ben gave the bandage peeking out from under her bandana a pointed look.

George took her time making her selection, debating the pros and cons of every weapon. Heavy weapons were a definite advantage when it came to big prey like the rogue werewolf, but were a definite liability when pursuing smaller, more agile supernaturals. She reluctantly returned the battle-axe to the rack, settling on a selection of smaller weaponry.

Ben fought a smile. With her candy-pink lipstick and nails, George looked as though she'd spend hours on fashion choices—not weapons. "Passing on the werewolf then?"

"A girl's got to make ends meet. And with all the big guns in town going after the werewolf, the pickings are good for the small freelancer."

"Glad to hear it." Insurance agents refused to cover supernatural hunters. He knew she had big hospital bills following her close escape from death, but she'd refused his offer of financial assistance.

She nodded, experimentally twirling a throwing knife. "Matter of fact, I've been picking up a steady stream of small targets. I got this really interesting gig—"

Ben held up a hand. "No details."

"I'm not asking you to help me. Just telling you about the job."

"I know. I'm serious about living an ordinary life from now on."

She tilted her head, studying him. "So this is by way of cleaning house as well as helping me? You're not worried about what you'll do in an emergency if you get human status?"

Ben shook his head. "My dad had that covered too." He stepped out of the armory and faced the bookcase. There was a hidden catch in one side that allowed the shelves to swing forward, revealing a room beyond. It was small, barely larger than the single bed it contained, but it was completely undetectable.

"A panic room?"

"Dad called it the VIP room."

"It smells of vampire."

"And that's why." Ben motioned to the lock. "Once you're inside, you can lock it and no one can enter. No windows, so no risk of sunlight. And it's warded, like the rest of the apartment."

George shook her head. "I can't get over the idea of a hunter working with vampires. It's too weird."

Ben stayed silent. How to explain that even though he'd worked for ARX just like his father, it had taken his own death and resurrection to truly understand the danger of vampires? "Hunter isn't like a revenant. He's entirely different."

"You'd hope. Ugh." George stepped out of the safe room. "You need some air freshener in there, stat."

Ben swung the bookcase shut, hiding the room once more. He was thoughtful as he locked the armory, the file cabinets sliding back into place.

"You look really serious all of a sudden."

Ben smiled ruefully. "Just thinking that it's going to be harder than I thought to go back to normal."

George watched him sympathetically, leaning against the office door. "You really think you can cut the supernatural out of your life?"

"I have to try." Ben took a deep breath. "Look—you know I worked for ARX even before I became a vampire."

"You were one of their top agents. I couldn't get much info on you, but I got that much."

Ben smiled thinly. "What you don't know is that I was living with vampires since the age of ten—master vampires, I should say."

George's eyes widened. "So the rumors are true? The vampire at ARX's head is over a thousand years old?"

"Nearer two thousand at this point. You can imagine the amount of influence he had." Ben looked down. He didn't need to tell George that he wasn't talking about normal influence, but the power of suggestion that all vampires, creatures that harnessed the powerful forces of blood magic, possessed.

"Shit. I don't want to imagine that kind of power." She looked at Ben. "But he's a good guy, right? I mean—"

"He uses his influence for what he believes are good motives," he said slowly. "And while he is definitely more altruistic than most vampires, he's still an autocrat. And his will is strong enough everyone around him agrees. It's just—what happens when you get a vampire that old." He bit his lip. This was still a sensitive subject. "I spent the most formative years of my life under the same roof as him. During that time, my interest in the supernatural became an obsession. The only thing I cared about was joining my father—and the vampires—in a career in ARX. Hell, I was majoring in supernatural studies when—" Ben swallowed. It was still hard to talk about his death.

George dropped her gaze sympathetically. "You think that the presence of the vampires dictated your interest in the supernatural? I don't know. You said you were interested even before then, right? And something about you suggests to me that whatever your interests, you were going to geek out over them."

"I just don't know." Ben frowned at the bookcase. "That's the problem. I don't know who I would have been without their influence—or who I am now. That's why I need to cut everything supernatural out of my life. To—"

"Figure out who you are without it?"

Ben swallowed the nervousness in his throat. "Right. If I'm going to convince the Register of my humanity, I have to figure out who I was before my interest in the supernatural developed."

"Wow, Ben."

"You don't think I can do it?"

"If anyone can, it's you. But I don't think you realize what a tall order that is. How many years of your life is that?"

Ben squared his shoulders. "I have to do it."

"And where does Nate fit into this? He is a lot of things, but ordinary is not on the list."

Ben grimaced.

"You're cutting him out too? He's your boyfriend!"

"It's not permanent! It's just until my application is approved."

"Does he know about this?"

Ben nodded. "We talked about it. Just last night."

George looked at him a long moment before shaking her head. "You're taking a big risk, resting a relationship on red tape. What if your application is turned down?"

"It won't be. I'm human. I have a pulse, a—"

"Yeah, I know. But best case scenario, you could be waiting months. You really think Nate's going to stick around all that time? He's used to a lot of attention. What if he gets bored, finds someone new?"

It was what Ben was most afraid of. "He'll wait. He has to. Otherwise—"

"Look. Pro-tip for you from someone who didn't grow up in Dracula's castle. Hanging out with their hot boyfriend is high on the list of things twenty-somethings do." George smirked at him.

Ben tilted his head. He was reminded again just how much he didn't know about George. "What would you do? If you could do anything right now."

"Anything?"

"Not hunting, I mean." He tilted his head. "You don't want to spend your entire life hunting, right?"

"Nah. I'll retire eventually. But until then, I gotta make ends meet." George shrugged. "I might have got into it for revenge, but now... Well, I got the skills and I got the know-how to protect other people. Might as well do it."

"But if finances weren't a problem, and you figured you were due some time off?"

George grinned. "That's easy. Pennsylvania road trip."

Ben blinked. "Pennsylvania?"

"They got the highest number of coasters in any state. And I'm going to ride them all."

Of all the answers he'd expected, this wasn't one of them. "You like roller coasters?"

"Love them. Don't know if you've noticed this about me, but I'm an adrenaline junkie." George smirked. "Your turn. What's the first thing you're going to do now you're human?"

"I—" Ben's brain stalled. "I don't know."

"College? Paragliding? Learn a new skill?"

Everyone at college knew him as the promising supernatural major who was already taking advanced postgrad-level courses as an undergrad. Ben swallowed. All the books he'd read had involved the supernatural in some way, and for relaxation he'd played Monster Wars Online. Ben looked around the office, casting for inspiration. His hand brushed the acorn in his pocket. "I'm going to make my will."

"*Ben.*" George groaned. "That's so—boring."

He raised an eyebrow. "You're not going to say morbid?"

"Given our friendship was cemented when we promised that the first of us to die gets put down by the other, I can't object to morbid. But really." George elbowed him. "You realize you can still have fun as a human."

"I will," he promised. "But until then, I've decided to embrace boredom. After all, this is my life from now on, right?"

A DAY LATER, Ben stepped into the apartment elevator with distinct satisfaction. Making his will had not been difficult. His father's lawyer joked that making a will was a lot more straightforward than his request to have his identity validated. It had been simple too. The apartment building and his possessions to Nate, his father's armory to George. Even though he hoped it'd be a long time before his will had to be used, Ben felt pleased knowing he'd have a connection with both of them even after death.

Even better, he'd treated himself to coffee on the way home, and not one person had asked him what he thought of the werewolf case. And he had no reason to leave his apartment for the rest of the day. Ben hit the button for his floor. *I might actually be able to pull it off—an entire day of ordinary.*

The elevator doors opened. Ben's first thought was that he'd got the wrong floor. Two men stood in front of the door. Ben's penthouse was the only apartment on the top floor—but as they heard the elevator, the men turned toward him.

"Bennet Hawick?"

Ben nodded. "That's me."

"We're from the Registry." The taller of the two men handed him a business card. "We'd like you to come with us."

Ben looked down at the card in his hand. He recognized the Registry logo, but not the name. "What's going on?"

"You submitted an application for declassification to the Registry?" The tall man did all the talking. His companion moved to Ben's other side, watching him wordlessly. "The Committee has requested further information."

"Ah." Ben forced himself to respond. "Give me a moment, and I'll just grab some things—"

"Your immediate presence is required."

Ben looked from one man to another. "Is that—normal?"

"Where irregularities are noted, the Registry prefers to address them promptly." The tall man threw his hand to the elevator door to stop it from closing. He motioned Ben inside.

It wasn't until he was sitting in their car, the tall man driving and his silent companion watching Ben from the back seat, that Ben realized this could be very bad. *What if they want more tests? Or I'm arrested?* Not being a vampire wasn't exactly a criminal charge...but the way the men had hurried him into the car was not exactly reassuring.

They're treating me like a criminal. The way the second man kept his eyes on Ben was very disconcerting.

Ben cast around for a question to break the ice. His gaze ranged over the man's hands, resting on his knees, and he froze.

Hairy palms—the guy is a werewolf!

He resisted the urge to look the man in the face, knowing that he'd read his alarm on his face. Instead, Ben breathed out. *Think!*

The most important thing to do was notify someone of his whereabouts. Ben felt in his pocket for his phone. He could send Nate a message, saying that if he wasn't home in a few hours to notify Department Seven—

His fingers closed on something small and smooth. Ben pulled it out of his pocket.

Nate's acorn.

His fingers wrapped around it. It was solid in his hand, solid and comfortingly warm—like Nate. And thinking of Nate gave Ben a feeling of strength.

So what if the guy's a wolf? It makes sense that the Registry would employ supernaturals—and werewolves make great guards. Ben returned the acorn to his pocket but kept his hand locked around it. *I can't freak out anytime something unexpected happens.*

Before long, they pulled up outside the Registry. Leaving the car parked on the side of the road, Ben's guard led him past the reception area—still empty—and down a musty hallway. They paused in front of a door.

The tall man fixed Ben with a sharp look. "Stay here. I'm going to inform the council that you've arrived."

Ben nodded. *He has tawny eyes, too. Another wolf?*

As the door shut behind him, Ben became aware of a strange sound. It was soft, but steady, a regular whisper. He glanced at his companion, but the werewolf didn't seem bothered by whatever it was.

Must be normal. Ben looked around for the source and his eyes fell on an open doorway. He took a step toward it and gasped.

At first glance it looked like a library, but a closer look revealed it to be the Register's collection of records pertaining to the city' s supernatural citizens. Most of the books were in uniform volumes, safely contained in cabinets with glass fronts and locked doors. But in the center of the room, nine desks were arranged in a circle, with a tenth desk in the center. On the surface of each desk lay an open book. As Ben watched, an invisible force whipped through the pages of the ten books, giving rise to the sound of pages turning.

It's not wind. Ben didn't need to glance up at the closed windows to know they weren't open. The library smelled equally of stale air and magic. *This is magic.* And incredibly powerful magic to have created a self-perpetuating repeating spell.

Magical books? Ben took a step closer to the door. He could see now that the ten books were chained to their tables. *Must be. Magical books, old enough to have taken on the power of their owners. That's what is powering the spell—the books' own magic.* And that magic would be renewed by the very spell the books were performing, effectively turning them into a renewable magical generator.

And the spell's object? Ben looked to the book resting at the center of the circle. It was an important looking book, leather-bound with its title painted in gold leaf. *The Register itself?* Ben took another step toward the door. *Is this how the city protects itself and monitors its supernatural residents?* He couldn't read the contents of its pages, they turned too fast—

"Get out of that." The werewolf abruptly stepped in front of Ben, shutting the door. "That's off-limits."

"Sorry." Ben took a deep breath. He couldn't let the man rattle him. "I didn't know."

The man growled low. "You know now."

Ben was very still. *That's definitely hostile behavior—and entirely unwarranted.* What was going on? As an ARX agent, he'd had run-ins with werewolves, but those had always been wolves that had broken New Camden's laws. He couldn't hold that against Ben, could he?

The first door opened, revealing the tall man. "The council is ready to see you now, Mr. Hawick." His words were polite, but Ben detected a definite coolness.

Ben fingers searched for the acorn in his pocket. He stepped through the door.

The room he entered was a cross between an old-fashioned chapel and a court of law. Wooden chairs of varying styles, none of which originated in this century, formed a half circle around a raised wooden podium. Before it, seated at a wide table, were two men and a woman.

Ben recognized the woman as New Camden's mayor, but the men gave him a moment's pause. One was tall and thin, his white hair swept loosely back over his skull. His gray suit appeared a few sizes too big for him. The other's suit fit perfectly, but he managed to give the impression of being ready to burst out of it at any moment. He sat alertly, his eyes appraising Ben. He sneered slightly. "The stand, if you would, Mr. Hawick."

Ben climbed the steps into the stand, holding the edge of the podium tightly. "I'm afraid you have me at a disadvantage."

"This is Councilor Wisner, New Camden's newly appointed security head," the white-haired man said. "Diane Chandler, our mayor. I, myself, am Roger Hartman, the council's advisor on supernatural rights."

Ben felt dizzy. *What are councilors doing looking into my application?* "I don't quite understand why we're all here."

Wisner sneered. "You don't? I'll tell you, Hawick. You lodged a highly irregular application—one that has never been requested before in the history of this city. Naturally, we can't let it go unchallenged."

"Perhaps we should start with the preliminaries." Hartman looked at the paper before him. "Your name is Bennet Hawick? Your parents were Austin and Audrey Hawick, and you were born in New Camden?"

Ben nodded. *Maybe this won't be so bad.* "That's correct."

"I knew your father. He was a model of supernatural tolerance. His death was a great loss to our community."

Ben ducked his head. "Thank you."

"If we could confine ourselves to the matter at hand?" Wisner didn't wait for his companions' agreement before launching into his questions. "You're applying for human status? Our records state you were a Class Seven Vampire."

"Class Five." Ben took a deep breath. "As an ARX employee, I was subject to rigorous training to suppress my vampiric instincts and kept under close observation. I was not considered a risk to the public and was employed by ARX as a field agent. The Class Seven rating referred to the level of clearance I had with regards to magic use and research material to aid me in the course of my investigations."

Wisner kept his eyes on Ben. "Class Seven magical knowledge is still Class Seven. And you're asking to be completely declassified, to take that knowledge into the city, where we have only your word that you won't act on it?"

Ben stiffened. "As I wrote in my cover letter, I feel strongly about leaving my past behind me. I want to be normal. There would be no place for that knowledge in my new life."

"So you say," sneered Wisner. "But you can't prove that can you?" He turned to the mayor. "We have only his word for his intentions."

The mayor frowned. She was a tiny woman, dwarfed by her two companions. "What I don't understand is how a vampire ends up applying for human status at all. You claim to be human?"

Ben nodded. If she could feel the way his heart was pounding, she'd have no doubt of the truth of his claims. "You've looked at my medical records? I'm alive. I have a pulse, I walk in sunlight with no ill-effects, I eat, I sleep—"

"We've examined your medical records and talked to the doctor who examined you." Hartman removed his glasses. "He was not aware that you were once a vampire?"

"I thought it was better not to tell him. To ensure the results were not impacted. The Department Seven tests on the other hand—"

Wisner slapped the table. "You see? He is prepared to cover up the truth when it suits him. I don't think we can take his word that he will behave."

"I disagree. The doctor didn't need to know Mr. Hawick's past in order to examine him." Hartman glanced down. "What I am curious about is how exactly the transformation happened. You do not go into much detail, Mr. Hawick."

Ben swallowed. "The necromancer kidnapped me for my connections to Saltaire. As a member of his colony, I was not only powerful, but he looked on me as family. I was useful as a tool for revenge, and as a source of raw power. The necromancer had made preparations for a complicated magical ritual. It was after this ritual that I became human again."

Wisner's lip curled. "That's not my idea of revenge."

The mayor nodded. "What was the purpose of the spell?"

"He wanted to combine his considerable power as a necromancer with the power of a vampire. If he'd succeeded...he'd have been a huge threat to the city."

The mayor's mouth was a flat, unimpressed line. "Tens of people killed, and a panic that overtook the entire city... I consider the necromancer was a huge threat. And we have only your word as to the intent of the spell? You can't prove it?"

"Prove it?" Ben looked blankly at her.

"Provide a diagram of the spell," Hartman suggested. "So that the magical department could confirm it."

Ben shook his head. "My memories of that time aren't the clearest. I'd been kidnapped and subjected to an incredibly draining magical ritual. I can remember a few bits and pieces, but I never saw the entire circle. There's no way I could recreate it for you." *Even if I wanted to.* As far as Ben was concerned, the magic that the necromancer had created belonged with the necromancer—dead.

His audience exchanged glances.

Hartman shuffled his notes. "You had a long acquaintance with the necromancer?"

Not this again. Hadn't he been subjected to endless hours of grilling by Department Seven? "We were both ARX employees. We knew each other for a number of years, but we weren't well acquainted. He resented me, and I had no idea he was anything but Hunter's personal assistant."

"So you say." Wisner leaned back in his chair. The gesture was insolent.

Ben narrowed his eyes. "He tried to kill me. In fact, he did. He was behind my murder."

"It's very easy to make accusations against a dead man."

Not in New Camden. Ben bit back the retort. "With all due respect, Councilor, I didn't put a hit out on myself."

"But you weren't the only one who died, were you? You lost your father in the attack." Wisner turned to his colleagues. "Hawick has a background of violent deaths. There is also the mystery surrounding his mother's death, and even without the ARX records, we can imagine the sort of career he had."

Ben leaned heavily against the side of the podium. They couldn't imagine he had anything to do with his parents' deaths, could they?

"Even if we accept Hawick's statement as truthful, the impact these deaths would have on his young psyche would be immense—and harmful. His time spent with ARX as a vampire would only exacerbate this. Do we really want to release such a damaged individual into our city with no way of monitoring his behavior?"

"I was a model employee throughout my time at ARX. And before then, too. Look at my high school reports, my university transcript—"

"The necromancer was a model ARX employee, too." Wisner crossed his arms. "And look how that turned out."

"Is there anyone at ARX who can confirm your statements?" The mayor demanded, her hands folded on her lap.

Ben shook his head. "As part of my desire to separate myself from my previous life, I cut ties with ARX."

Hartman sighed. "It is a difficult case. Without any evidence to back up your statements, well—you understand why we have to be cautious. Your case would be much strengthened if you had a statement from ARX as evidence of your claims."

Ben winced. He didn't think his outstanding record as an ARX investigator would win him any fans from this crowd. He hadn't just been responsible for tracking down multiple supernatural threats but eliminating them. *They're more likely to take one look and write me off as a dangerous killer—regardless of the fact that I was saving human lives.* "Impossible. Even if I hadn't cut ties, the ARX members I was most strongly associated with don't do daylight hours."

The mayor shuddered. "We don't really need to see Saltaire, do we?"

Hartman raised his eyebrows. "I understood the committee appointed to look into ARX's involvement with the debacle cleared him of personal responsibility?"

"We had to, didn't we?" The mayor muttered. "What choice do you have with a master vampire in the room?"

"Another factor to take into account. Hawick may have a good record of behavior—but that was while he lived under Saltaire's roof, subject to Saltaire's...guidance. Without it..." Wisner shrugged. "He is an unknown. We cannot sign off on this extraordinary request. It's simply too risky."

The mayor shot him a sideways look. "Like allowing a young wolf to roam freely around the city?"

Wisner's growl sounded out of place in the dignified surroundings of the study. "He will be found, and found quickly. And I am already taking steps to ensure that it does not happen again. As New Camden's Security Head, I plan on making sure the city stays safe—and that starts with tighter regulations to prevent cases like the necromancer."

The mayor nodded. "Agreed."

"I don't think anyone's arguing with that," Hartman added.

Ben took a shuddering breath. "But—"

"It's usual in these sorts of cases to allow you time to put an appeal together," Hartman told Ben. "In the meantime, we'll want you to attend regular counseling sessions. To monitor your progress."

Ben swallowed. His cheeks burned. *Like I'm a raw revenant.* He hadn't fought death and survived to be subjected to this humiliation!

"In the meantime, an interim classification." Hartman turned to his colleagues. "Class Six?"

"*Six?*" Ben stared in horror.

The mayor frowned. "Six is—"

"No contact with anyone who lacks sufficient supernatural clearance to defend themselves if necessary, or is supernatural themselves, and a curfew." Wisner grinned. His tongue lolled on his jagged teeth.

Ben stared at his teeth, fascinated despite the circumstances. *Of course. Werewolf.*

"We're all in agreement? Very well." Hartman turned back to Ben. "We will see you back here in two weeks for an additional report."

"And in the meantime, we'll be keeping a very close eye on you." Wisner said. "You're dangerous, Hawick—and don't think we don't know it."

BEN GRIPPED HIS phone tightly. It rang and rang. *Please. Please pick up—*

"Hello?"

Hearing Nate's voice brought relief so strong that Ben felt dizzy. He steadied himself against the stone wall of the Registry building. Among the many thoughts racing through his head in the wake of the committee's ruling was the memory of Nate's premonition. What if he was right? What if he literally never sees me again—

"Hello? Any one there?"

Ben forced himself to take a deep breath. "Nate? Can you hear me?"

"Ben!" Nate's pleasure at the call was obvious from the warmth in his voice. "Yeah? What's up—good news?"

Ben shut his eyes. Sharing this with Nate was going to be harder than he thought. "The opposite actually." He tightened his free hand around the loose fabric at the collar of his T-shirt. "Can I see you?"

"Sure. I was about to leave for Century—I got a cleaning shift, but—"

A movement in his peripheral vision caught Ben's attention. There was a woman waiting for him, a woman he'd never seen before. She wore a crisp black jacket and skirt, but the professional effect was countered by the electric-pink scarf looped around her neck and outsized earrings dangling from her ears. Her eyes were fixed on him.

Ben frowned. "I'll meet you there." He pressed end call, turning to face the woman. "Can I help you?"

"I believe I can help you." The woman held out a business card. Her nails were the same bright pink as the scarf. "Diya Patel. I'm employed by the Registry as an advocate for the supernatural."

Ben's fingers tightened around the card. He stared at Diya with a feeling of horror. *Does she know...?*

Diya's brown eyes met his sympathetically. "I was present for your hearing."

"I didn't see you."

"I'm not surprised. I can imagine that was a very difficult ordeal."

"Difficult is not the word." Ben took a deep breath. "Look, it's very kind of you to offer your services, but I don't need an advocate."

"You need me," Diya said. "You see, Mr. Hawick, you're in even greater trouble than you realize. Are you familiar with the measures New Camden City Council adopted after the necromancer's death?"

Ben shook his head. "I've been somewhat preoccupied with other matters."

"I thought you might be. Which is why you need to listen to me." Diya tucked a strand of her dark hair behind an ear. "You're familiar with the varied classifications that enable the city to create magical wards governing specific groups of supernatural citizens?"

Including me. Ben nodded. "The names of those classified are recorded in books held in the Registry, and those books are used to power the spells." He'd seen the spell at work when he'd passed the library. "And before you ask, I know the limitations imposed on me by this ruling."

"What you don't know is that a new class was added to deal with extreme cases of harmful supernaturals. In an effort to deter future cases like the necromancer, a new book was created in the Register. One in which the names of those deemed too dangerous to have any kind of contact with anyone will be recorded."

Ben stared at Diya. This was starting to make a horrible kind of sense. "You're not telling me that—"

Diya nodded. "Unless we can convince the committee to accept your humanity, you risk being added to the Final Register."

Ben had a sudden suspicion. "And if that happens?"

Diya's eyes were sympathetic. "You'll exist only to yourself."

Chapter Four

"HELLO? BEN?"

The only response Nate got was a few seconds of dial tone and then he was left looking at his phone screen. He dropped the phone into his pocket and turned to find the dog looking at him.

"That was Ben." Nate picked up Aki's hair dryer. "He's my boyfriend, but it's complicated. We're not dating, but it's not like we're on the rocks. It's just timing."

The dog barked.

"You're as bad as Aki." Nate hit the switch of the hair dryer. "Speaking of, don't worry about him. Yeah he freaked out about you being here, but that's just who he is. Underneath his 'I don't care about anything but me' front, he's a really great guy."

The dog let his tongue hang out and his eyes roll back. He might have been rolling his eyes, or really enjoying the hot air.

"You'll see. As long as you don't eat his hair gel or sleep on his clothes, you'll get on great." Nate ran his fingers over the dog's fur. When he'd first smuggled the dog inside via the emergency stairs, the dog's scruffy appearance had made him look disreputable. A bath had revealed that the dog's fur wasn't gray, but a fluffy white.

Nate ran his fingers through the dog's fur. "You don't look like any dog I know. Too big to be a shih tzu—or even a poodle. But you're too skinny to be an English sheepdog..."

The dog barked and nudged Nate's hand with his head.

Nate took the hint and ran his hand over the dog's smooth head. "I always wanted a dog as a kid," he said. "A puppy that would be all mine. Twins, you know. We shared everything. But Pa said no. We had chickens and they roamed around the garden. He said a dog would worry them. But when I was ten, I noticed a stray cat hanging round. I started secretly feeding it. Thought I could tame it and make it my pet. Well, it followed me back to the farmhouse, and Pa saw it near the chook house and shot it. And that was the end of me and pets." Nate sighed.

The dog stared at him.

Nate smiled ruefully. "I can see how dog owners get so obsessed with their pets. The way you sit there... It's like you understand everything I say."

The dog let his tongue loll out again.

"Dunno why you're looking so pleased with yourself. I did all the work here." Nate put the hair dryer back on the bathroom counter and surveyed the mess. Most of the water had been soaked up by the towels he'd laid down, but the bathroom looked as though a tornado had ripped through it—or Aki had used it. Nate bundled the towels into the laundry hamper. "Let's get you something to eat."

The dog wolfed down the leftover macaroni in huge bites. "Dog food's going to have to wait until my next paycheck," Nate warned him. "Speaking of, I'm going to have to get to work."

The dog followed him to the door.

"We'll be back late," Nate said. "Don't wait up. Just you know. Do whatever things dogs do—but don't pee on anything. Or eat Aki's stuff."

The dog gave another bark and wagged his tail.

Nate hoped that was agreement.

AS NATE APPROACHED Century, he couldn't help a feeling of anticipation. Yeah, he was looking forward to an evening of cleaning, rather than the club's risqué entertainment. But the sight of the club always gave him a thrill. Tonight though... Nate grinned. The thrill had nothing to do with Century's myriad attractions and everything to do with Ben's phone call.

He's never offered to visit me here before. Usually, I have to twist his arm to get him to go out...and he still says no.

Century started life as an opera house way back when New Camden still had designs on respectability. The building was a baroque masterpiece, with architectural flourishes that made it a landmark, even without containing the most notorious nightclub in all of the city. Century had built a name making prostitution classy, combining elements of a regular nightclub with that of a brothel, and devoting the same amount of lavish spending to both. The result was a venue that was respectable enough to visit while still exciting its clientele.

The main entrance already had a considerable line of people outside it. Nate ducked down the alley beside the building to the staff entrance. Like all of Century's escorts, he wore a thin black wristband. Containing GPS, transaction functions, a light to indicate Nate's availability, and considerable security features, the wristband was developed specifically by Century to protect its staff. Today, Nate simply waved it before the door's sensors and stepped inside. Cleaning was far from his preferred job, but beggars couldn't be choosers, and Nate was really lucky to still be employed by the club at all.

It did not take long at all to pull the uniform jumpsuit worn by the cleaning staff over his regular clothes. Nate assembled his cleaning gear and glanced at the clock. It was still relatively early. *Time to find Aki?* He knocked on the dressing room door and walked in.

Century splurged on clothing and stylists for their escorts, cultivating an allure about them that justified the high prices their services commanded. For the staff, this meant their pick of the latest fashions— a choice that could take fashion-conscious Aki upward of an hour.

Nate spotted Aki digging into a clothing rack. "They got the new styles in already?"

"Right? It's like they want me to be late on the floor." Aki blinked. "Nate? What are you doing here? It's supposed to be your night off!"

"Don't look so happy to see me." Nate motioned to his uniform. "They had a cleaner call out sick. I'm filling in."

Aki frowned. "But you hate cleaning."

"I don't hate it. And I like getting paid." Nate hesitated. "Especially now we have a dog to provide for."

Aki chewed his lip. "You sure you should be here at all? I hear dogs don't do well if you leave them alone."

"Um." Of all the things Nate was expecting, concern for the dog was not it. "Are you—okay?"

"Of course I am."

"It's just that you seem a little—" Nate hesitated.

"You've thrown me off my groove showing up out of the blue." Aki turned back to the clothing racks.

"I thought you'd be happier to see me." *And angrier about the dog.* "Are you feeling okay?" Nate reached for Aki's forehead.

Aki batted his hand away. "I'm a complex person! I'm allowed to have different opinions about things!"

A static crackle had them both glancing up at the speaker in the dressing room ceiling. "All staff to the floor in five minutes for an important staff meeting."

"Thank god." Aki grabbed a shirt off the rack and ducked into a changing booth. "Let's go, Nate. Can't miss a staff meeting."

Nate frowned at the closed curtain. *Now I know something's wrong. No one likes staff meetings...*

When they reached the dance floor before the stage, most of the staff was already there, milling around.

Tybalt smirked, nudging Javier as he spotted Aki and Nate arriving. "So, Nate. What have you got us into this time?"

Javier counted off on his fingers. "We've had vampires, demons... Please tell me you're not dating the rogue werewolf."

Nate frowned at them. "You're not funny."

"This has to be about the werewolf, right?" Aki looked around the club. Security was clustered around the stage. "Why else would security be here?"

"Everyone's here." Nate hesitated. "You think maybe they're announcing Denise's replacement?" He'd been the one to discover Denise's death. The manager was murdered during the necromancer's attempt at killing Nate. The only flaw in his plan was the fact that Nate hadn't died.

Aki winced sympathetically, placing his hand on Nate's arm.

"About time," Tybalt said. "Yeah, she was murdered. Very sad. But Century needs someone in charge who knows what they're doing. And the interim managers—" He broke off midsentence, eyes widening as he took in the stage.

Nothing makes Tybalt pause. Nate turned to look—and felt his breath catch. There, exactly as he'd seen her last, if you discounted being a bloodied, dead mess, was Denise.

The club went very still.

Denise smiled. "Thank you for giving me your undivided attention— and for your patience with the interim management team. I'm back now, and I'm pleased to announce that things should be back to normal very soon."

Aki's fingers had tightened painfully on Nate's skin.

Tybalt leaned in. "You're sure she was dead?"

Nate could only nod. He couldn't take his eyes off the woman on stage.

Denise wore her signature suit—or a very good copy of it. Her lipstick was her usual rich shade, and there was no mistaking the assurance in her voice—that was all Denise. *But how? How is this possible?*

"I am resuming full manager duties from tonight," Denise continued. "And on that note, we have some precautionary security measures to address. Century made the news for all of the wrong reasons during the necromancer attacks—"

"She's talking about her death," Aki said. "Isn't she?"

Denise's eyes glittered. "And we need to do serious work promoting Century as a safe place for customers."

Although there was no way she could have heard them from her position on the stage, Nate felt she was looking right at them. He felt Aki's nails dig into his skin as he flinched.

Denise paused a moment to nod to Century's head of security—looking as pale as everyone else. "To that end and to ensure the safety of our employees, our security team are following the latest briefings from Department Seven and are on the lookout for the rogue werewolf. We've also increased our defensive wards and urge all our employees to familiarize themselves again with our emergency procedures."

"Emergency procedures—like your dead manager returning to life and holding a staff meeting?" Tybalt muttered.

"I don't know," Nate said. "If anyone's going to raise from the dead, I'm glad it's Denise."

"The last thing we need is another supernatural in the place. We're getting overrun—sorry, Nate. But it's true." Javier frowned at the stage. "You think she was always this way and now she can't hide it?"

"One way to find out." Tybalt raised his hand.

"I hardly have to remind you all that Century takes a hard line on illegal supernaturals—yes, Tybalt?"

Tybalt sneered. "So what exactly are you—" With every word he said, the atmosphere in the club seemed to grow colder. Denise settled a hand on her hip and waited. Nate felt an urge to take a step back. Tybalt swallowed, lowering his hand. "—your plans now you're back?"

Denise smiled. "I should be back up to speed in no time. And then it's back to the business of making sure Century remains the best club in New Camden." She looked across the silent crowd. "Any other questions, I'll be in my office." She gave them a crisp nod before walking off the stage, the security chief hurrying to match her pace.

Nate suddenly rediscovered breathing. "Wow."

"Shit." Aki's gaze didn't relax. "I skipped out on her funeral. You think she knows?"

"This is Denise." Javier ran his hand over his face. "She knew everything even before she died. And now—"

"Now, who knows what she can do?" Tybalt headed toward the bar. "I think we were safer with the fucking werewolf."

AT LEAST THERE'S something you can say for cleaning. Nate moved his cart to the next booth. *It's not exciting in any way.* Denise's unexpected return was all he'd been able to think about that entire night. He couldn't imagine how Aki was faring. *Trying to keep your mind on a client when your scary manager has returned from the dead is...* He shook his head.

As he bundled the sheets into his cart and remade the bed, Nate told himself he'd just have to get used to it. *I came back from the dead and management was cool with it—is that why?* Nate smoothed down the sheet, automatically fluffing the pillows. "It'd explain a lot... But man, we are so screwed." There would be no excuses for calling out of work when the manager refused to call in dead...

Maybe Ben will know what to do. Nate cheered up. The last time Ben had visited Nate at his place of work had resulted in a passionate encounter that left their feelings for each other exposed. Ben had purposefully avoided visiting Nate at his place of work since. *If he's changed his mind about that...* Nate couldn't help a feeling of anticipation. *Maybe he's changed his mind about the rest of it.*

Nate pushed his cleaning cart into the back corridor. The clock at the end of the hall indicated his shift had finished and he was free to wait for Ben in the club.

There was no sign of Ben at the table booths, so Nate joined the guests at the bar. Although it was midweek, it seemed to him like the crowd was smaller than usual. *Because of the negative publicity Denise mentioned?* Nate leaned against the bar. *That's my fault...*

"You're still here?" Aki leaned against the bar next to him.

Nate shook his head, turning his attention to his companion. "Man, Aki. If I didn't know we were friends..."

Aki shrugged, depositing a tray of empty glasses on the bar. "You've become so boring since meeting your not-actual-boyfriend. I figured you'd be heading back home to pine at the first available opportunity."

"For your information, Ben's on his way here." Nate looked around the club again. His eyes fell on a group of patrons just entering the club. "Hey, there's Rick."

"Who cares? Do you know who I saw?"

Nate straightened. Rick had been his first regular client when he'd started at Century. "I should say hi."

Aki grabbed his arm for the second time that night. "I don't think that's a good idea."

Nate frowned. "Why not? I haven't seen him in weeks. Not since—" Nate's eyes widened. "Not since my supernatural status was added to my Century profile."

"This way." Aki tugged Nate after him, heading across the dance floor to the shadows.

Nate followed numbly. His heart beat fast, his head pulsing in time with it. *But that means—*

"Okay." Aki turned around to face him. "Let's talk."

"That's deliberate, isn't it? He changed his night to my night off." Nate turned his head back to look at Rick, deep in conversation with another host. "Because I'm supernatural."

"He's an idiot." Aki spoke with heat. "Seriously. Supernatural doesn't mean dangerous—or that you're not still you. If he's too stupid to realize that, that's his problem."

Nate looked down at his friend. Aki complained about anything and everything, but he wasn't usually this vehement. "You knew. And you didn't want me to find out—that's why you've been acting so weird all evening."

Aki squirmed. "I knew you'd be upset. You're way too invested in your clients."

Too invested? Nate leaned against the wall. "I thought we were—not friends, exactly. But cool. And he couldn't even tell me himself." That hurt as much as Rick's desertion.

"See? You care too much, Nate. No one at Starbucks tells their barista when they're changing their coffee shop."

"I bet some people do." But Aki had a point. Nate breathed out. *I do care too much what people think of me. Part of being supernatural means facing this kind of reaction. And that means—it's time to toughen up.* He straightened. "You're right. His loss."

Aki watched him. The shadows made his brown eyes even darker. "You're really okay?"

"Yeah. I got you and Ben—what do I need a graphic designer for? Shitty business cards?"

Aki laughed. "That's right." He turned his gaze back to the dance floor. "I guess I should get back to work."

Nate followed his gaze. The night had picked up, with a good-sized crowd swaying to the music blaring out of the club's speakers. "Want to dance?" He let his hand rest on Aki's arm. "It's been ages since we worked a crowd."

"And show Rick what he's missing at the same time?" Aki leaned into Nate's touch. "Didn't think you did that now you're"—he sketched quotation marks in the air—"dating."

Nate gave Aki a push toward the crowd. "Dating doesn't mean I can't have fun with my friends."

Aki snorted, leading the way onto the floor. "How much fun can you be? You've been rusting in Little River, a place that, from everything you've told me, is too uncool even for barn dances."

Nate grabbed Aki's arm. He gave a sharp tug that pulled Aki snug against Nate's chest. Keeping Aki trapped against him, Nate moved, knowing Aki had no choice but to move with him. "What was that about 'rusty'?"

Aki's mouth curved. He moved as if his body were adhered to Nate's. "Challenge accepted. But I warn you—I'm not going to play nice."

"You've never played nice in your life."

Aki grinned. "Just so long as you know what you're in for."

Nate placed his hands on Aki's hips, spinning him around. "I'm aware." He ground against Aki. "Are you?"

Aki planted his feet squarely, looking back over his shoulder. He didn't say anything. His look was challenge enough. Shutting his eyes, Aki began to rock with the beat pulsing through the club.

Nate felt a spark of exhilaration. When Aki danced, he put his entire self into it—and it was impossible not to do the same. He let the music wash over him, his hand on Aki's hip, reading his rhythm. When Aki moved, Nate moved with him, as seamlessly as if they'd rehearsed it.

The lights flashed in time with the music, catching the dancers for a split second before losing them to the darkness. Nate caught glimpses of bodies moving in his peripheral vision but kept his eyes locked on Aki. He set a fast pace, daring Nate to match it.

Speed wasn't Nate's strong suit, but he let Aki have his way. The dance was about him after all—and Nate was pretty sure that the pace of the dancers immediately surrounding them had slowed as they watched.

He glanced around, seeing a space had formed around them. *Time to step it up.* The next time Aki cruised by him, Nate pulled him close. He put his hands on the small of Aki's back, as Aki settled his hands on Nate's chest. "Ready?"

Aki's mouth curved. "Always."

They had rehearsed this, but the combination of moves always felt fresh. A lot of that was Aki. He invested whatever movement he made with the sexuality he freely embraced—and he wasn't above changing the rules. His hand wandered toward Nate's fly.

Nate caught Aki by his hips, holding him midair a moment before tossing him up, and on the downward catch, sliding him through his legs across the floor.

The crowd murmured with appreciation. Aki smoldered, body rippling as he caught Nate's hand and levered himself back to his feet. It was only too easy to imagine the same maneuver beneath the sheets.

That's Aki's specialty. Now for mine. Nate made his movements preemptory. His strength kept Aki locked tightly against him, their movements like one.

Nate was keenly aware they were practically alone on the floor. *Everyone's watching.* The thought excited him. He loved the feeling of being on display, and the next time Aki rippled against him, Nate swayed with him.

When the music stopped, Aki was pressed against him, breathing rapidly. There was a long pause before the house lights came on.

As the DJ announced the end of his set, Aki licked his lips. "Okay. So maybe you haven't forgotten everything I taught you. But we should probably do that again. To practice."

Nate snorted, stepping back. "And keep you from your adoring public? Pass."

"Your loss." Aki released Nate, before stalking toward the bar. As Nate watched, a couple of men slipped out of the crowd to follow him. Aki would have no trouble finding his next client.

Once Nate would have been content to join the crowd and find a new partner for the next set. Now, as much as he enjoyed putting on a show, the audience couldn't hold him the way it once had—the way only one man could.

Nate made his way to the shadows. He didn't need to see Ben to know he was there—and had been for some time. His heart beat in a way it hadn't throughout the entire dance. "Enjoy the show?"

Ben's gasp was breathless. "Nate." Without another word, he broke the distance between them, throwing his arms around Nate.

Nate grinned, settling an arm around Ben comfortably. *If this is the reaction I get, Aki and I need to dance more often.* He raised his other hand to brush Ben's hair. "I'm taking that as a yes."

Ben didn't reply.

Nate's forehead furrowed. This was—unusual. Yeah, he was used to making an impression on the floor, but Ben seemed less turned on, more—

More needy. Nate swallowed. Ben was never needy. He thought back to their brief phone call that afternoon. "Something's happened, hasn't it?"

Ben's body tensed beneath Nate's touch.

"What's the matter?"

Ben sighed, settling his face against Nate's shoulder. "Let's leave it at I had a really bad day."

A bad day for Ben could involve anything from kidnapping by necromancer, to having to put down multiple undead, to being found by the vampire family he had left. "Anything I can do?"

Ben tightened his arms around Nate. "Exactly what you're doing now."

This is really serious. Ben wasn't just hugging him. He was hugging Nate in a public place—and didn't seem to care that anyone could see them. Nate stroked his fingers over Ben's skull in what he hoped was a comforting gesture. "Let's go outside and you can tell me all about it." Nate shifted his arm to settle on Ben's back. "Or if you'd rather, we could just go home."

Ben lifted his face to Nate's. He looked tired. "Can we just stay like this for a while?"

Nate's heart constricted. He liked it when Ben leaned on him, but to hear him sound so lost was—wrong. "Yeah. Whatever you want."

Ben leaned back against Nate. He shut his eyes. "Sorry to ruin your evening."

"You kidding?" Nate gave him a squeeze. "You've got no idea how long I've been wanting to get you out on the dance floor."

Ben snorted. His breath tickled Nate's neck. "And when you succeed, no one's dancing."

Nate looked across the floor. The DJ was signing autographs at the bar and most of the crowd had dispersed to find drinks. The house music was turned up, and a few hardcore couples remained on the floor. "Just means more floor for us."

He'd hadn't meant it as anything more than a throwaway comment, but he felt Ben tense. "I can't dance. I've never even tried."

"And if you had, you'd know there's nothing to it." Nate gave Ben's hand a reassuring squeeze. "Trust me. I've seen you fight. I know you can move."

Ben raised his head to look at Nate. "There's a big difference between fighting and what you and Aki were doing."

"Wanna bet?" Nate shifted, rocking gently to the music filling the club. "What you saw was the continuation of a long-running argument between us."

Ben snorted. "Is that what you call it?"

Nate cocked an eyebrow. *Now he's teasing me? Am I sure this is Ben?* He studied the man in front of him. The club's lights caught Ben's pale skin, making him look skeletal and vulnerable. "You're not jealous?"

Ben had relaxed enough to loosen his grip on Nate, looking around the club. He studied each of the groups of people nearest to them in turn, seemingly reassured by the fact that none of them were looking their way. "No. I know how close you and Aki are, and that it doesn't change how you feel about me. I also know you like to dance—and I could never dance like Aki does."

Nate felt a warmth settle over him. Ben spoke like he'd given serious thought to the nuances of their relationship. "You don't have to dance like Aki does. The way you focus so intently on whatever you're doing... That'd translate really well to the floor. Especially once you've found your vibe."

Ben tilted his head. "You've thought about this."

"I think about you a lot. This shouldn't be a surprise."

"But about us dancing, specifically?" Ben frowned.

"Yeah." Nate wrapped his arms around Ben, rocking him in time with the music. "There's a power on the dance floor. Once you get into it, the energy of it just picks you up and carries you along. It's like unfurling new leaves—you never want to stop."

He saw Ben's mouth quirk. "You're the only person I know who could compare dancing to growing leaves." He glanced toward the floor again. "Let's do this."

Nate paused. "You really want to? I know you've had a bad day. If you'd rather talk—"

"I don't want to talk. Or think." Ben tightened his hold on Nate. "I want to feel—and you always make me feel good."

Nate's breath caught. *Don't pull any punches.* He lifted Ben's hands from his shoulders, squeezing them before drawing one hand over Ben's head, guiding him around in a circle. He dropped his hands to Ben's hips, pressing against his back. "You can start by relaxing. You're not going to enjoy yourself wound up that tightly."

"Easy for you to say." Ben's movements were abrupt. "You know what you're doing."

Nate settled his arms around Ben, drawing him back against his chest. "Feel the rhythm. Go with it." He felt Ben relax, starting to sway with him. "Yeah, like that." He let go of Ben, raising his arms above his head as they moved.

Ben glanced back at him. His eyes gleamed in the dark and then he looked away, mirroring Nate's motions. "How's this?"

"It's a good start." Nate stepped back, circling Ben. "Use your whole body. Let it flow." He demonstrated, letting the music pulse through him.

Ben shut his eyes. The intermittent flashing lights caught his blush. "Promise you'll tell me if I'm making a fool of myself."

"No one would see you even if you were. There's a reason Century keeps its lights low."

Ben glanced up. His smile was wicked. "To prevent patrons embarrassing themselves? I thought they had a different purpose." He swayed toward Nate.

Nate felt his breath catch in his throat. There was an intent in Ben's gaze that sent an immediate surge of need through him. "So, maybe there's more than one reason."

Ben took hold of Nate's shirt with both hands, tugging Nate toward him. With every step they took, he brushed against Nate.

Heat coursed through Nate's skin at the contact. He couldn't resist, wrapping his arms around Ben, pulling him closer. "Knew you'd be good at this."

Ben straddled Nate's leg, sliding against him. "Know what else I'm good at?" His fingers closed around Nate's fly.

Nate's body reacted with immediate interest, his hips thrusting toward Ben. *Is this really happening?* Him. Ben. On the floor, in full view of anyone. "Are we still talking about dancing?"

Ben smiled. "That depends"—his gaze settled on Nate's mouth—"on how you define 'dancing.'"

Nate cupped Ben's chin. The friction between their bodies was nothing compared to Ben's tongue, slipping between his lips like this was all part of his master plan—

"You guys really are dating then."

Nate winced. As he turned to face Aki, he settled his arm around Ben. "I told you it was complicated." He frowned at Aki. Surely he could see they were in the middle of something?

Ben bumped his elbow against Nate's. "Nice to see you too, Aki." He settled his hand on the small of Nate's back. "You joining us on the floor?" He sounded like he meant the invitation, and Nate was relieved.

Aki scowled and shook his head. "It's nothing. Sorry to crash your date."

"It's not nothing." Aki could be thoughtless, but he wouldn't have interrupted without a reason. "What's up?"

"Can you spot me?"

Nate straightened. He looked over the heads of the people on the dance floor to the crowd at the bar. "Did something happen?"

Aki shook his head. "It's just a feeling—it's probably nothing." He crossed his arms over his chest. "I wouldn't be asking, but it's been building all night and keeps getting stronger."

Ben tilted his head. "By 'spot you,' do you mean—"

"Spot like in training. You know, when you get someone to keep an eye on you, make sure you don't get into trouble?" Nate placed his hand on Ben's arm. "Aki and I spot each other. If there's a situation or a client that gives us a weird vibe, but there's nothing concrete enough to call in security—"

"You look out for each other." Ben considered Aki. "And you don't know why you've got this feeling?"

Aki shook his head, shooting Nate an apologetic glance. "I thought it was to do with Rick. But he left early, so your guess is as good as mine."

"Could it be a client? Something someone said?" Ben looked toward the bar.

"Forget it. It's just a feeling." Aki wheeled around. "Enjoy your date."

Nate hesitantly placed a hand on Ben's shoulder. "So—" The moment was definitely gone. "What now?"

"Now?" Ben tangled his fingers in Nate's. "We spot Aki."

"You mean that?"

"He's your friend," Ben said. "And if we didn't, you'd spend the rest of the evening fretting about him."

Nate felt a warmth entirely unrelated to the previous heat between them. "You know me too well." He led the way across the club. There was a couple just leaving the bar, and Nate and Ben took their place, a few meters from where Aki was deep in conversation with one of his admirers.

Aki didn't halt what he was saying, but his eyes rested on Nate a moment and the corner of his mouth turned up.

Really worried then. Nate weighed up the guy talking to Aki. He was a well-dressed man in a suit. He played with his tie, leaning in to whisper something that made Aki smile. *Looks like a professional of some sort— but you can't always tell.*

"Here." Ben placed a glass beside him. "I needed something and I thought you might too."

Nate picked up the glass. "A coke?"

"No sense in tempting fate. Especially if Aki's right and something is going to happen."

Nate toyed with the drink. "You don't have to buy me anything you know."

"Why not? You bought me groceries." Ben made a motion as if to brush his hair out of his eyes, but his fingers closed on nothing. He dropped his hand to his glass. "I never thanked you for that, by the way."

"It's cool. I figured you had a lot on your mind."

Ben pursed his lips. "I did. But that's still no excuse. You were looking out for me—even if you did go about it in a backward way."

"You're being way kinder than you should to a guy who broke into your apartment." Nate's fingers tightened around his glass. "At the time, I didn't think that through, but now—"

"I wouldn't let anyone else get away with that," Ben said. "But you're always the exception that proves the rule."

Nate glanced at him. "Is that a good thing?"

"Depends what the rule is." Ben took a sip of his coke.

Nate followed suit. He wanted something a lot stronger than the soft drink, but Ben's call was wise. Nate glanced down the bar. *I really hope Aki's feeling clears up soon.* "Huh."

"What have you seen?" Ben was instantly alert.

"Check out that guy in the denim jacket." The guy was middle-aged and swarthy, overdue a shave by a good couple of days. He made his way down the bar, interrupting conversations to show people a photo, oblivious to the looks of annoyance shot his way. "Anything goes at Century—but he's way underdressed."

"He seems very intent on getting people to look at that photo," Ben agreed. "And he's not making very many friends in the process."

Nate had a sudden hunch. He took a step toward the man, but he'd already reached Aki and his client.

Aki shot the man a glare. He glanced at the photo, his lip curling. He made some comment to the man and turned back to his client.

The swarthy man was having none of it. He grabbed Aki's arm, jerking him back to face him. "What did you say?"

Aki tried to pull his arm back. "Let go of me."

"You think I'm going to let a little runt like you insult me and get away with it?" The man slammed his hand down hard on the bar, centimeters away from where Aki stood.

Aki flinched. "Once again. I'm sorry your hot boyfriend ditched you, but face facts. If you're looking for him here, then you already know it's over."

The man growled. "How dare you! I'm not some fag—" He raised his fist again, but before he could swing, Nate caught his arm from behind.

"Not a good idea." Nate hoped his tone was calm. Inwardly, he was anything but. "Century doesn't tolerate violence. You got the choice of leaving now or getting tossed out by security."

The man stiffened, turning to face Nate. His eyes flashed in the light from the bar. His nostrils flared. "What the hell are you?"

Nate stared at him. The man's eyes were yellow. He was suddenly reminded of the man he'd seen at Department Seven. "Aki, call security."

"Done," Aki reported immediately. Each of the hosts had an alarm built into their wristbands that could be activated with a single touch. "They're on the way."

They might even be making their way to the bar now, but Nate couldn't risk taking his eyes off the guy to check. His heart beat fast, like an animal suddenly realizing it was cornered.

"Aki? We need to leave." There was movement in Nate's peripheral vision, Ben hauling Aki away from the bar.

"Why? Nate's got this."

Nate clenched his fists, readying himself for the attack that could come at any moment. "Do it. This isn't a regular asshole."

The guy met his eyes and smirked. He knew the power he had, and he wasn't afraid to use it. "That's right. And I can tell you now—you're going to regret ever picking a fight with a werewolf."

Chapter Five

"YOU'RE GOING TO regret ever picking a fight with a werewolf."

Already do. Ben stayed where he was. Sudden movements and werewolves were not a great combination—especially when the wolf was already agitated. *He must have scented Nate's abilities.* As Ben watched, the man's nostrils flared again. His lip curled back, exposing his teeth in a snarl that was too canine for comfort.

Nate held his ground. His mouth pressed together thinly, but he refused to be intimidated, staring down the man before him.

Doesn't he know not to meet a wolf's eyes? Ben couldn't look away from the two of them.

Someone hit the lights. Ben heard the sound of protest quickly muffled as those on the dance floor realized the reason for the disturbance. *There must be at least fifty people in here. Fifty untrained civilians—and one wolf.* Ben forced himself to take his eyes off Nate, sizing up the club's escape routes. *Where's security? We need to get these people out of here!*

Aki drew a deep breath beside Ben.

The werewolf's eyes flickered toward them. His eyes narrowed.

Ben grabbed Aki's arm. He stepped backward, pulling Aki with him. "Aki, we have to get out of here."

"What are you doing?" Aki hissed, refusing to budge. "We can't leave Nate!"

"We need backup." Ben dragged Aki back another step. "You need to call Department Seven."

"For this loser?" Aki scoffed. "Look, security's already here. The guy's going to be tossed out on his tail faster than you can say 'karma.'" He tugged his arm free of Ben's grip.

"He's a werewolf."

"So? He's just one guy."

Ben glanced around the bar. Thankfully, the club-goers kept a safe distance—you didn't get to legal drinking age in New Camden without acquiring a sixth sense for supernatural situations—watching the altercation with varying degrees of concern and alarm. Ben scanned their faces, looking for anyone who seemed more than usually alert. *Wolves are never alone.*

"What's going on here?" A uniformed guard jogged up. He paused to size up the situation. "How about we step outside and see if we can sort out this misunderstanding, gentlemen?"

"There's nothing to misunderstand!" Aki folded his arms across his chest.

"An eight-oh-eight. The guy threatened Aki." Nate took his eyes off the wolf, turning to the guard.

No! "Nate—"

It was the opening the wolf had been waiting for. The guy swung, his fist catching Nate in the throat. He fell heavily into a bar stool.

"Hands above your head!" The security guard brandished his Taser. "Now!"

"You don't tell me what to do, human!" The man's voice was laced with a vicious snarl. He lashed out, catching the guard with a direct punch to the head. As the guard slid to the floor stunned, the wolf turned, looking for Aki.

Someone screamed. As if that was a cue, mass panic broke out. People ran for the door, or dived for cover behind the bar.

Ben was roughly shouldered aside by a passing club-goer and lost his balance. He fell, catching his head against the edge of a stool. The room swayed, tipping crazily. *That's me. I've fallen.*

There were hands on his side. Aki knelt beside him. "Ben! Are you— oh fuck."

Ben raised his head with difficulty to follow Aki's gaze.

The wolf watched them. He seemed to be enjoying the panic. A smile played across his face as he stepped over the unconscious guard toward them. "I'm not going to make you regret those words," he promised, not taking his eyes off Aki. "I'm going to make you regret ever learning to speak."

"Don't move," Ben croaked. "Whatever you do, don't run."

"Who said anything about running?" Aki murmured. "I've forgotten how to move."

The wolf snarled again, gathering himself for a leap—and was suddenly jerked backward. Before he could regain his balance, Nate had swung his fist in the wolf's face. It connected with a powerful crack—one that sounded wooden. The wolf stumbled backward.

"Nate! What are you doing?" Aki sounded hysterical. "That's a werewolf!"

Ben winced as Aki's shout went straight through his throbbing head. *About time Aki's survival instincts kicked in—but did they have to kick in so loudly?*

"The guy's a bully and a jerk." Nate watched the wolf, readying himself to meet his next attack. His voice sounded calm. "I'm not letting him hurt you—or anyone else."

He's done something. Ben let Aki haul him into a sitting position. *Nate's not using any ordinary strength. If he's tapped into the tree part of him—* Ben transferred his gaze to the werewolf, noticeably swaying as he regained his footing.

Something warm trickled down his lip. Ben absently brushed it aside with his hand. The scent of copper brought a sudden surge of hunger. *Blood.* He looked at the red smear on his hand and put his fingers to his lip. *I'm bleeding...?*

The wolf snarled, launching himself at Nate. They grappled furiously for the upper hand, sending another bar stool tumbling. The wolf tried to overpower Nate with increasing desperation, but Nate was as immoveable as an oak tree. He met a full-body tackle without flinching, throwing the wolf back to the floor.

The wolf hauled himself up onto his elbows, using a nearby stool as support. "What the hell are you?"

"Someone who is done holding back." Nate clenched his fists. "You want to fight, fine. Just don't be surprised if you bite off more than you can chew."

The wolf reacted to Nate's words with another snarl and threw the bar stool.

It was hard to think past the blood. It filled Ben's senses, demanding attention. *Think.* He swayed unsteadily to his feet. "Aki, call Department Seven. And then alert your manager."

This time, Aki didn't argue. He scurried off, the wolf not giving him a glance. All his attention was concentrated on Nate.

Careless. Ben's teeth bared as he smiled. *The wolf has made himself open.* He was oblivious to the security team hurrying across the floor to surround him.

"Tasers?" A younger man asked.

The security chief shook his head. "We risk getting Nate."

The conversation alerted the werewolf to their presence. His eyes rolled and he growled. As the security team took an alarmed step back, the guy dropped to the floor.

Ben's skin tingled as magic surged nearby. "Nate! Pin him—now! You need to end this quickly!"

"We have him outnumbered." Nate looked to Ben. "It's over—he just doesn't know it."

"He's changing into wolf form. You've got to stop him before he transforms."

The man screamed. The horrible sound of twisting bone echoed through the club, and the sound of tearing fabric followed. He rocked forward on the floor, twisting as they watched.

"Shit!" Nate dropped on top of him, an arm around the guy's neck. He was joined by the security team, all piling on him in an attempt to subdue the guy before he could reach the final stages of his transformation.

They're too late. Ben licked his lips, standing still as he waited for the result. He felt eerily calm. His senses worked overtime, weighing the various threats that surrounded him, but he felt a confidence that was completely disproportionate to his human state.

Maybe I'm not a vampire—but I still have my ARX training. Now that they had the very real prospect of a wolf in the club, the first priority was getting the remaining people inside far away. Ben pulled himself up to address the people crouched behind the bar. "Into the kitchen. Now."

They didn't argue either. Ben looked across the club but saw that once the people crouched under the table booths had seen the stream of movement, they'd also made their way to the nearest exit.

Good. Ben felt a moment's exultation—he wasn't sure why—but another horrible crack brought his attention back to the wolf. This was followed by an ominous silence.

The security guards shouted as they felt the body beneath them move. They slid off as the wolf raised himself onto two legs—and he really was a wolf now. His torso had expanded, and his muscular body was covered in thick fur. Worst of all were the teeth bared as he snarled—a single snap from those could end a man's life. And Nate was still hanging on to the guy's neck. As Ben watched, the wolf dropped to all fours and shook itself furiously. Nate lost his grip and was thrown.

No one hurts what is mine. Ben drew himself up. His hands flexed and he regretted his lack of weapon.

The wolf turned, locking eyes with him. Awareness glittered in its eyes and it snarled a warning.

Ben drew back his teeth in disgust. *You do not intimidate me, wolf.* He stepped back as the wolf began to prowl around him, the two mutually circling each other. Some part of Ben's brain shouted that this was unusual—that a werewolf wouldn't waste time intimidating a human like this, especially when it had shown itself so contemptuous of the security guards.

Another part of Ben, a much louder part, gloried in it. *The wolf recognizes a fellow predator.* The effects of being a vampire for so long?

Not the time. Ben noticed the slight pause in the wolf's rhythm. He readjusted his weight. *Building up to a pounce.* He watched the wolf's hindquarters for the telltale giveaway of the leap and flung himself out of the way. He was back on his feet before the wolf managed to turn.

Not bad for a guy without vampire speed. Ben permitted himself a slight smirk, keeping his eyes on the wolf. It would leap again. And with every leap, there was the chance of it catching him. *I need a weapon. Something to end this.*

Something long and thick intruded into his vision. One of the guards had dropped his Taser. *Perfect.*

Ben darted forward as if making a break for escape. As the wolf pounced, Ben dropped, launching himself at the Taser. He grabbed it, but before he could lift it, the wolf's paw slammed down on the other end.

The wolf growled low, an obvious warning. The sound seemed to go all the way through Ben, just as the wolf's yellow eyes stared him down. His teeth bared, the growl built to a more ominous rumble.

Ben's nostrils flared. The scent of the wolf mingled with the coppery traces of the cut on his lip. It urged him to fight.

So I fight with the only weapon I have. Ben stared the wolf full in the eyes and snarled back. Werewolves, with their ingrained hierarchy, were particularly sensitive to influence. If Ben could make the wolf believe he was a stronger predator, they might just have a chance—

No if. You're going to do this. Ben leaned closer to the wolf. He summoned all the arrogance of master vampire, projecting the cold confidence that characterized Saltaire. "Heel, dog."

The wolf wavered. Its snarl dropped and it hunched back. A whine escaped it. It took its foot off the Taser as it stepped back—

And was suddenly raised in the air by someone behind it and slammed into the side of the bar. It slid to the floor and was still.

Nate placed an arm against the bar to steady himself, looking down at the wolf at his feet. It didn't even try to rise. "Guess that settles that." He looked up, caught Ben's gaze, and smiled.

Ben smiled back—and something sharp dug into the side of his cheeks. As the security team set about securing the stunned wolf within a net, Ben ducked into a darkened corner. Carefully, he ran his tongue down the row of his teeth. *This isn't possible.*

Where there should have been only teeth there were now fangs.

Ben ran his tongue over their edge, tasting again the faint tinge of copper in his mouth. *This shouldn't be possible.* He felt for his pulse, steady and regular. *I didn't die. There's no way I should be a vampire— no way.* Ben leaned heavily against the bar. He spotted a spoon on the bar beside him and picked it up. Where there should have been a reflection, there was nothing.

Shit. Ben let the spoon slide from his fingers. Police sirens sounded outside, indicating that Department Seven had arrived. *I've got far bigger problems than a werewolf.*

"SO MUCH FOR 'staying out of trouble,' blossom." Kenzies shook her head as she surveyed the scene. She'd wasted no time sizing up the situation, directing her staff to load the werewolf into the secure van Department Seven had brought with them and dispatching her staff to reassure and take statements from the club-goers. She'd opted to interview those directly involved with the incident herself—starting with Nate.

Ben, watching from the sidelines, had to suppress the urge to snarl. He didn't like Kenzies's proprietary attitude toward Nate, and he liked even less the way that Nate appeared genuinely glad to see her. Nate didn't understand that Department Seven were not his friends. Instead, Ben stayed where he was. His tongue flicked up, but the fangs were still there. He shut his eyes, trying to will them aside. Until they vanished, he couldn't risk attracting any attention.

"This isn't my fault," Nate protested. "The guy just lashed out. He could have done serious damage—"

"Is this true?" A woman in a pale-green business suit walked in, Aki hovering at her elbow. She picked her way through the scattered debris as if she walked down a catwalk. Several of the surrounding Department Seven officers paused in their duties to size her up.

Ben breathed in sulfur and power. *Dangerous!* Denise was powerful, that was obvious—but it was hard to pinpoint the source of her power. The sulfur indicated some sort of demonic origin, but her face, as she scanned the mess left in the club, gave no hint of her thoughts. *Doubly dangerous. This woman is a master at whatever she is...*

Force her into revealing herself with a surprise attack! You can be off and away before she knows what hit her—

Ben pinched the bridge of his nose. *Great. Now I'm thinking like a vampire.* He took firm control of himself. There would be no sneak attacks tonight. *I'm a totally normal citizen caught up in an extraordinary event. That's all.*

As Denise looked around, her eyes fell on Ben. She immediately stiffened. "What is he doing here? I thought I made my instructions clear. No vampires on Century premises without express permission from management."

"It's cool." Nate walked over to put his arm around Ben. "There's a long and complicated story behind it, but Ben's human now."

Ben pressed his lips together in what he hoped was a convincing smile as Nate drew him back toward the group. The last thing he wanted to do was join the discussion—but if he remained close to Nate, then Nate's own power would hopefully prevent anyone sensing the vampire's presence.

Nate leaned down to whisper to Ben. "Everything okay? It's not like you to be quiet when there's a situation like this going down."

Ben hesitated, glancing round to see if they were observed. Denise was talking, expressing her desire that Department Seven would get to the bottom of the matter quickly. Kenzies appeared to be listening to her, but Ben knew from past experience how good a werewolf's hearing was. There was one option available to him. *Here's hoping the werewolf scared off anyone without supernatural links.* Otherwise the restrictions on who could see Ben were going to make Nate look really weird. He tugged Nate around to face him, pulling him down for a kiss.

Nate took the hint eagerly—so eagerly that Ben felt a moment's guilt that this wasn't the spur of the moment expression of affection Nate imagined. He relaxed his grip on Nate's shirt, letting his fingers stroke the back of Nate's neck in apology. He felt the moment that Nate encountered his fangs. His body tensed, and he drew back to stare down at Ben with wide eyes. Ben pressed his lips together and nodded.

Nate looked as if he only just stopped himself from glancing around to see if they were observed. "How?" he whispered.

Ben squeezed his hand. "I don't know. But let's keep this between us."

Nate nodded, the muscles in his throat tensing as he swallowed. As they turned back to watch the discussion unfolding, his hand settled around Ben again.

Ben knew more about the supernatural than Nate—but the gesture made him keenly aware of how close Nate stood, how right it felt whenever he brushed against Ben. *Focus! You can't get distracted now.* But with the wolf contained, the energy in his body wanted a new outlet. It wanted Nate.

Ben fought the urge to tug his shirt down. *At least if anyone glances this way, they'll put our odd behavior down to mutual attraction.* That gave him an idea.

He squeezed Nate's hand, turning toward him. "We need to get out of here," he said, letting his need color his words. If Kenzies was listening, she'd interpret them as a couple wanting privacy, not Ben needing to escape. "Take me home?" It was bad enough being surrounded by Department Seven staff, but at any moment, they risked—

"Not so fast." Gunn had arrived.

Ben tensed. *Of course, we wouldn't get a break.* He turned to see Gunn lighting a cigarette in full view of the club's no-smoking signs, surveying the gathered crowd with a smirk. "Trying to skip out on the party you started, Bennet? I find that very curious. A guy might think you didn't want your statement taken."

How long had he been there observing? Ben took a moment to calm his racing heart. "We've given statements."

Gunn marched over to him, brandishing his cigarette like a weapon. "Not to me you haven't. And I want a full explanation of all of this." He paused, leaning in to Ben. "What on earth have you been up to?"

There was a firm denial on Ben's lips, but with Gunn in his face, he was frozen. He took a deep breath, immediately regretting it. This close, Gunn's signature scent of smoke and stale air was almost overpowering. *I have to say something—but the longer I hesitate, the more suspicious I become.* His mouth twitched as Ben fought the instinct to bare his fangs and snarl back at Gunn. The vampire recognized another master predator in the *lemur,* a fact that only amped up Ben's reactions.

Gunn's mouth curved in triumph. "No answer, huh? I find that most suspicious." His eyes glittered as he paused to take a drag of his cigarette.

Denise had other ideas. Her heels clicked as she marched across the floor. "Officer Gunn. You're well aware of Century's no-smoking policy."

Gunn turned to face her, raising an eyebrow as he sized her up. His gaze lingered on the low-cut bosom of her suit jacket, before settling on her face with studied insolence. "Nonsmoking, Ms. Levin? Could have sworn I caught a whiff of brimstone earlier."

Denise's eyes narrowed. Before Gunn had sensed her intention, she had snatched his cigarette and ground it out on the floor beneath the toe of her high heel shoe. "I'm surprised you can smell anything. Your considerable personal odor gave me the impression you'd lost the use of your nose a long time ago, officer."

Gunn smirked, crossing his arms as he applied himself to this new victim. "I don't miss much. May I commiserate with you on your return to work? First day back, only for your club to be gate-crashed by a werewolf." His eyes glittered. "That doesn't say much for your management."

Denise wasn't having any of it. "That doesn't say much for the werewolf. My staff responded to the situation promptly, and we avoided any serious injuries to our clients. Your medical staff assure me that Jackson will recover soon. I'd like to know what you intend to do about the werewolf."

"What is going on here?" A belligerent figure shouldered past the watching security team and walked up to Gunn and Denise. "I had a phone call from your office informing me that one of my pack had accosted a civilian—an allegation I find incredibly hard to believe—and now I see that he is confined to a police van like a common criminal. This is highly irregular and I protest vehemently the handling he has received." He looked from Gunn, to Denise and the watching crowd. "Well? I demand a full explanation."

"We were just getting to that." Gunn made a gesture as if to reach for another cigarette, but a glance at Denise stopped him.

Kenzies glanced at the notebook in her hand. "Preliminary interviews with witnesses at the scene indicate that Carl Grossman, listed as a member of your pack, launched an unprovoked attack on a civilian, ignored the attempts of Century's security to deescalate the situation, and instigated a brawl culminating in his transformation in a crowded public place, and seriously injuring at least one guard."

Wisner didn't even glance her way. His eyes remained on Gunn. "Well? I'm waiting."

Kenzies bristled, but apart from drawing in a reflexive breath, said nothing.

Gunn's eyes narrowed. "Preliminary interviews with witnesses at the scene indicate that your fucking wolf attacked a civilian, blew off security, transformed in a manner dangerous to civilians, and knocked out a guard."

Wisner crossed his arms. "I find that hard to believe. What proof do you have?" His eyes lingered on Ben and Nate and he sneered. "I doubt the veracity of these so-called witnesses—"

"In addition to the civilian he harassed and his friends, Department Seven is currently taking statements from the bar staff, and between twenty to thirty of the civilians who stuck around. They all agree on the facts of the situation, Councilor," Kenzies reported. "And that is that your wolf acted entirely inappropriately."

Wisner frowned.

"I don't have the fucking patience for another round of musical whispers," Gunn said. "You heard her."

"I'd like to know what action you intend to take, Councilor Wisner." Denise had her hands on her hips. "You've been very vocal about keeping the city safe from supernatural threats. What happens when the threat is caused by your pack? And don't deny your wolf was responsible. My staff are reviewing the security footage as we speak." She indicated a camera above their heads. "The camera doesn't lie."

Wisner made a stiff bow. "Carl was part of a team of wolves I assigned to go door-to-door through the club district, looking for sightings of the rogue werewolf currently threatening the city. It is deeply regrettable that he found himself involved in an altercation in the course of his search. I regard the locating and securing of the rogue werewolf as paramount to the safety of the city."

"And the safety and security of my staff and customers is paramount to me," Denise said.

"Naturally, your guard will be compensated—"

Denise wasn't deterred. "I demand a public apology, Wisner."

"The matter is still under investigation." Wisner tugged his jacket straight. "Although, I do concede that before he was sent to canvas Century, Carl should have been better briefed on what is appropriate behavior for your establishment—"

"Appropriate behavior for anywhere!" Ben felt Nate tense as Aki pushed his way into the circle. Department Seven had patched him up when they'd taken his statement, so he had a bandage on one cheek. He waved an angry finger at Wisner. "I know you've got license to do what you like within your own pack, but that doesn't give you the right to force it on other people! Keep your creepy Neanderthal beliefs to yourself."

Gunn chuckled. "Sounds like someone wants to make a statement."

"I have so many statements—"

Wisner snarled viciously.

Aki froze, as if the fact that he was face-to-face with a second werewolf had just registered.

Nate stepped forward, silently putting his hand on Aki's shoulder. "Pretty sure that intimidating a witness is a big 'No.'"

Wisner's eyes rested on Nate speculatively. "You're the man responsible for Carl's unconscious condition."

Ben felt a thrill of horror at Wisner's appraisal of Nate. "Actually, Carl is responsible for Carl's unconscious condition, Councilor." Wisner turned his gaze on him, and Ben forced himself to continue. "It's extremely lucky Nate was here. If he hadn't stopped him, Carl might have severely injured a civilian, or worse."

Wisner frowned, but before he could voice his thoughts, Denise spoke.

"Severely injure a civilian or worse. That's hardly likely to inspire confidence in the city's head of security, is it?"

Wisner's nostrils flared. "I'll review the incident. If I consider Carl at fault, he won't leave the pack compound until he's been sufficiently educated on the inappropriateness of his behavior." He glanced to Gunn. "I'll leave it to you to deal with these miscreants."

His words were met by an immediate outcry. "I resent the dismissal of my staff as miscreants—" Denise started.

Aki was just as upset. "And what about his punishment? He attacked me—what if I want to press charges?"

Wisner permitted himself a slight smile. "That is unfortunate for you." He walked out, making a point of forcing the security team to move aside to let him pass.

"What does he mean?" Aki said. "He can't stop me from pressing charges, can he?"

"Werewolves fall under a gray area in the law," Kenzies explained. She was just as tense as anyone else. More, Ben realized. The presence of Wisner must send her own lupine instincts into overdrive, while the man's insolent behavior tested her professionally. "They're bound by the rules set down by their pack leader, not those of the city. But their pack leader is responsible for making sure that no member of his pack breaks the rules. When a crime is committed, as long as it can't be demonstrated that the pack leader ordered it, punishment is left in the hands of the pack."

"That is bullshit! That is the most bullshit thing I have heard tonight!"

Denise put a hand on his arm, and Aki subsided angrily. "I agree with Mr. Fujino. The steps that Councilor Wisner is likely to take do not reassure me to the safety of my club. I demand action, Officer Gunn."

"Kenzies is our lupine expert." Gunn nodded to his deputy. "She can discuss your options with you. In the meantime, I'd like a word with Nate and Ben."

Ben swallowed. "Of course." His voice sounded stiff. He followed Gunn reluctantly across the club to one of the table booths on the ground floor. *Hopefully Gunn doesn't read too much into that—what am I thinking? Gunn already knows.* As a *lemur,* Gunn was tuned in to negative emotion.

As Nate sat down beside him, he felt for Ben's hand, squeezing it under the table.

Ben felt a rush of gratitude. At least this time, he wasn't facing Gunn's interrogation alone.

"So, Nate." Gunn leaned an elbow on the table, casually putting his feet up on the seat on his side of the booth. "Fighting werewolves, huh? That's really keeping a low profile."

"I didn't realize he was a werewolf at the time," Nate protested.

"And when you did?" Gunn looked at him. "From all accounts, you didn't seem reluctant to throw your weight around."

"What was I supposed to do, let Aki get hurt?" Nate leaned forward. "He's just human!"

"And you, on the other hand, aren't." Gunn tilted his head. "Out of curiosity, how did you manage to stand up to a fully transformed werewolf? They're supposedly unstoppable."

"You don't have to answer that question," Ben said.

Nate hesitated.

Gunn shot Ben a look of dislike. "Using magic of any kind in a public space is a serious offense, Nate."

"You don't know he used magic," Ben said. "His strength could be inherent."

Gunn sat up, giving Ben a flat look. "I find that difficult to believe."

"Nate is an unknown," Ben said. "No one knows how his powers work. So before you throw out accusations of magic use, maybe you should gather more facts."

Gunn snorted.

Beside Ben, Nate suddenly started. "Ow!" He rubbed his shin, staring at Gunn. "Did you kick me?"

"Inherent strength my ass." Gunn folded his arms. "I'm going to have to make a note of this on your file. Probably recommend further counseling. Maybe even a spot of community labor."

"I can't believe you kicked me."

"That's not proof," Ben said. "And you know it. What's the point of harassing Nate anyway? You know Wisner's wolf was behind this."

"The point is that totally normal people do not wrestle werewolves."

Ben froze. Gunn couldn't know—could he? *Department Seven works closely with the Registry—but no, it hasn't even been a day since my hearing! There's no way—*

"But you know I'm not...totally normal." Nate frowned.

"Yeah. I know. But it's not a good idea to advertise that fact in front of pricks like Wisner." Gunn felt in his bomber jacket for his packet of cigarettes. "Take it from me, Nate. The guy is itching to make an example out of someone. You want to keep your head down."

Ben felt cold. If Gunn shared his fears, the situation had to be serious.

"Show up to community service, and do an exemplary job. Avoid all further contact with any werewolves. If you see Wisner or his goons, call me, and get the fuck out of there. You got that?"

Nate nodded, frowning. "What's going on? Is this because of the rogue wolf?"

"The brat's certainly not helping. But the tide is changing." Gunn twirled a cigarette in his fingers. "Wisner's looking to make New Camden a pack concern, and he might just pull it off."

"You're not going to light that cigarette I presume, Gunn." Denise stood over their table.

Gunn paused in the act of reaching for his lighter. "I'm in the middle of an interview."

"Wasting our valuable time, you mean." Denise's hands rested on her hips. "Your subordinates have already interviewed Nathan. As the wolf has been removed from the club, and you tell us there is no chance of prosecution, I fail to see what point there is to prolonging this interview."

Gunn stood slowly, drawing himself up to meet her gaze. "You're in a hurry to get us out of here. Afraid of what we might find if we stick around?"

Denise raised her jaw. "Century has nothing to hide from Department Seven. In fact, if you'd like to stick around, I can offer you the staff discount."

"Very generous." Gunn leered, leaning against the booth. "And which member of the staff would that discount apply for? I'm hoping management is included."

From the way Nate tensed beside him, and the silence in the club, Ben was braced for something far worse than Denise's smile. It was sharp and dangerous, drawn tight like a whip. She stepped forward, her fingers trailing across Gunn's chin, gently stroking his stubble. "You couldn't afford me, Gunn. I'd take all you have and more. And you—" She dropped her hand.

Gunn, leaning into her touch, overbalanced. He stumbled, clumsily.

Denise's smile was satisfaction personified. "You have nothing left to lose." She turned her gaze on Nate. "Nathan, if you wouldn't mind joining us in the break room. I'd like to refresh your memory of our employee safety measures."

Nate stood.

Ben watched them go. People drew back as Denise stalked through the club, Nate trailing behind her. She collected Aki and the remaining staff members not already involved in the debriefing the security team was having in a corner. He felt like he'd had a narrow escape—

Gunn sighed. "That is a woman worth losing your soul to."

Ben shot him a look. "You don't have a soul to lose."

Gunn glanced at him with pure dislike, but before he could act on it, Kenzies appeared at his elbow.

"We done, boss?" She gestured to the Department Seven staff milling behind them. "Only we're none of us getting overtime to watch you get shot down."

Gunn's snarl was reflexive. "Move out. And Ben?" His hand fell on Ben's arm. "Mind stepping outside a moment? I want a word."

NEW CAMDEN WAS still wide awake, even at this time of night. Century's lights flickered overhead, the neon hum just audible beneath the sound of music and voices from neighboring clubs.

Ben wrapped his arms around himself. How many of Century's patrons promptly took cover in other clubs? For many of them, witnessing an altercation with a werewolf would not be enough to throw them off their groove. He felt a sudden appreciation for New Camden's resilience.

Gunn took a deep and noisy pull of his cigarette. "That's better."

Ben's nose twitched. "For you, maybe."

Gunn snorted. "When I picked it up, everyone was doing it. Doctors recommended it for patients. To calm the nerves. You should try it."

"Pass." Ben spoke carefully, avoiding breathing in through his nose.

"Sure? You seem plenty nervous tonight."

Ben stayed still. *He's just guessing. Probing for a reaction.* He risked a quick swipe of his tongue over his teeth. The fangs were gone. "Your imagination is getting overtime."

"It and everyone else in the department. Everyone's got extra shifts, tracking down Wisner's lost puppy—on top of everything else we got to do. And that's not all. You know, the Registry wants us to do its work for it, too."

Ben froze. This was bad. "People wanting you to do your job. Yeah, that does sound rough."

Gunn drew a crumpled letter from his pocket. As he smoothed it out, Ben caught a glimpse of the Registry's letterhead—and his own name. "It's an interesting request. I'm to fill out an appraisal of one Bennet Hawick, and indicate whether I would support his application for humanity."

"You must get requests for security appraisals all the time." Ben took a deep breath and immediately regretted it. The smoke made his eyes tear and hung uncomfortably to the back of his throat. "I'm sure you're too much of a professional to allow any personal vendettas to sway your opinion."

Gunn chuckled. "First time anyone's accused me of being professional. But as a seasoned officer, I got to admit tackling a transformed werewolf does not strike me as the actions of a"—he glanced at the letter—"well-adjusted citizen to me."

Calm! He can't know how serious this is. Ben narrowed his eyes. "Gunn. You're amoral, irresponsible, and prey on the negative emotions of weak, suffering, and vulnerable people. You refusing to vet me is pretty much a shining seal of approval."

Gunn shook his head. "Compliments will get you nowhere, Benny. You want me to sign off on your clearance, I got a job for you."

Every instinct Ben had warned him that nothing good could come of working with Gunn. *But what choice do I have?* "A job? What kind of a job? I'm not breaking the law—"

"You'll be assisting Department Seven in the pursuit of a dangerous fugitive. And quite possibly, preventing another scene like the one you saw tonight."

Ben blinked. "The rogue werewolf?"

"Yeah. Daddy wolf's not happy that one of his pack is AWOL—sets a bad example to the rest of his tame dogs. The longer it takes us to locate the pup, the worse his temper becomes—and the more likely it is that someone is going to get hurt."

He couldn't disagree with Gunn there. Wisner—well, nothing about the guy suggested that he was a reasonable man. "You're not asking me to find him are you? Because my days as an investigator are behind me."

"I'm sure the god-fearing people of this city sleep more soundly for it. No. We don't know where the wolf is, but we know who might. Before he turned tail, the wolf was a member of a counseling group run through Department Seven. We think the members of that group know something they're not telling. If you infiltrate that group, you might hear something of use to us."

Ben frowned. "You're asking me to spy for you? I refuse."

Gunn grinned at him. It was not a pleasant sight. "As you wish. But I'm not signing any reports until that wolf is found and secured."

He'd been right to be afraid. "You can't do that!"

"Can't I?" Gunn took another pull of his cigarette. "That rogue wolf is our top priority right now. Until he's found, it's entirely in order for us to suspend non-urgent business such as performing security clearances. Public safety is our priority, you know."

Public safety had never been Gunn's priority—and both of them knew it. Ben narrowed his eyes. "This is highly questionable—even for you. You can't do this."

"Can't I?" Gunn dropped his cigarette butt into the street. "See you tomorrow. Nine AM sharp, Benny."

Chapter Six

"C'MON, AKI." NATE put his hand over the kitchen doorway, preventing Aki from squeezing past him into the kitchen. "The dog needs a walk. Look at him! He hasn't been out since yesterday."

"So walk him yourself." Aki folded his arms. He was already dressed for running, with a fluorescent jacket over his shorts and singlet. "You made the ludicrous decision to adopt the thing, so it's obviously your responsibility."

"But I have to go to Department Seven for community service, and you're going to the park anyway."

"Not my problem." Aki gave up dignity and crawled under Nate's arm. "Anyway, I'm going to run. Not dog sit."

Nate cast an eye at the dog. He sat hopefully, the piece of rope Nate had found, looped through his collar. "Dogs like running." They must, right? "And this dog's used to taking care of itself. You won't even know he's there."

Aki snorted as he refilled his water bottle from the sink. "Believe me, I will know."

The dog gave a soft whine.

"Please?" Nate said. "I did kind of save your life last night."

Aki groaned. "You would bring that up, wouldn't you?"

"It is a pretty big deal. I mean, a friend agrees to spot you. A true friend punches a werewolf in the face for you."

Aki smirked. "I should not be encouraging you to punch werewolves—even if they are incredible jerks—but fine. I'll walk your stupid dog—but only this time."

"Thanks, Aki." Nate looked to the dog. "Ready to go, Fluffy?"

He was already on his feet, his tail wagging happily. As Aki adjusted his headphones, the dog danced happily around him.

"We're not calling it 'Fluffy.' That's cruel and unusual."

"Well, what would you call him?"

"An unwanted encumbrance." Aki wiped his hand on his shorts before taking up the rope. He resisted the dog's attempts to pull him toward the door. "I warn you. If this mutt gives me fleas, I will be exacting a heavy and painful revenge."

"Thanks, Aki."

"You hear me? *Painful.*"

DEPARTMENT SEVEN MIGHT not have been filled with hunters, but the office was obviously busy. Nate leaned against the front counter, waiting for the receptionist to end her call. The moment she replaced the receiver, it rang again. She picked it up, giving Nate a grimace. *With you in a moment*, she mouthed.

Nate looked around the reception area. Although it was early in the morning, there were a couple of people dozing in seats. A couple were dressed for clubbing. *Have they been waiting overnight?*

"Hold and I'll reroute you directly to the officer in charge." The receptionist put down the receiver. "Hey, honey. You here for—"

The phone rang again.

"You've reached Department Seven. How can I help?" The receptionist pushed a pad of paper and a pen toward Nate.

He wrote down "Community Service" and pushed the pad back.

"Can you describe the nature of your complaint?" the receptionist asked. She cupped the phone to her chest and jerked her head toward the internal door. "Same room as last time."

"Thanks." Nate pushed open the internal door with misgivings. A sign on the door indicated that you were only allowed past the door in the company of a Department Seven officer. *Then again, people don't exactly break into police stations as a rule.* Nate took a deep breath and tried to look as if he knew where he was going.

He found the interrogation room without difficulty. To his surprise, Charlotte and Vazul were already there.

"Nate!" Charlotte greeted him with a wave and a smile. "You're joining us again? What a nice surprise."

Vazul smirked. "Glad to see that you're joining us in marked opposition to the current suppressive regime."

"I don't know about that," Nate said. "Gunn just said something about community service."

"It's supposed to cure us of our uncooperative attitudes by fostering a sense of pride in our community, or at least the part of the community consisting of the parks." Vazul sneered. "In reality, a morning picking up cigarette butts engenders nothing but scorn for my so-called peers—"

Charlotte sighed. "You saying stuff like that is why we keep having to do community service." She looked at Nate. "Kenzies dropped off some jackets and gloves for us to use. Vazul and I already have ours."

The jackets were high-visibility vests with "Dept. 7" emblazoned across the back. There were two pairs of gloves on the table. Nate reached for the bigger pair. They were a tight fit, but they'd do. "What's with the extra pair? They're not expecting your werewolf friend to show up for this?"

"According to Kenzies, there's one more person joining us. As soon as he shows up, we can leave."

As if on cue, the door opened. Ben stood there, wearing a hoodie and a pair of jeans so new they still had the shop crease. "Is this the interrogation room?"

Nate felt a huge grin split his face. "Ben! What are you doing here?"

"The same thing as you. Community service."

"No way. You?" Nate frowned. Gunn could boss Nate around all he wanted—as a supernatural, Nate came into the officer's jurisdiction. But Ben was human.

"I don't want to talk about it." Ben pulled on the gloves with resignation. "Let's just get this over with."

"Right." Nate turned to their companions. "Charlotte, Vazul, this is Ben. He's a friend of mine."

Ben gave a grimace that might have been intended to be a smile. Charlotte waved hello.

Vazul sneered. "If we wait until someone in Department Seven remembers us, we are likely to be here all morning. I suggest we leave now and make a start. Kenzies will find us." He grabbed some of the rubbish bags on the table and stuffed them into his jeans pockets

"You've done this before?" Nate asked, following Vazul's example.

"Numerous times. And yet, for some strange reason, it doesn't make me any more charitably inclined to our human 'friends.'"

Nate glanced worriedly in Ben's direction. "Not everyone litters."

"Wait and see," Charlotte picked up a pair of tongs. "I like people, and by the end of these sessions, I'm left feeling pretty upset."

Ben snorted. "Nothing like cleaning up someone else's mess to really make you feel for them. Let's go." He walked out of the room, leaving the others to catch up.

THE PARK VAZUL referred to was a small square of grass not far from Department Seven. Nate was relieved. He didn't mind telling Aki about having to do community service, but he drew the line at Aki spectating. Once the morning sun cleared the surrounding buildings, the day was pleasant. As they spread out to look for trash throughout the park, Nate hummed.

"You cannot be enjoying this." Vazul had a metal spike which he used to skewer soggy pieces of paper and plastic wrappers.

Nate squirmed. "It's a good day for this, at least. It'd suck if it was raining."

"It does suck," Vazul confirmed. "Just you wait. This is hardly the last time we'll be picking up trash together." He moved off in pursuit of a piece of newspaper. Charlotte drifted after him, leaving Nate alone with Ben.

Nate felt a smile crease his face. He turned aside to pick up a discarded water bottle but was conscious that Ben was studying him as he pulled his gloves on.

"Vazul is right. You are way too cheerful."

Nate shrugged. "I didn't expect to be hanging out with you this morning. Or even last night. It's almost like we're dating." He bit his lip but Ben only snorted.

"I hate to break it to you, but picking up trash in the park is a terrible date."

Nate frowned, extricating a soggy cigarette packet from under a bush. "You know something weird? We've never actually been on a date."

"And if you enjoy picking up trash, that might be why." Ben stood on tiptoe to grab a plastic bag caught in the branches of a tree.

"I'm serious. Our entire relationship has been back to front. We fucked the first time we met—"

"Not so loudly! Charlotte and Vazul might hear." Ben's hand fell just short of the bag.

"Then we got to know each other," Nate continued. "And we've both met each other's families before we've even been out for coffee." He placed a hand on the trunk of the tree.

Ben took a step back as the branch he was trying to reach suddenly lowered. He raised his eyebrows when he saw where Nate's hand was. "That's cheating."

"Not when I'm being helpful."

"Show-off." Ben plucked the plastic bag out of the tree.

"Aren't you going to thank me?"

Ben shook his head, proceeding down the park. "I'm not encouraging this behavior."

Nate followed after him. "You mean me using magic, or me flirting with you?"

Ben's shoulders tensed. "You know why we can't date, Nate."

"I don't know. I think I did a pretty good job of sticking up for myself—and Aki—last night. That werewolf never knew what hit him."

Ben's mouth curved. "That's certainly true."

"So, what do you say? One entirely normal date."

Ben shook his head. "Sorry, Nate."

"At least pretend to think about it, jeez! I'd even let you pick where we go and what we do."

"I've got a lot going on right now. My application's more complicated than I first thought."

"How do you mean?"

Ben hesitated. "I need to get additional clearance. They've set me up with a caseworker. She's lined me up for an interview with an expert today, and then I'm meeting her again tomorrow."

Nate frowned. "Isn't that a little excessive?" He studied Ben with a frown.

The daylight made the angles of Ben's face appear abrupt, highlighting the shadows under his eyes. His expressive mouth wobbled, and his brows pulled together in thought. "It's nothing you need to worry about." He looked up and caught Nate's eyes on him. He smiled. "You would not believe the amount of red tape involved in this. It's more time-consuming than anything else. In fact, picking up trash with you might be the highlight of my day."

"Now who's flirting?" Nate elbowed Ben, who retaliated by nudging Nate's shin with his foot.

"Do you mind? We're supposed to be picking up rubbish, not fooling around!" Vazul called out from across the park. Reluctantly, Nate returned to work.

The park was frequently used as a shortcut by office workers on their way to the surrounding buildings, dog walkers, a few joggers and two people that Nate just couldn't place. They circled the park, stopping pedestrians and waking the guy stretched out on a park bench. As the two guys moved on, the man on the bench hastily grabbed his possessions and hurried out of the park. "Ben, you see those guys? What's with them?"

Ben paused a moment to size them up. "From the sheer amount of camouflage they're wearing, my guess is hunters. And since we're in New Camden and not a forest, I'm going to say supernatural hunters."

Nate looked again at the men. "They couldn't be plainclothes police or something?"

"No way those beards are regulation," Ben said with certainty. "And you see how both of them are wearing bulky jackets that look way too big for their bodies? They've got a crossbow concealed under there, or an axe—some manner of weapon aimed at werewolves."

Charlotte shivered. "I wish you hadn't said that. I hate thinking about hunters. Having so many of them in a city with a large supernatural population just doesn't seem safe."

Vazul snorted. "It depends who you want to keep safe. The needs of the supernatural population don't really figure in the official reports. Another example of the—"

"Many oppressions leveled against us. I know." Nate continued to watch the men make their way around the park. "They're coming this way."

"Ignore them," Ben said, turning back to picking up rubbish. "We're keeping a low profile, remember?"

Nate frowned. He'd talked over Gunn's warning with Aki on their way home from Century. They both agreed that it was like Gunn to try to scare Nate and that he wasn't above twisting facts. But if Ben was taking it seriously...

They smelled the hunters before they heard them. Not content with the known werewolf protections, they'd taken the precaution of dousing themselves liberally in garlic before setting out.

"Well, well. What do we have here?" One of the hunters sneered. "Department Seven trash. How appropriate." He was a tall young man, whose dirty-blond hair was worn in a mullet.

His companion elbowed him. "So what are you four anyway?" He was shorter than his companion and built like a football player. His face had a sour, watchful look about it, not helped by the fact his nose had obviously been broken at some point.

"That is none of your business," Vazul said at once.

Mullet stepped forward, looming over Vazul. "It's very much our business. We got a license to investigate the supernatural—and I find your attitude very suspicious."

Nate straightened up, putting his rubbish bag down. He stood next to Vazul with his arms crossed, using his height to its full advantage. "We're not under investigation. You're looking for the werewolf, right? Do any of us look like a wolf?"

The hunters looked at Charlotte's pencil-thin arms, Vazul's stout chest and Ben's overall skinniness, before looking back at Nate. "Well—"

"He's not a wolf," Ben said. "His palms aren't hairy."

Charlotte was unsuccessful in muffling a snort.

Broken Nose glared, turning his attention on Ben. "You think you know a thing or two about hunting, punk? Let us tell you something. You don't know shit."

"Actually—"

"It's cool, Nate." Ben went back to work. "I don't know shit about the supernatural."

"Yeah," Vazul said. "That's why we're all picking up trash in a park courtesy of Department Seven."

Mullet tapped Vazul in the chest. "I don't like your attitude."

"I don't like yours."

"Vazul," Charlotte said in a warning tone.

"You want to question us about the wolf, get on with it," Ben said. "But we haven't seen him, none of us know where he is, and we've got work to do, so if you don't mind, we'd like to get on with it."

Broken Nose smirked. "By all means. Get on with your work. In fact, let us help." He grabbed Nate's bag, upending its contents on the grass.

Mullet followed suit, snatching up Vazul's bag, scattering trash everywhere. He flung the bag at Ben and jogged after his companion. Their raucous laughter drifted back.

"I will put such a curse on you!" Charlotte yelled after them. "Creeps! Jerks! You—monsters!"

"Deep breaths," Vazul told her. "Do that calming thing you do."

Nate was not feeling calm himself. He peeled off his gloves, taking a step after the hunters. "They can't do that."

Ben grabbed him by the arm. "You are not picking a fight with a bunch of hunters. Have you forgotten what happened last night?"

"But—"

"Ben is right," Vazul said. "As irritating as it is to see stupidity like that go unpunished, doing so would only bring further punishment upon ourselves. Trust us."

Charlotte's eyes were shut, but with an obvious effort, she relaxed her body. "That's why we're here."

"Picking fights with hunters?" Nate couldn't believe his ears.

"The entire industry needs an overhaul," Vazul grimly began to shovel rubbish back into his bag. "It is almost entirely unregulated—"

"Subject to Department Seven oversight," Ben protested.

"And the Department is severely understaffed and underfinanced," Vazul said. "Unable to properly regulate hunting. At the same time hunting tends to attract totally unprincipled people. It's a powder keg of disastrous proportions."

Nate thought of George. "I don't know if I'd go that far." He looked to Ben, helping Vazul scoop up the trash. "What do you think?"

"Hunting is one of those gray areas," Ben said slowly. "They must be licensed to hunt, and that involves an interview and background check. If they break any laws, they're subject to prosecution—"

"Assuming the victim is a human." Vazul skewered a chip packet with surprising violence. "Don't get me started on the double-standard there."

Nate looked across the park, but the two hunters had moved on. "That's disgusting."

"Not that the hunters are alone in being intrusive." Ben nodded his head toward the park gate. "You see that guy there?"

Nate transferred his gaze to the man, a youngish man wearing a baseball cap and jacket. "Yeah."

"Werewolf."

Nate shot Ben a startled look, but he was retrieving Nate's rubbish bag as if he'd merely remarked on the weather. "Him? No way."

Vazul narrowed his eyes at the distant figure. "What makes you certain?"

"He scented the air a moment ago. You know how wolves do? And he moved his position to avoid being downwind of those two hunters."

Nate knelt to help Ben shovel trash back into his bag. "What's he doing? Do you think he's spying on us?"

Ben nodded. "I hate to say it, but it makes sense. After last night, Wisner's probably got an eye on both of us."

"On all of us," Vazul corrected. "And it wouldn't be the first time either."

Charlotte sighed. "I really wish he wouldn't do it. It's such an unpleasant feeling, knowing you're being watched."

"That's probably why he does it. Intimidation tactics." Vazul glared at the werewolf. "Wisner's getting more and more out of line."

"Councilor Wisner?" Nate frowned. "If he's a councilor, how is he allowed to get away with this?"

"Because he's a councilor." Charlotte paused to scoop her hair out of her face. "He justifies it on the grounds that his werewolves are keeping the city safe, using their success in hunting the rogue werewolf as an example. My guess is that he plans to replace Department Seven with his own private werewolf militia."

"But he hasn't found the rogue werewolf."

Vazul grinned. "And that's the problem, isn't it?"

Ben shook his head. "If the rogue werewolf hadn't run away, Wisner wouldn't have an excuse to put his wolves out on the streets so blatantly. There would be no cause for the media panic, no justification for Wisner's actions."

"Just FYI, Ben." Charlotte scowled. "Victim blaming is seriously uncool."

Nate looked at her in surprise. Charlotte was the last person he'd expect to snap at someone. "You think the werewolf is the victim here?"

Charlotte nodded. "Grant is a great guy."

Ben cocked an eyebrow. "You know him?"

"He used to be a member of the counseling group before I joined," Nate explained.

"Right." Ben hesitated. "I didn't realize."

"The media don't have the full story." Charlotte said quickly. Her cheeks were flushed. "You think Wisner's overbearing as a councilor. Imagine having him as a stepdad, living with him..."

Nate winced. "Sounds horrible."

"Agreed. But even then, there's a process for wolves to follow to emancipate themselves from a pack. It's well-established." Ben nodded.

Charlotte clenched her fists. "Maybe he wasn't given a choice. Maybe—"

Vazul waved a can at her. "Char, is aluminum recyclable or not?"

Charlotte was jarred out of her rant. "Recyclable, of course."

"And if they're squashed? Does that make a difference?"

"Let me see." Charlotte moved over to Vazul.

Nate caught Ben's frown. "We haven't looked for trash over there yet," he said, putting a hand on Ben's shoulder and steering him toward a cluster of trees. "Let's go." He waited until they were out of hearing distance of Charlotte and Vazul. "Something on your mind?"

Ben's smile was a little bit too quick. He shook his head. "No, not at all. Why would you think that?"

"It's just that I figured in our current situation you'd be more sympathetic to a guy who is obviously getting the full Wisner treatment."

Ben smiled thinly. "I wouldn't wish Wisner on anyone—except perhaps Gunn. But no, I'm fine. A little rattled from last night, maybe, but fine." He elbowed Nate. "You know things are bad when Gunn's giving good advice."

Nate snorted, but his gaze remained on Ben. "You don't even feel slightly curious about the rogue werewolf's story?"

Ben shook his head. "If I knew where he was, I'd report him to Department Seven. And you should too. It's entirely due to this runaway wolf that we're in so much trouble right now."

"Trouble? What can Wisner, do? Seriously—we got an entire room of people who can testify that we acted in self-defense. So long as we don't get into any more fights, we're fine."

Ben hesitated. "Wisner doesn't strike me as a good person to make an enemy of. I'd be really careful to stay out of trouble if I were you."

The second time he's told me to be careful. Nate frowned, placing his hand on Ben's shoulder. "There's something on your mind," he said quietly. "I'm sure of it. Whatever it is, you can tell me."

Ben came to an abrupt decision. "You ever feel like you're fighting a battle you just can't win? That no matter what you do, it's not going to make a difference?" Ben's mouth twisted deprecatingly. "Maybe I'm kidding myself thinking I can have an ordinary life."

"Don't say that." Nate squeezed his shoulder. "You've fought so hard to get where you are now. It makes sense that you'd be ready to take a break. But think how far you've come. You've moved back into your old apartment, you're living on your own for the first time—you're a landlord now. All of those are a big deal, Ben."

Ben smiled faintly. "But compared to the power of the City Council or even Department Seven..."

"You don't have to be big to be powerful." Nate looked around, spotting a crack in the pavement. "Look over there."

"At the sidewalk?" Ben frowned.

Nate crouched by the crack, beckoning Ben to join him. "See there?" A few green leaves showed above the surface of the concrete. "Hardly the best environment for life. Entirely surrounded by concrete and it probably gets trampled several times a day. But it's still growing."

Ben eyed the plant with a raised eyebrow. "It's a weed."

"Look again." Nate pulled his glove off, placing his palm against the concrete. Just like he had with the tree earlier, he reached out to the plant, this time lending it some of his energy.

Ben's breath caught as new leaves sprouted and the plant pushed itself higher. It turned a bud toward the sun, unfurled petals, and revealed a brightly colored flower. "Did you do that?"

"I hurried it along a little," Nate said. "But I didn't change the plant in any way. It's no robust weed, but a delicate flower—and if it can survive in the middle of a concrete jungle, then you can too."

Ben's mouth twitched. "That is the weirdest pep talk I have ever received—but thanks, Nate. I appreciate it." He looked down at the flower, his fingers gently stroking one petal.

"That's beautiful," Charlotte said in a hushed tone behind them.

Nate jumped to his feet. Charlotte and Vazul had gathered behind them, entirely unnoticed. "How long were you there?"

Vazul smirked. "Long enough to see your party trick—but don't worry. Your secret is safe with us."

Charlotte nodded. "If it wasn't for our spy over there"—she nodded to the watching werewolf—"I'd show you my specialty."

Vazul's phone suddenly emitted a blaring noise. "That's my timer," he said, fishing it out of his jacket pocket. "Finally, we can end this farcical maneuver. We're free to go."

"It's really okay to just leave?" Nate asked, helping stack their collected bags of rubbish beside the park's trash bins.

"Yeah. Kenzies usually finds the time to come out and check on us once, but she trusts us to knock off on schedule. Besides, I'm sure the werewolf will be making notes."

Nate slowly peeled off his remaining glove. He was sorry to see the community service come to an end. Ben was already looking at his phone. "So, um—"

"We usually hang out after we finish." Charlotte looked hopefully at Nate and Ben. "Want to join us?"

"Sounds great," Nate agreed. "Ben?"

To his disappointment, Ben shook his head. "Sorry. I've got another appointment." He nodded to Charlotte and Vazul. "Nice meeting you. Nate, I'll see you later."

Vazul watched him go with narrowed eyes. "I am dismissive of society's expectations around dating, but even so—your boyfriend's a jerk. No offense."

"Ben's got a lot on his mind right now," Nate said. "Once you get to know him, you'll see he's a really great guy."

Charlotte shook her head. "I don't know. I can understand someone who doesn't know about the supernatural making blanket statements about werewolves, but for one of us to do it—"

"Give him a break. We kind of got into a fight with a werewolf last night, so it's probably that."

Charlotte and Vazul exchanged a look. "A werewolf?"

"You can tell us all about it over coffee," Vazul decided.

Nate winced. "Sorry, guys. I'm broke—"

"Our treat," Charlotte said. She gave him a smile, tucking her hair out of her face. "Us supernatural types have to stick together."

Nate returned her smile, but he couldn't help a twinge of misgivings. *If supernaturals stick together—where does that leave me and Ben?*

"NATE! WHERE HAVE you been?" Aki scrambled to his feet, brandishing his phone. "I have been waiting hours for you to come back! No, don't answer that—you will not believe what happened to me."

Nate held up his hands in surrender. "At least let me walk in the door, Aki." He stepped inside their shared apartment, dropping his bag on the floor beside him.

The dog came padding up to greet him, his tail wagging.

"You have a good walk, boy?"

"We had the best walk. You would not believe it." As Nate took a seat on the sofa, Aki plopped onto the seat beside him. "As soon as I got to the park your stupid dog yanked the rope out of my arms and ran away."

"What?" Nate looked down at the dog. He rested his chin on Nate's knee, looking up at him soulfully.

"I know, right?" Aki knelt on the sofa, waving an arm excitedly. "I took off after him, but Shaggy here can run when he wants. I lost him in the trees. I'd just decided that it was no use looking for him and was wondering how to break the news of our dog-less state to you, when out of nowhere, this chiseled god appears and offers to help me look for my dog."

Nate snorted. "Chiseled god, huh?" *Should have known. Aki only gets excited about one thing.*

Aki punched Nate lightly in the arm. "Don't smirk at me. This guy was seriously hot. He had the whole package—a dangerous amount of stubble, killer body and eyes that fuck you. Like, he was hot. And really into helping me find my dog."

Nate bit his lip to avoid smiling. "A dog lover?" Beside him, the dog's tail beat the floor rapidly.

"Naturally I pretended to be really devastated about my missing dog, and when it was becoming readily apparent that despite the efforts of the single most attractive single guy in the city this dog was gone, never to be found again, he bought me a hot dog to cheer me up."

"That's sweet of him." Nate stroked the dog's ears.

The dog's eyes shut in pleasure. His tongue lolled happily as he leaned against Nate. In fact, if Nate hadn't known better, he'd have sworn that the edges of the dog's mouth turned up in a smile.

"And that's not even the best bit." Aki waited until Nate was looking at him. "He bought me a hot dog with chili and cheese. He knew my toppings without asking."

"A man of taste then."

"He is literally perfect in every way. He even manages to eat a hot dog attractively. It was unreal."

"And what is the guy's name?"

Aki's smile faded. "He didn't say."

"You didn't get his name?" Nate sat up. "Phone number?"

The dog nudged his leg with his nose. Nate absently resumed patting it.

Aki shook his head, slumping back against the side of the sofa. "No. I was pretty much on the brink of asking him if I could blow him, when he thanked me for hanging out, said he'd like to get to know me, and took off." Aki frowned. "He'd like to 'get to know me.' What do you think that means?"

Nate snorted. "If I had to guess, I think he wants to get to know you." He eased himself off the sofa, heading into the kitchen to grab a drink. "How did you find Shaggy—Fluffy?"

Aki followed Nate to the kitchen doorway. "That's the weirdest thing about it. When I got back to the apartment, Cousin It was just waiting for me by the side of the stairs. He even wagged his tail at me like he was happy to see me or something."

"Maybe he was."

Aki hesitated. "Can I borrow Scruffy again tomorrow? Just to put the guy's mind at rest. I mean, he worked really hard at finding my dog—"

"You remember the discussion we had about how faking an interest in stuff to get a guy's attention is ultimately self-defeating?"

"Yeah. So?" The dog padded over to Aki, nudging his leg with his nose. Aki patted him. "Maybe your gross mutt is growing on me."

"I knew you'd come around." The sight of the dog reminded Nate that he was going to have to find something to feed it. He turned to the fridge, scanning the contents. "What do you want for lunch?" He looked back— just in time to find Aki wiping the hand that had touched the dog with a tissue. "He's really growing on you, huh."

"I like the dog. I don't like its germs."

Nate hesitated. "Maybe I should come with you to the park tomorrow. I don't have any appointments with Department Seven."

"Great idea. You can hold the lead while I talk to mystery god."

"Deal." But as Nate started taking the ingredients for a salad out of the fridge, he couldn't help a feeling of unease. Aki fell in lust at the drop of a hat, but it never lasted long and the fallout was not fun.

Chapter Seven

BEN WASN'T SURE what exactly he'd expected from a psychiatrist's office, but carnival masks were not it. He lay on the psychiatrist's sofa, staring at the two masks attached to the opposite wall.

"So, Mr. Hawick. Or do you prefer Bennet?" Dr. Wellbeloved asked.

Ben transferred his attention from the masks to the doctor. His desk was beside the sofa, so Ben had to crane his neck at a ninety-degree angle to see him. "I prefer Ben, actually."

Wellbeloved made a note of that. He was probably in his late forties, but had an energy that made his exact age hard to pin down. He wore an eggshell-blue shirt with long sleeves buttoned at the wrists, and despite the warm weather, an argyle vest. "Why are you here, Ben?"

Ben swallowed. His throat felt dry. The room felt stuffy and he longed to throw open a window. "Ms. Patel didn't explain when she made this appointment?"

Wellbeloved steepled his fingers together. "Diya explained the circumstances and the urgency of your case."

"It was really good of you to fit me in on such short notice," Ben said quickly. He'd bypassed a packed waiting room to see the doctor.

"Anything for Diya. But you have not answered my question. I would like you to tell me, in your own words, what you think you are doing here." He had a musical lilt to his words.

Ben wondered if that was the reason for the doctor's obvious popularity. "Because the Registry Select Committee thinks I'm a danger to others." He shifted restlessly, trying to find a comfortable position on the sofa. *What should I do with my hands?* If he laid them flat beside him, the glossy fabric of the sofa made him feel like they were going to slide off. After a moment, he rested his hands on his chest. Better—even if it now meant he felt their weight every time he took a breath.

"And are you?"

"No!" Ben sat up at once. His heart beat fast. The degrees on the wall of Wellbeloved's office indicated he'd had a full grounding in psychiatry but divulged nothing about his supernatural knowledge. Diya had told him the doctor was skilled in dealing with paranormal cases but not how. *Does he know...?* He swiped his tongue over his teeth, but there were no traces of fangs.

"That is a strongly defensive reaction." Wellbeloved raised his eyebrows. His hazel eyes regarded Ben steadily. "Obviously the suggestion bothers you."

Ben forced himself to breathe in and out. "The suggestion would bother anyone. Look. I'm not comfortable being here, but I don't have any choice about it, so can't we just get on with the interview?"

"As you wish. But we can fix one of those problems of yours right now. You are not comfortable on the sofa?" Wellbeloved waved to the armchair set before his desk. "Then perhaps you will find a chair more to your liking?"

Ben fought a blush as he sat in the chair. After a moment, he wriggled out of his shoes, curling up in the chair.

"Better? Good." Wellbeloved leaned back in his chair, watching Ben. "But I am curious. Why did you take the sofa at all, with the chair right there?"

"I thought it was expected." Ben reached to tuck his hair behind his ears. He caught the doctor's gaze on him and dropped his hand. Much as he resented the old-fashioned look of his hair, he found comfort in its screening length—a fact which he suspected was not lost on the psychiatrist.

"And do you always do what is expected?" Wellbeloved met Ben's frown with an open expression. "It is a serious question. Diya gave me something of your history when she made your appointment. Looking at your application, I can see that you excelled academically both at high school and what university classes you took before your most unfortunate death."

Ben hoped his wince wasn't apparent.

"You were equally proficient in your professional career as an investigator for ARX, and now that you are no longer a vampire, you have swung in the opposite direction and wish to prove yourself a human. If I had to venture a guess, I would say that you are someone who likes rules."

Ben stiffened. "Is there anything wrong with that?"

"Please, relax. I am not trying to trick you. I just want an insight into your personality." Wellbeloved laid down his pen. "Did I touch a nerve?"

Ben looked at his knees. "I don't—miss being a vampire," he said. "But I'm lost without the routine. I don't know what I'm doing any more. It's really—hard. A lot harder than I thought it would be." Ben described his problems remembering to eat and his difficulty in making up his mind to do things.

Wellbeloved made sympathetic noises as he scribbled on his notepad. "It sounds as though you are suffering mild depression."

"Depression?"

"Do not be alarmed. Most people experience some form of depression in their lifetimes without it being clinical. It is important that you recognize it for what it is, and do not let it keep you from moving forward."

Ben hesitated. "I don't leave my apartment, except for things I have to do."

"And friends? Hobbies?"

Ben shook his head. "I think about reaching out to my university friends or the people I knew in high school, but I never do. When I look at their lives, what they're doing... It's like a different world. One I'm not part of."

"But what of your interests? What do you do in your apartment?"

Ben played with the cord of his hoodie. "Not much. I've been trying to set up my apartment, but I never get very far before I run into a decision I can't make. Where to put a picture or something." He found himself describing his paralysis. "That's not normal, is it?"

"What is normal in one circumstance is not normal in another, and what is normal for one person is not normal for the next. If I spent an hour wondering where to hang a picture, my secretary would cancel my appointments and book me a vacation. But for you, I think it is a symptom of something deeper."

Ben felt his chest constrict. "Go on."

"It is early days yet, but from what you have described and what Diya has told me, you have faced a lot of change in a very short time. You lost your father tragically at the same time that you died and became a vampire. It is my thought that in pushing yourself to meet the demands of your new situation, you did not allow yourself time to grieve for your father—or for yourself."

Ben blinked. "I—"

"It is not surprising, in those circumstances, that you would cling hard to anything that gave your life a direction or purpose. And equally understandable that now that you find yourself outside of that world, you are at a loss about how to deal with it."

Ben's throat tightened. He had to force the words out. "I'm normal?"

Wellbeloved nodded. "What you have described is a very normal reaction to trauma—and I can imagine that life as a vampire was traumatic indeed. I have a few vampires among my patients, and their cases tend to be very complex. The trauma of their own deaths, coupled with the violent lives that most of them must lead... It is not difficult, and it is no surprise that it would leave a lasting impact on you, especially at your young age."

The relief was so strong Ben had to shut his eyes. "Thank you."

"For giving what is only my professional opinion?" Wellbeloved tapped his pen against his desk. "In your circumstances, I imagine that it is a great comfort to have a goal to work toward. Is that why you applied for humanity?"

"One of the reasons." Ben wriggled back in the armchair. "I don't want to go back to my former life."

"And that is why you have cut ties so dramatically with your past. Is that wise, I wonder?"

Ben blinked. "But they're vampires! You know the effect vampires have on those around them—"

"It is a great challenge in treating them," Wellbeloved agreed. "I have to put on the crucifix just to make sure I do not tell my vampire patients what they want to hear."

Despite himself, Ben's mouth curved. "There's a difference between counseling vampires and living with them."

"And that is my point! They were your family. I'm not going to urge you to renew dangerous relationships, but I think it is important to acknowledge the importance of such ties. Diya tells me you have made no new friends since then. You have not made the effort?"

Ben fought the urge to blush. Diya had asked him if there was anyone besides George who could attest to his personality and actions since becoming human, and he'd been forced to admit to his complete lack of social life. "No. I don't—feel like it. It's hard to summon energy for anything but the really important things."

"Like?" Wellbeloved raised his eyebrows at him. "You're a young man in his twenties. What could be more important than establishing a social group?"

"My application for a start." Wellbeloved knew how crucial this was. Ben forced himself to breathe evenly. *Maybe it's a test.*

"Could it be that this application is a crutch? Do you say to yourself, when my application is accepted I will apply to jobs or to school or find friends."

"Um—"

"You do not need to say yes. The answer is on your face. You have put your life on hold while you pursue this application."

Ben looked down. "It's not for long. The application—well, I never expected it to be this complicated—but it shouldn't take more than a few weeks."

Wellbeloved was not impressed. He leaned his elbows on his polished wood desk. "It is most important not to deceive ourselves. Could it be you're afraid of living?"

"That's ridiculous," Ben snapped.

Wellbeloved raised his eyebrows, and Ben immediately felt foolish. Instead of pointing out that Ben was again on the defensive, he asked in a mild tone, "What does living mean to you?"

The question took him by surprise. "Well—freedom." Ben frowned as he considered this. "Feeling things—emotions, I mean. Getting close to people without hurting them."

"And freedom means also the risk of failure. Of having your feelings hurt, or friends leaving you."

Ben shook his head. "I've been hurt. As a vampire—" He paused, not sure he wanted to get into this with the doctor. Sympathetic as the man seemed, he was an employee of the Registry.

But Wellbeloved's expression was simply thoughtful. "Judging current relationships by the past is not fair."

"Nate—" Ben cut himself off abruptly.

Wellbeloved straightened up. "So there is a special someone in your life? Diya will be delighted. It will help your case immensely to provide evidence that you are forming relationships—a support network, if you will."

Ben shook his head. "Nate is not being brought into this."

"Why not? It is very important to show that you are a rounded personality—"

"I can't expose Nate to the scrutiny of the Registry," Ben said flatly.

Wellbeloved tilted his head. "He is supernatural too, then?"

"This is—confidential, isn't it?"

Wellbeloved nodded. "When I make my recommendation, I will speak in general terms of your state of mind. The details will remain between both of us. If it would make you feel more at ease, I will put down my pen." He capped it and laid it on his desk with a flourish. "There you are!"

Ben looked down. Far from reassuring, Wellbeloved's actions had left him on edge, wondering how much he'd already exposed. "Because of me, Nate got caught up in the necromancer's attacks. He almost died. In fact, for a long time, I believed he had died."

Wellbeloved made a sympathetic clucking sound. "And his near death was...?"

"Devastating." Ben wrapped his arms around himself. Just the thought of it made him feel cold. "I couldn't go through that again."

Wellbeloved simply nodded.

Ben stared at him. For the first time, the chill he was experiencing made sense. "I *am* afraid."

"Again, it is a perfectly natural reaction. The mind does not like emotional pain any more than it likes physical pain. It will come up with ways to protect you from it. But if you allow it to fool you and hold yourself back from life, you risk life passing you by."

Ben swallowed. His skin felt clammy. "What should I do?"

"That is something you need to work out yourself."

"Your job—"

"Merely to assess your state of mind. And I will tell you, Bennet, that I have found you to be a young man who has been through some very tough times but is showing remarkable strength of character in how he deals with them."

Ben's mouth was dry. "Thank you."

Wellbeloved wagged a finger at him. "I will not add that in some ways he makes things more difficult on himself than he needs to. You have been given a great burden for one man. You need not feel ashamed to ask others for help." He took a business card out of the holder on his desk and turned it over to jot down a number on the back. "If you discover you need help, I am here. This is my after-hours number."

Ben took the card with a hand that was strangely tremulous. "Thank you."

Wellbeloved shook his hand. "You have a lot of work to do still," he said. "And I trust I will see you again, if only to hear how it goes."

Outside in the street, Ben took a deep breath and leaned back against the brick wall of Wellbeloved's offices. The sun warmed his face and he shut his eyes, reveling in its warmth. *Normal! He thinks I'm normal!*

One sliver of cold remained. *But you didn't tell him about the vampire, did you?*

That was a fluke. It's not happening again. Pushing the thought aside, Ben fished in his pocket for his phone.

Nate answered on the third ring. "Ben?"

"Hey." Ben turned aside, so the pedestrians passing by wouldn't see his grin. "I was rethinking that normal date suggestion of yours."

"You're serious?" There was no mistaking the enthusiasm in Nate's voice.

Ben nodded, forgetting Nate wouldn't be able to see him. "Very."

"I'm working tonight, but if you wanted to hang out—"

"Not Century." Ben bit his lip. In all the excitement surrounding the werewolf and having his statement taken, he'd not been able to keep his curfew. Kenzies had assured him that since he'd been in the company of Department Seven officers it didn't count, but he wondered if the review committee, of which Wisner was one, would see it in the same light. "I was thinking tomorrow afternoon."

"An actual date, huh?"

"I was thinking we could just hang out. Maybe get a coffee together."

"Sounds good," Nate said promptly.

"All right. I have one appointment tomorrow. I'll call you after that." Ben hung up and dropped his phone into his pocket with a smile. His heart gave conflicting signals. It beat rapidly, as if warning him of danger, but his entire chest was infused with warmth.

Ben placed a hand over his chest curiously. *Is this living at last?* For so long he'd been cold, this warmth seemed unbelievable. *And it's because of Nate.* When Wellbeloved said that he shouldn't feel ashamed to ask others for help, did that mean maybe—

Some warning sense pulled Ben's attention to his peripheral vision. A man lingered in a doorway. As Ben caught sight of him, he ducked out of sight, but not before Ben had recognized him. *The werewolf watching us at the park.*

His feeling of warmth gone, Ben started walking toward his next appointment.

"So YOU AGREE that it is likely Wisner is having me followed?" Ben leaned out the window of Diya's office. It was on the second floor of the Registry and afforded an excellent view over the pavement. He couldn't see the werewolf, but the man was loitering outside the apartment building when Ben had left that morning. He knew the man was out there, somewhere. "And there's nothing we can do about it?"

"I'm afraid not." Diya watched him with a concerned expression. "As part of this process, the committee is free to pursue an independent inquiry into your circumstances. That includes placing you under surveillance for the period of time that your case is in question."

Ben narrowed his eyes. "If he's hoping to find evidence of me being anything but a model citizen, he's out of luck. The only thing his spies have seen was me picking up rubbish and attending my psychiatric evaluation yesterday—which went very well, by the way."

"I know. Wellbeloved already rang to let me know the results were on their way. He's very impressed by you." But Diya didn't smile.

Ben glanced over his shoulder at her. She sat at her desk, wearing a charcoal-colored trouser suit, with a vibrant scarf around her neck as a burst of color. Bright colors seemed to be Diya's trademark. Her office furniture was sleek and monochrome, but there were accents of color around the office in the forms of an electric-pink cushion on the chair, the picture frames of her black-and-white photos, and the case of her laptop. He made his way back to the chair but, instead of sitting, leaned against it. "What's on your mind?"

Diya's smile was more rueful than amused. "The psychiatric report is only the first step. We need to build a complete case. I've forwarded the necessary paperwork to Department Seven—"

"I know. Gunn told me." Ben slid into the chair properly. "Bad news on that front. Gunn as good as told me he isn't going to sign it." He gave Diya the bare bones of his conversation with the *lemur*.

Diya frowned, leaning forward. "Did you stress the urgency of your situation?"

Ben snorted. "To Gunn, that's even more of a reason not to fill out my application."

Diya hesitated, picking up a pencil from her desk. "There is an alternative." She dropped her gaze to her desk surface. "If you allowed ARX to examine you—"

"No way." Ben scrambled to his feet.

Diya gripped the pencil tightly. "ARX's reputation has suffered recently, but they are still a widely respected source of knowledge in supernatural affairs, and the City council relies on them greatly. They're also the most respected authority on vampires in this country. What's more, they know you, know your history... Surely you see that a recommendation from them carries much more weight than from someone only casually acquainted with you."

"No!"

Diya flinched. Her fingers clutched at the scarf tangled around her throat. The movement was so slight that if Ben had not once been a vampire he would not have noticed it—but he had been. And he saw.

There was an ugly patch of raised skin on Diya's neck. *That's no ordinary scar.* Ben looked down blankly. *That was caused by fangs—*

When a vampire fed with permission, the result was two deep puncture wounds. When the victim struggled, it looked more like an attack by a wild animal. Ben was in no doubt about what he'd seen. *That was a vampire.* "Sorry," he said. "I guess my past with ARX is still a bit raw." He sat down.

Diya swallowed. "I'm aware of your feelings about ARX, but I have to urge you to reconsider. Without Department Seven or ARX approval, your case is extremely shaky."

"I know." Ben put his palms on his knees. "Believe me, I've been considering the risk—and the risk that ARX poses to my freedom is just not worth it."

Diya pursed her lips. For a moment, Ben thought she was going to argue with him, but instead, she looked down at the paper in front of her. "As you feel that strongly, I'll look into alternatives. But I hope that you'll keep what I've told you today in mind. The Final Register is just that—final. There can be no appeals—because no one will remember you."

BEN RAISED HIS hand to the doorbell of the apartment Nate and Aki shared. His interview with Diya still troubled him, but if anything, their talk had made him more aware of how important Nate was. It was as if his interview with Wellbeloved had released a pressure inside of him, allowing feeling to flow again. *Maybe I didn't have to try so hard. Maybe I was human all this time.*

When he pressed the buzzer, a noise rose inside the apartment—a noise that sounded suspiciously like a barking dog.

"Fluffy, stop that! Shush—no barking!" Nate's voice. "Quick, Aki. Take him in your room!"

"I don't want it!"

"We have to hide him somewhere—"

Ben tried the door handle. The door wasn't locked. It swung open, revealing a scene straight out of a sitcom.

Nate was holding the dog, a woolly vaguely tribble-like collection of fur and teeth. As the door opened, he twisted in Nate's arms, continuing to bark.

"Ben!" Nate had guilt written all over his face. "This isn't what it looks like."

Ben raised an eyebrow. "That you've adopted a stray dog? You know the apartments all have a strict no-pet rule." He pulled the door shut behind him, nodding to Aki, who was leaning in the doorframe of his room. "Hi, Aki."

"We haven't adopted him," Nate said. The dog continued to bark, fighting to free himself from Nate's hold and finally, with a twist of his entire body, succeeded. He immediately ran over to smell Ben's legs. "He's got an owner. We're just looking after him until his owner collects him."

"And who is his owner?" Ben stretched out a hand to pat the dog, but it leaped back out of range.

"That's the question." Aki snorted. "Whoever it is, they didn't even put their phone number on the dog's collar. Which is pretty smart if you ask me. They knew there'd be no way anyone could trace the dog back to them."

"Where did you find it?"

The dog had continued to back away from Ben. It now stood beside Nate, starting to bark again.

"Mason's Park." Nate absently scratched the dog's ears. "He's really friendly. He can't have been on his own long. I'm sure we'll track down his owner in no time."

"Can I see his collar?" Ben took a step forward.

The dog bared its teeth and snarled.

Ben froze in surprise. "Friendly?"

"Stop that! Jeez—" Nate crouched, keeping a firm hand on the dog's collar. "I don't know what's come over him. He hasn't reacted like this to anyone else."

"Clearly the dog has good taste." Aki smirked.

"Maybe he's just surprised. I mean, as far as he knows this is his home. You're the first visitor we've had." Nate fished the dog's collar out of his voluminous fur. "There? See what I mean? They're not words, they're just symbols."

"Runes." With a wary eye on the dog, Ben took a step forward to peer at the collar. "That's not a name. It looks like an inscription—no. A spell—"

The dog twisted frantically in Nate's grasp. It managed to wrest itself free and darted across the room.

"Oh no you don't!" Nate ran after it. The dog feinted one way and then the other, and Nate narrowly missed colliding with the coffee table.

Ben straightened, watching the chase. The apartment was small, much smaller than his own, and the furnishings were definitely not in the same league. The surface of the coffee table had obvious stains and was littered with Aki's notes—he was in the third year of a degree in physical therapy. The sofa the dog now ducked behind and the two armchairs filled the room completely. Any more and it would have been crowded. *And it's still miles more comfortable than my apartment.*

Ben stepped out of Nate's way, considering the furnishings. They weren't likely to win any interior design awards. None of the chairs matched, being castoffs from those of Aki's college friends who had graduated to real jobs. The bookcase had been scavenged from a dumpster, and the TV was secondhand. But the divergent elements were linked. A hand-knit woolen blanket was thrown over the sofa, and bright cerulean cushions were dotted about the sofa and chairs. The same color had been used to paint the bookcase, the pot beside the TV which was home to a spiky plant, and the frames of two black-and-white photographs. Ben stepped forward to take a closer look at the pictures.

"Why would anyone want to cast a spell on some dumb mutt's collar?" Aki watched the chase with a frown. "Not on the sofa, you pest!"

"Lots of reasons. It could be to keep the wearer of the collar from wandering off or meant to ward off danger. I'd need a close look to identify the spell." Ben considered the photos. Although both were black-and-white, there the similarity ended. One captured a figure caught in a spotlight. The person's features were blurred as they moved at a speed too quickly for the camera to follow. The lighting suggested a stage and the figure suggested dance. The combination said "Aki" as clearly as if his name had been on it.

The other photo just as clearly said "Nate." It played with the contrast of light and dark, but this time the medium was sunlight falling through a canopy of leaves and onto on a mossy log. The light illuminated the furry tendrils of the moss and made the drop of water on the end of a single toadstool shine like a diamond. It was stillness, and Ben felt a sense of peace just looking at it.

"Beatrice," Aki said. "A house-warming present. Mandy made the cushions."

Ben turned hastily. He hadn't realized his scrutiny had been so obvious. "The place looks great. Already you've made it look so—lived in." As he spoke the words, he couldn't help but think of his own apartment above their heads. *Is that what it's missing? Being lived in?*

Aki sniffed, opening his mouth—but before he could correct Ben, the dog dove through his legs, seeking shelter in Aki's room. "Get out of there! My room is strictly off-limits—Nate! It's under my bed!"

Nate lay down on the floor to try to grab the dog. "I can't reach him. Guess he's staying there."

"He is not!" Aki stamped his foot.

"He'll come out once we leave and then you can shut the door." Nate got onto his knees. "If anything, this is a compliment. The dog chose your bed to hide under, right? He obviously likes you."

Aki shot him a withering look. "Fuck off on your date already."

Nate pressed the button for the elevator and wiped his palms on his jeans. "Sorry about that. Look, I promise we won't keep the dog any longer than it takes to track down his owner."

"It's cool. Just as long as you keep it out of sight of any other residents. I don't want more people deciding to pet sit."

Nate shot Ben a glance as they stepped inside the elevator. "You're not angry about this?"

"More amused than anything else." Ben hesitated. His fingers seemed to reach for Nate's of their own accord. "Let's just say that I always pictured you as a dog person."

"You've thought about me and pets?"

Ben nodded. Better than divulging how strongly Nate's hurt reminded him of a begging dog. "In passing. Don't worry. Our date doesn't involve stopping by a pet store."

Nate's fingers twitched as if he wanted to take Ben's, but instead, he hit the button for the ground floor. "Where are we going for our date?" The question sounded stiff, oddly formal.

Ben shrugged, putting his hands in his pockets. "I figured Ikea was as a good a place as anywhere else." He gave Nate a quick look, noticing he'd changed his clothes since that morning. His hair was messed up, thanks to his escapade with the dog, but had a sleek look, suggesting that he'd had a shower not that long ago. *Made an effort.*

"The housewares store?"

"Is there any other Ikea?" Ben nudged Nate. "I was hoping you could help me choose some new furnishings for my apartment."

"You're taking me furniture shopping? I don't know if you're allowed to make fun of my lack of romantic ideas for dates." Nate nudged back.

"We can go somewhere else. I just figured that they've got a cafe, and maybe you could give me some pointers—I mean, you and Aki have made your place look really good."

"You think so?" Nate ran a hand through his hair. "We've been pretty lucky with our friends. Beatrice is really artistic, you know, being a photographer, and Mandy's hobby is sewing."

"But one of you had to come up with the color scheme."

"We both did," Nate said. "And you don't want to know how long it took us to agree on something. But Aki's right—the color brings everything together."

Ben nodded. "That's what I need. My apartment—" He hesitated. "It needs personality. I haven't managed to make it feel comfortable, and well, I thought you'd be able to help."

"I don't know." Nate tugged his collar. "I mean I'll try, but I'm no expert or anything."

"Believe me. An interior decorator is the last thing on my shopping list." They reached the lobby and the elevator doors opened. Nate hit the hold-door button as Ben stepped through. "I could hire someone to make it look good. But I want someone who can make it look real."

"Huh." Nate walked a step behind Ben, obviously considering what he was saying. "Something less showroom, more a place where people actually live?"

"That's right." Ben waited on the steps for Nate to catch up.

Nate smirked. "That's easy. Borrow Aki for a day. At the end of it, your apartment will look as if there's an entire football team living in it."

"Pass." Ben had glimpsed the mess in Aki's room when Nate had tried to get the dog out from under the bed. "I mean if you don't want to—"

"I never said that." Nate held out a hand. "Let me see your list?"

Ben's hand was into the pocket of his jacket before he realized what Nate's question implied. "How did you know I made a list?"

Nate grinned at him. "You really need me to answer that?"

Ben shook his head, smoothing out the paper and handing it to Nate. "I guess not."

He watched Nate scan the page as they walked down the street. He'd relaxed, losing his earlier stiffness. Ben felt something in his chest give way to warmth. *This is right. Him. Me. Neither of us thinking—just being.*

"This is quite a list." Nate looked up, catching Ben's eye. His eyes sparkled. "I've worked out your plan."

Ben's mouth quirked. "Really."

Nate handed the paper back. "Yeah. You dragged me along, not for my interior decorating skills, but to carry all your purchases home at the end of this."

Ben laughed. "You offering? Thanks, Nate. It's appreciated."

"Hey! I didn't say that."

Ben shot him a playful grin. "I'll make it up to you." He let his gaze linger over Nate's torso, following the sculpted line of his chest down before flicking his gaze up to Nate's eyes. "Somehow."

From the sudden interest in Nate's expression, his mind had gone exactly where Ben was intending. "What do you have in mind? Because I'm warning you—when Ikea says they're happy to let customers test out the beds, they're not talking about more than lying on them."

Ben smiled. The knowledge that he had Nate's full attention made him powerful. He trailed a finger down Nate's arm, letting his touch linger, and stepping back just as Nate leaned in. "You'll have to wait to find out."

He turned, walking the remaining distance to the corner, scanning for a passing taxi. He was conscious that Nate jogged to keep up. Ben felt a surge of joy. *Have I been overthinking?* Nate stood close enough that Ben could feel the heat of his body. He didn't need to touch him to feel the extra sensory awareness he felt whenever they made love. *Human is easier than I thought.* A cab turned down the street. "Taxi!" Ben raised a hand.

The driver didn't even glance in their direction. He continued to cruise down the street.

"Wow. Rude." Nate waved. "Taxi!"

The man reacted immediately, pulling over. "You want to try signaling a little sooner next time," he scolded, turning to watch Nate scramble into the backseat. "If there had been a car behind me, I wouldn't have been able to stop."

"But—"

Ben elbowed Nate as he drew his seat belt on. "Let it go." He squeezed Nate's hand. "We're on a date, after all. Tell him where we want to go." As Nate frowned, Ben thought of an excuse. "You're the people person."

Nate obviously wasn't buying it, but he turned to give instructions to the driver.

Ben breathed out, settling his hands on his lap. *I'd almost forgotten.* He was Class Six—Restricted. To normal people he was invisible.

He reached for Nate's hand. *At least Nate can see me.* The thought of the Final Register filled him with dread. *No. Ordinary date.* Ben swallowed. *I'm not letting this spoil our time together.*

Chapter Eight

"OKAY. THIS IS cool." Ben came to a stop before a painting. "What do you think?"

Nate halted to consider the painting. It was some kind of modern art statement. A woodcut that didn't quite line up. The color looked like it was sloppily applied with a sponge by a graduate arts student who had half-assed every other assignment and felt that making an effort now would ruin his vibe. But despite that, it still had something. The detail of the lines of the pier, stretching out in mathematical precision over the blurred, indistinct shape of the water, and the dark shadows of the building behind—a boathouse maybe—wasn't obscured by the slapdash nature of the color. Or maybe the sloppiness was what made it? "The Lady in the Lake." Nate peered at the painting. "I don't see anyone."

"I don't think it's a literal title." Ben leaned back against Nate as he considered it. "The Lady in the Lake's part of the Arthurian mythos. You know—she gave Arthur Excalibur."

Ben's body was warm where it rested against Nate. He readjusted his posture and felt Ben relax against him. His close-cut hair tickled Nate's neck. It was really hard to think of something intelligent to say. Nate made a valiant effort. "So, kind of a modern take on the old legend?"

Ben nodded, ticking Nate's neck further. "I guess so. Do you like it?"

Nate considered it. He liked paintings that looked like what they were meant to be. But this... You had to admit that the artist knew what a lake in the woods looked like. Morning mist hung above the water, making the shapes of the trees beyond vague. "Now that I stop and look at it, yeah. It's the sort of painting you give a second look."

Ben made a sound of acknowledgement, not taking his eyes off it. "Above the bookshelf in the dining room?"

Nate pictured the painting hanging on Ben's wall. "I think it would look good there—but it's not my dining room. It's yours."

Ben nodded. He straightened up to peer at the label beside the painting. "The artist isn't listed. That's odd."

Nate hung back a step. "Ask a shop assistant?"

"Good idea." Ben sized up the shop and strode down an aisle.

Nate followed slowly. He was out of his league, and he knew it. Nothing said 'different worlds' like a painting that cost Nate's entire month's pretax earnings with the cut that Century took. But Ben had barely glanced at the price.

I know he's rich. Nate hunched his shoulders. *But this is way out of my comfort zone.* Just one more difference to add to the growing list of things they couldn't agree on—

Nate looked up—and stared.

In his search for a shop assistant, Ben had wandered into bathroom fittings. He'd glanced around and then suddenly flinched. While Nate watched, he took a step backward, bumping into a sink. Ben jumped, his arm catching on a display fern.

"I got it!" Nate snatched the fern out of midair. He replaced it on the countertop. "There. No harm done." He turned to Ben. "Are you all right?"

Ben let out a slow breath. He smiled, placing his hand on Nate's arm. "Thanks to your reflexes." His mouth twitched ruefully. "Were you coming to my rescue—or the plant's?"

But Nate wasn't going to let himself be teased. "What's wrong?"

"Nothing's wrong."

"Don't try that. I know you too well. This entire day, you've been acting, well—off."

"Is it bad that I want to spend time with a friend?"

Nate glanced around. There was still no sign of any staff member, which for now was a good thing. "Please, Ben? I know something's not right. You were silent practically the entire taxi ride. And now that we're here…" He hesitated. There had scarcely been a moment when Ben didn't have his hands on some part of Nate—but how to bring that up without making Ben sound clingy? "You've been more—physical than usual."

Ben forced a smile. "Making up for lost time. And isn't physical what you do on dates?"

Nate hesitated. *I don't want to fuck this up.* Inexplicable or not, it had been far, far too long since he and Ben had spent time together that wasn't fraught with tension. *Just enjoy it—*

No. Nate's eyes fell on the dark shadows around Ben's eyes. *I have to know.* "I'm definitely not complaining. But I can't help but think there's something else going on here. You don't jump at nothing."

"Just my imagination." Ben tugged him. "Let's go back. I think we passed an assistant in the bedding department."

Nate looked around. His gaze fell on a wall of mirrors, and he felt Ben's fingers tighten on his wrists. "That's it, isn't it? The mirrors."

"Vampire instinct takes a while to forget," Ben said quickly. "I got a fright. I wasn't expecting them."

"That's all?"

Ben nodded. "What more are you expecting?"

Nate looked around. There was a middle-aged couple slowly browsing their way toward them. He took Ben's hand, leading him out of bathroom fittings, into the sample living room. He nudged Ben to sit on the sofa, taking the seat beside him. "The last time we talked about us, you told me that we couldn't have any contact while you were working on your humanity application. You're still working on it, but now you're acting like we never had that conversation. I have to know. Is this you—or the vampire?"

Ben tensed. He didn't reply.

Nate squeezed his hand in apology. "What happened at Century? I have to know, Ben."

"I—don't know." Ben stared down at the charcoal-gray carpet sample beneath their feet. "It doesn't make any sense."

"It shouldn't be possible, right? To be a vampire but still have a heartbeat?"

Ben snorted. "If we're talking about what is possible, then I shouldn't have a pulse at all. The encounter with Sandy should have finished me. This—this is just one more unlikely coincidence. And I'm starting to think that I'm not just incredibly lucky, but that something has gone incredibly wrong."

With every word, his grip tightened on Nate's arm.

"Hey." Nate placed a hand on Ben's shoulder. "Let's talk this through. When you say incredibly wrong, you just mean that this hasn't happened before, right?"

"Right."

"But as far as you know, no vampire ever switched back to human before either. So this might be totally normal. We just don't know."

Ben lifted his head to look at Nate. His brow furrowed. "That's—a point. But I don't see how it helps us."

"Maybe instead of concentrating on what you think should be happening, we can focus on what is." Nate stroked Ben's back. "Talk me through what happened. When did you first notice…?"

"The vampire? Not until you'd knocked the werewolf out. That's when I realized I had fangs. I think they showed up before then and I was just unaware—there was no way I could have dodged the werewolf's leap without vampire reflexes." Ben's voice sounded less strained, more natural as he applied himself to the problem. "And there are thoughts that I put down to old habit that could have been the vampire…in fact, was the vampire." He relaxed his death grip on Nate's arm. "Blood."

"Blood?" Nate was startled. He looked up to make sure they were still alone.

Ben nodded. "Someone knocked me down in the panic to evacuate. When I got up, I tasted blood. I had cut my mouth. That and the danger are probably what triggered the revival of the vampire."

"Meaning it could happen again?"

Ben tensed. "It's not happening again. I'm not going back, Nate."

Nate took a deep breath. "It's happened twice. I don't think you can be sure of that." He hurried onward, hating himself more with every word. "It's worth experimenting to see if you can make it happen on purpose. Then you can make sure—"

"It's not happening again." Ben didn't need to raise his voice to make a statement final.

"But if you know you can prevent it—"

"You don't understand, Nate. It can't happen again." Ben was never healthy-looking on a good day, but he seemed to have lost what little color he had. "Convincing everyone I'm normal is the only chance I have."

"Only chance?" Nate echoed. *I don't like the sound of that.*

Ben nodded. He let go of Nate's arm to pull the slate-gray sofa cushion onto his lap. "The Registry's investigating my case. They're keeping a really close eye on me."

Nate's eyes widened. "You mean the werewolf at the park yesterday. That wasn't Wisner keeping tabs on us—"

Ben nodded. "He was keeping surveillance on me. I can't let them know about this—and I especially can't let Department Seven know. If anyone gets even the slightest idea that I've retained some form of vampiric power, the first thing they're going to do is get ARX in to investigate—"

"And there's no way that Saltaire is going to let you go after that," Nate finished. "Fuck."

"It's the end of everything." Ben took a deep breath. He addressed his next words to Nate's chest. "I've got no right to ask you to keep my secrets—"

"Hey." Nate felt his heart contract with sympathy. He gently put his fingers beneath Ben's chin, raising his eyes to meet Nate's gaze. "You keep my secret. And Ethan's—and you don't even like Ethan. You don't have to take me shopping to get me to help you."

Ben's cheeks flushed. "You—this isn't some attempt to bribe you! That—honestly never occurred to me. I just—well, given how coldly I've treated you, I felt bad about putting an even greater burden on you."

"The thing about burdens is they're meant to be shared." Nate pulled Ben toward him. "Try me."

Ben looked as though he wanted very much to pull away, but with a sigh, he shut his eyes, leaning against Nate. His fingers gripped Nate's T-shirt as if he wanted to be very certain that Nate wasn't going anywhere. "My appointment yesterday was with a psychiatrist. The Registry wants to make sure I'm—normal."

Nate bit his lip. There were many things he could say to that, but he wasn't sure that Ben would take any of them well. He was such an intensely private person that the experience of baring his thoughts to a stranger would be tough no matter why he did it.

"He was—good at his stuff. He made me see that I've been making excuses. Putting off living because I was afraid."

"Afraid?" Nate stroked the spiky hair at the base of Ben's skull. "He knows you stood up to a demon, right?"

He felt Ben smile against the bare skin of his neck. "He was right. Everyone I love died. Including you."

Nate's fingers stilled. "I got better!"

"Even knowing you—survived—I can't forget. I thought that with the vampire gone, I could move on. I wouldn't have to worry about endangering the people I care about. But now—"

"You're trying to deny the vampire—just like you tried to deny that you had feelings for me?" Nate settled back so that he could study Ben's expression.

Ben straightened, nodding his head. His cheeks had a guilty flush. "Well—"

Nate squeezed his hand and stood. "Come on. I want to show you something."

As Nate nudged Ben forward into the Ikea's toilets, he gave the stalls a quick scan to check for feet. Nothing. They were entirely alone, and to make sure they stayed that way, Nate stuck the 'cleaning in progress sign' on the door before he closed it.

"What are we doing here?" Ben gave Nate a nonplussed look. He turned, catching sight of the mirror and froze.

"I noticed you flinch," Nate said gently. "Mirrors still give you problems, huh?"

For a moment, he thought Ben might deny it, but then his shoulders sagged. "It doesn't matter how many times I see myself in one, it just doesn't seem real. I keep thinking that my reflection won't be there, and someone will realize—realize I'm faking it."

Nate put his hand on Ben's shoulder, steering him toward the mirror. "The best way to deal with fear is to face it. Keep your eyes on the glass." He planted a kiss to Ben's neck, peeling his jacket off.

"What—are you doing?" Ben tensed.

Nate planted a second soft kiss, putting his hands on Ben's hips before he replied. "I figured that maybe you wouldn't have such a hard time with mirrors if we gave you some positive associations." He began to work his way down Ben's neck toward his shoulder.

Ben squirmed in his touch but—Nate noticed with triumph—made no attempt to free himself. "What if someone comes in?"

"Then it's their fault for not obeying the cleaning sign." Nate looped one arm comfortably around Ben's torso, inviting him to lean against Nate. His other hand stroked the bare skin beneath Ben's T-shirt.

Ben shivered. "You've got an answer for everything." His eyes fell half shut.

"I try." Nate glanced at the mirror and saw that a flush was spreading across Ben's cheeks. He wasn't surprised—his own skin was on fire. The thrill of holding Ben after so long at arm's length was playing havoc with his senses.

And I'm not the only one. As Nate watched, Ben's body quivered. Repressing the urge to do what exactly? Nate nuzzled Ben's neck, before dropping his mouth to Ben's skin again. This time, Ben couldn't resist the urge to thrust his hips toward Nate's roving hand. "Nate—"

Nate's hips jerked in automatic response to Ben's breathless whisper. "Open your eyes."

Ben shook his head. "It's better with them closed. I don't—don't need the reminder—"

Nate's fingers paused on Ben's fly. He could feel heat beneath the denim and knew Ben longed for his touch. "Reminder?"

Mortification flooded Ben's cheeks. He squirmed, and this time it wasn't in pleasure. "I look so—dead. Like I crawled out of a coffin to get here."

Nate felt his heart constrict painfully. It was no good saying that some people found the fresh-out-of-the-coffin look really attractive. "Nothing wrong with your pulse at any rate." He pressed another kiss to Ben's neck. "Look at yourself now. No one could accuse you of being pale or emotionless."

Ben's eyes snapped open. He gulped at his reflection, raising one hand to his cheek as if he needed the reassurance that what he saw was real.

I can see it—but can he? Ben's complexion wasn't merely flushed. His eyes shone darkly, the pupils expanded. To Nate, he looked like perfection, but he cast a worried look at himself in the mirror. Next to Ben, his natural tan looked as garish as if it had come straight out of a fake-tan bottle. He took a step back, not wanting the contrast to overshadow Ben's view, but Ben's fingers gripped his arm, stopping him from moving.

"This is all you." Ben swallowed. His fingers stroked Nate's skin. "Your effect on me—"

"You don't see yourself with your guard down." Nate leaned against Ben, wrapping his arms around him. "This is the Ben I see."

Ben shut his eyes. "I want so much to believe you." His body arched as Nate's hand continued to stroke his trapped erection.

"I'm not making this up." Nate watched Ben's mouth fall open in a silent gasp, always mindful of their location and the need to be careful. "I didn't fall for Ben the vampire. I fell in love with you—" Nate bit down on his tongue. Was using the l-word a mistake?

Ben went very still.

I've gone too far. Nate knew he should step back and release Ben, but he couldn't make his arms obey. He could only wait for the rejection he knew was coming, as Ben turned his back on the mirror, taking Nate by his shoulders.

"Kiss me." There was a breathless note in Ben's voice.

For a moment, Nate didn't think he'd heard correctly. And then with a rush of elation, he pressed his mouth to Ben's.

Ben draped his arms over Nate's shoulders, devoting himself to the kiss. And the next. Nate tasted faint traces of toothpaste—*had Ben hoped their date might go in this direction?*—and felt the mixture of control tinged with abandon that was all Ben. His erection pulsed painfully, drawing his attention to its trapped state—and calling Nate's attention to the state of Ben's need.

He unbuttoned Ben's fly, easing his erection out of his jeans. He broke the kiss, only to lift Ben by the hips, placing him on the countertop. Nate took a moment to study him, flushed with need, his cock a bold rejection of any claims that Ben was not alive.

"Nate—" Taking him by the collar, Ben pulled him back to his lips.

He'd wanted to take Ben's cock in his mouth, but there was a special pleasure in giving Ben what he wanted. Nate continued to kiss him, matching Ben's leisurely pace, as he wrapped his fingers around his shaft. He stroked him slowly, echoing the rhythm of their mouths. He felt Ben gasp, knew the moment when his need reached the point of no return. And he gloried in it all. He slowed his hand, trying to make the moment last, but with his fingers gripping Nate's shoulders, Ben came.

They didn't speak afterward. Nate listened to Ben's breathing even out, as he tidied him up. He couldn't resist using his mouth to catch the drips adhering to Ben's cock and got a breathy hum that made his whole body tingle for his pains.

"You—" Ben started.

A blaring phone alarm interrupted them.

"Shit." Nate dug his phone out of his pocket, glancing at the alert. "That's my 'time to leave for work' alarm."

Ben made no effort to move. "You don't want to be late again."

"Hey, if you discount necromancers, I'm a model employee."

"And werewolves?" Ben's eyes creased with amusement.

With his cheeks flushed and his eyes still dark, Nate thought he'd never looked better. "Um—" Denise wouldn't mind if he was a little late, right?

But as if reading his thoughts, Ben slid off the counter. "Come and see me after work." His breathing hadn't quite returned to normal, and there was a haste to his words that underscored his message. "We can continue this—" His gaze dropped to the bulge in Nate's jeans. "—conversation then."

Nate swallowed. Work was going to be difficult.

STANDING IN THE corridor outside the manager's office, Nate took a deep breath. He'd been back in the office many times to speak to the interim managers and he'd been fine—so there was no need to feel like he was in danger. They'd done a thorough cleaning of the office, and no traces of the necromancer's manipulations remained. He raised his hand to the door, steeling himself to knock—

"Come in, Nathan."

Nate gulped. *That's new.*

He pushed open the door.

Denise sat at the desk, her perfectly styled head bent over some paperwork. She finished whatever she was writing and then looked up. "Is this about last night? I trust that the community service Department Seven assigned you does not conflict with any of your duties here."

"No." Nate shook his head. He made his way over to stand before the desk, fighting the urge to wipe his hands on his jeans. He was nervous enough without calling attention to it. "That was this morning—the first at any rate. It went okay."

"Glad to hear it." Denise leaned back in her chair, considering him. She'd switched out her usual suit and skirt combo for a sleek green dress in a shade of emerald.

Nate stared at her with a sense of despair. What did you say to the woman whose death you were partially responsible for?

Denise's eyes narrowed. "Any sympathy you may want to express is entirely misplaced. You don't run a business in this industry on sentiment. Escorts face a greater risk of violence and death than any other profession in this city, and although we do what we can to protect our workers and ourselves, it's always a possibility." She flicked a piece of fluff off the sleeve of her dress. "When I was still on the floor, I decided to—let's say, I took out some extra insurance. It paid off. That's all."

Nate nodded. He had no idea what she implied, but Denise was still very much master of herself and everyone else. "I see."

"And I have to admit that the new form does come with some...interesting advantages." Denise's mouth curved.

We are in so much trouble. Nate gulped.

"If that's all, Nathan?"

Nate took an involuntary step toward the door. Only the thought of Ben, eyes screwed shut as he refused to look at his reflection, stopped him. "Actually, there was something else." He turned heavily toward Denise. "I was wondering... How much of my indenture is left?" He flinched, expecting a reprimand.

Instead, Denise studied him thoughtfully. "Are you unhappy with us, Nate?"

"No! No. Um. It's just—well, lately it has been harder to keep my mind on the job and well..."

"And you are thinking of leaving us." Denise rested her hands on the desk. "Mr. Hawick's influence?"

"He doesn't know I'm thinking about this," Nate said miserably. He had no idea what Ben would think of this move. "But...yeah. Since meeting him...well. My heart's not in the game so much."

Denise sighed. "It happens to the best of us. Let me see..." She opened the laptop on her desk, typing in a command and scrolling through files until she found what she was looking for. "Nathan Granger... Assuming there are no further interruptions to your work schedule, you should be a free man in six months."

"Six months?" Nate echoed with dismay.

"I hate to say it, but the episode with the necromancer tarnished your reputation. And your decision to be open about your supernatural status, while admirable, does affect your earnings ability—"

"What if I take extra shifts?"

Denise shook her head. "The rules limiting the hours you can work are designed for your protection. Working in this industry takes a toll on many levels."

"What about if I took on cleaning shifts?"

"That's a possibility." Denise clicked to a new file and brought up a different spreadsheet. "Actually, one of our permanent cleaning staff is moving next week. Would you be interested in replacing Kathy in laundry?"

"Totally," Nate said. "Please."

Denise typed something into the computer. "I've added you to the roster. That brings your expected time of release down to three months."

"Thank you, Denise. I really appreciate this."

Denise closed the laptop. "Just make sure there are no further altercations with werewolves. Wisner is paying for last night's damage, but if he wasn't, it would be coming out of your paycheck."

"Trust me," Nate said. "There will be no more altercations of any kind."

"I CANNOT BELIEVE you, Nate." The roof was shadowed, but even in the dim light of the one fluorescent bulb, Aki's displeasure was obvious. "As if saddling me with your embarrassingly boring pseudo-boyfriend wasn't bad enough, now you want to abandon me."

"It's not like that." Aki was seated on a deck chair, and Nate carefully picked his way across the roof to join him. Maybe waiting until the end of the night to have this conversation had been a mistake. "You were working at Century before I showed up—and I seem to remember that you were pretty adamant back then that you didn't need me hanging around, cramping your style."

Aki snorted. "I was mad at being saddled with the clueless country boy. I had to teach you everything you know—it's only thanks to me that you even made a success of yourself here. And you want to throw it all away!"

Nate, who remembered a very different version of events, stayed silent. He'd known Aki would be upset, but he hadn't realized how upset.

"All my hard work, wasted! And none of the newbies are any fun to hang out with. You give them a hint and they just stare at you. Ugh." Nate tried to take Aki's hand, but Aki wrested it away. "And what are you going to do instead? You don't have any qualifications or job experience. I bet you haven't thought about this at all."

Nate hadn't. "I've got three months to figure it out."

"And if you can't think of anything?"

Nate winced. "I have to try. I mean, Ben—" He felt a shiver across his spine, a sudden awareness of the depths of the shadows around them.

"Yes," said a voice from somewhere above their heads. "Tell me about Ben."

Aki yelped, scrambling to his feet. Nate swore, pushing Aki behind him as a figure dropped from the roof of the doorway.

"Hunter!"

The vampire stepped into the light, the glow of the humming bulb catching his bared fangs perfectly. He moved with the sinuous grace of a snake, stalking toward them with complete assurance. The light and shadow made his habitual pallor look deliberate. Nate heard Aki moan and couldn't blame him. Hunter was using every weapon he had—not the least of which was his extraordinarily provocative looks.

We are so fucked. It wasn't merely the threat Hunter posed, but being in the presence of a vampire of his power was a danger all in itself. Nate swallowed, concentrating on staying where he was and meeting Hunter's gaze. He couldn't repress a shudder.

Hunter came to a halt. "Hello, Nate. You are a curiously hard man to track down, but as you can see, I managed to find you—as I find everyone I look for." The sentence started urbane and ended with grim satisfaction.

"What do you want?" Nate croaked. It was hard to form words—hard even to think—with Hunter's air of decadence and power surrounding them.

Hunter's eyes flashed. "My brother." There was no amusement in his voice, just the threat of a garrote drawing tight. "What have you done with Ben?"

Nate's heart rapidly accelerated, but his body was curiously slow to react. "Nothing."

"Come now." Hunter's smile was flat, his eyes unamused. "You can't expect me to believe that. Be reasonable—I will find him, whether you help me willingly or not."

That was a definite threat. Nate forced himself to look not at Hunter's eyes, or his teeth, but over his shoulder. "He doesn't want to be found."

"I don't believe that." Hunter's voice was abrupt. "We're his family."

"Saltaire tried to kill him." Nate croaked. Every second that passed made it harder to breathe. He could feel Aki, standing frozen behind him, but didn't dare take his eyes off Hunter to see if he was all right. "You know what happened while you were in the vault?"

Hunter's lips pressed together thinly. "I do not. And I want Ben to tell me. You do not know our ways. You can't make this decision for him."

Nate clenched his fists. "And if he's made it himself?"

Hunter raised his jaw, staring Nate down. His jaw clenched. "Nate. Tell me where Ben is."

The words were on his lips. Nate forced his mouth shut with difficulty. A voice whispered inside his head that there was no point in being so obstinate.

Compulsion. Nate shut his eyes. It was the vampire's greatest weapon—and one no human could resist. His body strained to take a step toward Hunter. His mind urged him to give in to the pressure he felt. *But I'm not human.*

Nate imagined the acorn in his hand. He remembered its cool smoothness, and the tiny imperfections in its shell. He remembered standing with the tree it came from at his back, while revenants circled, unable to reach him and Ben under the tree's protection. He imagined that same strength in his veins. Nate dug his roots in. "No."

There was a moment in which the only sound on the roof was Aki's hastily indrawn breath.

Hunter took a step forward. "Tell me—"

"That's not going to work anymore." It was as if a fog was lifting. Nate's thoughts came faster, the heaviness in his body melting away. Nate raised his hand to the button on his wristband that summoned security. "You can't compel me."

Hunter's eyes glittered darkly. "I asked you for the information freely first. You will regret not giving it to me—one way or another, I will find him, Nathan."

Nate took a step back, saw Hunter's eyes follow him with predatory awareness. "You—"

There was the rattle of footsteps on the stairs and the door to the roof was flung open. Security shone their flashlights on the scene. "What's the situation?"

Nate raised his hand to screen his eyes from the sudden glare. "He's a vampire. Threatening me."

"Where?"

Nate lowered his arm and glanced around. The security guards swung their flashlights over the roof, but the only thing they uncovered were the other deckchairs and the potted palm. Hunter had vanished.

"He was here." Nate turned to his friend. "Right Aki?"

Aki didn't immediately respond.

Nate placed a hand on his shoulder. "Aki? Are you all right?"

"All right is not the word." Aki sucked in a deep breath. "Holy crap, Nate."

Nate winced. "I'm sorry you had to see that—"

"Apologize for him? Never!" Aki shook his head, as if attempting to shake off his lethargy. "That is the sort of meeting you spend an entire lifetime waiting for!"

Nate glanced at the security guards, who had stopped scanning the rooftop to watch. "Uh—"

"Did you see his mouth? Like—that was indecent exposure right there. And all he did was lick his lips! And when he moved..." Aki raised a hand, as if hoping to find the appropriate adjective in the shadows.

"Vampire," said one of the guards with a nod. He spoke into the radio he carried. "Roger, this is Bill. On the roof. No immediate danger. The perp has left—"

"Heard you coming," Nate said. "You got here just in time. Thanks."

The other guard motioned the two of them toward the stairs. "You'd better report to Denise."

As they made their way down the stairs, Aki frowned. "That man— that was tall, dark, and deadly, right? The one you totally embarrassed yourself over?"

Nate winced. He did not want to be reminded of his first encounter with Hunter. "Yeah. That's Hunter. Who, as you so rightly pointed out, is a bad idea in every respect."

"You didn't tell me he was hot!"

Nate rolled his eyes. "Actually, I did. Repeatedly."

"But clearly not in any meaningful way. I was entirely unprepared for—" Aki came to a halt so sudden that the security guard nearly crashed into him. "For that—greatness!" He shook his head. "No, your vampire obsession totally makes sense now, except for one thing—how on earth can you prefer Ben to that vision?"

"You're crushing on the guy at the park, remember?" Nate took in Aki's flushed face with concern. "Remember? The chiseled god?"

"Him?" Aki waved a hand dismissively. "He likes dogs."

Nate hesitated and then gave Aki a nudge toward the employee quarters. "Go, have a cold shower or something to clear your head and join us, okay? I'll let Denise know what happened."

Denise was not impressed. "You're sure it was Mr. Hunter?"

"Absolutely. I mean, even if I forgot a face, you don't forget a presence like that." Especially when he tried to kill you. Nate ran a hand through his hair. "What do we do?"

"That's a very good question." Denise frowned. "You say he didn't harm either of you. What was his purpose in coming to the club?"

Nate swallowed. "I'm—not sure. At the time, I didn't really think about it. I was more focused on, well—him." Something warned him that sharing the news that Hunter was looking for Ben was not a good idea.

"Perhaps he thought you might oblige him at another house party." Denise crossed her arms. "I hope I don't need to tell you I strongly disapprove of any such arrangement."

"Totally," Nate said, nodding hastily. "The last thing I want to do is entertain vampires."

"I'll see that the rooftop is better illuminated and make sure that our security team looks into extending the protective wards to cover the roof as well as the club," Denise decided. "And I'll also issue an internal memo, reminding everyone that Century has a strict no vampire policy."

"Are you going to inform Department Seven?" Nate bit his lip.

Denise considered him for a long moment. "I don't believe so. There's little they can do about this incident. Unless you don't consider my precautions adequate?"

"No! You're doing everything possible," Nate said. "Cannot be happier. Absolutely."

Denise didn't look convinced, but as she crossed her arms, there was a knock at the door. "Come in, Bill," she said without taking her eyes off Nate.

Bill looked as disconcerted to be greeted by name as Nate had been earlier. "We've just finished patrolling around the club. No sign of the vampire." He hesitated. "Or of Mr. Fujino."

Aki. Nate's chest tightened painfully. "He's gone?"

"Ducked out soon after you went to report. The doorman didn't think to stop him."

Nate grabbed his phone, dialing Aki's number.

"Did the vampire speak to Aki directly?"

Nate shook his head. "I don't think so. In fact, I know he didn't. He only spoke to me." Aki's voicemail message started to play. Nate ended the call. "He's not answering."

"Akihiro is a New Camden native. He knows what measures to take for his own safety, and how to protect himself. He has a level of self-protection that others could learn from." Denise gave Nate a meaningful look. "I'm sure that the only thing on his mind was skipping out on a tedious meeting."

Nate shook his head. "He's gone after Hunter. I know he has."

Chapter Nine

"IF ANYTHING HAPPENS to Aki—I'll never forgive myself." Nate sounded like misery personified. He sat on the sofa of his apartment, the dog lying mournfully against his leg. "It was my idea to go up onto the roof to talk, me that Hunter came to see..."

The dog whined softly. Nate dropped his hand to his ears but, after the initial first pat, forgot what he was doing. The dog didn't complain. Its worried eyes gazed up at Nate, every bit as unhappy as he was.

Ben rubbed the back of his neck. He felt helpless in the face of such anxiety. "Hunter won't hurt him. Not badly, anyway. It's against ARX policy."

"But ARX denies any involvement. According to them, Hunter's taken leave for the rest of the week." Nate's shoulders hunched miserably. "I made Denise call and check. They couldn't tell us anything—they suggested that maybe I had my vampires mixed up." He sounded outraged.

Ben caught his breath. "You didn't tell them why Hunter visited the club?"

Nate shook his head. "I didn't say anything about you to them—or to Denise." His eyes rested on Ben worriedly. "She knows about you. Hell, she saw you at Century the night of the werewolf. It's not going to take her long to put two and two together and realize that Hunter might be looking for you. And if she doesn't, Department Seven definitely will."

"Don't panic. Let's think about this calmly." Ben took the space on the other side of Nate from the dog. He reached for his hand. "Denise was reluctant to call Department Seven in because she doesn't want the club getting bad publicity, and there's no evidence that Aki is with Hunter."

"I know he is!" Nate raised his head to Ben immediately. Beside him, the dog gave a low growl. "You didn't see him on the stairs! There's no way I should have left him alone—"

"You can't help that now." Ben placed his hand on Nate's shoulder. "I agree with you. I think that Aki definitely went after Hunter. But it's equally possible that he lost him and will make his way home when he gives up."

"Then why doesn't he answer his phone?" Nate looked at his smartphone lying on the coffee table.

"He's probably intent on whatever he's doing." Ben let his hand rest on Nate's arm a moment longer. "And then there's Aki's..." He hesitated. He hadn't realized how strong Aki's abilities were until he was able to see Ben at Century despite the class six restriction placed on him.

"Foresight?" Nate said miserably. "He puts too much weight on that. It makes him reckless."

"All this speculation is only upsetting you. Try to remain optimistic." He walked into Nate and Aki's kitchen, scanning the shelves for anything that looked like it might be helpful. *What did you give people for emergencies?* Godfrey made tea—but surely extra caffeine was the last thing Nate needed right now.

"I don't know how you can be so calm." Nate frowned, stroking the dog's side. "You more than anyone know what Hunter is like."

"Right." Ben hoped he sounded reassuringly confident and not as if he was dismissing Nate's concerns. "And I know that Hunter follows Saltaire's rules about not harming innocent bystanders. If he has Aki, he won't harm him." He spotted a packet of herbal tea on the shelf and took it down. He turned the kettle on.

"That would be more convincing if I didn't know that Hunter has a track record of breaking the rules where you are concerned."

Ben stuck his head out of the kitchen. "What do you mean?"

Nate winced. The dog gazed up at him with concern. "Did I ever tell you what happened between me and Hunter, after you dumped me, and Saltaire dragged you home?"

Ben shook his head. "I know Saltaire ordered Hunter to deal with you."

"Implication: kill me. Or at least scrub my mind of any knowledge of you and your family." Nate placed his hand on the dog's head. "What he actually did was to compel me to stay inside Century unless someone I knew was with me. In other words, preserving my life—and my memories."

Ben frowned. "Surely that proves my point. Hunter won't harm Aki—"

Nate shook his head. "He didn't do it out of a fondness for me or any sense of regard for humans. He did it solely because I was important to you." He raised his head. "You see? When you're involved, Hunter's an unknown. We don't know what he will or won't do."

Ben stared back at him. He couldn't argue with Nate's conclusions, even though he badly wanted to. *Hunter's not—it's not like that!*

Nate's phone buzzed.

The dog yelped as Nate lunged forward to grab it, unceremoniously dumping the dog on the floor.

"A message? Is it from Aki?" Ben hurried forward.

Having great time. Don't rescue me. I've got this totally under control.

Nate typed furiously in response. "He can't mean that."

Ben crossed his arms, leaning back against the wall. He wasn't as familiar with Aki as Nate was, but he knew Hunter—and Hunter's effect on people. He wasn't convinced that Aki hadn't intended his message exactly as he'd sent it. "You did say that he seemed...attracted to Hunter."

The dog made a piteous sound in the back of his throat. Absently, Ben crouched to pet it.

"Yeah, but when I fell for you, Aki was vehemently against anything to do with vampires. I can't believe he'd just change his mind—" The phone beeped again.

Seriously, if you rescue me now I will never forgive you.

"Damnit, Aki! Just tell me where you are!"

Ben glanced out the window. "It's almost dawn. Hunter will be retiring—and he'll have made arrangements for Aki's safety during the day. We should head to bed."

Nate's head jerked up from the phone. "What—and just leave him there?"

The dog barked.

"No. While Hunter sleeps, we will continue to investigate. But you've been working all night. You're going to crash soon. And you can't help Aki if you're out cold."

Nate stood reluctantly. "It feels wrong, but I know you're right—and Aki doesn't seem like he's in any pain." He hesitated. "Stay with me? I'm too wired to get to sleep on my own."

"Of course." Ben followed Nate into his room.

Every time he visited, it seemed that Nate had added another plant to the collection already filling the window sill. He sat on the bed as Nate discarded his T-shirt and climbed into bed.

"I really appreciate you coming by," Nate said, reaching for the light. "Sorry your date night didn't end how you wanted it to."

Ben shook his head, even though Nate couldn't see him in the dark. "Don't give it a second thought. Aki comes before date nights."

"Even so. It means a lot, having you here for this." Nate found his hand in the dark and held it.

Ben stretched out, trying to move as little as possible. If it had occurred to Nate that Aki wouldn't have been taken if not for Ben's presence in his life, he hadn't given any sign of it. Instead, he shifted restlessly, the bed shaking as he moved, until at last his breathing evened out and he fell still.

Nate... Ben felt something catch at the base of his throat. He swallowed it with difficulty. His rolled onto his side. He could make out Nate's outline in the dark. *We will find Aki. I promise you— I won't leave your side until we do.*

There was a click behind him. Very carefully, Ben raised his head.

The dog nosed the door open. With a glance at Ben, he slipped through the door, dragging with him a bright orange T-shirt that could only belong to Aki. Ben fell asleep to the sound of him making a nest out of it at the base of the bed.

"No, YOU CAN'T come and look for Aki with us. You have stay here and guard the apartment." Nate carefully squeezed himself out the door of the apartment, slamming it shut before the dog could escape. "Good dog." He locked the door.

On the other side of it, the dog barked loudly.

There is no way that the other tenants aren't going to notice. Ben looked down the hallway, but there was no sign of any of the apartment building's other occupants. So far, Ben was pretty sure that none of them knew of his and Nate's relationship, but he was not looking forward to when they figured it out. *The dog is going to look like special treatment for sure.* "You haven't had the chance to search for the owner at all, have you?"

Nate looked at him oddly, hitting the button to call the elevator. "With everything else that's going on?"

"That's what I thought." Ben stepped into the elevator, still frowning. *Is it bad that Aki is gone, and I'm worrying about something so trivial? Or is that what Wellbeloved would describe as a defense of the brain? After all, if anything happens to Aki, I'm partially responsible...*

"Where are we going?" Nate asked as the doors closed.

"I thought we'd take the direct approach. Signal a taxi and tell them to head to twenty-one Rueful Crescent."

"Hunter's house?" Nate stared at him.

"I did say the direct approach."

"Yeah, but just showing up on his doorstep... I thought we'd be a little more subtle than that."

"Hunter doesn't know that I can go out in daylight," Ben told Nate. "Last time he saw me, I was still a vampire."

"So, he won't be expecting us to show up until evening?" Nate mulled that over as he waved a taxi down. He held the door open for Ben. "What about Godfrey?"

"Godfrey already knows."

"What?"

Ben motioned to the driver, waiting patiently for instructions.

"Oh right." Nate gave the address.

Ben pressed a finger to his lips and frowned. With any luck, Nate would assume that Ben was being extra paranoid about being overheard—and not worried about revealing that the taxi driver couldn't see him. *Why am I so determined to keep this from Nate?* It hadn't been a conscious decision, just a shying away from it that had turned into a concentrated effort. *It's not as if Nate would be repulsed by me or angry—just worried.* Ben cast a look at the deep frown that furrowed Nate's expression. For a moment, he looked more like his grim brother than himself. *He would worry about me—and I don't want to add to everything else that he's got to deal with right now.* Aki being missing was bad news enough.

The taxi pulled up in front of a Victorian townhouse in the hills overlooking the city. As Nate paid the taxi fare, Ben cast a critical eye over the house. From the outside, it was as immaculately maintained as ever. When he reached out his hand to the gate, he felt a faint humming in the air, traces of protective runes. Godfrey, the housekeeper, had clearly been working hard restoring the mansion's wards, but he still had a long way to go.

I'd forgotten that the townhouse's security was breached. Ben frowned up at the house. *Was Hunter still using it?* With their location exposed to every vampire in the city, they'd want to find a new base... For the first time, Ben felt misgivings.

"Second thoughts?" Nate stood behind Ben, looking up at the house.

Ben shook his head. "It's strange to see the place in daylight. Let's go inside."

The gate opened at his touch, indicating that either Godfrey had rebuilt on what remained of the previous wards or had made a deliberate allowance for Ben.

Ben rang the bell, watching Nate sniff the lavender growing in terracotta pots on the steps. He heard a step inside the house, and then the door was pulled back.

"Ben! This is a delightful surprise." Godfrey stood on the doorstep, looking as correct as he always did. He wore an apron over his suit, and brightly colored rubber gloves. The smell of ammonia hung around him. Clearly they'd interrupted cleaning. "And Nathan, too! You really are spoiling me."

Nate shook hands awkwardly. "You can call me Nate."

"Can we come in?" Ben stepped into the hall. Underlying the strong smell of floor wax was a deeper, earthier smell. Ben swallowed, instantly taken back to the many long nights he'd spent in the house. The feeling was so strong that he felt with his tongue for the edges of his fangs and was surprised not to find them.

Nate stood so close to him that his shoulder bumped Ben. "I hope we're not interrupting."

"Not at all," Godfrey lifted a mop out of the way, motioning them down the hall. "I have been looking forward to your visit."

Ben and Nate exchanged a glance. "You knew we were coming?" Ben asked, at the same time that Nate said, "Do you know where Aki is?"

Godfrey looked up. His tawny eyes, as sharp and alert as a bird, alighted on them curiously. "We seem to be talking at cross-purposes. I imagined you'd want to use the library. I have been putting aside books I thought would be of interest to the pair of you as I find them."

Ben felt Nate shift restlessly behind him. "That's very kind of you," he said quickly.

"Go ahead into the library. I'll join you in a moment."

"But—"

"You haven't seen the library yet, have you Nate?" Ben took him by the hand. "It's very impressive." He pulled Nate down the hall after him.

The library had been one of Ben's favorite rooms in the entire house. He opened the door, taking a moment to savor its peculiar smell of books and herbs.

"Why didn't we just ask him about Aki?" Nate shoved his hands into his pockets as he walked into the room. "We don't have time to read!"

"Nothing is going to happen until after sunset," Ben reminded him. "And you've had a message from Aki this morning, haven't you?"

"He updated his Tumblr," Nate said reluctantly. He looked around, seemingly taking in the library for the first time. "Wow. I've never seen so many books outside an actual library."

"It's an impressive collection. Godfrey and Hunter have been working on it for a number of centuries."

Nate extended his hand as if to touch a leather-bound volume on the shelf and then thought better of it. "And all these books are supernatural?"

"About the supernatural," Ben corrected. "Yes. Except for the mystery novels." He waved a hand toward a solitary bookcase, lined with thin, brightly colored volumes. "Godfrey collects them. He refers to them as his vice."

Nate scratched the back of his head. "Do you think Godfrey knows about Aki?"

Ben frowned. "If he did, he'd not have mentioned the library," he said slowly. "No matter what books he'd set aside for us, he'd know that a friend came first."

"So that means what, exactly?"

"Hunter's acting alone. Which makes sense. Godfrey would not approve of kidnapping, and if he knew Hunter was looking for me, I'm almost certain he would have found a way to let me know." Ben hesitated in front of what had been his favorite armchair as a teen but sat, instead, on the sofa. "Hunter's acting alone."

As he hoped, Nate joined him. "Which means Aki's not here. We're wasting our time."

"We're gathering information." Ben leaned forward to look at the two piles of books on the table. "An Encyclopedia of Plants and Their Use in Spellcraft and Healing—I think this is for you." He slid the larger pile over to Nate.

"Huh." Nate frowned at the book. "I was thinking about learning some witchcraft. I mean, everyone already assumes that I'm a witch, so it makes sense..."

"I think it's a really good idea." As Nate opened the encyclopedia, Ben turned to the books laid out in front of him. There were only three books in this pile, and one was simply a folder. Ben opened it and discovered a faint facsimile of what looked to be a scrap of an illuminated manuscript. A saint stood, bedecked with halo and holy book, radiating the rays of the sun. The sunlight spread outward from him, striking a group of black-clad figures with exaggerated teeth and claws. The group writhed and died, disintegrating under the light, except for one, a figure that turned, oblivious to the light, and shook his fist.

The door opened, and Godfrey backed into the room, his hands full with a tray upon which rested all the accoutrements of tea. Nate immediately stood up to take the tray and Ben made room for it on the coffee table.

"Thank you. I didn't ask if you had time for tea, but I hope you'll indulge an old man." Godfrey smiled at Ben. "It has been a long time since we took tea together. And Nathan—Nate, I believe I owe you an apology for the last time."

"It's all right," Nate said. "No harm done."

Godfrey turned the delicate china cups over to sit on their saucers and carefully poured three cups of tea. "Milk?" he asked Nate as he added sugar and a dash of milk to Ben's cup.

Ben wasn't surprised that Godfrey still remembered how he liked his tea, but it gave him a feeling of warmth nonetheless. "Thank you, Godfrey."

The old servant didn't respond until everyone had a cup of tea and a cookie in front of them. "If I had thought of it, I could have made your favorite cookies."

"These are great," Ben said, and Nate, wiping crumbs from his mouth, nodded hasty agreement. "It's been too long since I've eaten any of your cooking." Ben motioned to the pile of books. "What are these?"

"You will find that my research has been piecemeal. I have been chiefly occupied redoing the wards on the house, so I have not had as much time to look into our collection as I had hoped."

Ben looked down at the folder. "What have you been looking for?"

"Cases of vampires that have returned to life."

"Wait," Nate said. "There have been others?"

"A very few," Godfrey said. "Not much is known about them. Knowledge is limited to rumor only, as there are no firsthand accounts. Any vampire who was able to restore himself to life was regarded as a threat by not only vampires, but his fellow man as well. I imagine that their survival would have rested on disguising what they were. But rumors..." Godfrey rested a hand on the folder. "A note in the margin of an illuminated manuscript. A paragraph in an account of a vampire outbreak in Ratisbon. And of course, the first treatise ever written on vampires, which includes a lot of theory about the origin and nature of vampires, now dismissed as speculation by an ignorant churchman with a naive belief in the ability of faith to heal even vampirism. But if my suspicions are right, and the author was himself a cured vampire or knew a cured vampire—well. The implications are clear."

Ben looked down at the slender clothbound volume. He wasn't sure why his throat suddenly felt so tight, or why there was a sudden heat in his eyes. "It's really kind of you to look these up at all. I know how busy you are."

"Nonsense. I am an old man, and it gives me pleasure—especially since with Hunter not in residence, I have a lot of time on my hands." Godfrey beamed at them. "Nate, I'm sure your books need no explanation. I thought that given your ability, plants should be our starting point."

Nate sat up straight at the mention of Hunter, shooting Ben an urgent look.

Ben kept his tone casual. "Don't encourage him. There's too many plants in his apartment as it is."

Godfrey smiled. "I am most grateful for his attention to our little garden. It thrives as it has never thrived before."

"While we're here, do you want to take a quick look at it?" Ben suggested. "I know you'll want to admire your handiwork."

Nate frowned, clearly wondering what Ben was up to. "If you don't mind," he said, looking at Godfrey.

The old man beamed. "By all means! I should be delighted."

As Nate pulled the door shut behind him, Godfrey set his cup of tea in his saucer. He rested his long hands on his knees and waited.

Knows me too well. Ben swallowed. "Why are you doing this?"

"Do I really need to answer that question?" Godfrey's voice was kind.

Ben felt his cheeks heat. "No. Sorry—I mean, thank you. I've spent so long second-guessing myself that I've lost sight of who my friends are."

"We were all very fond of you," Godfrey said. "It had been so long since we had a child in the house. Watching you grow was a privilege. I felt it. Saltaire felt it, and I know that Hunter could not have been more pleased with his brother." Godfrey watched Ben. "I have kept my word and respected your desire to make a life of your own. Hunter and Saltaire have no idea that you are alive—"

"Hunter knows," Ben said. He gripped his teacup firmly. "He went to Nate's family farm to look for me. And last night he confronted Nate at Century."

"He said nothing to me." Godfrey frowned. "I have not seen him this past week. Not since—he took leave to travel. Said that he wanted some time to pursue a private inquiry."

"Me." Ben set his cup down. "Do you know where he is now?"

Godfrey shook his head. "He has an apartment of his own somewhere in the city. I know that much. He uses it to entertain guests privately. He has always kept it secret, and I saw no reason to pry. We all need our privacy on occasion." Godfrey hesitated. "Does this have something to do with the 'Aki' Nate mentioned?"

"His friend. Aki saw Hunter call on Nate and disappeared soon after. We think they're together."

"Ah." Godfrey looked at the sofa where Nate had been sitting. "He will be concerned, of course. I understand that Hunter and Nate did not part on good terms."

Ben's mouth twisted. "Strangely enough, he resents that Hunter tried to kill him."

"A natural reaction. But you can reassure him that Hunter means no harm to his friend."

"I don't think Nate will be able to relax until we find Aki."

"I regret that I cannot be of help to you there. After sundown, I can call Hunter and urge him to reconsider."

"No. His business is with me. I'll handle it."

Godfrey hesitated. "Is Hunter's wish to see you again really such a bad thing? He regards you as his brother, and he will do much for you. At your request, he will keep your secret from Saltaire."

"So long as Saltaire doesn't order him to do otherwise." Ben immediately felt guilty. Hunter couldn't disobey the vampire who had created him, just as Ben was incapable of so much as a disobedient thought in his presence.

"Saltaire is on sabbatical in Europe," Godfrey said. "He is making a pilgrimage of the places of his youth. He warned me we need not expect him for several moons."

Moons? It was an unusual way to put it— Was Godfrey also thinking of the rogue werewolf?

But Godfrey was as inscrutable as ever, tidying up the tea things onto their tray. "I imagine that you will wish to be on your way in search of Nate's friend. As happy as I am to see you, I will not keep you. I will merely add that you are welcome any time, and that if there is anything you would like from your room sent to your apartment, I am happy to oblige."

Ben set down his cup of tea. "Actually, speaking of my room—do you mind if I take a look at it?"

It was a very strange feeling standing in the doorway of the room that had been his since he was ten years old until his untimely death at twenty-one. Ben looked around the room, his eyes moving from the familiar movie posters to the controllers for his gaming unit. On the one hand, everything looked exactly as he'd left it, so familiar that it hurt. On the other hand, he felt curiously disconnected from it, as if he looked at the room of a stranger.

"You okay?"

Ben turned to see Nate walking down the hall toward him, carrying the books Godfrey had lent them. He made room for Nate to stand next to him in the doorway. "Just thinking. I didn't expect that the sight of my room would move me so much. Godfrey's kept it exactly how it was. It feels—" Ben caught himself. *It feels more like mine than my entire apartment.*

Nate looked around. "You want to take anything with you?"

It was surprisingly tempting. The room's clutter was evidence that Ben had lived here, really lived, and his interests asserted themselves proudly all over the room. From the framed poster of Bela Lugiosi's *Dracula,* to the Monster Hunter figurines on the bookcase, the room said "geek—with very specific interests." "Maybe later." With one last look at the room, Ben turned down the hall. "We still have work to do."

"We're sneaking into Hunter's room?"

"I'm sneaking in. You're keeping guard." Ben stepped through the grand master bedroom and into the adjoining study. Hunter's desk was a Victorian monster, filled with tiny drawers and secret hiding places. It did not seem to have been used recently. The newest of the letters stacked neatly on the desk was from the month prior, and a thin layer of dust coated the surface. Clearly Godfrey had been very busy with the wards if he hadn't had time to keep the house up to his usual standards. Ben tried the drawers and wasn't surprised to find most of them locked. The ones that did open revealed nothing more innocuous that a selection of fountain pens and a spare power cord for Hunter's laptop.

"Any luck?"

"No. But then again, this was a slim chance." Hunter had been maintaining his secret apartment for years. He would have had plenty of time to perfect his hiding places for any information about it. Ben scanned the room, reluctant to leave. His gaze fell on an open calendar. Godfrey's mention of moons came back to him. "Nate, when is the full moon?"

"Tuesday," Nate said promptly. "Only reason I know that is the rogue werewolf. The papers are counting down. Why?"

"The fifth day before the Ides." Ben stared at the calendar. "I'd totally forgotten."

"The Ides?"

"It's a Roman thing—an Ancient Roman thing. The Ides were observed on the day of the full moon and used to calculate the date. Today is the fifth day before the Ides, a day of meeting." Ben squeezed past Nate and out the doorway, pulling Nate after him. "It's also the day of the month when the Vampire Senate gathers."

"And you think Hunter's going to be there?"

"He has to be there. With Saltaire in Europe, Hunter is the only vampire in ARX. If he doesn't show up, ARX won't be represented, and that is as good as dissolving the company."

"Even if he's kidnapping?" Nate hurried down the stairs after Ben.

"He'll expect me to remember the date and show up." Ben knew he was right. Hunter was operating under the assumption that Ben was still very much a vampire, and that he still felt the obligations that went along with his link to Saltaire. "He may bring Aki with him."

"So what do we do?"

Ben smiled. He was not sure why Nate's assumption that he was going to walk into a meeting of New Camden's vampire elite beside Ben warmed him—but it did. "We show up."

THE STORE WAS sparsely furnished in the way of expensive stores. Ben's changing room was so wide that it had space for an armchair, and the mirrors covered three of the four walls. Ben took a deep breath, but as he raised his gaze to the glass, he wasn't met with the usual feelings of panic and revulsion. He still looked strange—Ben ran a hand over his hair, discovered that it was just long enough to have lost the spiky feel—but not in a way that made him jump.

Ben's mouth twitched. *Did Nate's cure for mirrors actually have an effect? If so, we need to try that again.*

There was a rustle of cloth in the next changing room. "Are you sure about this?" Nate asked. "I mean, shopping for suits doesn't seem like it's going to help us find Aki."

"Trust me, it's necessary." Ben turned his attention back to the glass. He tugged his suit jacket straight, wriggling his shoulders, and surveyed the results. The suit fit him like a glove. The muted gray the shop assistant had recommended downplayed his pale skin, and the crimson shirt gave him a touch of color. A black vest and tie completed the ensemble. Ben looked down at his sneakers. Next stop would be shoes. "Vampires are only impressed by power. We aren't getting into the senate meeting unless we look the part."

"If you say so." Nate sounded uncertain. "I don't know why we don't just go there now. Aki and an entire room of vampires just says 'disaster' to me."

"He won't be there now, and there's no way we could hide our presence from an entire gathering of vampires while we wait for Hunter to show up." Ben took one last critical look at himself in the mirror and nodded. "I'm ready. You?"

"I can't help but feel like we're getting ready for a funeral." Nate threw back the curtain. The shop assistant had given him a darker shade of gray than Ben, and the strong lines of the suit gave definition to Nate's already well-defined body. He motioned awkwardly to the suit. "What do you think?"

"You look good. Definitely not funeral material." Nate's tie was already straight, but Ben was unable to resist stepping in close to adjust it. He stroked his hands down Nate's vest, smoothing it before buttoning his jacket. "Aki's been sending you messages, right? Has he indicated that he feels in danger?"

Nate shook his head. "He's not telling me anything useful or answering my questions. He wants to know what I know about Hunter and if he has a type."

Ben snorted, looking around for the shop assistant. "Curvy redheads."

Nate paused, phone in hand. "Are you sure? I mean—he seemed really into you."

"We never had the discussion, but the impression I got is that Hunter is bi with a strong preference for women. It is a very special man who holds his attention longer than one night."

Nate winced. "Aki's not going to like that."

"Good. Maybe Aki will tell you where he is, and we can take him home." Ben caught the shop assistant's eye, and he immediately came forward. "The suits are perfect. We'll take them both." He handed the man his credit card.

Nate tugged at his necktie. "You didn't ask how much they cost."

"This sort of store, if you have to ask, you can't afford it." Ben caught Nate's frown. "What's the matter?"

Nate shook his head. "It's stupid. We're preparing to walk in on a bunch of vampires on their home turf, and I'm worried about you buying me a suit that I could never afford."

"Hey." Ben took his hand. "That's not stupid. This is something that bothers you a lot, I know."

Nate smiled faintly. "We've never had a lot of money. It freaks me out. If anything happens to this suit, I'm going to feel terrible."

"Don't," Ben said, as the shop assistant returned with his card and receipt. "It's your suit now. It's meant for you to wear. And that means it probably will get dirty at some point."

"But I can't repay you."

The shop assistant busied himself folding their street clothes up and tucking them into a shopping bag. Ben took advantage of his distraction to lean against Nate. "You give me presents I can't repay."

"What, acorns?" Nate snorted.

"Like your belief in me. No matter what happens, you've always been confident that I had the strength to deal with it. And thanks to your belief, I have." Ben looked down. "A week ago, there would have been no way I would agree to confront the Vampire Senate—or even return to Hunter's house. But with you beside me, it doesn't seem impossible at all." He squeezed Nate's hand. "You give me strength, Nate. And that's worth so much more to me than anything in this entire store."

Nate's hand tightened around Ben. "So. Vampires?"

Ben nodded. "Vampires."

Chapter Ten

WAS IT A vampire trait never to pay for their own taxi? As soon as they pulled up to the street in downtown New Camden, Ben handed Nate his wallet and climbed out of the cab. *It would make sense, I guess. A true vampire would never do something so menial as pay for something.* And Ben had been silent all of the drive, probably psyching himself up for what they were about to do.

As he joined Ben on the pavement, Nate looked around. He was surprised to find their surroundings very familiar. The neon glow and crowded pavement could only be the nightclub district. "We're only a couple of blocks from Century."

"That's right." Ben had only waited for Nate to join him to start walking.

"The Vampire Senate has its meetings in a club?" It made sense. From Nate's limited experience of vampires, they were adept at combining business with pleasure.

"Don't mention the V-word out here." Ben gave the order without looking back. "There will be fellow attendees on the street, and they have very good hearing. We don't want to be obvious."

He was really getting into the vampire mindset—or was there another explanation? As Nate hurried after him, he noticed that Ben's shoulders were hunched. *Nervous.* He caught up with Ben. "We don't have to go in right away, do we? Let's take a walk around the block."

For a moment, he thought Ben would refuse, but after a moment's thought, he nodded. "I'm that obvious?"

Nate squeezed his hand. "Only to me."

Despite New Camden's blanket ban on smoking in public places, a faint trace of tobacco hung on the air. The night was cool, and many of the club-goers standing outside on the pavement wrapped their arms around themselves. Nate was conscious of gazes thrown his way and lingering. He walked a little taller, unconsciously adopting his Century manner. "Shit! I never called out of work! They're going to be wondering where I am." Nate hastily dug in the pockets of his suit for his phone.

Ben cleared his throat. "I've got a confession to make. While you were finishing your dinner, I called Century. I booked you for the evening."

Nate felt his cheeks heat. "You know I don't want our relationship influenced by my job—"

"I know," Ben said. "But I thought it was necessary. I need your full attention tonight, and I didn't want you to be even slightly worried about what might be happening at your work." He took a deep breath. "To get into the club, I'm going to have to bring out my..." He hesitated.

"Inner Dracula?" Nate guessed.

Ben snorted. "That works. I—I'll be trusting you to make sure that I don't lose control." He stopped walking, turning to look at Nate. "You won't let me hurt anyone innocent?"

Nate nodded, unable to take his gaze away from Ben's. "You know I won't." Inwardly, he soared. Ben trusted him to protect him! He depended on Nate! *I'm someone he can rely on.* Had he succeeded in proving himself at last? *Wait till Aki hears about this—*

Nate's elation faded abruptly. With every moment that passed, Aki spent longer under Hunter's influence.

"It's a lot harder to do this on purpose," Ben continued. "I'm not even sure how it worked the last time."

"There was blood, right? And danger."

Ben nodded. "Lucky that cut on my lip hasn't healed." He ran his tongue over it and then looked up to meet Nate's gaze. "Let's walk back. Slowly."

Nate's eyes were better adjusted to the dark as they made their return journey. He weighed the people they passed. How many of them were not what they seemed? Did that lipsticked smile conceal fangs? Was there something pointed in the attention the pair of men were giving himself and Ben?

As a woman paused her conversation to run her gaze up and down Nate, Ben inserted himself between them. "We don't have time to waste flirting with strangers."

There was an abruptness that Nate thought he recognized. *The vampire's pretty possessive.* "Just trying to help. You feeling this?"

Ben paused. He swiped his tongue across his teeth and nodded. "It's now or never."

To Nate's amazement, he led the way to the club with the longest queue outside. "We're not going into Royal, are we? But they're incredibly exclusive. They don't let anyone in who isn't on their list."

"Yes." Ben walked right past the line.

Nate hurried after him. "But it's VIP only. Celebrities."

"Yes."

The bouncer was a wiry man in a suit that didn't disguise his bulk or the fact that he'd been on the losing side of more than a few fights in his time. He sized up Ben and Nate as they approached and scowled. "No cutting in."

"We're for upstairs," Ben said casually.

The man snorted. "No one gets into upstairs."

Ben pressed his lips together in a thin smile, as if he'd been expecting this. "You will let us in." He stared at the doorman.

The doorman stared at him dully. There was an unfocused look in his eyes. His mouth parted, but he didn't speak. He simply stared back.

Nate's heart thumped in his chest, uncomfortably loud. He was aware that the people standing in line had fallen silent, as if they too were affected by the unbearable pressure growing between Ben and the doorman. Nate tugged at his collar. *I can't stand any more of this.* In a minute he would scream or run or something—

He fumbled for Ben's hand, squeezing it.

Ben gripped his hand tightly, not taking his eyes off the doorman. He raised his chin arrogantly, projecting his gaze. "Let us upstairs."

The doorman shook his head, as if trying to clear his mind. "Upstairs," he said. He opened a nondescript door, painted the same black as the exterior of the club. Beyond it, an unremarkable tradesman's entrance was revealed.

Ben stepped through the door. Nate looked over his shoulder, to see the doorman looking after them with dislike. He shut the door behind them.

"Did you compel him?" Nate's voice echoed alarmingly. He winced at how rattled he sounded.

"I had to. That's how you get in." Ben was breathing hard. It had clearly been an effort. The entrance was empty apart from a metal staircase that spiraled upward. Ben began to climb it. "The doorman has slight magical abilities himself. He's able to resist most lower-level vampires. Only a higher-level vampire can successfully compel him."

"Fuck." Nate stared blankly at the staircase. "So if you'd failed, you wouldn't just be denied entry—"

"I'd be a target for any vampires watching," Ben agreed. "Which is why I couldn't fail."

Nate started to climb. "And the doorman? Is he—okay?"

"He took the job knowing what it entailed. I imagine he is paid extremely well for his services." Ben waited for Nate to join him before opening the door at the top of the staircase. "Stay close," he warned.

For a startled moment, Nate thought they'd stepped into another world. The long wood-paneled room was a distinct contrast to the stairwell, or even the street outside. It was large enough to hold two hundred people comfortably. Wooden chairs with stiff cushions were placed around the edge of the room, and at the end closest to Nate and Ben, a string quartet played classical music from a raised stage. Three large chandeliers hung from the ceiling, sending out a warm glow. Candles were placed in wall mounts intermittently dotted around the room, and waiters drifted around the room, offering their trays to the exquisitely dressed people who had formed small pockets of conversation. Only two things broke the illusion. The faint sound of pounding bass from the nightclub on the floor below underscored the performance of the quartet. And the air was permeated by the smell of decay, a loamy smell of leaves in autumn. Nate recognized it immediately. *Vampires.*

"It's maintained exactly like an old-fashioned ballroom," Ben explained. "Vampires tend to get hold of an idea and stick to it. There's bound to be a bowl of punch somewhere—yes, there it is."

Nate looked. Along the far wall were three long tables, elaborately draped in cloth and flowers. They held a selection of refreshments that didn't seem to have been touched at all. The centerpiece, an elaborate crystal punch bowl, was nearly full. "This place is unreal." He looked around the room again. "Do you think Aki is here?" As he turned his head, he was met by the sight of the other guests turning away, just in time to avoid meeting his gaze. "We're being watched."

"Of course we are." Ben cast a sharp look around them, summing up their companions. "They're curious. They haven't seen me in a few months. There will be rumors about my death. I've also—never brought a companion to one of these events before. You're likely to come in for a lot of scrutiny."

Nate tugged his jacket straight reflexively. "Bring it on."

Ben's mouth flickered into a smile. He nodded toward a pair of doors in the center of the adjoining wall. A bored-looking man leaned against them. "It's patron-only beyond the doors."

"Patron?"

"Sorry. A term adopted by the vampires. A patron's a vampire with at least two clients—that is vampire followers. They make up the senate."

"That's not confusing at all." Nate looked at the door. "You think that's where Hunter is?"

"It's a possibility. I'll check it out." Ben walked toward the doors.

"I'll stay here. Obviously." Nate pulled the sleeves of his suit down as he watched Ben walk across the floor.

Ben didn't try to skirt the groups that had gathered on the floor. He simply lined up the most direct route and took it. When he approached a cluster of conversationalists, the group seemed to shrink, people melting out of the way.

Nate was amused. *Ben might not like it, but he puts on a mean vampire when he feels like it.* He watched the group. Although there were no obvious looks sent in Ben's direction, Nate got the impression that they were very much aware of him. Those that were aware, at least. Most people seemed to be there in pairs. One pale, glassy-eyed individual to each healthy-looking attendee. *I guess people brought a snack?* But that didn't fit with the impression Nate got of vampires, which was that they liked to downplay their appetites as much as possible.

A waiter approached. He paused, giving Nate an obvious once-over, and hesitated.

A drink would be a very good thing, Nate decided. He needed something to take the edge off his nervousness. He walked over to the waiter. "What have you got?"

"A fine selection of reds. All fresh." The man frowned. "You would be a newcomer here?"

Nate nodded, looking at the wineglasses on the tray with foreboding. "When you say fresh...?"

"Drawn today and kept at body temperature before serving."

Nate swallowed, looking at the crimson liquid. *I should have known it wouldn't be wine.* "Do you have, um. Anything...vegetarian?"

The waiter lifted a glass. "This is one hundred percent vegan blood."

"Fantastic. Thank you." Nate took the glass with relief.

The waiter still paused. He seemed on the brink of saying something when an imperious gesture from a nearby group sent him on his way.

Nate strolled the length of the ballroom. It was extremely unlikely that he'd see Aki among the revelers, but he had to look. He finished his explorations in front of the stage where the musicians played. He raised the wineglass to his lips.

"You don't want that." Ben took the wine glass from him, slipping his arm through Nate's. "Not unless you've taken on the blood-drinking characteristics of that plant from *The Little Shop of Horrors.*"

Nate recoiled. "He said it was vegan."

"Blood of a vegan." Ben took a sip and made a face.

"They didn't—"

"Kill a vegan?" Ben gave him an amused look. "It will have been donated. This crowd makes a point of being extremely civilized—at least when anyone is around to see."

Nate looked around. "Who are these people?"

"They're the highest-ranked members of the vampire families of New Camden and their followers." Ben nodded. "They're here to play politics, show off, and gather information about what their rivals are up to. You can tell the really important ones by the fact they're all wearing a gold ring and something purple."

Nate considered the plum-colored waistcoat of a man with a monocle. "And their escorts?"

"Some are human. They're the ones looking glassy-eyed. Probably overwhelmed by the presence of so many vampires." Ben narrowed his eyes. "You've attracted attention."

Nate looked up. A woman with fine, ash-colored hair tied up in an elaborate cascade of curls, and a flowing silk gown drifted over to them. She didn't appear to be more than a few years older than them. "Bennet," she said. "It has been some time. I thought you were no longer with us."

Ben smiled thinly. "Rumors are not always reliable, Lila."

"You seem to be spreading your wings quite thoroughly." She watched Nate through her lashes. "Will you introduce me to your charming companion?"

Ben snorted. "Nate, this is Lila. She is the representative of the Family Furia."

She shook Nate's hand and let her hand linger on his arm. "I am delighted. It is not very often we see fresh blood of such obvious quality. Where did Bennet find you?"

Her eyes were the soft blue of forget-me-nots, framed by delicate lashes that gave every look the effect of a furtively stolen glance. Nate felt somehow flattered. "We met in New Camden."

"Indeed? And what brought you here tonight?" It wasn't what she said. It was how she said it. A low tone layered with invitation, while her eyes remained fixed on Nate.

Nate opened his mouth, but it was Ben who replied. "You're wasting your time. Nate's with me."

Lila cast Ben a sideways look. "Are you sure about that?"

"Very." Ben put his hand on Nate's arm.

Lila watched the gesture through half-closed eyes. "If you feel so strongly, why haven't you claimed him?"

"All in good time," Ben said abruptly.

Lila smiled. She touched her fingers to Nate's cheek, still talking to Ben. "I wonder that you are willing to let him wander the ballroom unchaperoned, knowing that you have not marked him. He is practically an invitation."

Nate froze. His Century training had covered what to do in a wide range of situations. Being felt up by a vampire making pointed conversation with your boyfriend (sort of) was not on the list. He opened his mouth to say something but never got the chance.

Ben's fingers tightened on Nate's arm. "If anyone tries to sway him, they'll regret it."

Lila's mouth curled. It was not a nice smile, and for the first time, Nate had an awareness of danger. "It is not only other vampires you must guard against, but his wandering attention. A word of advice, Bennet. Your power may be sufficient to captivate him when you are alone, but you were most unwise to bring an unclaimed companion to a gathering of this nature. With so much power on display, I am sure that Nate will not have trouble finding someone who can give him what he wants."

"Good advice," Ben said. "Acquired, no doubt, through experience."

Lila's eyes flashed. She turned to Nate. "You're wasting your time. He will not turn you—he is too afraid for that. But there are others who would be happy to oblige."

She's offering to make me a vampire. Nate swallowed. "Thanks, but Ben's right. I'm not exactly looking for anything like that just now."

Lila's smile curled ironically. "You say so now..." She drifted back to her companions, leaving a cloud of expensive perfume in her wake.

Nate lowered his head to Ben's ear as she walked away. "I was only looking for Aki—"

"I know. She was simply trying to throw me off guard, undermine my confidence." Ben swallowed the remaining liquid in his glass. He held it out and a waiter collected it. "Let's dance."

There were a few couples on the floor already, but to Nate's relief, they didn't seem to be attempting anything formal. "Shouldn't we be looking for Hunter?"

Ben placed one hand on the small of Nate's back and took his hand with the other one. "We need to talk," he said. "This gives us the best opportunity."

"Right." Nate placed his hand on Ben's shoulder.

In sharp contrast to their dance the previous night, Ben took control at once and kept it. He held Nate close, guiding him when to change direction with a peremptory tug.

This isn't like Ben. Nate glanced around. No one was obviously watching them, but he knew that they must be attracting a fair amount of attention. "Is everything all right?"

"No sign of Hunter," Ben said in a voice so slow that if Nate hadn't been pressed against him, he'd have missed it entirely. "But I can sense that he is here."

"Do you know where?"

Ben shook his head. "The problem with having so many vampires gathered in one place is that they drown out each other's signals. All I have is the certainty that he is close by."

"Could he be in the club? That's more Aki's scene."

Ben shook his head. "Somehow, I doubt it. If he doesn't make an appearance for the senate meeting, we can search there, but—he *must* make an appearance for the senate."

Another dancing couple passed into their orbit. Ben snarled softly, and gripping Nate tightly, steered him away.

Okay, this is getting odd. Nate hesitated and then leaned toward Ben, capturing his lips.

Ben didn't hesitate to return the kiss. Trying desperately not to think about the copper taste, Nate ran his tongue against the line of Ben's teeth until he encountered something sharp.

A fang. Nate's mind raced. *He's gone full vampire.*

There wasn't time to think. Nate dropped his mouth to Ben's ear. "I want you," he whispered. "Can we go somewhere private?"

The vampire leaned his head against Nate's chest. His eyes were half-closed, and his mouth was supremely satisfied.

Nate allowed himself a faint, animal whimper. "Please?"

"All right," the vampire allowed. "But only because I want it." He stalked off the dance floor, leading the way to the sidelines.

Nate spotted a staircase to one side of the door they'd entered by. "Where does that go?"

"The gallery?" The vampire squeezed Nate's hand. "A good thought." He tugged Nate up the narrow staircase.

At the top of the stairs, Nate could see a thin platform running the length of the wall, elegantly screened with wooden railings. It was just wide enough for two people to walk arm in arm and gave a bird's-eye view of the dancers on the floor below. Paintings in heavy frames were placed on the wall at intervals, with candles in holders between them.

The vampire didn't give Nate time to take in their surroundings, he simply hurried him along the corridor to the area above the stage. There was space here for a sofa. The vampire nudged Nate toward it, but while they'd been moving, Nate had time to come up with an attack. He held his ground, using his physical proximity deliberately as he leaned over Ben.

The vampire growled, turning to meet him. He initiated the kiss, but Nate did his best to wrest control of it. He gripped the vampire by his shoulder, holding him in close as he battled.

As Nate had hoped, the vampire responded wholeheartedly. He pushed Nate backward onto the sofa, planting himself on top of him. His fingers tangled in the hair at the base of Nate's skull, squeezing a warning.

This shouldn't be this hot. Nate's thoughts were a confused whirl among a series of impressions. A fang pressed against his lip, and Nate felt an immediate surge rock his body. His hips jerked up against Ben, and he gripped the arm of the sofa, trying to prevent himself from arching into Ben's body. *This is too much—*

He'd been trying to distract the vampire, but it was he who'd been caught. Nate broke the kiss. He gasped for air, hoping desperately that the oxygen would do something for the fire that was raging through him.

The vampire's arm tightened on his shoulder and then relaxed. "Nice work, Nate."

Thank god. "Ben. You're—"

"Not thinking like a vampire." Ben breathed out. "You've got this down to a fine art." After a moment he stood, turning aside from Nate as he tugged his jacket and sleeves back into order.

Nate got to his feet and followed suit. "My pleasure." He wondered if Ben knew how far he'd come to losing control himself. The jacket was long enough to hide his erection. *As if he hadn't already felt it.*

Ben placed a hand on his hip, letting his fingers ghost up beneath the suit jacket. "I gathered." He licked his lips. "I'm reminded that I owe you a date night."

When had sardonic become so sexy? Nate shifted. "There are many nights."

"Indeed." Ben's smile was pointed. "And tonight is one of them."

Nate was conscious that his heart was beating faster. "Once we find Aki and Hunter."

Ben squeezed his hand. "Agreed." He leaned over the railing, looking down at the floor below.

In the short time they'd been occupied, the floor had filled with even more elegantly dressed people. No man wore anything less than a full suit, replete with vest. A few had shown up with canes and tail coats. The women vied in elaborate gowns with intricate hairstyles.

"That's Family Quinctia," Ben said, nodding toward a middle-aged man with a rakish air, accompanied by three men and a woman in matching suits. "Led by Allard who was—or tries to pretend he was—a courtier during the reign of Louis XIV."

Nate frowned over the bannister. "He'd be old then?"

"One of our—I mean, ARX's main rivals. He's one of the consuls—it's a mostly honorary title. There's two, and for a year they share responsibility for calling the meetings." Ben nodded to a lady with dark hair left to fall sleekly around her neck. "She's the other—Genevieve. She's the oldest vampire present. With Saltaire absent, she is probably the biggest threat to other vampires. Notice how everyone gives her a wide berth."

There was a conspicuous amount of space left for the woman and her companions. The lady who had flirted with Nate dropped her an exaggerated curtsey, and waited to be acknowledged before joining her train of followers.

"They're forming groups?" Nate looked around. "Where is Family Saltaire?"

"Family Postumia." Ben leaned on the railing. "Saltaire despises the acquisitive nature of his fellow vampires. He has always refused to arrive with a contingent. Hunter will be here alone."

Nate looked down at the groups. "Won't that look odd?"

"Yes." Ben hesitated. "Saltaire's power is resented by his fellow vampires, and they know that ARX has lost standing with the mayor following the necromancer's attacks. There's a good chance that things might get messy. Hunter should never have involved Aki with this."

"You think there'll be a fight?" Nate looked again at the elegant outfits on the floor below.

"It's always possible. With vampires, civilized is only ever a veneer."

Nate looked down at the floor. It was hard to imagine the people below in the same category as the revenants he'd narrowly escaped on New Camden's streets, but Ben's voice held a certainty that couldn't be refuted. "Look. That's the waiter that served me earlier. Where is he going?"

The man had set his tray down on the end of the punch table and walked rapidly toward the staircase at the other end of the ballroom. He climbed it, bringing himself to the end of the long corridor that linked the platform where Ben and Nate were to a matching platform at the other end of the gallery.

As they watched, the waiter approached a large painting. He looked around, noticed that Ben and Nate were watching, and came to an abrupt halt. He stared at the painting, before moving his attention slowly to the next painting.

"Very odd." Ben put his arm through Nate's, and they started walking slowly toward the other end of the room. "If you intend to study a painting, you don't approach it at a run."

"And you don't study paintings at all while on a job," Nate agreed. "Very unprofessional."

Ben paused and they pretended to study the painting before them.

"He keeps glancing our way," Nate reported, watching the man's reflection in the polished glass of the painting frame. "Doesn't seem happy that we're here."

"It occurs to me that if Hunter is here, he's probably posted people to keep an eye out for us. You asking for vegan blood probably got his attention. He's trying to report."

"He's given up." The waiter had cast a look back at the painting and then marched quickly toward the stairs. He strode toward a staff-only door. "Should we follow?"

Ben shook his head. "I've got a feeling about this gallery. Let's take a closer look at that painting he was in such a hurry to reach."

It was a landscape, showing a ruined castle set among a steep, rocky outcrop. A range of mountains rose up in the background like a jagged dagger. It was painted in the muted tones of centuries past, but the strokes had a frenzied note to them that kept it vivid long after it was first committed to canvas.

"It's pretty striking." Nate tilted his head as he considered it. "Gives you a really strong feeling." It was hard to pinpoint that feeling exactly. The ruin was desolate, but there was something in the castle's grim determination to cling to its exposed position that made it feel triumphant. "Where do you think it is?"

"If I had to guess, I'd say the Carpathian Mountains." Ben studied the painting with a rueful air. "Hunter grew up there."

Nate gave the painting a startled glance. "You think—"

"This is no coincidence. Is anyone watching?"

Nate looked over his shoulder, standing so that he screened Ben from anyone watching. "No."

Ben pushed the painting aside. "There's a door here." He met Nate's eyes. "I've got no idea what's on the other side of this."

"I'm going with you."

Ben's mouth curved. Nate felt a rush of pride—*that smile is because of me*—and Ben nodded. "Be quick." He opened the door. Nate, his heart beating fast, stepped after him, pulling the door shut behind them.

NATE'S IMMEDIATE IMPRESSION was of a modern studio apartment, furnished with castoffs from the rooms they'd passed through. He looked over Ben's shoulder, scanning the apartment, and his eyes came to rest on a figure on a chair in front of them.

"Hunter." Ben spoke before Nate could, his tone crisp.

Hunter looked up. He was in the act of pouring a glass of wine, but although he affected surprise, the stream of wine never so much as wobbled. "Ben. And Nathan too." He sat up, holding the glass out to the figure seated in the armchair immediately before the door. "This is a pleasant surprise."

Ben stepped aside, and Nate got a clear view of the person in the chair. "Aki!"

Aki turned around to scowl at him. "Yeah. Very pleasant."

Nate hurried to his side. "Are you okay?"

Aki shifted, careful of the wine glass he held. "Totally fine. Hunter's been the perfect gentleman," he said, adding in an undertone pitched for Nate only, "unfortunately."

"I have found Akihiro a very interesting companion."

Nate shot Hunter a sharp look. Was there emphasis laid on that interesting? "You—"

Hunter placed his own glass on the table and stood, acting as though Nate hadn't spoken. "We were just about to share a glass of Loire Valley chenin blanc. You are most welcome to join us." He stood, taking two more wine glasses from a cabinet beside the kitchenette.

"You know we must decline." Ben stayed where he was. "It's no good pretending this is a social call, Hunter. You didn't invite Aki for the pleasure of his company, just as we're not here to catch up on old times."

"Hey—" Aki started to protest, but Nate nudged him.

"Not the time."

Hunter glanced over his shoulder at Ben. "I can't be forgiven for wanting to spend time with my brother—a brother I haven't seen or heard from in over a month?"

Ben pressed his mouth together thinly. "We are no longer members of the same family. Saltaire took care of that when he turned me out."

"Our relationship means so little to you that you discard it so easily?" Hunter put down the wine glasses and turned to Ben. "I am hurt." His eyes glittered, and his tone of voice was mournful. Nate, who still remembered how it felt to realize that Hunter had no qualms about ripping his throat out, had a moment of hesitation.

"That's really cold," Aki said vehemently. "Just to drop someone like that—he thought you were dead!"

Nate put a hand on Aki's shoulder, squeezing it in warning. "You don't have the full story."

"Am I to be blamed for Saltaire's actions?" Hunter continued, keeping his eyes fixed on Ben. He spoke as if they were alone in the room. His muted manner gave a quiet dignity to his words. "You know how closely we are tied and that it is not always possible for me to resist him."

Ben raised an eyebrow. "Saltaire did not tell you to kidnap Aki."

"You seem to have a false idea of the situation. This arrangement was at his suggestion." Hunter inclined his head toward Aki.

"You didn't!" But as Nate met Aki's smirk, he knew that no compulsion had been necessary.

"All my idea," he said. "And you have to admit, it worked perfectly." He motioned to the room. "Here you are, exactly as Hunter wanted, and here I am, having enjoyed a day and night of Hunter's...excellent hospitality." He cast a meaningful look at Hunter that the vampire ignored.

"How did you know we'd find you?" Nate asked.

"You're more resourceful than you think," Aki said. "I knew you'd come up with something."

"You couldn't have just told us where you were? I was so worried!"

"Would you have rushed to my rescue if you thought I was enjoying myself?" Aki shook his head. "No. It had to be this way—and I have to say, I think I did a really good job of coming up with this plan."

Nate wrapped his arm around Aki's neck. "You're so lucky Denise didn't call Department Seven in—"

Aki thumped his arm. "Let go! This is twenty-year-old wine! If you make me spill it—"

"You took a big risk yourself," Ben told Hunter. "If Gunn got wind of this, he'd have made all the ground he could out of it."

"I can handle Gunn." Hunter dismissed Gunn with a shrug. "Besides, it is worth it—to see for myself that you are all right." He smiled. "It is very good to see you, Ben."

Nate looked up in alarm. He knew firsthand just how effective Hunter's charm could be.

But to his astonishment, Hunter didn't seem to have turned on his considerable charisma. There was a bittersweet note to his smile, and he made no attempt to join Ben at the door.

Ben's mouth twisted sardonically. "And the fact that you've got me here for the first senate meeting since the necromancer attacks is pure coincidence?"

"It is a fortunate coincidence," Hunter allowed. "I would be glad of your presence...but I would be foolish to assume that having distanced yourself from your family, you would join me in a public appearance."

"You are right."

"Oh, come on!" Aki said, almost spilling the wine as he put his glass down. "You were a vampire for ages, you know how important it is to make a strong impression! And it's not Hunter's fault that you almost got killed."

Ben raised an eyebrow. "You've evidently found a lot to discuss."

Aki drew himself up. "I find vampire politics fascinating. It's like the West Wing, only sexier."

"And more people get killed," Nate added.

Aki shot him a look. "I think you're both being really close-minded. ARX works really hard to protect the people of New Camden." He jabbed Nate in the chest with his finger. "As you pointed out when you were making a case for dating Ben."

"It's not that I don't appreciate the situation," Ben said stiffly. "But I've got an unparalleled chance to live my life on my own terms, free of Saltaire's influence. I have to go for it."

Hunter drew a sharp breath. For the first moment, his control wavered. "This is your influence." He shot Nate a look so venomous Nate blanched. "How else could my brother, who felt so strongly about his duty to the living that he spent every moment of his un-life preparing himself to better protect the innocent, desert his beliefs so completely—"

"You're making a big mistake, Hunter." Ben approached him.

Nate took a deep breath. "You really think we should?"

Ben nodded. "He is my brother," he said simply. "We may not always agree, but I have been unfair by avoiding him." He took Hunter's hand, wrapping it around his wrist. "I know I can trust him with my secret."

Hunter waited, clearly expecting Ben to speak. He frowned as Ben remained silent, then his eyes widened, his gaze dropping to Ben's wrist. "But this—"

"I have a pulse," Ben said. "Sunlight does not burn me. I'm—"

"Alive." Hunter made no move to let go of Ben's hand. "But this is impossible!"

Ben spoke quickly. "No one is really sure how it happened, except that it was the result of Peter's spell. He wanted to combine the power of a necromancer with that of a vampire, so he transferred my vampiric abilities to himself—"

"And you gained his humanity." Hunter still hadn't moved. "I see."

Ben squared his shoulders, raising his face to Hunter's. "I know this is hard to take. You must be upset—"

"Why upset? Do you think I would begrudge you this happiness?" Hunter squeezed Ben's hand. "I am astonished. And in a moment, I will be glad. I knew you were never happy as a vampire." He let go of Ben's hand, stepping toward the bottle of wine. "We must toast your good news."

"You really mean that?" Ben followed him to the counter.

Hunter looked up with a smile, but his expression softened as he looked at Ben. "Did you really think I would hold your good fortune against you?"

"It's what every vampire wants," Ben said simply. "And you've been a vampire much longer than I was. It's not fair."

Hunter laughed. "Nothing in life or death is fair. I learned that long ago—and I learned that it is no good expecting all things to be equal. Enjoy your life, Ben, and do not imagine that I am anything but pleased for you."

After a moment, Ben nodded. "Thank you, Hunter." He bowed his head. "I owe you an apology. I should have listened to Nate when he said my brother would be glad for me."

Hunter's eyes flashed over Nate in surprise. His ample mouth curved. "Nathan is somewhat of an expert on brothers, I fancy. I met yours."

"He told me," Nathan said with a feeling of resignation. He could feel the look that Aki was giving him.

"A very unusual man." Hunter hesitated. "Individual."

"Yeah." In another moment, he was going to be apologizing to Hunter.

"Nate's family have been very kind to me." Ben's tone was firm. He took the wine glass Hunter handed him.

Hunter raised an eyebrow but poured a second glass, handing it to Nate. "I am glad to hear it." He raised his glass, looking to see that Aki had some wine remaining. "Let us toast to your incredible good fortune, and to fam—" He broke off as the door swung open.

The waiter from earlier stepped into the room. He shot Nate and Ben a harassed look and stood at attention.

"As you can see, my guests have found me," Hunter said with a wave. "Or is this the other matter?"

"The councilor has arrived," the waiter said stiffly. "He's brought an escort."

"You explained that it is our rule that we provide the escorts for our guests?"

"He insists."

"What a tiresome man Wisner is." Hunter put down his glass.

"Wisner?" Nate echoed with a sense of dismay. He saw Ben tense.

Hunter was already turning toward the door. "I have to go. We will celebrate your news another time, Ben."

Ben tilted his head. "You're making arrangements for Wisner's escort?"

Hunter smirked at him. "It is customary for the owner of an establishment to provide for the safety of his guests."

"You own Club Royal?" Nate couldn't help his surprise.

"It is my little secret," Hunter said, tugging his jacket straight with an air of complacency. "I hope you don't mind keeping it. I fear my fellow vampires would not enjoy themselves as much if they knew it was my hospitality they were partaking of." He gave Ben a conspiratorial look. "Did it never occur to you to wonder why the Club was so well suited to our purposes?"

"You designed it that way." Ben shook his head. "Does Saltaire know?"

"I'm almost certain he has worked it out, but he says nothing." Hunter waited while the waiter checked that the exit was clear and then slipped out of the room. "Akihiro, once again, it was a pleasure."

"Anytime," Aki said fervently.

"I am not sure I will see you again after this, Ben. I will not try to look for you—"

"I'll keep in touch." Ben said.

Nate swallowed. *He'll keep in touch with Hunter—but I don't get any contact!*

Hunter paused in front of Nate. "It occurs to me that I owe you an apology. I should have remembered that you have Ben's best interests at heart."

Nate felt himself ungainly and in the way. He muttered something unintelligible, even to himself. Hunter smiled, and with a last look back over his shoulder—"Don't be a stranger, Ben."—stepped through the door, leaving a disconcerting silence behind him.

Chapter Eleven

BEN BREATHED OUT slowly, taking stock of his mental state. It was only after a master vampire left that you realized how far under his influence you had been. With Hunter in the room, he'd felt drunk, his thoughts filtered through a crimson lens.

"So even Ben's hot vampire brother has met your twin—and I, your best friend, don't get an invite? How is that fair?" Aki rounded on Nate.

"Ben's vampire brother didn't wait to be introduced." Nate held up his hands. "And like I keep telling you, Ethan doesn't do relationships."

"Whatever." Aki downed the remainder of his wine and put his glass down. "Hunter agrees that you've been very rude."

Ben winced. Hunter had ample time to pump Aki on the details of Nate's past. Although... He interrupted the argument between Nate and Aki. "You didn't tell Hunter that I was human."

Aki shrugged, stretching as he stood. "He never asked. If he'd asked, I don't think I'd have had a choice." His gaze flickered to Nate. "I figured that was classified info, so I played down that angle—so you can stop telling me that I didn't know what I was doing."

"You—!" To Ben's surprise, Nate pulled Aki into a hug. "Don't scare me like that. I was that worried—"

Unacceptable! Ben took a step toward them, his fists clenched. *My consort should know better—*

Consort? Ben came to an abrupt halt. *Where did that come from?*

He unclenched his hands, taking stock of his reactions. The stab of unreasonable anger melted away, leaving his shoulders tensed. There was no increase in his breathing. Ben pressed his fingers to his mouth, knowing what he would find before his fingers even brushed his fangs. *The vampire's back.*

Aki wriggled free of Nate's hold, brushing his hair back into order. "Look, after all the heart attacks you've given me, Mr. 'I Run Toward the Danger,' I think I'm allowed one vampire." He dusted off his shoulder with a casualness that didn't fool anyone. "So...do you think I made an impression on Hunter?"

Nate gave him a distinctly unimpressed look. "What happened to all the advice you gave me about why getting involved with a vampire is a terrible idea?"

Aki stuck his tongue out. "You ignored it. I can, too."

Nate let out an impatient huff of breath, turning toward Ben in silent entreaty. The vampire purred in satisfaction. Ben found the unconscious gesture touching. He put his hand on Nate's arm. "Let's go. It's already been a long night."

"Yeah." Nate opened the door. "Here's hoping we've seen the end of it."

AS THEY MADE their way toward the gallery, loud voices floated up from the ballroom beneath them. Wisner's strident tones were instantly recognizable. Ben drew back. *If he sees me here, I'm finished.*

Aki had no such misgivings. "God. I cannot believe the guy just invited himself into a Vampire Senate meeting. He's practically asking to be politely beaten up."

Ben winced—Aki had clearly bought into the polished veneer vampires liked to present—but before he could stop him, Nate had joined Aki at the railing.

"You're very well-informed about vampires suddenly."

"Hunter gave me a primer on vampire politics."

"Thrilling."

Aki sighed gustily. "I could listen to him talk about patron client relationships all night. That voice, Nate!"

Ben hesitated. *Have they forgotten I'm here?*

"So why is Wisner here?" Nate asked, looking down at the gathering.

Aki shrugged. "I don't know. I think he just insisted on having a hearing, and the senate decided to indulge him. I bet they regret that now—listen to him!"

Wisner was not taking pains to endear himself to his hosts. "I was under the impression that the vampire families conducted their meetings in a more formal setting. Standing around, addressing a crowd from the middle of a dance floor is not my idea of civilized."

"How we conduct our meetings is our business, Councilor."

Who spoke? Was that Genevieve? Despite himself, Ben crept closer to the railing. He could see the back of Wisner's head and took some comfort in the fact that Wisner was fully occupied with the vampires surrounding him in a loose half circle.

Genevieve inspected her nails with studied indifference. "No nonvampire is ever admitted to our meeting. It is an honor to be allowed to address our gathering at all."

One of the two men standing on either side of Wisner gave a low growl. An answering ripple went through the crowd, with several of the younger vampires baring their teeth and adjusting their posture.

"I believe one of the conditions of your escort accompanying you was your word that they would not provoke any quarrel." Hunter spoke with the same indifference, but there was a note of warning in his voice. "Perhaps you wish to leave?"

Wisner made an effort to control himself. "You will forgive my men. They are on edge. The current situation in the city is most unsettling."

"At last," drawled a vampire from the back of the crowd. "I fancy the councilor is finally getting to business."

Wisner shot him a venomous look. "My message is simple. I come not only to request your cooperation in the speedy recovery of the missing werewolf, but to make you an offer."

This time it was the senior vampires who reacted. Genevieve shared a look with Hunter and Allard, before she turned to Wisner. "We were not informed of this."

Wisner smiled. "I'm informing you now."

"Changing the script on a vampire," Aki whispered. "Not a good idea."

Ben nudged him. "Quiet."

Wisner glanced around the crowd in front of him, assured that he had their full attention. "Vampires have long enjoyed the hospitality of the city of New Camden. For many centuries, you've had homes here, and you've been long invested in the city itself. In fact, you've come to view the city as yours. You enjoy a special position in its hierarchy and enjoy preeminence among its supernatural citizens. That ended with the necromancer's attacks."

The ballroom was still. Wisner had the vampires' attention, all right.

"You may have permission to speak," said Allard stiffly. "But I wouldn't suggest you try our patience. We do not take being insulted in our own place lightly."

"What insult? I speak of the truth. You must all have noticed that with so many of your number...culled...in the riots that followed, vampires have lost their former eminence. Your numbers have declined—"

"Those who died were no loss." Allard wiped dust from his sleeve. "They were impetuous youths who had not learned to master their hunger. They are as different from us as you are from a true wolf."

Wisner's eyes flashed. "That isn't how the public sees it. Or how the council does. I'm here to warn you that your way of life is under further threat—unless you take action to undo the harmful impressions acting against you."

"What does he want?" Nate murmured.

Ben cast a look down at the crowd. Fortunately, all the attention was on Wisner. "Nothing good." He stepped back from the railing and gave Nate a tug. Reluctantly, Nate stepped back.

"You have two choices. Cling to your traditions and see your influence and power wane, until you lose all your privileges and are hunted from the city. Or adapt to your changing circumstances by joining an unparalleled alliance of werewolves and vampires."

"So that is your game." Genevieve did not sound surprised. "It would be a feather in your cap to present such an alliance to the Council."

Wisner's tone was conciliatory. "I think only of the benefit to the city. Having its two most powerful groups of supernatural citizens united in a common cause will surely be a deterrent to any harmful elements— and endlessly reassuring to the citizens whose goodwill enables us to live here at all."

"And who will head this alliance? Yourself, of course?" Hunter sounded suitably neutral.

"That is up for discussion," Wisner said stiffly. "Perhaps, if the senate would like to convene we could discuss it in more detail—"

There was a definite stir. Ben felt his mouth twitch as he fought the urge to bare his teeth. *He dares?* He could only imagine the reactions to Wisner's assumption of entry to the senate. He was not surprised to hear a startled growl—Wisner's men had probably not anticipated the strength of the vampires' pride.

"You presume too much," Genevieve said flatly. "We will discuss your offer amongst ourselves and let you know the result."

Wisner's growl was a mistake. He must be losing his temper. "This attitude of uncooperativeness is what allowed the necromancer to infiltrate your ranks so effectively—"

"On the contrary. The necromancer never set foot amongst our members or attended our meetings. You have seriously misjudged the limits of our tolerance, Councilor." Hunter sounded pleasant, if distant—which meant that he was very close to angry. Ben couldn't help a feeling of exultation. He flexed his fingers, curling them into fists. The councilor was on very dangerous ground. "Perhaps you should concentrate on locating your missing wolf."

There was a pause before Wisner spoke. "We know the wolf has aid. We ask that if any of your numbers are abetting his behavior, you turn him over to us at once."

There was a moment's silence. Ben could imagine the three vampire elders exchanging a look. "You have been assured that none of our kind have any knowledge of your werewolf. At the council's request, we have searched for him and found nothing."

"It is possible that you have been deceived," Wisner said. "I seek permission to look for him in your territories."

"Impossible," Allard said at once. "It is an insult to even suggest it—"

"I suggest we consider the councilor's request not as testament of how little he thinks we know our territory, but as a sign of how anxious he is to recover his missing pup," Hunter said. "Only four days remain until the full moon. Naturally the city is anxious to avoid having a werewolf loosed on the city..."

"Indeed," said Genevieve. "It would be as bad as the necromancer attacks—and we would not wish that on a fellow supernatural community."

Nate leaned down to Ben. "She's threatening him, isn't she?"

Ben nodded.

"See what I mean?" Aki said, not taking his eyes off the crowd below. "Sexy West Wing."

"I hope I shall not have to take a report of your lack of cooperation back to the council." There was a low growl to Wisner's voice.

"I believe we can set your mind at ease there," Hunter purred. "We'll report our decision directly to the council ourselves."

"You have delivered your message," Genevieve stated firmly. "Now, I suggest you leave that we may discuss our decision."

Wisner made an attempt to prolong his exit but didn't make another attempt to invite himself into the senate meeting. Perhaps, he'd finally taken the hint.

There was a buzz of conversation immediately after the door slammed shut. Ben felt for Nate's hand. "Let's go." The immediate reactions to Wisner's speech would cover their exit.

"Come on, Aki."

Aki reluctantly followed suit. "This is probably the only chance I'll ever get to observe a vampire party. Can't we just stay a little longer—"

"Hunter's going to be occupied," Ben said. "Vampires are very fond of the sound of their own voices. You probably won't see him before dawn."

"I'm not just interested in Hunter," Aki said with a complete lack of conviction as he reluctantly followed them down the stairs. "I'm appreciating the anthropological significance."

By the time they reached the bottom of the stairs, the council members were beginning to move toward the door. Genevieve took precedence, followed by Allard as was the custom. Hunter took a step to follow them.

"Not so fast." A long-haired vampire elbowed his way through the crowd. "I question Emeric's right of entry to our meeting."

Halfway to the door, Ben stumbled to a halt. Heart beating fast, he turned back to watch.

There was a stir of agreement. "We have never been so grievously insulted on our own turf," agreed a gentleman with magnificent sideburns. "It was ARX's oversight that allowed the necromancer to bring our kind into disrepute. Why should ARX's representative speak for us?"

Nate groped for Ben's hand. "This is bad, isn't it?"

Ben nodded. He didn't dare take his eyes off the scene playing out before them.

"I had hoped that you knew my qualifications well enough that I would not be forced to repeat them." Hunter sounded bored. "I have been a member of this council almost since its founding. I represent not ARX, but my sire—"

"Saltaire is ARX," the long-haired man shot back instantly. "And ARX has no love for vampires. It is only because of Saltaire's power that we tolerate it at all. You do not have his power—and your sire has abandoned the city. You have no claim on us—you alone do not even have a retinue." He motioned to the two women accompanying him.

Hunter raised an eyebrow. "Clients were never a condition of entry to our council, merely a demonstration that we possess power necessary to debate without influence. If I am not accompanied by one, that is because I do not need one."

Ben felt Nate shift beside him. He gripped his arm tightly.

The younger vampire snarled. "Wisner spoke truth about one thing. You have grown too used to having power to know how to defend yourself! I think it is time to shed our society of deadwood." He looked around. "Our rules state that any nomination to our senate must be seconded."

"I represent Saltaire," Hunter said. "I need no second."

"Saltaire isn't here. He has not been here for many months, and you alone remain of his clan." The long-haired man smiled in triumph. "You represent no clan but yourself. Unless you can produce a second—"

Ben stepped forward. "I trust that I am a satisfactory second?" His heart beat fast. Ben projected his voice over it. "Or do I need to introduce myself again?"

The crowd drew back to stare. Hunter was as astonished as the rest of them. Ben permitted himself a slight smile. *So there.*

"But we heard—you were dead." The long-haired vampire cast a disconcerted glance between Hunter and Ben.

"Aren't we all?" Hunter's smile curved in amusement. "It suited ARX for Bennet to remain out of the spotlight as we...tidied up some of the necromancer's loose ends."

"You made no mention of having a second," Genevieve said. She stood in the doorway to the meeting room. This comment was her first intervention in the challenge to Hunter's authority.

"I did not think it necessary. I have enough power of my own to stand up to any challenge that Julian cares to make," Hunter said with a bow toward the long-haired man. "But if you should like to test me..."

Julian. Ben gave the long-haired man a closer look. He had only been newly elected to the senate himself but was clearly already in search of more power.

Julian returned his stare. "It is not our way to settle disputes between principles," he said. "I am sure I need not remind you. I propose my retinue against yours."

He waved a hand and the two women stepped forward. Ben was sure they were disconcerted by this turn of events. One clutched a sequined handbag, the other smoothed her hands over her fitted gown.

"Two against one?" Hunter's acting was note perfect. He desperately wanted to get Ben out of the confrontation, but there was no sign of it in his voice. "I am equally certain that our charter forbids that."

Julian raised his shoulders in a shrug. "If you cannot provide a third—"

"You didn't ask for a third." Nate stepped up to stand beside Ben.

Ben felt a thrill. He glanced at Nate, saw him nod in response. His mouth was pressed into a line, but he didn't seem worried. He stood casually beside Ben.

"A new addition to our family," Hunter said. "I'd introduce you, but I'd only delay the meeting further."

"Two new additions to the clan in as many years." Allard sounded amused. "My. You *are* busy."

Julian was not pleased. "He's not a vampire. He can't take part in our assembly—"

"Our rules only prohibit nonvampires from joining the senate meeting," Genevieve said. "It is not against our rules to make a nonvampire part of a clan—in exceptional circumstances." She gave Nate an intent look.

Ben fought the urge to step closer to Nate. "If you don't like it," he said to Julian, "you can withdraw your challenge."

Julian snarled. He'd bared his fangs, and the vampire in Ben reared in readiness. *How quickly the young one loses control! He will be easy to defeat—*

"I think," Hunter said, in tones that were impossible to ignore, "that Councilor Wisner has filled our quota of empty posturing for the night. Instead, I propose a quick solution to all our challenges. If Nathan and Julian agree, of course."

Julian narrowed his eyes, but Nate turned to Hunter. "Me against him?"

Hunter smiled. "You are so marvelously direct. But yes—I propose a battle of wills. If Julian can compel Nathan, I will cede my place on the senate without a word. If he cannot, then I propose that we get on with business."

There was a stir of interest. The vampires seemed to approve.

Julian hesitated. "You will not interfere?" He looked at Ben. "Either of you?"

Hunter held his hands up. "Neither of us can loan our power to a human. You know that."

He can't be serious. Leaving Nate to this— Ben struggled to think past the vampire's overwhelming desire to throw Julian to the floor.

Nate placed his hand on his arm. "I am sure you were looking forward to cutting loose," he said. "But I got this. Trust me."

Trust me. Ben let the words settle over him. He looked up, found Nate was watching him. His hazel eyes showed no fear, only certainty.

Ben smiled. "You'll make it up to me. Later." He walked over to join Hunter.

"Nathan is in agreement," Hunter said. "Julian?"

The vampire pressed his lips together and nodded.

The vampires drew back, leaving Nate and Julian standing in a circle before them. As Julian took a step toward Nate, Ben felt his stomach clench. *If anything happens to him—*

Hunter laid his hand on Ben's shoulder. "Have no fear," he said, his voice low. "Nathan is a remarkable discovery."

Julian raised his chin. His eyes flashed with insolence, and he stood with full awareness of his power. "Kneel," he commanded.

The air in the ballroom grew heavy. How had he not noticed how stale it was? The power lacing through it made it feel heavy, like they were trapped in a much smaller room. Ben resisted the urge to shift, to find some means of escape. *I've faced much stronger vampires.* He wondered how old Julian was? He must have got lucky and surprised an older vampire. Although he had the strength of decades, he had not yet learned to hide his ambition.

Nate shifted, the slight movement bringing Ben's attention back to him. The vampire in him sprang to the fore. It wanted to snarl a threat at Julian for even daring to bring his power to bear on Nate. *He will regret this—he will regret this very much.*

Nate took a step forward.

A ripple went through the watching crowd.

Ben fought a growl. Every one of the watching vampires was tuned to Nate. Every sign of weakness would be noted and analyzed, its owners waiting for the first chance to take advantage of it. Every one of them was hungry—

I will fight them all, fang and nail. Ben's thoughts were fast and confused. *They will learn not to even look at him—*

Hunter's hand tightened on his shoulder in warning.

At the same time, Nate's head snapped up. He took a step toward Julian. "You kneel."

Julian was so startled that he took a step back and stumbled. His clumsy footsteps echoed in the complete silence of the hall.

Hunter smiled. He looked to Genevieve and Allard, who inclined their heads and turned without another word into the meeting room. This time, Hunter joined them without comment, and another five vampires filed in behind them.

Julian was the last to enter. As he passed Ben, he shot him a venomous look. "I'm not letting this go."

"I think a vampire who can't compel a nonvampire should think twice about making threats." Ben smiled pleasantly at him.

The doors were shut behind the council members, and the remaining vampires and their companions turned away with a sigh. After a moment, a desultory conversation sprung up, but it was clear that many considered the highlight of the evening had been reached.

Ben took Nate's arm in his, pulling him toward the door. "You have a lot to learn about vampires—"

"Am I about to learn?"

How dare he sound so—pleased with himself! The vampire spun around, intending to let Nate know just how seriously he had pushed his patience—and found the waiter hovering at their elbows. "What is it?"

The waiter took a step back. "In accordance with the instructions I received from the manager, I put Mr. Fujino into a taxi just as the situation started to get tense. There's a second taxi waiting for you."

The vampire paused. He was not so gone with anger that he couldn't see the advantages of waiting to get Nate out from under the eyes of the remaining vampires before educating him. "We'll take it. Our...thanks to the manager."

NEW CAMDEN SPED past beyond the taxi windows, a blur of neon lights and glimpses of scantily dressed people outside clubs or lingering in the glow of street lights. And wherever there was light, there was shadow, made even darker by the contrast.

There was good hunting in those shadows, favored by those who preyed on New Camden's human population. Another night, and the vampire would have itched to be out there, hoping to assuage the pain he carried in the thrill of the hunt, and the knowledge that he'd done, if not good, then less bad.

Tonight, his prey was much closer. Nate cast a look at the driver in the rear view mirror and then slid across the back seat. He placed his hand on Ben's arm. "So—"

"So?" The vampire looked up with a chilling reprimand but, instead, found himself struck by how dark Nate's eyes looked in the unlit cab, and how close his mouth was.

"I had the impression," Nate spoke quietly, leaning in to Ben, "that you had quite a lot to say to me."

The vampire growled. *If Nate thought he could tell him what to do—* He gripped Nate's shoulder, holding him in place as he kissed him roughly.

Nate gasped. *Serves him right.* The vampire did not try to gentle his fangs, pursuing Nate's mouth single-mindedly. Nate would have to look out for himself—

Nate did. He moaned, leaning in to Ben, his fingers clutching at Ben's shirt, drawing him close. Their mouths met again and again. Each time the vampire, who did not need to breathe, found himself breathless, given a taste of something warm and necessary but just out of reach. Need pulsed in him and, with it, a heightened awareness of Nate's presence. In the close confines of the taxi, he filled the vampire's senses with his peculiar smell of drying grass and fresh leaves. And beneath it, faint but growing, the salty scent of arousal.

The vampire pressed his fang against Nate's neck, not breaking the skin, but enough so that Nate would feel it and recognize it. He felt the shudder that went through Nate, and he sank back against the car seat, struggling to undo his tie. *Perfect.* The vampire took the tie from him, undoing it easily, and then bent to his work. He kissed his exposed skin and worked his way down Nate's neck, lingering on his collar bone before making his way up the other side.

Even if he hadn't known how sensitive Nate's neck was, Nate's reaction would have shown him. His eyelids fluttered shut and his mouth, usually so articulate, fell open. He clutched Ben's shoulders, his body jerking as Ben progressed over his skin. "Fuck, Ben. You—"

The taxi came to a stop, jerking them both back to awareness of their situation. "We've arrived," said the driver.

The vampire handed his wallet to Nate and climbed out of the car without another word.

He was astonished at himself. How had he let himself be so distracted as to let his guard down in front of a complete unknown? True, he would have detected any supernatural influence in the man, but many of New Camden's supernatural element employed humans as spies, trusting their brethren would overlook them. *I have been careless—and it is his fault.*

The one saving grace was that unless the driver had supernatural qualifications, he would have seen only Nate making out with someone imaginary. The vampire's lip curled. The idea of anyone thinking less of Nate did not sit well with him. He looked back at Nate, climbing out of the cab.

Nate straightened up. He turned toward Ben, automatically seeking his gaze. The suit, rumpled by their journey, looked right on him. The jacket lay open, and at some point, half of the shirt had been tugged loose. The vampire found his gaze drawn to the tie, hanging loosely around Nate's neck. He was immediately visited by an intense need to mark the clear skin at Nate's neck. Only when his fangs cut into his own lips, did Ben realize he had bared them.

This man is dangerous. He watched Nate's approach through narrowed eyes, taking in the cocky walk, the assurance of his gaze—how many men dared look directly into a vampire's eyes, knowing what they faced?

He withstood compulsion. The vampire frowned. He'd never been able to command Nate. It was one of the things that had made him so special. The fact that Nate was able to resist Julian was unexpected—but good. *I will claim him in other ways. Make him understand that he is mine—*

Nate keyed in the password to the automatic door, holding it open for Ben. "What now?"

The vampire raised an eyebrow at the inquiry. "Now?"

"We have the night to ourselves. Aki's back home, I got the night off Century..." The elevator arrived. Nate stepped into it but made no move to press the button to his floor.

The vampire was amused. He stepped into the elevator. Seizing the ends of the tie, he used them to tug Nate's mouth down to kissing level. Nate gasped, his body straining toward Ben's—but the vampire held himself perfectly still, not giving him the contact he wanted. *If I am to keep my head, I must take control.* "We will wait till we're inside my apartment to discuss this."

He stepped back, noting the ripple that went through Nate's body as he stood, pausing to readjust his trousers. The vampire felt a sense of triumph. *It will not be hard to control one who craves it.*

As soon as they were within Ben's apartment, Nate's hand dropped to the curve of Ben's ass. "You want—"

The vampire turned to face him. "I will tell you what I want—in good time." He saw appreciation flicker in Nate's eyes. "You will wait for me in the bedroom."

Nate made no protest. He found his way across the living room and hit the bedroom light, illuminating himself as he stood in the doorway. Only when he'd stepped out of sight into the room did Ben move.

He locked the front door behind them, sliding all three bolts home and testing his wards. They held true. Then, he hurried to what had been his father's office. Among the tools of his trade, his father had kept a bottle of wine, a present from a grateful client—there! Ben took the bottle from the shelf and wiped off the dust. He inspected the label critically and decided it would do. He went to the kitchen for a couple of glasses.

While he made his preparations, a portion of his mind dwelled on Nate. What was he doing as he waited for Ben? Was he thinking—as the vampire was—of what he intended? He hurried to the bedroom. Anticipation was one of the vampire's weapons, letting need grow to overwhelming limits before making his move. But Nate—Nate was unpredictable.

When the vampire slipped into the room, he found Nate's suit jacket and trousers, neatly folded and hanging off the edge of Ben's bedside table, his socks and shoes next to them. Nate stood in shirt and boxers, leaning out of the open window. The faint perfume of his plants floated in on the warm evening air. As the door clicked shut behind Ben, Nate turned. His eyes dropped to the bottle of wine and his mouth curved. "This a special occasion?"

"I intend it to be—memorable." The vampire was pleased to see that Nate had left the tie draped around his neck. "Shut the window." With anyone else, those three simple words would have had the effect of a command they could not disobey. Nate could—but chose not to.

Nate took a last deep breath of the night air before closing the window. "I don't know if I even need the wine. There's something in the air—I feel half-drunk already." He turned toward Ben. "I'm guessing that's you. You've got no idea how hard it was to keep a straight face at the vampire meeting, when every time you opened your mouth all I could think about was getting you alone."

The vampire placed the wine bottle and glasses on the bedside table and sat on the edge of the bed. Part of him gloried in Nate's blatant admission of need, but he knew from past experience that Nate's very enthusiasm was a source of his danger. "You made yourself conspicuous. It's not wise to attract the attention of so many vampires. They'll be wondering about you now."

Nate shrugged, running a hand through his hair. "I can't help that. What was I supposed to do—leave you and Hunter hanging?"

The vampire frowned. He did not have an answer to that—and he did not like that Hunter had been included in Nate's motivations. He stood, holding out his arms. "Come here."

Nate grinned. He held Ben's gaze as he sauntered over, standing in front of him. He ran his hands up and down Ben's sides, stroking him beneath the suit jacket.

Ben took the ends of the tie in hand and tugged Nate down to meet him for a kiss. Their mouths met in the same exploratory rhythm of Nate's hands, but the vampire sensed a growing need in his companion. His mouth quirked up in sudden understanding. *He left the tie on purpose, hoping I'd use it.* Nate enjoyed when the vampire took control of their encounters. *So I shall give him what he wants—and remind him that he is mine all at once.*

The vampire stepped back, stretching his arms out. "Undress me."

Nate's smile was immediate. "I love it when you get all authoritative." He ran his hands down Ben's front, before undoing his suit jacket buttons.

"I know." A disquieting thought cut through the vampire's satisfaction. "Did you know that Julian would be unable to compel you?"

"I was pretty sure I could stand up to him." The suit buttons undone, Nate stepped behind Ben. He pressed his mouth to Ben's neck, tonguing it as he slipped the jacket off. When he stepped back, the vampire felt the loss of his body heat with regret.

He turned to watch Nate search for a hanger for his jacket in the wardrobe. "What made you sure?"

Nate put the suit jacket on the hangar, draping it over the end of the bed. He approached Ben again, settling on his knees on the ground before him. "When Hunter showed up at Century, he didn't just ask me where you were."

The vampire felt Nate's fingers on his belt buckle and the warmth of his skin with only half his attention. *Nate wasn't able to resist Hunter's compulsion before… What has changed?* "How?"

Nate placed the belt on the bed. He glanced up at Ben, his fingers searching for the button on his trouser fly. "You know how I've been practicing using my powers? I imagined myself a tree. Solid as an oak, with roots deep beneath the ground, where Hunter could never see them." His smile lingered, even as he pressed his lips to the fabric covering Ben's erection.

Ben rocked on his heels, pressing against Nate's mouth. His mind raced. He did not realize that he'd placed his hand on Nate's shoulder until he looked down. "You—" He swallowed. He did not like this sudden threat to his mastery. "Could you resist me?"

Nate placed his hands on Ben's hips, and Ben felt his warm breath through the cloth as he breathed in deeply. "I don't want to. You're everything I want, Ben—"

It was more than he'd ever imagined he could have, more than he'd even dared to hope for. But it was not enough for the vampire. "And if I wanted you to resist?"

Nate looked up, startled, his fingers poised to undo Ben's fly. "What?"

The vampire stroked his cheek. "Do not touch yourself. Do not come. Not until I let you."

Color rushed immediately to Nate's cheeks. He licked his lips, the vampire noting with satisfaction that his breath shook. "Ben—"

Was that a plea? "You can't do it?"

Nate's eyes glittered darkly. He raised his chin. "Try me."

The vampire exulted.

Chapter Twelve

NATE'S HEART BEAT fast. His words—"Try me"—seemed to hang in the air between them. Ben hadn't moved, but Nate felt how tense his stillness was.

He ran his tongue over lips that were suddenly dry.

It was as if he'd turned a switch. Ben bent to him, gripping his chin and turning it up firmly to meet his mouth. His kiss was hungry, and he didn't seem to care that his fangs pressed into Nate's skin.

Nate barely managed to repress a moan, but he was sure that Ben was fully aware of the effect he had on Nate. *I'm in so much trouble.* Ben was hard to resist in any circumstances, but when he got the urge to take control, he was on fire.

Ben released him. Nate sat back on his heels, digesting the rush of lingering sensation—and then realized that Ben was talking to him? "Sorry, what?"

Ben's smile bared his fangs. "Remove my trousers," he ordered. "Then lie on the bed."

Fuck me. Nate's hands fumbled as he tugged Ben's trousers down. They'd played this game before—but not with the vampire involved. That gave the encounter a level of danger that had Nate's heart beating rapidly. He dared not think about his cock, pulsing with the same beat and demanding attention. *Have to get my head in the game!* If he gave way before Ben too easily, there'd be no need for further encounters.

As Ben stood and stepped out of his trousers, Nate saw his chance. He moved back, putting some distance between them as he folded the trousers. He let his gaze rake over Ben, standing there in shirt and briefs. Nate's mouth was dry, but he resisted the urge to swallow. Instead, he let his gaze linger pointedly on the evidence of Ben's own need, the bulge just visible through the shirt.

He saw Ben's fingers twitch. Fighting an impulse to cover himself?

Nate sauntered to the bed with confidence and settled himself on his back on the bed, leaning against the headboard. He felt the tie slide off and let it go. He had his hands full already. His fingers itched to stroke his cock, but he settled for running them over the smooth surface of Ben's sheets.

The vampire gave no sign of his interest, but the fingers undoing his tie struggled unnecessarily with the knot. Nate felt a rush of satisfaction. He shifted, ostensibly making himself comfortable, raising one knee and letting his hand dangle from it. He kept a close watch on Ben's reactions.

He'd gone still when Nate moved, and his mouth was open. He didn't seem to be breathing more rapidly, but there was color in his face that hadn't been there before, and he dropped his tie on the floor with what seemed like impatience. His eyes made their way up Nate's body, narrowing when they met Nate's gaze. He turned, flicking off the lights.

Fuck. Nate drew a shaky breath. Not knowing Ben's location was sensory deprivation—or was it overload? As his eyes adjusted to the dark, the smallest sound took on momentous importance. He heard the flutter of cloth and imagined Ben's discarded shirt falling to the floor. He shifted on the bed, straining to hear more.

He was acutely aware of every sensation in his body. The sheets beneath him had taken on his warmth, brushing across his skin like a caress. The feeling of his boxers against his straining erection was agony. Nate dug his fingers into the sheets in an effort to resist touching himself.

There was a movement in the darkness. The light of the alarm clock outlined Ben's shape and beneath it the gleam of his eyes fixed on Nate.

Nate bit his lip. *Vampire night vision?* The thought that Ben could see him perfectly had him squirming, raising his hips off the bed. He felt exposed in the best possible way. *I am so screwed. There is no way I'm going to be able to hold on—he's playing me from the inside out.*

Ben's touch, stroking his chest through his shirt, made him shudder. Nate screwed his eyes shut, tensing his body as he fought the urge to arch into Ben's fingers.

Ben's chuckle was low, and Nate recognized the tone of what he thought of as Ben's inner vampire. "It is just as well that we are alone. If New Camden's vampires suspected how responsive you are—"

"Only you," Nate gasped, not even sure what point he was arguing. It was hard to think with Ben's hand resting on his stomach, so close to where his cock waited, but making no move to touch it. "You, Ben."

Ben said nothing, but he began slowly unbuttoning Nate's shirt.

The cold air on his chest was sobering. Nate took a deep breath, fighting to get his body under control. He had to hold on, not get more aroused. "Um. There was a lady at the meeting. The blonde who tried to hit on me."

Ben ran his fingers down Nate's chest. "What about her?"

Nate gasped. After so much time anticipating it, Ben's touch had an electrifying effect. "You— I mean, she...she said something." He made a concerted effort to focus. "You hadn't marked me. What did she mean?"

Ben went still, his fingers resting lightly on Nate's chest. "It's not important."

"She meant biting, right? Feeding."

Ben's fingers gripped his arm. "It's not important, Nate."

"Isn't it? 'Cause I think who you feed from would be really important—and I am totally up for that."

Ben let go, sitting back on his heels. "It's not a simple matter. Feeding a vampire—even when done consensually and with as much care as possible—still creates a link between the vampire and the donor. Their destiny is forever entwined, as you saw with the necromancer. It ends only with death—permanent death."

Nate felt a chill settle over him. "Isn't that all the more reason for it to be me? We're already as entwined as it is possible to get."

"Nate." Ben gripped him by his collar, hauling him upright. "Do not tempt me. There are risks you don't know—"

"You're still afraid of hurting me—of thinking you have to protect me." Nate sought Ben's eyes in the dark. He placed his hands on Ben's sides. "I'm not the ignorant guy I was when we first met. I've grown— you know how much I've changed."

"It's true you've learned a lot," Ben said slowly. "But this is a really big thing, Nate."

"All the more reason it should be me and not some anonymous vegan." Nate licked his lips. "Don't you think?"

There was a faint glow from the window where New Camden's lights could be seen. Now that Nate's eyes were accustomed to the dark, he saw Ben's tongue flicker across his lips and pause, as if he'd caught himself in a reflexive motion. "You're not jealous, Nate?"

Was he? There was some resistance to the idea that Ben should lean on anyone else. Nate gave up trying to probe it. "I want to do anything I can for you. I—you're that important to me, Ben." Love came readily to his lips, but he didn't think Ben was ready to hear it.

Ben leaned in, his hand resting on Nate's cheek. "Hold on, and if you succeed in resisting me—I will feed."

Heat immediately surged through Nate's body as all his desire, momentarily held at bay by the serious turn of their conversation, rushed back in one overpowering wave. He felt Ben's fingers stroke his skin, and Nate was sure by the curve of his mouth that he'd felt Nate's need. *Cruel! He knows exactly what he's doing to me—and he enjoys it.* Nate moaned breathlessly.

Ben pushed him back down onto the bed, settling himself between Nate's legs. He parted Nate's shirt, pressing his mouth to Nate's exposed skin.

Nate dug his fingers into the sheets once more. It was a growing battle just to keep his reactions in check—a battle Nate knew he couldn't win. *Can't win on the defense—* But the idea of stopping Ben was intolerable. His dick pulsed, demanding attention. Just one touch—

Trying to keep his mind off his need, Nate concentrated on the discomfort of his situation. His muscles, straining for so long, ached. The slightly restrictive effect of the boxers. The cold night air settling over his skin. The feeling of release as Ben eased the boxers back, freeing his cock at last—

I'm in trouble. Nate swallowed. As much as he tried to focus his attention elsewhere, his cock pulled him back. He felt its angry pulse in his belly, spreading through his veins, beating in his forehead. One touch and it would all be over.

But Ben didn't immediately touch him. Nate heard the rustle of cloth over the sound of his own harsh breathing and looked up to see Ben's undershirt slide to the floor. He pushed his briefs off slowly.

Nate was aware that his mouth was parted and hungry. He couldn't see Ben's freed cock, but he could imagine it. In the dark, the pictures his mind created were so vivid he felt he could taste Ben already on his lips. His body strained, and Nate caught his hand reaching for his throbbing cock.

Have to hold on! Nate put his mind on the prize—the thought of Ben's mouth against his neck, taking him in a way no client or previous lover ever had. It would hurt, he was sure of it, but then—vampire addicts described it as a rush. There was something really hot about the thought of feeding Ben—

A breathy moan filled the air. Nate recognized it as himself too late. *Fuck. This is not working.* He felt the bed shift as Ben joined him and struggled desperately to take hold of himself. *I'm a tree—an oak. Time is nothing to me. Nothing shakes me—*

He felt the calm of the oak settle over him, just in time.

Ben's cock pressed against his leg as he positioned himself between Nate's legs. "Spread yourself, Nate. Legs bent."

Nate shifted himself, helped by Ben's hands, directing him the way he wanted him. His heart still beat at an accelerated rhythm, but he was able to distance himself from it.

Ben rested one hand on Nate's upturned knee. He rocked lightly on his heels, his cock sliding over Nate's skin, rubbing against the base of Nate's erection.

"Fuck me..." How was it Ben felt so good? It filtered through his thoughts of the oak, and Nate clung with difficulty to his resolve. *The breeze ruffles the leaves—but it doesn't go within.* Nate forced his tense body to relax. He was fighting Ben's battle for him, making himself even more aware of every move he made.

Ben must have interpreted Nate's relaxation as preparedness. "Condom?"

"Got it." Nate had placed it on the bedside table within easy reach. Struggling with the tiny packet between trembling fingers was a welcome distraction. Nate wriggled into a sitting position, taking hold of Ben's base with one hand. He couldn't resist running his thumb along the ridge of the frenulum, admiring how it felt beneath his hand.

Ben tensed. "Nate." It was equal parts command and warning.

Nate grinned in triumph. Perhaps he wasn't the only one in danger of letting go too soon? He slid the condom on, using his hand to gently pump Ben's length as he did. *Hard—so hard.* The smell of the plastic didn't obscure the heady smell of Ben's arousal. Nate let him go, to lick a smudge of precome off his fingers, and found Ben's gaze on him.

"As you were." His eyes were completely dark, only their gleam indicating where Ben looked.

Nate found himself on his back, spreading himself, his heart racing as he waited for Ben's next move. He swallowed, wondering if he should have tried to take the battle into Ben's territory—and then it was too late. Ben's cock trailed across his skin, its cool tip searching for—and finding—his entrance.

Tree! Nate tried to remain still. Every thought was on Ben's movements, his cock teasing across Nate's entrance. The bed tipped, Ben adjusting his weight, one hand resting on Nate for balance. And then he was slipping through the tight ring of muscle as easily as if he was coming home.

Oak. Nate tried to remind himself that he was an oak, but the thought flashed into his mind of the rowan, putting its roots down inside the oak, the two growing together. *Fuck me.* Ben paused, readjusting his hold on Nate's legs, before drawing back to slide into him and it was all Nate could do not to come right then.

"Ben—" He was a professional. He should not be going to pieces but it was everything exactly where he wanted it most. Ben moved inside him as if he were part of Nate, his treacherous body accommodating him perfectly.

"So greedy." Ben paused, holding himself still. He let go of Nate, so it was only his cock inside Nate, his skin pressed against Nate's ass. "Are you even trying to hold out?"

Nate bit his lip. His one chance was to get Ben so close that he lost control, that he forgot—

Deliberately he tightened around Ben's cock, raising his hips so that he could thrust against him.

Ben gave a vampire's growl and, seizing Nate's leg, went back to his work. His thrusts were fast, and Nate felt a sense of triumph. *I got him—*

And then Ben brushed his prostate, and for a second Nate couldn't even think.

He was next aware of Ben sliding out, rolling him onto his side. He moved his leg at Ben's urging, watching as Ben lined himself up again. Ben gripped his leg, using it to hold Nate in place as he slammed into him. Nate looked down his stomach. His neglected cock was red and swollen, jerking with every thrust Ben made. Nate's voice was hoarse. He didn't remember speaking, but he couldn't stop the tumble of words from his mouth. "Ben—please, Ben. I can't—can't wait. I need—"

Ben slowed. He deliberately pushed forward, striking unerringly at Nate's prostate. "You give up?"

Nate bit back his whine. "Yeah. Yeah, I can't—I'm going to—I'm so close."

Ben's grin was savage. He pulled out entirely. Nate found himself pushed face down onto the bed, felt Ben climb over him. He willingly spread himself wide. "Please, Ben—"

Ben's breath tickled Nate's neck before his kiss. He laved his tongue across Nate's sensitized skin, and Nate moaned. He felt Ben's hands slide across his cheeks, and raised his hips. Ben's cock found his entrance unerringly and slid home in one devastating move.

Nate's whole body trembled with it. "Fuck—" It would not be long at all, just another raise of Ben's hips—

Ben's mouth pressed wetly against his neck. There was a sudden scrape—teeth—and then two pinpricks that grew suddenly into lancing pain.

Fuck! Nate's body jerked in alarm, and Ben's hips snapped forward. Nate's body quivered, like he was caught in a spider's web, unable to free himself, caught between his need and the pain in his neck, throbbing in time with his racing heart.

The pain vanished, in its place a rush of warmth. Ben placed his mouth over it and sucked, sending exquisite ripples of pain through his skin. Nate felt something inside him unlock. His body arched of its own accord, his vision filling with light. His come splattered across his stomach, while his mind soared, riding waves of sensation he'd never dreamed existed.

And then—

This is too much. The awareness of danger came suddenly. Nate tried to formulate a warning, but his thoughts were slow. "Ben—"

The darkness was sudden, and equally intense. Nate fell.

Chapter Thirteen

A KNOCKING SOUND. Pain lanced through Ben's head.

He groaned, curling up on the bed. With every knock, his entire skull pulsed with fire. It blotted out everything but the sound.

It was a few seconds before he realized it had stopped, his head continuing to beat with the aftereffects of the pain. Ben breathed out in relief, burrowing back into the blankets. It was no good. His head continued to throb, duller but still painful. His lips cracked, and when he ran his tongue over them he tasted copper. There was a thick feeling in his mouth.

The knocking started again. This time, it was a determined assault, a stream of continuous banging. A few seconds was more than Ben could take. He levered himself upward and swung his legs over the side of his bed. He staggered as he stood, only preventing himself from falling by catching the back of the chair. His foot encountered cloth. He realized it was a shirt and pulled it on. *There should be trousers.* He had a dim memory of them folded over the back of a chair.

Something dry crackled under his feet as he stepped toward the chair. Ben looked down, but he couldn't see anything. The room's heavy blackout curtains kept it dark, too dark for his tired eyes to fathom. He could smell something sweet and rotten, and fought a wave of nausea.

The banging started up again, more energetically. Ben stepped into the trousers and made his way to the door. His legs didn't want to obey him, but by staggering from doorway to wall, he reached the front door. The pain increased with his proximity to the sound. Swallowing back bile, Ben opened the door.

Aki blinked at him, dropping his hand. "Jeez, Ben! You frightened me, looming up out of the dark like that." He peered closely at him. "Rough night?"

Ben stared at him. His brain struggled to process Aki's question—or even the searing yellow of his high-visibility jacket and the hot-pink running shorts he wore.

Something moved at his feet. He looked down and saw the dog straining at his lead to get into the apartment.

"Heel," Aki said, jerking the lead. "That bad, huh? You guys must have had quite the party after I left."

Ben swallowed. The thick feeling in his mouth had increased to the choking point. "Aki."

"Congratulations on remembering my name. Don't strain anything coming up with a greeting—seriously, you look terrible. I'm guessing Nate's even worse if you're the one answering the door?"

Ben felt a spike of alarm. "Nate—" Where was Nate?

"What on earth did you guys get up to? It smells like a forest died in here."

The dog began to bark. Each bark sent a stabbing pain through Ben's skull, ending any chance of thought.

"Stop that! God—" Aki hauled the dog back from the door. "It's like you've never been hungover, you sadistic brute."

Ben gripped the doorframe tightly. "Hungover?" He racked his aching brain, trying to place the word. A memory surfaced. "There was a bottle of wine."

"More than one, I'm guessing." Aki sounded amused, even as he struggled to drag the frantically barking dog toward the elevator. "Nate's with you?"

Nate. Ben looked blankly toward the bedroom. "Um—"

"Yeah, no." Aki snorted. "I do not need the TMI. I came to see if Nate wanted to take responsibility for his animal, but I'll do it. Tell him he owes me—and get some vegetable juice into him."

"Vegetable juice?" Ben swallowed and felt a burning sensation at the back of his throat.

"Nate swears by it as a hangover cure. Doesn't matter what kind—as long as there's some kind of vegetable involved, he's good. The key is to stay hydrated." Aki succeeded in wrestling the dog into the elevator. He yelled back, over the closing doors. "Seriously, hydrate!"

Ben stood still, staring after them. The noise had gone, but the twisting sensations in his stomach had risen up to take their place. His stomach heaved, and Ben realized that he was going to be sick.

He staggered to the bathroom on legs that shook, only just reaching the toilet in time.

It was some time before he could think. His stomach continued to roll, and he gagged, but this time the only thing that was produced was a dribble of spit and something hard that stuck to Ben's lip.

He sank backward onto the floor, shutting his eyes. For a few moments he just breathed. His skin was clammy, but the cold of the tiles beneath him was a relief. *What is the matter with me?*

He picked the hard thing from his lip and looked at it. It took him some time to recognize it—an uneven patch of some brown thing that looked leathery but was brittle. There were thin veins running through it. *A leaf?* Ben stared at it. *I don't remember eating any leaves—*

Memory flashed into his mind. Nate's body arched against him, the smell of his come mingling with the delicate sweetness of his blood—

Ben swallowed a fresh wave of bile and staggered to his feet. He stared at the contents of the toilet. *This is bad.* Blood, clotted and rapidly turning a dirty brown, in huge clumps, not that dissimilar from the dried brown leaves that stuck up out of the mass. *Not bad—this is—* His mind blanked. "Nate!"

His legs shook so violently that Ben found himself on his knees. He crawled toward the bedroom, fear building in his chest. Using the doorframe to pull himself up, Ben hit the lights.

It took him a moment to make sense of the scene in front of him. It looked like autumn had been and gone in his bedroom. Fallen leaves littered the floor, the bed—even the air was thick with the smell of them. The houseplants were wilted, leaning at crazy angles out of their pots. And on the bed, tangled in the sheet and lying very, very still, was a familiar body.

Ben hauled himself onto the bed, pulling back the sheets. "Nate?"

Nate lay on his side. His eyes were closed. Any hope that he was just sleeping was undone by how still he was. *I can't see his chest rise.* Ben crawled over to him, grabbing his hand. *Fuck, he's cold.* Humans weren't meant to feel this cold.

Ben pressed his fingers to the vein in Nate's wrist. He squeezed his eyes shut, concentrating—but there was nothing to feel. Ignoring the fear clutching at his gut, he pulled Nate over onto his back, so he could press his fingers to the artery in his neck.

The two deep incisions in Nate's neck seemed like an accusation. *No. No, no, no.* Ben snatched his hand away, becoming aware of the deep crimson stain on the sheets behind Nate. *Please, no.* He could almost taste the intoxicating richness of the blood on his lips, remembering how Nate's body yielded so perfectly to his own. Nate's blood, mingling with the endorphins of his release, was sweeter than anything he'd ever tasted—

I've killed him. Ben gasped, feeling as though he would be sick again, but there was nothing left in his stomach. *I've killed him—*

His hand stayed on Nate's shoulder. He didn't want to move. He couldn't. Without Nate, there was nothing—

No. I refuse—he can't die! Ben shook him. Harder and harder, trying to get a reaction out of him. "You promised you'd be here! You said you'd wait while I figured things out—that you'd be strong!"

Strong. Nate's peculiar strength came back to Ben in a rush. He staggered over to the window, drawing the curtain back.

On the fire escape, he could see Nate's collection of plants, still a healthy green.

Ben swallowed. *I don't know what it means...but it has to mean something.*

Not allowing himself to think about anything but what he was doing, Ben drew the curtains as wide apart as they could go. The sunlight didn't quite make it to the bed. Straining with all the strength remaining to him, Ben dragged Nate from the bed and into the light. It took him multiple attempts, but he didn't pause. Any time he was tempted to catch his breath, the chill of Nate's skin urged him onward.

Ben tenderly brushed Nate's hair out of his face. *Now what?* Plants needed sunlight and water. And soil, but how on earth was he meant to get soil into his apartment?

The plants! Ben climbed out of his window. He grabbed first one plant and then another, upending the contents of the pots onto the bedroom floor. It took several trips, and by the last one he had to close his eyes, taking a moment to will his body into obeying his instructions before dumping the soil onto the floor. He almost lost his footing as he dragged Nate onto the bed of soil.

Water. His body felt both heavy and weak. He swayed, dizzy and battling nausea as he reached the bathroom. There was a bucket used for cleaning in the cupboard below the sink. Ben filled it and dragged it back to the bedroom.

Nate hadn't moved. He lay still, even when Ben tipped the bucket over him. The breeze from the open window stirred the leaves, their murmur sounding like the breath he so wanted to hear Nate take.

"Please." Ben touched Nate's cheek. "I need you. Nate—please come back."

He shuddered, the breeze suddenly making him realize how cold he was. His stomach swelled, and Ben realized that he was going to be sick again.

This time, he made it only as far as the bath. Ben leaned against it, his hands clutching the cold edge of the tub. His body continued to shudder, even though there was nothing remaining in him but bile.

Nate. Ben shut his eyes. His thoughts were clouded and heavy, and there was a curious distance between himself and his body. He knew he should go to Nate, but he couldn't make himself move. Light exploded and dimmed in his head. *I have to go to Nate. If I don't—*

His stomach rolled again. *He's dead? You're fooling yourself.* Ben swallowed, but the feeling of Nate's skin, so unnaturally cold, rushed into his mind before he could dismiss it. *He's dead.* Ben choked back a sob at the memory of the vampire's exultation and the thrill of satisfying his hunger. *Dead—and I've killed him.*

THE PHONE WOKE him. Ben listened to it ring without stirring. He couldn't move. A heaviness had stolen over him, and he didn't want to exist at all. He just wanted to lie there, alone with his misery. He made no attempt to reach the phone, or even move. *Just leave me here.*

His eyes were shut, but as the phone continued to ring, he noticed that he lay on a pillow with a sheet over him. His brain digested these facts without curiosity. Ben didn't remember moving, but he didn't care. *What does it matter? Nothing matters.* His stomach rolled painfully. *Without Nate—*

There was movement nearby. The phone stopped mid-ring. "Hello?"

Nate's voice. Ben's eyes flew open in shock.

Nate stood at the foot of the master bed. He wore a T-shirt over his boxers, and one hand smoothed the jacket hanging over the back of the chair automatically. He had something wrapped around his neck. "Yeah, this is Ben's phone. I'm a friend—Nate. Can I ask who's calling?" Nate's fingers tightened over the back of the chair. "No—he's not able to take your call right now. He's not well." There was a pause. "Food poisoning."

Food...? Ben sat up. His head swam, dizziness warring with the bewildering thoughts racing through his mind. Nate—Nate was real. He felt a rush of relief, followed by an immediate thrill of horror. *Did Nate know...?*

"Diya? Okay, I'll give him the message. Yeah—thanks." Nate ended the call, replacing the phone within Ben's suit jacket. He turned around and Ben could see that the thing wrapped around his throat was a vine that started where the vampire had sunk his fangs into Nate's neck and extended down his arm.

Nate's gaze fell on him and he hesitated. "Man, I'm sorry. Was trying not to wake you."

"Wake me?" Ben swallowed. His voice was hoarse, barely a whisper. "Nate. You—" He held out a hand.

Nate sat on the edge of the bed. "I woke up in the sun. I'm guessing that was you?" He reached for Ben's hand. "You'd passed out in the bathroom. Scared me to death. Do you—you don't remember any of that?"

Ben reached out, pressing his hand to Nate's neck beneath the vines. He felt his pulse, loud and steady, and shut his eyes. The relief was so strong he just gave way, leaning against Nate's chest. He breathed in his warmth and felt the pinprick of tears threaten behind his eyes.

"Hey. It's okay." Ben heard the rustle of leaves as Nate wrapped his arms around him. "I'm fine. You—you're going to be fine."

Ben breathed out. "You're not dead. When I woke up, I thought—"

Nate's hold tightened reflexively. "I'm not dead, Ben. Not even close."

The words should have reassured him, but as Ben lay, watching Nate's chest rise with every breath, all he could feel was sick. Nate had survived—this time.

"I THINK THIS is a really bad idea. An hour ago you couldn't get out of bed without help, and now you want to go to Department Seven?" Nate stood in the bedroom doorway, watching as Ben struggled with the arms of his shirt.

Ben ignored the dizzy feeling. "Because I can't be sure that you will go unless I go with you."

Nate let out a frustrated breath. "I'm fine. You—you need to rest!"

"You're growing vines, Nate." Ben left his hand on the back of the chair to steady himself as he looked around for his hoodie. "Admittedly, that's more normal for you than for anyone else, but still—that's not a good sign!"

Nate opened Ben's wardrobe, pulling a hoodie from the shelving unit. He didn't have to search through the drawers to find it. "Ready? Catch." He threw the hoodie. "And the vine is the reason I don't want to go to Department Seven. You know they're going to ask questions."

I do not remember my wardrobe being that organized. Had Nate stayed in the bedroom with him all that time he'd been unconscious? Ben felt his stomach twist with something that felt like guilt. "Only if they see it. You've got a hoodie right? Wear that."

Nate hesitated. "You'll be all right in here on your own?"

Ben narrowed his eyes. "If you ask me how I'm feeling one more time, I will strangle you, Nate. You should be worried about yourself!"

"I am, I'm just—well, look at yourself! I'm not convinced we shouldn't be taking you to the hospital."

Ben shuddered. "Not the hospital."

"Then—"

"We're still going to Department Seven." Ben sat on the edge of the bed and began winding up his sleeves. "Please, Nate. Don't argue with me—this is really important."

"You're going to be eaten up with guilt until we do aren't you?" Nate ran a hand down his face. The vine extended all the way down his shoulder and the length of his arm—mirroring the flow of blood from the wound. Was that coincidence or deliberate? If Nate's magic was linked to his blood—

Ben's stomach rolled. He hastily reached for the bucket beside the bed.

Nate disappeared, coming back from the kitchen with a glass of water. "Drink this."

Ben shook his head. "I don't want to drink anything." The one good thing about how sick he'd been was that his stomach was nothing but bile, and he had nothing more to lose.

"Just rinse your mouth it. Trust me, you'll feel better." Nate pressed his hand to Ben's forehead. "You do not feel well at all."

Ben spat the water into the bucket and discovered that he did feel better. "I'll survive."

"Are you sure?" Nate stroked his arm. "You haven't been sick like this for a really long time. You don't know what it's like."

Ben frowned as a thought occurred to him. "What made you tell Diya I had food poisoning?"

Nate shrugged. "It was the first thing I thought of. To be honest, I panicked. When I found you unconscious in the bathroom, I thought the worst." Nate's fingers stilled. "That was—really bad, wasn't it?"

Ben shut his eyes. "You could have—"

"Don't say it."

"You could have died, Nate."

"So could you." Nate squeezed his shoulder tightly. "You're still weak. You want to go to Department Seven, but you haven't even tried to keep anything down—"

"Even the thought of food makes me nauseous. I can't, Nate."

"Let's see about that." The bed shifted as Nate stood, and Ben opened his eyes to see him walking out the door.

Carefully, Ben put the bucket back down on the floor. He pulled on the hoodie, and using the wall to steady himself, made his way to the wardrobe for socks. When Nate returned, Ben was sitting on the bed, pulling the last sock on.

Nate frowned, but instead of commenting, he held out a glass to Ben. "Here."

"I don't want it."

"Drink it." Nate closed his fingers around it. "It's just sugar dissolved in warm water. You need the energy." He watched Ben closely. "I'm not going to Department Seven with you unless you drink it."

Ben looked down at his knees. He couldn't help the rush of warmth he felt at Nate's concern—or the guilt that followed. *Looking out for you—which means you have to look out for him.* He took a cautious sip.

The water felt like the best thing ever to his aching, hurting throat. To his surprise, Ben found that the hard part was restraining himself to small sips instead of downing the entire drink at once.

Nate watched him anxiously.

Ben put the cup down on the bedside table. "You should go and get dressed. I don't mind you wearing only your boxers, but I don't think Department Seven would appreciate it."

"You'll be fine?"

"I can manage one glass of water by myself." Ben kept his voice firm. "Get ready, Nate." He settled back against the headboard, watching as Nate climbed out of the window. He'd tidied up the dirt, but there was still a muddy patch where Nate'd lain. The plants had been returned to their pots and stood against the wall.

Ben took another sip of water and then another. There was no way he was letting Nate get out of taking care of himself.

When Nate returned, with the vine tucked into the neck of his hoodie, Ben had finished the glass of water. He resisted Nate's attempt to make him rest and, instead, leaned on Nate's arm as they waited for a taxi.

"We must be costing you a fortune on cabs."

"That's not important." Ben was surprised to find how angry he was. "What's important is getting you checked out."

Nate looked down at him and immediately glanced away.

He was still withdrawn in the cab. Ben didn't like it, but he was too exhausted to question it—or argue with the arm that Nate slid around him. He leaned against him, his eyes closed. *Halfway there. We can do this.*

The woman at the reception desk looked curiously at them both. "No community service today," she said, "and even if there was, you're really late."

Ben realized that he had no idea what day it was or how long ago it had been since Aki knocking at the door had alerted him to the situation. "We're here for the lab. The morning-after vampire test."

"Oh." The receptionist looked very much like she wanted to ask and only the ringing of the phone prevented her. "Go back outside and around the corner—there's a door marked lab. Hit the intercom and tell them why you're here. They'll let you in."

"Morning-after vampire test?" Nate asked as soon as they were back outside.

"To check if you've—" Ben paused. "Caught" wasn't the right word, and neither was "infected."

"Picked up being a vampire?" Nate pressed the intercom button. "I had no idea Department Seven offered that service."

"Recent development." Ben leaned against the wall.

"And you think that I might be a vampire?"

"A vampire fed from you. It's a fifty-fifty chance."

"What happens if I've got it?"

"If you've got vampirism, that means you'll be fine and live a thoroughly normal life—until you die. And then—well, if you want to protect your loved ones, you've got to take steps. Most new vampires, acting entirely on instinct, return to the place they feel safest—their homes. And when they get there, they're overcome by hunger and—"

Nate shuddered. "That's enough—oh yeah, hi. The uh—the vampire test."

The door clicked open.

The steps down into Department Seven's basement laboratory were a challenge, but Ben took them one at a time, knowing he would have plenty of time to rest as Nate took the test. The lab staff ushered Nate into the lab and Ben was left alone in the waiting area. He took his phone out of his pocket. *Now to work out how long we've been out.*

Ben scanned the headlines on the news sites, but he felt entirely disconnected from it all. Even the realization that he had several messages from Diya didn't matter. He put his phone back in his pocket and settled back. *The only thing that matters is that Nate almost died—because of me.* He ran his tongue over his teeth. He couldn't feel the fangs, but he knew they were there—knew they'd always be there.

I'm not human. I'm a monster. And no amount of paperwork would change that.

"HEY." BEN DIDN'T know how much time had passed before Nate sat down next to him. "Good news." Nate was grinning.

Ben felt a spike of anger—did he still not understand how serious this had been? "What's the report?"

"Totally free of vampiric influence of—for lack of a better word—germs." Nate nudged him. "I guess my plant—whatever it is—doesn't agree with vampires."

Ben shut his eyes. The relief was too great.

"Ben? That's good news—don't freak out on me!" Nate's hand was on his shoulder. "Ben—"

"I'm just relieved." Ben swallowed. "I'm—really glad."

"Now, maybe we can get you home?" Nate offered his arm as Ben stood. "Or maybe even to a hospital?"

Ben resisted the urge to take it. "Home."

"If you're sure—" Nate noticed the bag on the bench beside Ben. "What's this?"

"Vegetable juice for you, a Coke for me. There's a store on the corner." Ben frowned. Nate was looking at him as if he'd done something extraordinary. "Aki told me you liked vegetable juice."

"Did he?" Nate picked up the bag, leading the way up the stairs.

The long wait, the fresh air, and the combination of sugar and caffeine in the Coke was having an effect. Ben's limbs were no longer as heavy and disconnected as they had been.

Nate looked down the street. "You really walked all the way to the store?"

"It was the least I could do after nearly killing you." Relief had given way to the tension headache that had been building throughout the long wait at the laboratory.

Nate winced, unscrewing the first bottle of vegetable juice. "Can we stop bringing that up?"

"And just forget it happened? Not happening, Nate! You—"

"Taxi." Nate stepped out into the road to hail it. "Let's continue this at home."

The cab ride was silent. Ben sipped his Coke slowly and carefully. Nate drank both bottles of vegetable juice and tried to make conversation with the cab driver.

They got into the elevator. Nate pressed the button for Ben's apartment. Ben leaned over and pressed the button for Nate and Aki's floor.

"You're still sick," Nate said immediately in protest. "You shouldn't be on your own, Ben."

The elevator lurched upward, and Ben had to steady himself against the wall. "And you should be a little bit more concerned with your health, not that of the guy who—"

"You didn't mean to hurt me! We both know that what happened was an accident!"

"Why are you making excuses for me? This is your life we're talking about—yours!"

The elevator arrived at Nate's floor, but he made no attempt to leave. "Look. I woke up feeling—not good, but not bad either. I was lying in sunlight, with my plants around me—I knew you'd done that. But I couldn't find you anywhere, and when I did—" Nate swallowed. "I poisoned you. My blood—that's what happened isn't it? You drank my blood and—"

"Neither of us knew that was going to happen," Ben said. "You—you're very lucky. Your plant nature not only protected you from vampirism, but it means that any vampire attempting to feed on you will—"

"And that's why vampire compulsion doesn't work on me anymore?"

"Probably. You'd have to do proper research to be sure." Ben held the door-open button down. "None of that changes the fact that if you hadn't been—whatever you are—you'd be dead."

"Or a vampire."

"Dead, Nate!" Ben felt his final shred of control snap. "All you would be is dead—like you were when I woke up!" Nate tried to speak, but Ben didn't give him the chance. "You didn't have a pulse—you weren't breathing—you just—you were dead."

"Not dead," Nate shot back. "I've got a pulse now. I'm breathing—"

"Only by pure luck!" Ben felt himself shaking, not in weakness but in anger. "Don't you care?"

"All right! I'm scared, okay?" Nate glared at him. "I am freaking out and trying not to show it because I've got no idea what to do. Maybe you could have killed me. But maybe you can't kill me? Did you think of that?" Nate motioned to his body. "Maybe I'm weird—weirder even than vampires. At least with a vampire there are rules, you know what's going to happen. Me—" Nate's hand came to a halt. "I've got no idea."

Ben resisted the urge to put his hand on Nate's arm. Anger had been replaced by concern. "Feel better?"

Nate let out his breath in a shaky burst. "Yeah. I guess I needed that. God." He buried his face in his hands. "I thought I was meant to be the expert on feelings."

Not when they're your own. "It's understandable to be confused. You need time to make sense of it." Ben nodded toward the door. "Go, lie down. You'll feel better for the rest."

"You'll be fine?"

Ben held up the Coke bottle. "Stop worrying and lie down already."

Nate stepped out of the elevator. "This—isn't something anyone can know about, right? Your application—"

"Forget my application."

Nate sucked in a deep breath. "But—"

Ben hit the button to close the elevator doors. "This changes everything, Nate."

He saw understanding flicker in Nate's eyes before the doors slid shut. Ben sank back against the wall.

Everything... When you'd lost everything, nothing mattered.

Chapter Fourteen

"FUCK." NATE DIDN'T need the click of the elevator doors sliding shut to recognize the barrier between him and Ben. It was there in the way that Ben held himself aloof, guarding his reactions. He was already impossibly distant. The closed doors were overkill. Nate clenched his fist. *How did I mess up so badly?*

Things had been going well. Ben had depended on him. And now... *Now I'll be lucky if he can look at me without experiencing a traumatic flashback.*

His reflection in the metal stared back at him—pale and scruffy, with his hoodie bunched weirdly around his neck. Nate winced, turning away.

As soon as he unlocked the door and pushed it open, the dog bounded up, its tail wagging. It barked, darting around in a circle.

Despite everything, a tired smile creased Nate's face. "Hey." He knelt down, holding his arms out for the dog. "You missed me, huh?"

The dog didn't seem to be able to decide whether he wanted to sniff Nate or lick him, so after a spirited attempt to do both at once, he stuck his nose down Nate's neck.

"Easy. You don't want to drown me—I've had enough near death experiences for one day." Nate's hand slowed, burying itself in the dog's fur.

The dog barked.

Nate raised his head to find the dog looking at him, his eyes filled with concern. "It's really hard to believe it happened. I know Ben wouldn't make it up—hell, I've got the vine to prove it. But..." He trailed off helplessly. "I can't believe I died again."

The dog barked again, darting back.

Nate peeled off his hoodie. It dragged on the vines and it took him a moment to untangle it. The vine had grown, winding tightly around his arm. As he watched, the leaves unfurled, stretching toward the light. "Ivy. It was ivy the last time, too." Nate caught a leaf between his fingers. It was smooth and glossy and felt cold.

He looked up and saw that the dog had backed away the length of the room. His tail drooped between his legs, his hind paws pressed up against the wall.

"It's okay. It's just me. You know, the one who feeds you."

The dog didn't move.

"Fuck. You're afraid of me?" Nate's stomach sank. He crouched down again. "Here, boy. Come here—see, it's still me."

The dog didn't move.

Wow. Dogs are supposed to like anyone. This... Nate swallowed and stood. "You're probably hungry. Let's get you fed." Then maybe the dog would remember him.

Nate stood in front of the fridge. There was some sliced ham. Nate put it in the dog's bowl, along with a piece of cheese—he was fairly confident that dogs liked cheese.

The dog watched from the kitchen doorway. He waited until Nate had returned to the fridge before slinking over to his bowl. In a couple of gulps, the cheese had disappeared.

Nate smirked. "Knew you'd like cheese. It's the protein, right? Dogs are all about protein."

Like vampires.

Nate found his fingers had drifted back to the raised bump where the ivy grew. He snatched them away, turning back to the fridge.

There was half a loaf of bread, but Nate didn't feel like making a sandwich. Or anything, really. The thought of food made his stomach heavy and his throat constrict. With a sigh, he shut the fridge door and grabbed himself a cup of water. He leaned back against the counter, watching the dog lick his already clean bowl, just in case he'd missed something.

"Good dog."

The dog glanced up at him, still wary.

Nate sighed. "Maybe you're smart to keep your distance. I fuck everything up." He sat down at the table with his cup of water.

The dog whined softly.

"No, it's true. Case in point—Ben. I pushed him to feed from me. It's supposed to be really hot—and I thought I could take it. But—something went wrong." Nate stared at the cracked surface of the table. His hand stroked the raised bump where the ivy left his skin. "I guess he took too much 'cause I passed out. And I made him sick. Literally. He was throwing up—I don't think he's kept anything down all day."

The dog made a plaintive sound. Nate looked down to find he had approached him, standing a few feet away and watching him with luminous eyes.

Nate smiled faintly. He knew it was nothing but the hope that there was more food to come, but the dog's actions touched him. Like it understood. *If nothing else, I can pretend he understands me.*

He groaned, hiding his face behind his hands. "Ugh. I am such a piece of shit. I was supposed to keep him from hurting anyone—that was the deal! And now— He must think I'm absolutely pathetic. The absolute worst."

A warm pressure had him looking down. The dog had crept close enough to rest his head on Nate's thigh, gazing up at him with what was, if not absolute trust, then well-disguised hunger.

Nate felt a knot form in the back of his throat. "It's true. I can understand how he feels. I'm—disgusted with me, too. I was supposed to be better than that. All my practice at being strong, at using my powers, at learning how to resist vampires... Apparently it all means shit when things really matter." Nate stood, returning his cup to the sink.

He caught movement in the window and looked up to see the ivy leaves rustle with his movement. His lip curled. *You can't look more like a freak, can you?* His fingers tightened on the ivy. Feeling a wave of revulsion for it, he ripped it away.

The wave of dizziness was immediate and intense. *Shit. I shouldn't have done that!* Nate reached for the counter, but he was too late. For the second time in twenty-four hours, he fell into darkness.

NATE STARED AT the ceiling above him. He was surprised to see wooden planks. He'd been expecting night sky and drizzle, and a few branches of the trees surrounding the Mason's park oak. At his neck, where there should have been cold mud, was a rough, warm presence. And the earth was soft underneath him, cushioning him.

"None of this makes sense." His voice cracked and Nate winced. *Is that really my voice?* What was happening to him?

"Quiet. Don't try to move."

He hadn't been about to move, but Nate stilled automatically. The voice—he didn't know the voice, but it was young, male, with an authoritative note.

There was the sound of movement beside him, and then something being set on the coffee table. A glass, perhaps?

The speaker bent over him and Nate saw a young man with a beard halfway between blond and light brown. The light in the living room was dim enough that Nate couldn't tell which it was, or what color the eyes that watched him so intently were. "Think you can drink something?"

Nate swallowed. At the question, he discovered he was suddenly very thirsty. "Yeah."

"Let's get you sitting up." The guy put his arm around Nate, and with the aid of a few cushions, Nate found himself settled in a half-reclining position.

The guy held a glass to his lips. "Easy—little sips."

Nate badly wanted to gulp down the entire glass, but he did as he was told.

After a few sips, the man withdrew the glass. "How are you feeling?"

"Terrible."

"Does the water help? You're not nauseous?"

Nate was about to shake his head and thought better of it. "No. The water's good." He paused. The last thing he remembered was ripping away the ivy. His fingers made their way to his neck.

The guy caught his hand. "I don't think you should do that."

Nate stared at him. He didn't have the emotional resources to be surprised. "What happened?"

"You passed out. I got you settled on the sofa, your head elevated. You don't seem to be bleeding, but— Better not do anything fast, okay?"

Nate considered his words. After a moment, he shut his eyes. "More water?"

The guy held the glass to his lips.

Halfway through the glass, Nate was too tired to swallow. The guy placed the glass on the coffee table beside him. "Go back to sleep," he said. "I'll be here to keep an eye on you."

I don't even know who you are. The thought was not urgent enough to keep him from sinking back into the comforting darkness.

ARTIFICIAL LIGHT FLOODED the dark living room. Nate winced at the sudden intrusion. He heard the bolts slide home and the jangle of keys. "Aki?"

"I'm home! Man—you just slept all day, huh?" Aki stood at the side of the sofa, looking down at him. "Geez, Nate. You really don't look good. Maybe you should lay off the partying—you're clearly way out of shape."

It was too much mental gymnastics to try to decipher Aki's words. Instead, Nate took slow and careful stock of his surroundings. He lay on the sofa, a full glass of water on the coffee table beside him. He was slightly raised, supported by cushions, and the rough hand-knit blanket that had been a present from his mother lay over him. There was a pressure on his feet, and Nate looked down the sofa to see the dog curled up on his legs.

The dog stretched and yawned, showing its teeth. He looked at Aki, his tail wagging hopefully.

"Yeah, I brought you something. Brought both you freeloaders something, actually." Aki fished in the bags he carried. He threw the dog what looked like half a kebab. The dog snatched it out of midair and gulped it down.

"I'm not going to make you catch your food. Sit up, Nate." Aki placed a bottle of his favorite vegetable juice on the coffee table. "I passed a kebab store on the way home. I got one of those weird-ass falafel things. They're vegetable right? No, they have to be—they taste like shit."

Nate placed his hand on the back of the sofa. Carefully and deliberately, he heaved himself into a sitting position. "You just got back?"

"I don't know what you're looking at me for. You ate all the food, and trust me, you don't want any of Nate's gross vegetarian stuff." Aki scratched the dog's ears. "Yeah. Obviously, Nate. You saw me walk in."

"That doesn't make sense."

"Are you high?"

"No. I—" Nate stared around the living room. It was exactly how it should be. The chairs were in all the right places, the dog and Aki watching him with bemusement. "You didn't move me to the sofa?"

"You're kidding, right? Look at the size of me compared to you. I couldn't move you off that sofa."

Nate looked around. "Did you have a friend over? I remember someone."

"I've been at work the entire night. No friends—nothing." Aki crossed the room, placing his hand on Nate's arm. "What's going on? You're starting to freak me out here."

You're freaked out. Nate swallowed, running a hand through his hair. His thoughts felt unbearably slow. "I don't remember exactly. I was in the kitchen when I got really dizzy. I think I fainted."

"Shit. Seriously? Dehydrated?"

Nate ignored Aki's question. "Someone had to have shifted me from the kitchen to the sofa because I know I didn't. And he tucked me in and brought me a glass of water."

Aki snorted. "He? Isn't Ben the obvious choice?"

Nate's throat tightened. "It wasn't Ben."

"Whoa. No need to snap." Aki stared at him. "Well, if it wasn't Ben and it wasn't me, that doesn't leave a lot of options. You probably hallucinated it."

"I didn't do that."

"How do you know? You said you fainted, right? Maybe you hit your head on the way down. Or maybe you're just so out of it that you imagined that, too."

"It didn't feel like a dream." But already he felt uncertain about the incident. It hadn't felt real at the time. He'd been curiously disconnected from his body throughout... Nate looked up and saw Aki's brow furrowed, his mouth pressed together as he studied him. He forced himself to smile. "No, you've got to be right. It's the only explanation." He reached for the kebab. "Thanks for the food, Aki."

"No problem. I know what you're like when you're hungover." Aki settled into one of the armchairs, watching Nate peel back the tinfoil surrounding the kebab. "So... You think Hunter was into me?"

The smell of the kebab set off an immediate chain reaction of hunger. Nate took a moment just to breathe it in before taking a small, careful bite. "No."

Aki glared at him. "At least consider the question."

"I have. And sorry, Aki, but I don't think there's anything happening."

The dog laid his head in Aki's lap, Aki stroking his ears automatically. "He seemed really interested in me. He only left me alone to attend to business and he always made sure I had everything I needed before he left. That's got to mean something, right?"

Nate shook his head. "You forget, I had dinner with the guy. That's how he is with everyone. He's even nice to his food."

"He wasn't nice to Wisner." Aki sighed gustily. "Did you hear that polite poison in his voice? Incredible. I was so mad when that waiter pushed me into the cab just as things were getting interesting."

"It was a lot better that you missed it." Nate swallowed his current bite and set his wrap down on the table.

The dog whined softly, pushing his nose into Aki's hand.

Aki resumed petting him. "What happened after I left?"

"Ben and I got into a vampire standoff against that guy, Julian. I won."

"You?" Aki's eyebrows raised. "But that's a good thing—right?"

Nate winced. "It was. But then—I fucked things up with Ben big time."

"Please tell me you didn't go for Hunter."

"No!"

"Well, then—"

"You know the deal between me and Ben? That I had to be strong enough to stop him hurting anyone?"

"Fuck. Seriously?"

Nate nodded. "Yeah. He ended up hurting me—and now he can't even look at me without flinching, and he's so remote he might as well be on the moon—"

"He hurt you?" Aki's voice was hard and flat. "Nate, what did he do?"

"It's not important—"

"Nate!" Aki was on his feet trying to tug the blanket off him. "What did he do?" The dog began to bark, reacting to his anger.

Nate clung to the blanket. "Leave it! Look it's not—it's my neck, all right?"

Aki insisted on taking a long look at Nate's neck, and once he'd stared at the two pin pricks, taking his pulse and temperature, and adding another blanket over Nate. He then went into the kitchen where he could be heard angrily banging cupboards. "You cannot be serious. Did neither of you think to get some sugar into you?"

"Ben got me two bottles of vegetable juice, which I drank." And planted him on his floor. Nate swallowed. The ivy had not grown back. His neck felt strangely bare without it. "And then you got me another drink."

"Drink it. And then drink this." Aki reappeared, stirring a glass of sugar water. "I am so mad at you. I thought we'd covered not scaring me."

"It wasn't supposed to end this way." Nate obediently drank the glass Aki set in front of him. "It was supposed to be hot—you know, like everyone says it is. And it was—but I guess— I don't know what went wrong."

Aki hesitated, wiping his hair out of his eyes before he perched on the coffee table. "Maybe this is a sign, Nate. You and Ben—you're not as good a fit as you think you are."

"Aki—"

Aki raised his hands in protest. "Just hear me out. How many times have one or the both of you got yourself into a seriously messed up situation for the other? That's not healthy—for you, for him, or for your relationship."

Nate swallowed. He couldn't forget Ben's expression as the elevator doors had closed. He'd already shut himself down. "I don't think there is a relationship anymore."

"That might be a good thing. Yeah, I know—he's totally changed your world, and shown you stuff about yourself you never knew, but—there has to be a point where enough is enough and if almost killing you is not that point, then I don't know what is."

Nate hunched his shoulders. "I don't want to talk about it."

"Just think about it, okay?" Aki didn't move. Nate could feel his gaze, studying him intently. "Is this why you're so down on Hunter? All vampires, by extension, are now bad news?"

Nate groaned. "Aki!"

"What? I had to ask!"

Nate took another sip of the sugary water. It tasted cloyingly sweet, but he thought his head was beginning to feel less cloudy. Too bad it couldn't do anything for the gaping hole in his chest. "What happened to your chiseled hunk?"

"Who?"

"The guy in the park?"

At the mention of the park, the dog's ears pricked up and its tail began to wag.

Aki snorted. "Don't get your hopes up, Fido. It's two in the morning. The park is locked—even if anyone wanted to take you for a walk. Which we don't." He settled back, drumming his fingers against the edge of the coffee table. "Chiseled god turns out to be a chiseled creeper. He—" Aki broke off suddenly. "You didn't tell him about me, right? This isn't some attempt to matchmake me against my will?"

"Aki, you told me that if I tried to set you up with anyone again you'd exorcise me."

"Eviscerate you. And I will." Aki frowned. "So you didn't communicate with him at all?"

"I've never seen the man. All I know is what you've told me."

"Right." Aki was silent, his fingers continuing their rapid beat. "So. After I went by Ben's apartment to see if you were up for taking responsibility for the dog you adopted and learning you were hungover—shit! You weren't, were you? That was when—"

"It's fine, Aki. Ben took care of me. Go on."

Aki looked like he badly wanted to argue but continued. "So, anyway, I take the dog to the park and immediately he runs away. I am super pissed, because just once I would like to be able to run without worrying that he's going to run into traffic or commit some other form of canine suicide, and while I'm looking for him, super bod appears." Aki pursed his lips. "I—might have run into him at the park again yesterday. He was nice then, seemed pretty happy to see me. But this time, he's really intense. Almost angry. He's trying to have this full-on relationship conversation with me, and he's talking like he knows me—like we've had more than an hour and a half of interaction, tops. So that was danger signal number one."

Nate set the glass down, staring at Aki. "Go on."

"He says he wants to talk to me alone and hauls me into the bushes. Which—yeah, I know, really bad idea—but I figured he was hot and at least I'd get something out of the time I spent crushing on this guy. Anyway, talking to me alone involves just about as much talking as you'd expect, and I'm up against a tree, his hand is on my cock, and I'm thinking that maybe he's just totally new to relationships and I can forgive him his assumptions when he says something about the vampire having no right to even look at me and that if he comes back, he will destroy him. Which is pretty messed up for a number of reasons, not the least of which being that I didn't tell him about Hunter, and you didn't tell him about Hunter, which means—"

"The guy was stalking you?" Nate's voice rose. He saw the dog flinch back out of the corner of his eye and held out a hand to pat it.

Aki's lips pressed together. "I really know how to pick them, don't I? This is what—the third time?"

Aki had been in serious trouble, and Nate would have had no idea. He swallowed. "What did you do?"

"I asked him how he knew about the vampire. And he stared at me, and his expression said he knew he'd messed up. So I kneed him in the groin and ran."

"Aki—"

"Nothing wrong with my self-preservation instincts! In fact, you could learn a lot from me. I was out of the trees before he'd even managed to get back on his feet, and I made it out of the park and back here in what I'm pretty sure is my best time ever."

Nate hesitated and then reached out to pull Aki into a loose hug. "I'm sorry, Aki."

Aki went with the hug with an eagerness that surprised Nate. "So am I. The guy seemed cool and he was hot—not Hunter level hot, but hot." He sighed. "And now—I'm just, like, fuck dating. I only ever seem to attract creeps and predators."

"You sure there's no other explanation?" Nate winced at the look Aki shot him. "Yeah, I know. I just hate seeing you unhappy."

Aki sank his head back against Nate's chest. "Better unhappy than dead. I'm a realist, Nate. I'm not so involved that I'm going to overlook the warning signs, even if it does mean that it's back to square one."

Better unhappy than dead. Nate tensed.

"Shit." Aki drew back, peering up at him anxiously. "I didn't mean it like that, Nate. I just—"

"No. You're right. I could learn a lot from you." Nate squeezed Aki's arm before sinking back on the sofa.

"At least you admit it." Aki ran his hand through his hair, frowning down at Nate. He looked absurdly delicate, with his carefully gelled hair awry and his clothes rumpled, and he was strong enough to escape a stalker and go to work as if nothing had happened. *He's strong. Stronger than me.* Nate hadn't even noticed the warning signs, too involved with Ben—

"You sure you're not going to pass out again? You're looking at me weirdly."

"Just thinking how glad I am for your self-preservation instincts, Aki. If anything had happened to you—"

"Don't think about it. I'm trying not to dwell." Aki stood, stretching. "But just so you know, we're going to need to find a new place to run."

"Agreed." Nate noticed the dog, hunched miserably by his feet, and scratched his ears. "How did the dog get home? You didn't—"

"No way I was going back to the park. But the dog's imprinted on us. When I went to leave for work, he was there at the door— Oh man, Nate! I didn't give you the good news."

"There was good news?"

Aki plonked himself on the sofa beside him. "You won't believe this. As soon as I arrive in Century, I'm called up to the office—like the instant I arrive. And Denise grills me about what happened and insists on checking that I wasn't fed on. And after an hour of this, she's finally convinced that, despite my best efforts, nothing happened, and she tells me that the club got an anonymous payment for me, covering last night and tonight."

"What?"

"And there was one for you, too. Twenty thousand each, Nate."

"What?" Nate shook his head. "Who—Hunter?"

Aki grinned at him. "Who else? It's got to be—and you don't drop that kind of money on someone you're not interested in, right?"

"Hunter's definitely not interested in me," Nate reminded Aki.

"Which is even more of a sign he could be into me. Trying to make nice with my friends."

"Or trying to pay off his debts. Vampires don't like owing anyone anything." Nate frowned. "Can we give it back?"

Aki gaped at him. "You're not serious. You're still sick, Nate—do you realize how much that is? I'm going to have my student loans paid off this year!"

"I don't know. Something about it doesn't sit right with me."

"You're just miffed because it's Hunter and Hunter has history with Ben that you don't." Aki said. "Besides, Denise already accepted the payment."

Nate frowned. His stomach growled, and he remembered the wrap Aki had brought him. "You're sure that's it?"

"Positive. I mean, how many rich people do we know? It was either him or Ben, and it's not Ben."

"No," Nate agreed. "It's not Ben." He took a bite and immediately managed to spill sauce on his T-shirt. "Fuck me. This was my last clean T-shirt."

"Not anymore." Aki had his phone out, skimming his messages.

Nate set the wrap down, pulling the T-shirt over his head. "Got any washing you need done?"

"You're kidding, right? You had a near-death experience. The laundry can wait."

"This can't. I'm seriously running out of clothes."

"So give it to me and I'll do it."

Nate stared at Aki. He could not remember seeing Aki ever wash an item of clothing. "Do you even know how?"

"You are so rude to me." Aki stood. "It's not rocket science. I can Google a tutorial."

Nate still hesitated, but he was too tired to protest. "Are you sure you don't mind? Because you had a crazy stalker to deal with."

"It's cool. Matter of fact, there's still so much adrenalin in my system that I need something to do. Trying to sleep now would be an exercise in frustration." Aki wandered into the bathroom, and Nate could hear him thumping around the laundry hamper.

He looked down. His wrap was there on the table, unattended, and in full view of the dog—who hadn't even given it a glance. He lay at the base of the sofa, looking mournfully after Aki.

Really odd. Nate stared down at him. *Maybe he's not hungry?* But the dog was always hungry. Nate stroked the dog's head, but the gesture didn't even produce the usual wagging tail. *Maybe he's sick—* "Aki, did you feed the dog anything weird?" Nate looked up and saw Aki standing in the bathroom doorway, his face pale and contorted by rage. "Aki?"

"You said you'd never seen the guy in the park, right?"

Nate nodded. "Yeah. That's right."

Aki took a step forward, brandishing a photograph. "So why do you have a picture of him in the pocket of your jeans?"

Nate stared at him. "I don't."

"Evidence begs to differ." Aki waved the photo at him. "Look at this, Nate! It was in your jeans!"

"But I don't—wait." Nate shook his head. "You remember the werewolf at the club, the guy who started the fight? He was showing everyone a photo. I figured it must be that missing werewolf they're all looking for. After all the excitement, I saw a photo on the ground and picked it up. I thought I should give it to Department Seven. Then it just went out of my head."

"This is that photo?" Aki stared down at it.

"Don't you recognize it?"

"I guess. I didn't look too closely at it at the time." Aki frowned, holding the photo up to the light. "I did notice that there was something familiar about it, but I didn't put it together. The first time I saw crazy stalker guy he was—not clean shaven, but respectably unkempt, you know? This photo looks like the missing link."

Nate heaved himself off the sofa, looking down at the photo. He'd barely glanced at it when he'd picked it up, the gesture automatic. The guy scowled at the camera. His beard was, if not out of control, rapidly approaching dangerous levels, and his eyes caught the flash the same way deer's eyes catch headlights. "A real winner."

"Shut the fuck up." Aki's hand tightened around the photo, crinkling it. "So not only am I being stalked, but the guy doing it is a werewolf. And not just any werewolf! The same fucking werewolf that's got the entire city by its balls—"

"Sit down." Nate pushed Aki back onto the sofa. "Let's think about this." He could see that Aki, already upset, was going to work himself up into a state.

"What is there to think about?"

"Let me see the photo again. There was something about it." Nate smoothed it out.

"Something stalkery?" Aki curled up. "Department Seven doesn't sleep, right? Ring your friends there, and tell them—"

"Wait." Nate swallowed. "This is the guy who helped me—when I passed out in the kitchen. You remember I told you?"

Aki stared at him. "Nate—there was nobody in the kitchen. That's impossible. The only people in this apartment are you and me."

"And the dog." Nate looked down but the dog was no longer at the base of the sofa. He looked up, seeing it slink through the door into Aki's room.

"What are you suggesting?"

Nate lowered his voice. "The entire city is looking for this werewolf, and they can't find him, right? What if he's been hiding here? Right under our noses. It would explain how he got into the apartment—and how he knew about you spending a night with a vampire."

Aki stared at him. "That's impossible Nate. Werewolves turn into wolves—not dogs."

"Can you think of another explanation?"

Aki stared at him and groaned, running his hands over his face. "I cannot believe this. Wasn't getting attacked by a werewolf enough without adopting one?"

"What do we do?"

Aki dropped his hands. "I'll tell you what we're going to do. We're going to handle this my way. The selfish way. No one is going to put themselves in the firing line unnecessarily, and no one is going to get hurt. You got that?"

What about the rogue wolf if Wisner got his hands on him? Nate bit his lip. *Thinking like that is what got me dead and Ben poisoned.* "Okay, Aki. We'll handle the werewolf your way."

Chapter Fifteen

THE PHONE RANG. Long, strident rings. Ben lay on the sofa and counted them. Eight, nine, ten... At ten, his answering machine took over. After a pause, the phone started again.

I should see who is calling. Or at the very least, put it on silent mode. Ben made no attempt to move. He hadn't stirred since he'd entered his apartment and collapsed on the sofa. It had been dusk then. In the time since, the dark shadows of the apartment had increased with night and retreated again with day. And he hadn't moved.

Bang! The door shook. Someone was intent on getting his attention.

Ben lay where he was. He knew only too well who was on the other side of that door, and the thought of facing Nate was too much for him to bear.

The pounding at the door continued.

He's not going to give up. Nate was quite capable of standing there all day, despite his injuries. He was going to attract attention, maybe even make himself sick... Ben pushed himself upright. He swung his body over the edge of the sofa, shuffling toward the door. Mentally he prepared himself for the barrage of conflicting emotions that was Nate. *I have to be firm. If I don't send him away—* He swallowed back the rush of fear at the memory of touching Nate's clammy skin, knowing he was dead—

The banging stopped the moment he pulled back the bolts. Ben took a deep breath before undoing the lock. He pulled the door open. "Nate. I—" He gaped at the woman standing in front of him. "Diya?"

She looked incongruously normal, wearing a black blazer over a bright-orange shirt and holding a briefcase in hand. "Hello, Bennet. I'm glad to see you out of bed. Are you feeling better?"

Ben stared at her. It took him a moment to remember her phone call. "I, um. Yes. Thank you."

Diya motioned to the apartment behind him. "May I come in?"

Ben stepped back automatically. It wasn't until Diya was inside, looking around at his furnishings, that it occurred to him how unusual this was. "What are you doing here?"

Diya turned her attention from the painting hanging over the dining room table to him. "You missed a counseling session yesterday, and an appointment with a legal representative with experience in supernatural rights. You're not answering my e-mails or my calls."

"I was sick."

Diya walked across the room to stand in front of him. "Not sick enough that you couldn't go to Department Seven yesterday."

Ben winced. "Wisner's spies?"

"He's making the most of your 'calculated disobedience.'" Diya paused to adjust her scarf, her eyes still watching Ben. "You must see how bad this looks?"

"I really was sick," Ben said. "Going to Department Seven alone exhausted me. I've been lying on the sofa ever since."

"I believe you. But we can't be sure the judges will. Not unless we can get this Nate to vouch for you?"

Ben leaned against the back of a dining room chair for support. "No. He—I refuse to let Nate be drawn into my problems."

Diya crossed her arms. "Even if it means that you fail your appeal?"

Ben gripped the back of the chair. "Even if it means I fail my appeal. Yes," he said, as Diya sucked in a sharp breath. "I know what that entails. But I stand by that. Nate's got no part in this."

Diya frowned. "But to remain Class Six—or even worse—be entered into the Final Register—"

Ben found the intensity of her gaze hard to bear. He looked down at the smooth dark surface of his table. It looked like a pool, reflecting the dining room lights, and dimly, Diya and his outlines. "Maybe that's for the best. I've spent so much time around, or as, a vampire. I think—" He swallowed. "It's changed me. Deep inside." He remembered the scar he'd glimpsed on Diya's neck and decided not to tell her about the vampire within. "I don't think I could ever be normal."

Diya eyed him in silence. When Ben glanced up, he saw that her lips were pressed together firmly and that she looked—upset. "I have no idea what this Nate guy said to you, but before you give up on your future, there's something you have to see." She marched over to the sofa, picking up Ben's jacket. "Put this on and follow me."

Ben was too surprised to argue.

BEN COULD HAVE easily picked out the car that was Diya's. The Ford was a bright, cherry red, perfectly suiting its owner's love of sleek design and eye-popping color. As she searched her handbag for the key, Ben couldn't help glancing up.

Nate's collection of plants spilled over the fire escape above them. The splash of green made something within him ease. It was stupid to think that just because the plants were fine, Nate was also fine—but he did think it. He lingered, wondering if Nate would step outside, but Diya found her keys.

"There! Take the front seat."

It wasn't until he was sitting in the passenger's seat that Ben realized he might be in danger—his last unexpected car ride had ended in interrogation at the Registry, after all. But the destination that Diya had in mind was not threatening, but baffling. She pulled into the parking lot attached to a high rise building in New Camden's outer suburbs.

"An apartment building? What are we doing here?" Ben turned to watch Diya.

She was intent on her rear view mirror as she parked. "You'll see."

She didn't talk as she led Ben through a door that required a security code and then into an elevator. By the time the elevator reached their destination, she already had her key in hand. As she unlocked the door of an apartment, Ben glanced around.

There were large pots with flowers on either side of the elevator, and the corridor they walked down was neat. The sounds of conversation floated out from an open door. It was a typical apartment block in other words—which made their presence there even more mysterious.

Diya stepped through the door. "Come on in."

It could only be her apartment. It followed the same decorating scheme as her office, only this time, vibrant color had been allowed to run amok. It was like looking at a modern art painting that you could sit on. There was a faint smell of perfume in the air—or was it spice?

"Make yourself comfortable," Diya said, putting her briefcase down on the bright-red sofa. "I'm going to let mother know we have a visitor."

But a harsh-faced woman had already stepped through a doorway, her gaze going through Ben and settling on Diya. She wore a sari, and her hair was tightly pulled back in a long braid. She asked a question in a language Ben didn't recognize.

She doesn't see me. Ben swallowed. No matter how often it happened, it didn't get easier.

"Mr. Hawick," Diya said. "You can't see him because of the restrictions, but he's a friend. He'll understand."

Ben resisted the urge to raise his eyebrows. Understand what?

Diya's mother added a few more sharp words, before turning into the kitchen.

"One moment." Diya hurried after the other woman, drawing the door closed behind her.

Ben looked around the room. The living-dining room area was modern and polished, everything sleek and bright. There was only one incongruous note—a statue of a many-armed figure on a shelf in one corner. Candles were placed before it and a photo in a brass frame. A young man in traditional garb. Ben suddenly became aware that he wasn't alone. He looked up to see Diya watching him.

"My husband, Rohit," Diya said. "He was killed in a vampire attack over a year ago."

Ben swallowed. "I'm sorry."

"Follow me." Diya beckoned Ben down a corridor.

It looked like a normal apartment with one exception. One door was fastened shut with five separate bolts. Instead of the usual lock, a heavy-duty steel lock had been installed.

Ben felt a sense of alarm. *This is not a good sign.* He stole a covert glance at Diya, sliding back the bolts with a grim expression. What did he know of her besides her brisk professional manner and her dedication to getting his application approved? She was the victim of a vampire attack and had lost her husband to one. She had no reason to want to help Ben, a former vampire—

Diya drew a chain from around her neck. There was a key on the end of it that she used to unlock the door. She stepped into the room. "The vampire attacked me first. I was pregnant. Rohit died protecting me and our child."

Ben remained in the doorway scanning the room. It was decorated in soft yellow, with low bookcases and a child-sized table and chairs. Stuffed toys were scattered across a cot and there was a changing table against one wall. Behind the cheerfully painted dresser were thick, blackout curtains. *Why does a child's room need blackout curtains? Especially if there's no child...* Ben knew the chances of any pregnancy surviving the trauma of a vampire attack were nil.

Diya stepped over to check that the blinds were tightly drawn. As she moved past the changing table, Ben caught sight of a familiarly shaped object resting upon it.

Ben stared. *That's not—a coffin?*

It was an infant-sized coffin. Diya paused in front of it, looking down. "Anjali wasn't supposed to survive, but I didn't give up hope. She was stillborn—or that's what the doctor said. I was allowed to hold her in my arms, and as I did, something very strange happened. My dead child started to breathe."

Ben sucked in a sharp breath. He joined Diya, standing before the coffin.

Diya opened the coffin, revealing a small baby, at first sight, sleeping peacefully. Her absolute stillness told a different story. "She was not supposed to survive. She is not supposed to exist now. When dawn came and her heart stopped, the hospital told me there was nothing to be done... But I brought her home."

Ben swallowed. He was no expert on children, but this wasn't a newborn. The little girl had thick, glossy curls that clung to her head, and her skin was not wrinkled. She was small, incredibly delicate-looking. "And when night fell?"

"She opened her eyes. She—there is no such thing as a living vampire. But her heart beats, she breathes, and she drinks milk. She is not even a year old, but her existence breaks every rule in the book—and that is all the Registry will care about."

Ben stared down at the tiny child. "That's why you're helping me."

Diya frowned, still looking down at her child. "Anjali is growing. For now, I can keep her safe inside this room, but realistically, I know that I can't hide her forever. And once people learn about her..."

Ben winced. "The laws on vampires are written for adults based on the assumption that a child doesn't possess the necessary self-control to hold their inner monster in check."

"She would be destroyed. For the good of the city—unless we can rewrite the rules surrounding vampires, prove that there are exceptions to what we know about them." Diya gripped the edge of the cot. "I know it's selfish of me to look at your case as helping our cause, but you— you're a benchmark case, Bennet. What the council decides will determine how other decisions are made in the future. If you can prove that being a vampire is reversible, that you can adapt to an ordinary life—don't you see how that opens up so many possibilities for others?"

Ben tilted his head at Diya. "Others?"

She stroked her daughter's hair. "I don't speak simply of myself and Anjali. There are others in New Camden in situations similar to yours, but they don't have your reputation or your resources—or your bravery."

Bravery? Ben opened his mouth to protest, but Diya continued.

"I fully believe that if we succeed in having your application approved, more supernaturals will come forward with their experiences—and we'll learn even more about living vampirism. Anjali might one day be allowed to go to school, make friends—you can have the life you want. And many, many others, living in fear or in hiding, unable to reveal their true selves, will have hope."

"And if we lose?"

Diya shut the coffin lid. "Then I am afraid we will see the restrictions on supernaturals tightened, and more pressure placed on those who don't fit the accepted understanding of supernaturals. Anyone different will either have to hide or be subjected to rigorous investigation and controls."

Ben stared down at the coffin without seeing it. His thoughts were on Nate. *Nate can't hide what he is any more than I can act human for an entire day. When Diya talks of supernaturals at risk, she means him—and others like him.*

"I know it's not fair to burden you with my struggles," Diya said softly. "But I wanted you to see that there is more than your future at stake. This decision—it could save lives, Bennet. But to win it... I need your full cooperation."

Ben's head snapped up. "You don't mean—"

Diya tucked her hair out of her face. "We're running out of time. The expert can't give us another appointment. If we want to prove that the vampire is gone, we have to go to ARX."

Ben stared at her and then abruptly turned to face the blackout curtains. His chest felt tight, his heartbeat suddenly tangible.

"I'm truly sorry," Diya said. "If there was any other way—"

"No," Ben said. "I understand." He took a deep breath. After the experience of waking up with Nate dead, he no longer feared what Saltaire might do. "You've made the appointment?"

Diya shook her head. "Not without your permission." She clutched the edge of her scarf. "You agree?"

Ben nodded. "Call them." It was a risk. ARX employed the best supernatural researchers in the world and gave them the best equipment. Convincing them of his humanity would be hard. If he failed—there would be no second chances. Saltaire would know—equally as unpleasant an option as anything the Registry could do.

But so what? Ben rested his hand on the bed, looking down at the child's toys. *She's totally innocent. A baby—it's not fair she has to go through this. Me... If Diya's right and we can win this, she'll have a better chance of having any sort of life. If we don't...* Ben put his hands in his pockets. *I'm already fucked up beyond all belief. Nothing can change that—so why not accept it and use it?*

Diya ended her call. "Great news. They're very interested in your case, and they're willing to see us immediately."

Ben nodded. He felt calm, as if a weight had been lifted. He knew what he needed to do. "Then let's go."

THE ARX BUILDING looked exactly like he'd seen it last. A modern, square-shaped building constructed from gleaming glass and metal. It was only when you got close that you realized the glass was tinted, hiding the interior from the view of those outside. It was just one of the myriad protections ARX took on behalf of its clients' privacy and protection.

Ben waited beside Diya as the security guard called to confirm they were expected before letting them in. He'd made no sign of performing anything but the casual inquiry, but Ben had felt a faint magical awareness wash over him. When they stepped over the threshold, he felt the powerful buzz of the wards around the building.

Just like nothing's changed. Diya paused to consult her phone, and Ben looked around. To the right was the reception area with screened booths for potential clients to wait for a security consultant in privacy. Ben had rarely consulted with the public. He looked down the corridor to the left. He'd spent his summers interning in ARX's labs and undertaken his first investigations. It was strange being back in the corridor, knowing that he was the subject of the inquiry.

"This way."

Diya fell into step beside him. "You're sure?"

"You forget. I used to work here."

Diya glanced at him. "Will it be difficult seeing your former colleagues?"

Ben shook his head. "It's going to be strange. But I was only here with the daytime staff for a few summers before...shifting to nights. After that, I didn't have much contact with the staff at all."

A tall man, old but with a vigorous crop of white hair, advanced down the corridor to join him. "There you are. I was just coming to fetch you. Ms. Patel, I presume? I'm Dr. Fagen." He shook hands with Diya before turning to Ben. "Ben, of course, needs no introduction."

Ben's heart sank. Fagen was the head of ARX's research department. That he was personally greeting them said a lot for how seriously ARX was taking his investigation. "It's been a long time, Dr. Fagen."

"Indeed." The man frowned at him, and Ben remembered that as a member of the board of directors, Fagen would have been privy to all the details of Ben's death and subsequent change in career. "A strange circumstance we find ourselves in. As far as I'm aware, a reversal of the type you claim is unprecedented."

"It's hard to believe," Ben said. "But it's true."

"We intend to put that statement to the test." Fagen led the way through multiple security checkpoints until at last they reached the labs. Despite Ben's past with ARX, the company didn't seem to be allowing him any leeway. *Fine by me.* The more rigorous the testing, the better the results—provided he passed.

"Can you tell us anything about what to expect?" Diya asked as they approached a meeting room.

"I could." Fagen opened the door and waved them in. "But I'm sure that Ben already has a very good idea of what is in store."

"An interview to establish I am who I claim to be and then a physical examination." Ben was not surprised to be greeted by a committee. A cross-section of ARX staff occupied the seven seats at the far end of the room, a conference table separating them from the two chairs set out for himself and Diya. As Ben took his seat, he realized he knew everyone on the panel. Fagen's second in command, who'd been Ben's supervisor during his internship. The magical expert that ARX commonly consulted and with whom Ben had collaborated on several investigations. His day and night liaison officers, responsible for following up the leads Ben was unable to. The security chief. And—Ben swallowed—Godfrey, his eyes twinkling as he took in Ben's surprise to see him.

Fagen took his place at the center of the row of colleagues. "This is an unprecedented case," he said. "We've had cases of dead returning to un-life, but never to my knowledge have we had a vampire return to life. With so many undead creatures who can change their form and tap into another's mind, we need to be sure that you are who you say you are, Bennet."

Ben nodded. "Naturally." His mouth twisted. "I've sat in on one of these before, you know."

The panel exchanged glances.

Fagen frowned. "If you don't mind, let's start the interview now."

The interview was intense. Ben was asked to describe the events that led to his leaving ARX in minute detail and was questioned about the necromancer's plans. As he was grilled, he was conscious of multiple waves of magical attention. *Checking that my aura matches that on record.* Ben pushed the awareness to the back of his mind and continued to answer questions.

Finally, Fagen held up a hand. "I think that's enough. Well?" He glanced at the panel.

"Nothing like this has ever come up before," said the day officer. "Not in all my years of working for ARX. It's not possible."

"That it hasn't happened before doesn't mean it's not possible," Godfrey said mildly. "It simply means that there is no precedent for it. And, if my memory of the necromancer attacks is correct, the notebooks recovered from de Silver's apartment suggested that he had taken his theories on advanced necromancy to new ground."

"Those notebooks are held in our highest security vault." Ben's former supervisor frowned. "We'll need express permission from the director himself to confirm their contents."

"Mr. Wilding is undergoing a separate appraisal by Department Seven—whose officers were first on the scene when the necromancer was defeated," Diya said quickly. "You need have no fears about that angle being unexplored."

"That may be so," Fagen said. "But there is the slight matter of confirming Bennet's identity." He shot Ben a penetrating stare. "You don't object?"

How can I? Ben braced himself for another round of questioning. "Go ahead."

This time he was led through his experiences as both a day and night employee of ARX, checking his memory of events against their own. The magic-user was silent, and Ben was conscious of a probing presence at the back of his mind. *Checking that I'm not possessed.* He realized that he'd trailed to a halt and forced himself to apply himself to the questions.

It seemed to go on for hours. Ben felt himself sagging in his chair, rapidly approaching exhaustion—and the panel seemed in no danger of running out of questions. *And this isn't even the hard part.*

As if echoing Ben's thoughts, Fagen turned to his committee. "I suspect that little more can be gained by this line of questioning. I propose we move on to the tests."

Ben was glad to leave the interview room. Once in the hallway, he stretched, taking the opportunity to massage some feeling back into his stiff legs.

Diya held out a soft drink she'd bought from the vending machine in the hall, and Ben took it eagerly. "What form will the tests take?" she asked Fagen.

"Finger prints, hair sample, retina scan—we need to assure ourselves that Bennet is who he claims to be." Fagen ushered Ben into a lab. "And then a series of general tests for the presence of anything...untoward. And finally, tests to determine that the vampiric element really is gone. I'm afraid that you'll have to remain outside. To ensure the veracity of the results, only myself, my assistant, and Ben will enter the lab."

Ben nodded at Diya. "I'll be fine. Don't worry. Dr. Fagen's an expert. I could be in no better hands."

Fagen simply frowned at the compliment. "In the interest of avoiding any preconceptions, my assistant is a new ARX employee who is unaware of your record," he said. "She hasn't been filled in on your history, and I hope that I can trust you to avoid giving any indication of what these tests are looking for."

Ben nodded. At Fagen's directions he stripped down to his T-shirt and shorts and took his place on a bed, much like that of a normal medical examining room. He sipped the soft drink, watching as Fagen pulled on a crisp lab coat and examining gloves. A few moments later, the assistant arrived, a young woman whose mask and cap didn't succeed in restraining her unruly curls. She raised her hand in what seemed to Ben like a cheery greeting and turned to Fagen for instructions.

The first stage of tests went quickly, and after a pause to confirm the results, so did the second. Ben was grateful for the support of the bed. The long interview and the tests were starting to take a toll on his already depleted energy.

The woman scanned the list of tests remaining. "I suppose you need clearance for a job interview?" she said. "Must be some job."

Ben smiled, conscious not only of the glance that Fagen sent him, but the tinted-glass windows of the lab. He was almost certain that the remaining committee members waited behind it with the clipboards. "This is more of a test. An experiment, I guess you could say."

The woman seemed like she wanted to ask more, but Fagen directed her attention to the items on the table. "We'll start with the garlic."

It was pungent, incredibly so. Ben frowned, wondering if the smell had always been this strong or if being a vampire had left him with added sensitivity. It felt cold and clammy on his skin, and he couldn't help shuddering as the paste was applied to a bare patch of his skin.

"A reaction?" Fagen said immediately.

"It feels gross." Ben said. "Not painful or anything. Just gross."

The woman snorted and quickly turned aside before Fagen could see her expression. When she turned back to apply a different paste to Ben's skin, her expression was serious.

One of these will be a control. The others varying degrees of garlic and other vampire repellants. Ben breathed carefully through his mouth. He felt on edge, unsure why. *It's daytime. I'm safe—the vampire can't make an appearance during the day.*

But the underground laboratory was completely cut off from any outside ventilation. The air was still and stuffy, and the two scientists worked in silence.

There was a movement to one side. Ben looked up to see Diya standing on the other side of the laboratory windows, watching. He grinned, giving her a thumbs-up. *She didn't have to stay.*

"We'll give those a bit of time," Fagen decided. "In the meantime, why don't we start on those blood samples now."

The woman picked up the tray and brought them over to him. "I wondered why these weren't going to the lab with the rest of them. Are we applying the holy water directly?"

"That's right. We'll start with an undiluted concentration—" Fagen picked up a test tube. It seemed to dance in his fingers and then leap.

There was the sound of shattered glass and then suddenly the smell of blood, overpoweringly strong—

I will feast! The woman had turned her back, leaving herself entirely unprotected. Her hair fell over her shoulders, exposing the clear skin of her neck. The vampire exulted, looking up into the watchful stare of Dr. Fagen—

No. Ben turned aside, clamping both hands over his mouth. He fought the fangs, forcing them back, pushing back the vampire. He breathed through his hands, trying to think. Had he bared his teeth at all?

Fagen stepped forward, pulling Ben's hands away from his mouth. With one hand on Ben's throat, he forced his teeth apart.

Every instinct Ben had told him to fight, shake the man off. He forced himself to remain still. "Satisfied?" he croaked.

Without a word, Fagen released him. He turned to the woman, who'd taken a step back. "Clean it up," he barked.

Ben rubbed his neck. He didn't allow himself to think of Diya's anxious expression, or the reactions of those watching behind the glass. "That was on purpose then. What were you hoping to prove?"

Fagen added a drop of holy water to one of the remaining vials. "It is impossible for a vampire to cease being a vampire. I've got no idea what you hope to gain by this pretense, but I won't sign off on it."

Ben swallowed. He could feel that it was teeth, not fangs, that pressed against the side of his mouth. "You taught me that a scientist keeps an open mind and let's the facts speak. Every test you've given me tonight, I've passed. Are you going to ignore that in favor of what you think my results should be?"

Fagen shook the test-tube vial and ignored Ben. He didn't speak to him directly until he'd concluded his tests. Ben was allowed to wash the traces of garlic and the other tests in a sink at one end of the room, while Fagen conferred with his colleagues.

Ben dressed slowly. He couldn't make out words, but he could hear the tone of the discussion had become heated. *I was so close...* He ran his lips over his teeth carefully, before pulling his sweater straight and making his way into the interview room.

"But that reaction to the spilled blood!" Fagen loudly demanded. "How do you explain that?"

"There are many possible interpretations," Godfrey's voice was mild but those gathered stilled to listen to it. "Disgust, for one. How many people do you know who can't look at blood?"

"But Hawick was an investigator. He should be hardened to the sight."

"He is not an investigator now," Godfrey continued placidly. "And he is striving to separate himself from his past. I suspect that the memory of his time as a vampire is painful for him and that is what was behind the reaction you saw."

Fagen sounded contemptuous. "You are growing soft in your old age. You cannot possibly believe this preposterous assertion! It is only because you were fond of the boy—"

"On the contrary. It is because I knew Bennet so well that I can be so certain that—strange as the circumstances are—he is who and what he claims to be."

Ben swallowed. *Godfrey—* He'd done nothing to deserve his championship. Instead he'd run away like an ungrateful child.

"With all due respect to your age and experience, I have to state again that I am not convinced," Fagen said. "Nothing like this has ever happened—"

"To the best of our knowledge," Ben's former supervisor cut in.

Fagen shot him a glance. "To the best of our knowledge. This— requires specialized knowledge. This requires Saltaire."

Ben drew a shaky breath. *I knew it.*

"Godfrey, can you contact him?"

"I can, but I don't know how long it will take him to get the message. He is deliberately taking a break from work."

"Mr. Hawick can't wait that long. His hearing is rapidly approaching."

"Perhaps I can be of assistance." An amused voice floated down the hallway. Everyone turned as one to see Hunter casually sauntering toward them. "Am I right in thinking this is a question that needs a vampire's input?" His eyes rested on Diya, who flinched before settling on Ben in mild surprise. "Ben. This is an unexpected pleasure."

"Pleasure is not the right word," Fagen said. "This man claims not only to be Hawick but to be Hawick cured of vampirism—an impossibility as you know."

"A few decades ago, vampires were widely held to be an impossibility," Hunter reminded him. "I don't suppose to know anything of the sort." His eyes raked Ben up and down in an insolent fashion. "I can certainly not detect any trace of vampire now."

Ben discovered his throat was dry. He swallowed.

"Then that means that this is something that has stolen Hawick's appearance, memories, and mind—"

"Dear me." Hunter raised an eyebrow. "And if he has so much of Ben, who is to say that he is not Ben?" As Fagen spluttered, Hunter turned to the rest of the group. "Suppose you fill me in on the results of the tests."

They did. Eagerly. Ben marveled that, without even being purposefully charming, Hunter still had people falling over themselves to please him. Diya caught his attention in his peripheral vision, taking a step back. Ben stood beside her, offering her a smile.

"That is an extensive series of tests." Hunter flicked through the reports. "And his reaction to the blood?"

"Sort of doubled up on himself and choked."

"Like he was going to be sick?" Hunter raised his eyebrows. "I can assure you, that is the last way a vampire would react to spilled blood. And that was the only unusual reaction?"

The group agreed that it was.

"Well. I certainly have no wish to tell you how to do your job, but I know what my conclusions are." Hunter carelessly straightened his collar. He was dressed down, wearing a blazer over a shirt, suggesting that he'd dropped by on a whim. *Was it a whim?* Ben looked closely at Godfrey. That the interview had lasted beyond sunset was unusual. Had that been deliberate?

Fagen scowled. "We should vote."

They did. It was close, but the scientists chose to sign off on Ben's report.

Ben's supervisor shuffled the papers together. "I'll prepare an official report of our findings and send that on," he told Diya. "And Hawick—if you're ever interested in recreating that accident scene, I think we'd all want to learn more."

Ben shook hands awkwardly. "I'll keep that in mind."

Once out of the building and back in Diya's car, Ben breathed out.

"That wasn't so bad, was it?"

"It's not over yet." Saltaire... Ben would be very surprised if Fagen wasn't sending Saltaire a detailed report of his misgivings at that very moment. And Hunter—it must have occurred to Hunter to wonder how Ben got into the club if he was truly one hundred percent human.

Diya pulled up outside the apartment building. "I didn't expect this to take so long. Will you be all right?"

Ben nodded. "I'm not sick anymore, just tired. I'll be fine."

It was a relief to step inside the still apartment. After all the prodding and poking, physically and mentally, the last thing Ben wanted was to deal with anyone. But there was still one thing he had to do.

Godfrey, Hunter, Diya...They're all putting their necks out for me. Nate, too— Ben hadn't let himself think of Nate all day. He felt his determination waver and quickly pulled out his phone. *They're doing all they can for me. Which means, I have to do my part, too.*

Gunn took his time answering. "Who the fuck is this and what do you want?"

"Hawick. I've got a proposition for you."

The phone crackled as Gunn growled. "Not interested."

"If I find this missing werewolf, you'll do my paperwork."

There was a pause. Ben could imagine Gunn raising an insolent eyebrow. "That is quite the change of heart. What happened, Benny? I thought you were too good to dirty your hands with the likes of us anymore."

"You don't care what my motivations are. The only thing that matters to you is that I have the skills, the experience, and am not hampered by the laws placed on Department Seven officers."

"Give me some credit. Does this have anything to do with a trip made to our laboratory yesterday?"

Ben was expecting that. He kept his voice steady. "More to do with Wisner's goon picking a fight in a very public place. I realized that there's more important things at stake than my normality."

"Oh, Benny." Gunn's voice was as close to amused as Ben had ever heard it. "You were never normal."

Ben could feel the start of a headache building. "Well? Do we have a deal? Full moon's approaching, Gunn. You need all the help you can get."

"Sure. If you think you can succeed where every hunter in the city has tried and failed, I'll put pen to paper for you," Gunn said. "We got a deal."

Chapter Sixteen

THE IRON GATES of Mason's Park loomed overhead. The padlock on the chain looped through them was entirely unnecessary. One look was enough to know that there was no way those gates would open.

"Told you the gates would be locked," Aki said behind him.

"It's not important," Nate said. "After all, we're not here to go for a walk." He looked down at the dog.

At the word "walk," the dog's tail began to wag. He looked from Nate to Aki with his usual optimism.

His usual optimism? Nate frowned. It seemed to him like the dog was forcing itself to act normal. *He must know something's up.* Or was this the usual reaction of a dog dragged out of an apartment at three in the morning?

"Nate." Aki's voice had a warning tone.

Nate realized that he was patting the dog on his head. He put his hands in his pocket and stepped back. "Okay, um. Listen."

The dog cocked its head. His tail still wagged.

Nate took a deep breath. "We know what—who you are—Grant."

"And we are not happy about it." Aki wrapped his arms around himself. "You wormed your way into our apartment—that was bad enough! Ate our food, let us think you were an ordinary dog—but to then try to worm your way into our lives!" He jabbed an angry finger at the dog. "All the time you were there, you were listening to our private conversations—spying on us!"

The dog's tail came to a halt. He drooped.

"We should be turning you over to Department Seven," Nate said. "But neither of us like the thought of anyone being in Wisner's power."

"You can thank your lucky stars that your stepdad's actions are marginally more reprehensible than your own. But if you come back, we're calling Department Seven at once. No hesitation." Aki scowled.

The dog looked up at them. His tawny eyes were mournful.

Nate knelt down to stroke the dog's fur. "It's not like he had a choice in disguising himself. I mean, with Wisner and everyone looking for him—"

"He could have transformed and told us the truth at any time," Aki said flatly. "And he didn't. All the time he was staying with us, he was endangering us. Can you imagine the trouble we'd be in if someone had traced him to our apartment? We'd be looking at a lot worse than community service. Especially after the fight in Century—no one would believe we didn't know who he was. We'd be charged with collaboration, at the least." Aki looked around the dark streets. "Let's go, Nate."

Nate reluctantly stood. "You'll be fine," he told the dog. "You're smart. You were doing pretty good before we found you."

"Nate. Let's go." Aki had already started.

"Good luck!" Nate jogged after Aki.

"Let's not stick around." Aki walked quickly.

Nate looked over his shoulder. "He's not following us."

"Doesn't need to. He knows where we live."

"And he also knows what will happen if he tries to take advantage of our hospitality again." Nate hesitated. It seemed like there was more to Aki's anger than the werewolf's deception. "Are you okay?"

"Don't ask stupid questions. That—wolf—was living with us for days! I feel cheated. Doesn't it make you upset knowing that all the time we were being nice to it, the dog was using us?"

Nate winced. "Yeah... But I also feel sad, too. He didn't have to do that. If he'd trusted us, I'd have wanted to help."

"You want to help anyway." Aki stuck his hands in his pockets, walking so fast that Nate was forced into a jog. "You keep looking back. Hoping the dog is following us?"

Nate started, snapping his gaze back to the street in front of them. "Wondering if he's going to be all right."

"What happens to him is entirely the werewolves' business. Put it out of your mind, Nate. From now on, you worry about you."

Nate swallowed. "Right." His chest felt heavy. It didn't sit right with him. *This is pathetic—I know the werewolf used us, and I still can't get angry about it. What is wrong with me?* Aki was so furious, he was shaking. Ben—

Nate swallowed. Ben's words at the park came back. *"If the rogue werewolf hadn't run away, Wisner wouldn't have an excuse to put his wolves out on the streets so blatantly. There would be no cause for the media panic, no justification for Wisner's actions."*

Nate chewed his lip. By hiding the wolf, had he and Aki given Wisner more control over the city? The guy had even wormed his way into the Vampire Senate... Nate groaned. *Once again, my desire to help only gets me and my friends into trouble.* Now, the entire city was in jeopardy.

SUNLIGHT FELL OVER him like a second blanket. Nate stretched out, intent on soaking up as much of its glorious warmth as he could. His body felt warm, more rested than he had in days. Nate shifted and became aware of the sheets beneath him. Something tickled his neck. Exploring it with his fingers, he discovered something smooth and glossy nesting at his collar bone.

Ivy. Shit.

Nate jerked out of his half doze. He sat up, finding himself alone in his bedroom. He caught a glimpse of himself in the mirror. His skin looked healthy, and the shadows under his eyes were gone. He looked thoroughly normal in fact—except for the ivy starting at the bite marks and draped around his neck like a scarf.

Nate fingered the ivy's starting point. He could no longer feel the individual incisions made by Ben's fangs. There was no pain, just the slightly ticklish feeling of a fresh scab. The leaves gently brushed his skin, disturbed by his movements.

Nate breathed out. *It's cool. I'm fine.* Already it felt like he'd never been hurt. In another day, the marks would be gone completely, and it would be like it had never happened—except for the distance between himself and Ben.

Nate shivered. He realized suddenly that the sunlight had shifted, leaving him cold. He swung his legs over the side of the bed. He picked up a sweatshirt off the floor, but instead of pulling it on, pushed the window up. He climbed out onto the fire escape and stood, feeling the sun directly on his skin. His collection of plants rustled as a breeze went through them. Nate took a deep breath, savoring their leafy aroma. *A little more of this and I'll be fine.*

But even standing on the fire escape, his skin soaking up the sun, Nate felt cold. He sat on the metal steps, the sweatshirt draped on his knee, and tried to pin down the chill. His skin was warm everywhere the sun touched, and his blood pumped the sun's rays through his body. He felt it everywhere—

Except here. Nate put his hand over his chest. An ache remained that even the sunlight couldn't soothe. *Am I just—sad?*

In the streets below, a movement caught his eye. *Ben!* He caught his breath and watched.

Ben was with a woman in a business suit, who gestured energetically as they walked toward a red car. Ben nodded. His body language was muted, and though it was hard to tell from a distance, Nate thought he still looked pale. As Nate watched, he turned his face up toward the apartment building, his gaze settling on Nate's plants.

Is he looking at me? It would have been easy to wave, but Nate found that he couldn't move. He could only stare at Ben across the distance between them. His chest gave an unhappy lurch, and he felt the ache anew.

Ben's companion said something. He turned away,, getting into her car without a backward look.

It was only as the car turned the corner that Nate was able to grip the railing and pull himself to his feet. *Ben—*

He'd needed Nate's arm to make the return trip to the apartment. Now he was talking business with strangers and—as far as Nate could judge—pulling it off without any sign of weakness. *Stupid. Did I forget how strong he was?*

Nate swallowed. *Did I really think I could protect him? He's got more strength in one little finger than I have in my entire being—strength of an oak or no!* He gripped the railing tightly. Learning the truth about his magical abilities hadn't changed who he was. Deep down inside, he was still the same attention-starved kid who would do anything to be needed. *What was I thinking? You can't make a daisy into an oak... No matter how good I get at using my powers, I'll still be weak inside. My need to be needed—it's like rot. It's in too deep...*

And a rotten heart was no use to Ben—or anyone.

There was a quick knock, followed by the sound of his bedroom door opening. "Hey, Nate. You— Nate?" Aki's voice raised.

Nate placed his hand over the vines, but he knew it was too late. There was no chance of hiding the ivy. "Aki."

Aki approached cautiously, his eyes wide. "Is that...*growing* out of you?"

"So what if it is? I told you about the plant stuff." Nate winced at the sound of his voice. *Defensive much?* How had he ever thought that he'd accepted his plant self?

"Yeah, but— I didn't think it'd be like this." Aki took a step closer, plainly fascinated.

Nate fought the urge to tug the vine away. "Is it really that weird?"

"Totally." Aki managed to drag his gaze off the vine and up to Nate's face. "But if this is what saved your life, then as far as I'm concerned, it's cool."

Nate breathed out. "Thanks, Aki."

"Anytime. So, are you going to mope for the entire day, or you want to join me for lunch?"

"Shouldn't that be breakfast—" Nate dropped his gaze to the clock by his bed. Two PM. "Never mind."

NATE SAT AT the table, a mug of coffee in front of him. He knew he should feel hungry, but there was no desire to eat. No desire for anything.

"This is a one-time-only offer to make food," Aki said, digging through the pantry. He had a loaf of bread, ham, and butter already on the bench. "You really going to turn that down?"

Nate smiled faintly. "Yeah. Sorry, Aki. I just...don't want anything."

"Well, when you're totally jealous of my great sandwich, remember it was your decision to mope that cost you a sandwich of your own." Aki shot him a look. "You're not going to make moping over your coffee a regular thing, are you?"

Nate picked up his mug. "I'm waiting for it to cool."

"Sure you are. Seriously, Nate. You're not yourself. In the time it took me to shower, dress, update my social media, and shave, you walked into the kitchen and sat down."

"I've got a lot to think about."

"Ben practically killed you and dumped you. That's pretty obviously a sign the relationship is over."

Nate sucked in his breath. Even knowing Aki didn't pull punches, that hurt. "He took me to Department Seven for the vampire test first." Nate looked down at the dark surface of his coffee. Unbidden, the memory of Ben's skin, clammy beneath his fingers, his pulse so faint that for a few terrifying seconds Nate couldn't feel it at all, came back.

Nate shut his eyes, but the memory came with him. Ben staring at him, his anguish written all over his wild, scared expression, and then that moment of blankness, when he locked his feelings down—locking Nate out. *I can't blame him. I wouldn't trust me either.*

"At least one of you is making smart decisions."

It took Nate a moment to pick up the thread of the conversation. "How rude. You're supposed to be my best friend. Be nice to me."

"Let's be real. If Ben walked in here right now, with a bunch of flowers and an apology, what would you do?"

Nate put the coffee down with a sigh. "I don't know."

"Would you take him back?"

"He's not going to want me back. And if he did—" Nate traced the grain of the wooden table with a finger. "I don't know. I miss him—but I can't bear the thought of hurting him again."

"I guess that's a start." Aki licked butter off the knife he'd just used. "I mean, it'd be even better if you were anxious about your own well-being, but baby steps."

"You're going to cut your tongue doing that. Also it's gross." Nate's gaze fell on the bowl of water in the corner of the kitchen, an empty plate beside it. The dog would not be joining them for another meal. "You think we did the right thing?"

"Absolutely," Aki said at once. "The more I think about it, the angrier I get. That was a total invasion of our privacy."

That was...vehement. Even for Aki, who never made a statement without making it clear what his opinion was. Nate raised his head to watch Aki. "Is that all you're upset about?"

Aki's shoulders hunched. "Isn't that enough?"

Nate set the coffee cup down. "You're acting as if— Did something happen I don't know about?" He saw Aki's jaw clench. "You know I won't tell anyone."

"I'm holding you to that." Aki looked down at the sandwich he was assembling. "So. When you were out, the dog was hanging out with me and I talked to it. Like, a lot. I told it some—really personal shit. Stuff I haven't even told you. And the dog just looked at me with its dumb dog eyes, and— Anyway, finding out that I wasn't talking to a dog? I feel—violated."

"Shit." Nate stared at Aki with dismay. "I had no idea—I'm so sorry, Aki."

"And then armed with my deepest darkest secrets, he tries to make my acquaintance—that's seriously creepy levels of stalker!" Aki slammed the fridge door shut. "No, we are way better off without the dog in the house."

"You're right." Nate stood, picking up the dog's bowl and plate. He dropped them in the sink, starting the tap.

"Obviously. I said so, didn't I?" Aki opened the fridge. "Where's the ketchup?"

"In the pantry." Nate picked up his coffee cup for the third time.

How long ago was it that he'd been getting groceries for Ben? It felt like an age ago. *I can't believe I thought I had anything to offer that he wasn't capable of himself... Guess my need to be needed was so strong it reached delusional levels...*

"This is hot sauce, Nate." Aki brandished a bottle accusingly.

Nate stared at it a moment before pulling himself back to the moment. "You tried the fridge?"

"First place I looked."

Nate stood, levering himself up to peer inside the fridge. "Guess we're out then."

"We can't be out of ketchup!"

"So use the hot sauce."

"On ham?"

"Why not? You like hot sauce."

"Not on ham!" Aki jabbed a finger at him. "There are limits, Nate."

Nate leaned against the fridge. "Try it. You might like it."

"I don't want to like it." Aki waved a hand toward his unfinished sandwich. "There are times when you want ketchup and only ketchup will do. Not hot sauce. It doesn't matter how good the hot sauce is, if it's not ketchup, it's not right."

Nate frowned. "It doesn't matter how good the hot sauce is?"

Aki nodded enthusiastically. "Sometimes only ketchup will do." He paused. "What? Why are you starting at me?"

Nate drew a deep breath. "You're right. It's like how you can't make a poppy into an oak, any more than you can make an acorn grow a poppy. You can't change what you are—but you can grow what you are."

"Um—"

"All this time, I was trying to be something I wasn't. Someone who was strong, who didn't get pushed around. I used my powers to fight, thought that made me powerful—I forgot that I like taking care of people. That I'm good at it—that it means a lot to me. So when Ben needed something from me, I didn't think about it—that part of me had been starved, I ignored all the danger signs."

"I don't—"

"But taking care of people is my strength. Think of a forest. You've got the tall trees—yeah, they're strong. But they also shelter the plants around them. The leaves they drop feed the plants beneath—it's called a parasol eco-system. That's me." Nate straightened, his heart thudding with the magnitude of his discovery. "And you realize what that means?"

"Nate." Aki ran his hand over his face. "I just want a sandwich."

"We need to find Grant." Nate made his way toward the door.

"The werewolf? What—why?" Aki made no attempt to follow.

"After everything that happened, I still want to help him. I think that means a lot." Nate pulled on a slightly fresher T-shirt and fished his jacket out of his wardrobe.

"You just admitted that you need to be needed. How do you know this isn't some—rebound thing? You can't help Ben, so you're focusing on Grant."

Nate's chest tightened. He felt a sense of sadness at the thought of Ben, but mingled with it was a sort of pride. "Ben doesn't need our help." Nate pulled on socks and stepped into his battered sneakers. "Grant does. And we're possibly the only ones in New Camden who can help him now." He grabbed his wallet and strode into the living room.

"Just because we can doesn't mean we have to!" Aki stood in the kitchen doorway. "Where do you get this 'we' from anyway?"

"Grant's got no reason to trust us right now. We threw him out. He knows we're mad. He might not listen to me, but I've got the feeling he'll listen to you." Nate stepped into Aki's room, scanning the floor. Aki kept most of his wardrobe strewn across his bed and floor and it took him a few moments to identify Aki's jacket, flung over the foot of the bed. "Here." He held out the jacket to Aki.

Aki made no move to take it. "Nate, I'm not kidding when I say I'm mad at the guy. What on earth makes you think I want anything to do with this ludicrous impulse of yours?"

"Remember what you said in the park—that you didn't think you'd ever find someone interested in you if they knew the real you first?" Nate motioned to the surrounding apartment. "The dog lived here with us. He saw us—both of us—at our most honest. Without trying to impress. Hell, you weren't even very nice to him."

"Yeah. Smart me. What's your point?"

"It was after he'd seen the real you that the wolf tried to get to know you. He was interested in you—the real you—and he was willing to risk getting captured by Department Seven or Wisner's pack to try to get to know you."

Aki stared at him. "Are you serious? You're just guessing—you can't possibly know that."

Nate knew he was right. "He's been on the run for weeks now. You think he'd risk his freedom for anyone who wasn't important to him?"

Aki looked at the jacket he held. His expression was conflicted. "I don't know about this, Nate. I really don't know."

"You don't have to come with me," Nate told him. "And I won't bring him back here without your permission. But my gut says that you're the key factor here."

"Key factor. Ugh. Nate, you really need to work on your flattery." Aki rubbed his hand over his face. "Okay, fine. I'll come with you—but I'm only doing this to make sure you're not getting taken advantage of."

Nate felt his chest ease. "Thanks, Aki."

"You should be thankful!" Aki grabbed his keys off the coffee table. "And just remember—I have not agreed to this."

MASON'S PARK HAD the usual crowd of small children with their parents, retirees on the jogging track, and serious runners weaving through the crowd with expressions of serious concentration. Nate walked slowly, scanning the ground for the dog's familiar white-gray coat.

"No sign?"

He looked up to see Aki jogging toward him from the other area of the park. "Nothing."

"It makes sense he'd go somewhere else. After all, he doesn't know that we won't change our minds and turn him in to Department Seven."

Nate looked around the park with a sense of defeat. For the first time since the elevator doors had closed behind Ben, he'd had certainty, a sense of purpose. The feeling was so strong, he hadn't even considered what they'd do if they couldn't find Grant.

Aki watched him, stretching idly. "You want to search another park?"

But the dog wasn't there either.

"The problem is that we don't know enough about the guy," Aki said. "Our interactions with him have been all one-sided. So you don't know he needs our help—any more than you know how to find him now."

Nate's shoulders sagged as he followed Aki down the road to their apartment. "I guess you're right." Mentally, he berated himself. *Stupid! Have I learned nothing?*

"Don't feel bad, Nate. You've already gone above and beyond by even looking for him—trust me, no one else in this city would have done what we just did."

"And it didn't work." Nate trudged along.

Aki was quiet a moment. "This is that important to you? You barely know the guy."

"I know he needs help," Nate said quietly. "And that we can help him. And—well, none of what I've seen of his stepfather makes me think that the guy is good news."

"His stepfather didn't force him to spy on us," Aki said. "But yeah, I will give you that point. I still think you're taking this way too personally."

Nate's smile flickered tiredly as they turned the corner onto their street. "When I went into Department Seven for my first counseling session, the reception was full of hunters. They were all armed, and every one of them was there for information to try to catch this guy. They didn't ask what he'd done to deserve being hunted down. They only cared about the price on his head. It—made me think. When—the hunter was found dead on our farm, and all our neighbors thought Ethan was responsible... It was the worst feeling ever, Aki. I felt really trapped—like there was nowhere we could run."

Aki drew a sharp breath. "This guy's not Ethan, Nate."

"I know. But—part of me thinks we need to stick together. Help each other out. And Charlotte and Vazul insist he's a cool guy."

Aki snorted. "He'll need to be more than a cool guy. Seriously, Nate—" He ground to a sudden halt.

Nate barely avoided clipping Aki with his elbow. He looked up, wondering what Aki had seen.

A man stood in the alleyway. He wore a charcoal-gray hoodie with the hood pulled up, but that did nothing to disguise him. His wild blonde beard, shaggy and unkempt, exploded out of the hoodie. More than a few leaves stuck to his jeans, and he had a duffel bag slung over his shoulders. His tawny eyes were fixed on Aki. "Talking about me?"

Aki clenched his hands into fists. "So what if we were? You have to admit you've given us a lot to talk about."

Not the least of which was what Grant was doing in human form in full daylight. Nate glanced around the street, but no one seemed to have spotted them.

"I know. That's why I'm here." The man hesitated. "I owe you an apology and an explanation. That is, if you're willing to hear it."

"This is really dangerous." Nate kept his voice pitched calmly. "If anyone saw you—"

Grant winced slightly. "Considering the risk I put the two of you under, I think that's fair."

"Fair?" Aki's voice hitched incredulously. "Do you really think anything you say can make up for what you did?"

Grant's eyes were fluid, resting on Aki with deep pain. "I know it can't. But this is all I can offer, so I had to try."

Aki hesitated, his mouth screwed shut.

"Your call," Nate said.

"*Thanks*." Aki jabbed a finger toward Grant. "If we change our minds about this, you go. Understood?"

"You have my word," Grant said fervently.

"And you're taking a shower and a shave as soon as we get back to the apartment." Aki shoved his hands in his pockets, walking off.

"Thank you." Grant hurried after him.

Aki snorted. "Don't think I'm being kind," he threatened. "Your body odor is an attack on the senses. And do not get me started on that beard—"

Nate fought a smile as he brought up the rear. Grant was about to discover just what he'd let himself in for.

Chapter Seventeen

NOTHING HAD CHANGED, but the university had taken on the subtle difference of a nightmare. With his breath sticking in his throat, Ben navigated the crowd of students. He couldn't avoid being jostled, stepped on, or bumped into. Thanks to the Class Six restrictions, he was invisible. *If the crowd turns, I'll be trampled or crushed—and no one would ever know.* By the time he reached the supernatural department, his skin was clammy and his heart beat fast.

I've never been happier for the department's open campus policy. The door opened at Ben's touch and the wards, allowing for the presence of supernatural guest speakers, did not expel him.

The secretary looked up and frowned, clearly wondering why the door had opened if there was no one there. Ben winced. Clutching the strap of his backpack, he walked down the hall to the office at the end. He knocked and was greeted by a voice within. He exhaled in relief. He didn't have a backup plan if Professor Winnaker was unable to see him. He was on shaky ground as it was. Knowing Grant was friends with Charlotte and Vazul, he'd looked into the pair online. Both were students of supernatural studies at the University of New Camden, making the department the starting point of Ben's investigation. He stepped into the office.

Professor Winnaker was one of Ben's favorite lecturers. He was the department head of supernatural studies, an elderly man with a bald head and eyes as gentle as a baby's. His absent-minded manner was at odds with his sharp intellect. Many careless undergraduates had been dismayed to discover that their seemingly kindly professor strictly abided to his high academic standards. Ben enjoyed being challenged to push himself and had turned out some of his best essays for Winnaker's class. He felt an ache for something lost as he settled in the armchair opposite Winnaker's desk. "It's been a while, professor. Do you have a moment?"

"Any time." Winnaker moved the pile of books on his desk to one side, and beamed kindly at Ben. "It is very good to see you again. Are you thinking of rejoining us?"

How much did the professor know of the circumstances surrounding Ben's abrupt disappearance from the university? "I'm not sure yet. I'm actually wondering if you taught a guy called Grant. He'd be a second year. Blond, a slight beard—"

"Grant, yes." The professor's eyes rested on Ben. "It has been a few weeks since he's been at the university. As a matter of fact, I'm quite concerned about him."

So his professor hadn't connected his absent student to the missing werewolf? Ben fought to keep his surprise off his face. It made sense—Grant's physical description hadn't been circulated to the newspapers, citing fears that vigilante citizens might endanger themselves. "You don't know why he hasn't shown up for classes?"

"No. His absence is most out of character. He's usually an extremely dependable young man. One his classmates could learn from." Professor Winnaker frowned at Ben. "I hope you're not here to ask me for his personal information. I had a visit from his stepfather, demanding the names of Grant's friends—really the man was most off-putting."

"Did you give him the info?"

"Of course not. I consider that information classified. And his stepfather—but I'm speaking out of turn. What did you want to know about Grant?"

Ben took a deep breath. He hated lying to his professor. *It's for a good cause.* "I'm looking for someone to share my apartment. Grant gave you as a reference."

Winnaker thawed. "He really should have asked permission first, you know. Of course, I'm happy to act as a reference, but a little warning is nice."

Ben grimaced sympathetically. "So what can you tell me about Grant?"

"Only that I'm sure that you'll get on fine. I've always found him to be responsible, well-organized, a little too serious perhaps—but that is rare among young people. I've got no doubt that more time in the company of his peers would cure him of that."

Ben jotted down the professor's description. "Do you happen to know if he's lived with anyone before?"

"As a matter of fact, there is a story there." Winnaker rested his clasped hands together on the desk. "It's really very odd. Grant was awarded a full scholarship in his first year here. It included tuition and accommodation. He was really passionate about his studies and he had the marks to back them up—an astounding application. I was personally interested in him, so I looked out for him amongst my students. Only three weeks into the school term, he vanished. I was concerned enough to visit him at his hall of residence, and he wasn't there. His family had shown up and moved him out without notice. Very inconsiderate—no mention of his intention, which is very odd considering how hard he worked to get the scholarship and how considerate he was in every other respect. My colleagues were rather put out, but I was concerned enough to try to visit him at his home."

Ben found that he was sitting on the edge of his seat. "And? What did they tell you?"

"Nothing." Winnaker spread his hands wide. "I wasn't even allowed in the gate. The rudeness of it—" He shook his head. "When Grant came back to school two weeks later, I took him aside to ask about it. I gathered there was some family situation that had necessitated his return. I don't think he was altogether happy about the situation, and there had been threats to prevent him from returning to school if he didn't keep his grades up—which after taking him out of school for those two weeks I felt was a bit much! Still, Grant rallied and his grades have been consistent. He was awarded a second scholarship for this year, and if it hadn't been for his current absence, I'd say that he was almost assured a third scholarship for next year." Winnaker frowned. "When you see him, let him know that I've put aside a copy of my lecture handouts for him. And I'm willing to discuss a makeup essay."

Ben raised his eyebrows. Grant had to be a keen student if Winnaker was talking about makeup projects. "I'll definitely pass that on."

"YOU DO REALIZE we're not going to find the missing werewolf in a library, right?" George announced her presence with a thud as her bag hit the floor. She flung herself into the chair across the study desk from Ben, ignoring the pointed looks surrounding students sent her way. "Or do I have to give you a refresher of how hunting works."

Ben grinned despite himself. "Glad you could make it."

"I knew that you were bound to come to your senses eventually. Didn't expect it quite so soon, but hey. The lure of the investigation." George leaned her elbows on the table, casually returning the stare of a glowering student. "You do realize we're cutting this really fine? The full moon's tonight."

"I know." Ben looked at the table in front of him. The desk in the university library was spread with a number of thick, leather-bound volumes, numbered with Roman numerals. He'd had a really hard time, both gathering them and then stopping the university students from taking what was, to all appearances, an unoccupied table. "I wanted to refresh my memory about the laws surrounding werewolves on the full moon."

"I can tell you that. Transforming in public? A huge no. Biting or attacking anyone while transformed counts as manslaughter—"

"The argument being that a werewolf can't claim any attacks were accidental because the influence of the full moon is a known constant that a responsible wolf would have made arrangements for." Ben patted the book in front of him. "Grant's successfully evaded an entire city looking for him. He's got to have a plan."

"So you thought you'd look up the specifics?" George studied the book. "It's an original approach, I'll give you that. Most hunters are patrolling the entertainment district, figuring that a wolf on the prowl is going to be in search of victims."

"The hotels will have been warned to look out for him. It's far more likely he's got a secure place lined up." He turned the page. "The question is, what is he aiming to do?"

"How do you mean?"

"We don't know why he's run away from home."

George snorted. "And the wolves are doing their best to make sure we don't know. Have you seen the Department Seven brief?" As Ben shook his head, she dug into her courier bag. "Let's just say brief is accurate."

It was. Ben frowned at the flyer. First name only, a physical description, the clothes he'd last been seen in, and two photos, one of a young man with bloodshot eyes and a beard that dwarfed him, and the other of a sandy-colored wolf, its teeth bared in a snarl. "This is everything?"

"Yeah. Needless to say, there have already been near misses with civilians." George sniffed scornfully at the paper. "Not even a last name, so we don't even have his social media. It's almost like they don't want us to find him."

"Maybe they don't." Ben frowned. "If a hunter does what New Camden's head of security can't—that's not going to look good for Councilor Wisner, is it? But if his pack find the rogue werewolf after Department Seven fails—"

"He's going to look real good." George wrinkled her nose in disgust. "Politicians—but you think they'd really risk people's lives to score points?"

"New Camden's supernatural population can't afford more deaths. Not after the necromancer backlash," Ben said promptly. "Wisner's smart enough to know that."

"You don't think this is a scheme cooked up between him and his stepson? That he knows where he is?"

Ben hesitated then shook his head. "A wolf searching for this missing werewolf caused a major scene at Century." He detailed the incident quickly. "Wisner's too smart to want that kind of publicity. If he knew where Grant was, his wolves wouldn't be so stressed searching for him that they lose their cool. The only explanation is that as the full moon approaches he's getting desperate."

George whistled. "Lucky Nate was there. If he hadn't been—"

Ben winced. "Yeah. Aki... Lucky doesn't even come close."

"The idea that Wisner's wolves are continuing to prowl the city is doing nothing for my personal sense of security," George said. "The guy just got a warning?"

Ben nodded. "There's something more to the situation. And I think I've got it. I spoke to someone who knows Grant—"

George straightened. "Inside information? And here you said you were retired."

Ben fought the urge to blush. "This is a one-time thing." He took a deep breath. "Anyway, my unbiased source described Grant as a grade-A student who took his responsibilities seriously. I also heard from someone, who claims to be his friend, that he'd tried establishing his freedom legally. I thought I'd look up how a werewolf goes about leaving a pack." Ben looked down at his notebook. "He's got to turn in the Werewolf Independence Form to the Registry. Once the form is handed in, the werewolf must prove to an agent of either the Registry or

Department Seven that he or she has made sufficient preparation to meet the full moon, including a secure room with only one means of exit, no windows, and a door certified to withstand a werewolf that locks from the outside."

"That makes sense. What about magical wards?"

"Magic may be present to provide mental protection and calm the werewolf contained within the room, but may not be the primary means of containment as in the case of anything happening to the rune's caster their protective value would be diminished." Ben picked up his pen. "I'm pretty sure that Grant's trying to establish his independence, and for whatever reason, his stepdad is trying to stop him."

"A werewolf certified door..." George pulled her laptop out of her bag. "How many security services offer those?"

Ben nodded in approval at the line of inquiry. "Not very many. It's highly unlikely that Grant made the inquiries himself. Ask about any inquiries from individuals in the last two months."

"Why two months?"

Ben bit his lip. "It's just a hunch...but I don't think Grant had very long to prepare for this. The fact that he's in hiding is not doing his cause any favors. If he'd had time to plan, he'd have disappeared shortly before the full moon, instead of weeks ahead of time, and he'd have lodged a change of address with Department Seven openly. The fact that he hasn't is the only thing that Wisner has against him, and he's milking it for all its worth."

George narrowed her eyes at him. "You're not on his side, are you?"

Ben blinked. "What? No. Whether justified or not, the fact remains that as long as he is on the loose, he's doing untold damage to the reputation of all New Camden's supernaturals—and my case with the Registry in particular." He took a deep breath. "I'm on thin ice. The council decided my application presented several red flags. We've got to do this strictly by the book."

"If you say so." George cracked her fingers before opening her laptop. "Just remember that there's no sympathy in hunting." She glared at a nearby student who had stopped her work to stare at them. "What are you looking at?"

Ben breathed out as the student devoted herself to her notes rather than reply. He'd been conscious of the weird looks sent their way by people who could only see one half of the conversation, even if George wasn't. *I don't know how much more of this I can take.*

BY THE TIME they left the library an hour later, they had a list of possible leads. George was going to visit the city's pounds, while Ben took his chances at Wisner's compound.

"Better you than me." George shouldered her courier bag. "I bet you don't even get in the door."

"You're probably right." But with his Class Six restrictions, meaning that many civilians couldn't see him, Ben was stuck talking to supernaturals or those with supernatural clearance. "But it's about the only thing I can do."

Almost an hour and a half later, Ben walked down the residential street that contained Wisner's house. The bus alone had taken almost an hour, winding its way through a distinctly upmarket residential suburb. As he'd done his best to avoid getting sat on, Ben's mind returned to the contradiction between Winnaker's description of Grant and the information given Department Seven by his pack mates.

A conscientious young man who made it into the university on a full scholarship. Ben frowned. To do that—and keep his marks up—would have kept Grant too busy to indulge in the sort of delinquent activity Wisner had accused him of. *Looks like Charlotte and Vazul are telling the truth... Or maybe there's more than one truth about Grant?*

As he approached the road that Wisner's house was on, Ben encountered a thick wall, twice his height, in pale-yellow stucco. The wall continued all the way to a metal gate that extended across the road.

Ben frowned. *A gated community?* They were rare in New Camden, but it shouldn't have come as a surprise that Wisner would have invested in one. He was that type.

A bearded man slouched in a small shed beside the gate. He cast scornful eyes over Ben's weedy form and made no attempt to rise, even when Ben stood directly in front of him.

"Excuse me," said Ben. "Can you help? I'm looking for 14 Grace Drive."

"State your name and business." The man reached for a battered-looking pad in front of him.

Ben frowned. "I'm here to see Mrs. Wisner."

"Forget it." The man thrust the pad back.

"Shouldn't you at least ask her if she wants to see me?"

"Don't have to." The man cast his eyes back over Ben. "No one sees Mrs. Wisner without the permission of her husband."

Ben raised an eyebrow. "Is that even legal? Last I heard, the rules regarding the head of a pack of werewolves having control over access to his pack was limited only to cases where the pack member was considered a threat to public safety. Is Mrs. Wisner a danger?"

The man growled, getting to his feet. "What are you trying to pull?"

"Nothing. This is all freely available information. Don't you know your rights?"

The man narrowed his eyes. "No one gets in or out of here without Wisner's permission."

"That sounds like an overreach of the councilor's position," Ben said. "You should bring it to his attention." He turned, walking away. His heart was pounding, but the wolf clearly didn't feel comfortable abandoning his position of lookout to chase him down. After a few minutes of fast walking, Ben reached the relative safety of the corner.

He slowed his steps. He hadn't expected anything to come out of trying to visit Wisner...but the strength of the refusal had thrown him. *If Grant goes back to that, ten to one he is never getting out.*

Ben slowed to a halt. Could he be responsible for turning Grant in for what was starting to look a lot like imprisonment? *You don't know enough about the situation. Mrs. Wisner might be perfectly happy with her husband choosing her guests...* But he didn't know she was.

A sudden buzzing in his pocket made him jump. Ben pulled his phone out. "George?"

"Hey." George's voice was muted, cautious. "I've got a situation." In the background a dog barked insistently.

"No." He'd told her how important it was to keep things discreet. "George—"

"Not my fault. It's so incredibly unnecessary. But I was getting a weird vibe from the third kennel I visited. The guy who runs the place invited me to look around and see if any of the dogs looked like my wolf. Next thing I know, I'm locked in."

"What?" Ben's grip tightened on the phone. "And it's not an accident?"

"Heard him making a phone call just outside the door. Sounds like someone told him that if anyone came by asking about Grant, he was to hold them."

Ben caught his breath. He had a very good idea who was behind that order. "There's no way out?"

"Who do you take me for, an amateur? This room is a prison—with a werewolf-proof door."

"I'll be there as soon as I can. Stay calm." Ben brought up the location of the kennels. "I'm closer than I realized."

"Can't be close enough," George said. "This entire situation is bogus."

Ben had to agree. He set off at a jog for the kennels. If it was Wisner behind George's kidnapping, then what did he possibly think he could gain from it? *Unless...*

Unless we're getting close to something Wisner doesn't want us to find.

The kennel was at one end of a large junkyard. The guy in charge lingered by the entrance, smoking a cigarette, with his sunglasses pulled low over his eyes. He had a number of tattoos down his muscled arms and startled every time a car went past. He was so focused on the road, he missed Ben swinging himself over the fence entirely.

Ben kept the wreck of an old SUV between himself and the man as he turned his attention to the lock. Although the door was solid and made of steel, amply fitted out to deal with the security needs of werewolves, the lock itself was straightforward.

Just like riding a bike. Ben pulled his father's skeleton key out of his pocket, slipping it into the lock. *You don't forget.* The lock clicked and Ben pushed the door open.

At first he didn't see George, just the rows and rows of caged dogs. Across one wall were five larger-than-usual cages with human-sized mattresses at the bottom. *Makes sense that a werewolf pack would use this place.* Ben looked around, his heart sinking. Was he too late? Had George been taken somewhere else—

"Didn't expect you to be quite that fast." George's statement made Ben jump. She squeezed herself out from under one of the cages. "Figured I'd make it hard for them to get to me."

"Smart. I only saw one guy." Ben turned his attention to outside. "He's still waiting at the gate—shit." An SUV with tinted windows had just pulled in. "We're out of time."

"Hide." George immediately wriggled herself back under the crates.

You can't hide from wolves! Their noses—

Ben decided he had no choice. He ducked outside, and spotting a handy dumpster, swung himself up onto the roof. Lying flat against its surface, he barely dared to breathe. Would this be enough?

"That's right. A girl, on her own. She had a hunter's license. Looked legit." The tattooed man was leading Wisner and a contingent of two burly men to the shed. "Are you sure about locking her up? What if she complains?"

"So let her complain. You've got a right to protect your private property." Wisner spoke with assurance.

"Easy for you to say. But I'm a working man. I got my reputation to think of. It was bad enough turning the kid in to you, but this—she's no wolf." The voices were rapidly approaching. Any moment now they'd be at the shed.

One of Wisner's men growled. "You think what the boss wants you to think."

"Don't get me wrong, I'm not about to question your judgment, Boss. But I got to say. I don't like it." There was a pause.

"What's wrong?"

"I locked the door. It's not locked now." The man pushed the door open. "Gone. Motherfuckin' hunter had an accomplice!"

There was the unwelcome sound of all four werewolves inhaling deeply. Ben winced. In their human forms, the werewolves' sense of smell would not be as acute as it was in their wolf form, but it was still far too accurate for his peace of mind. In the kennel, George's scent would at least be overpowered by that of the surrounding dogs—who had scented the wolves and were going out of their minds, to judge by the frenzied barking going on below.

"Shut that door." Wisner growled. There was silence until the door slammed shut, and then a pause, which Ben could only read as ominous. "You got that scent?"

"Smells like vampire. But in daylight?"

"Left here through the fence." A second voice sounded from a short distance.

"Vampire now?" The kennel owner sounded aggrieved. "You've got to be kidding."

"It's of no matter," Wisner said. "I've got a very good idea of who is responsible for this."

"Well, you can tell them I've had enough of this. I was happy enough to do you a favor and let you know if anyone came sniffing around after your missing pup, but this is where I draw the line. It's hard enough running an honest business without getting involved in anything shady. If the motherfucker had let the dogs out—shit, I'd be done for."

"If you're that unhappy, I can remove your pack from our ranks."

There was a pause. "I didn't say that," the kennel owner said.

"No? Because it sounded like you'd forgotten the reason why our packs have aligned." Wisner's voice was a collar pulled tight enough to choke. "To bring order to New Camden, and to restore the werewolf to its rightful place as the city's protector and master."

There was a sound that sounded very like a whimper.

"Obey the pack's directives, and you'll be fine. But stick your neck out—and you'll find what it feels like to have the might of the city turned against you and yours."

"You're right. I spoke out of line—I wasn't thinking." His voice was so muted that it was almost impossible to recognize it as belonging to the same man who had greeted Wisner on his arrival.

"A smart decision. Change is coming to New Camden—and you do not want to be on the wrong side of it." Wisner paused. "That is—if you're willing to prove you belong."

"Anything, Boss! You name it!" The guy sounded desperate. Ben couldn't blame him. When Wisner dropped his voice to that commanding growl, Ben had chills the entire length of his back.

Upstart wolf!

Of all the times for the vampire to make an appearance. Ben deliberately forced the thought down. Instead, he thought of Nate. The scent of the decaying leaves littering the apartment came to him at once, along with his terror that Nate might not wake up.

"I have a job for your pack." Wisner started to speak. At the same time, the wolf that had prowled over to the fence traced his way back to the kennel, opening the door. This set off a fresh range of barking from the trapped dogs. He quickly shut it—but whatever Wisner had said to the man was lost.

"You got it. The Juggawolves will take care of it."

"Good. Then I leave it to you."

There was the sound of one set of footsteps hurrying away. A few moments later, the junkyard owner came into Ben's view, heading toward the main garage. Presumably to call the rest of his pack. *Just what we need—more werewolves.*

"Is that really okay, boss? Grant getting captured by those lowlifes will make the rest of us look really weak—"

"They will fail," Wisner said. "They are clumsy and headstrong. Not only will they not find Grant, but they may well bring the law down upon themselves. Fortunately, we are here to provide the strong pack leadership that New Camden so obviously needs."

There was a chuckle from one of his companions. "You've thought of everything."

"I have. So don't question me again." Wisner strode off, the two men at his heels.

Ben waited until he'd heard their truck drive away before cautiously raising his head. *Not good.*

GEORGE PEERED OUT the window of Ben's apartment, keeping an eye on the street below. "You were right about your hunch. Wisner doesn't want this kid found—unless it's by him."

Ben looked over to her. He had his phone to one ear, listening to the Department Seven answering machine music on seemingly endless loop. "I could have done without being proved right so ominously." He wasn't prepared for a werewolf pack. Balancing his phone on one shoulder, Ben carried his candles, salt, and herbs into the living room. "Hello?" The music had stopped—only to be followed by the beep of a line disconnected. Ben swore. "They cut me off!"

"What can Department Seven even do? Wisner's a councilor."

"They need to know about this." Ben started to make a pile of everything he would need to strengthen the runes around the apartment. He ran a mental checklist to make sure he had everything.

"Hey, it's your boyfriend."

"Nate's not—" Ben started automatically. The words stuck in his throat. Nate wasn't—and never would be. He'd lost even their nebulous connection to each other.

George turned her head to stare at him. "Not?" Her eyes narrowed. "Did something happen?"

"I don't want to talk about it," Ben said. "But we're not together. By mutual agreement."

"Mutual? You're kidding."

Ben shook his head, coming over to join George at the window, looking down at Nate in the street below. Three days without Ben's presence had restored his health. He looked like any young man his age walking down the street. Aki was gesticulating wildly with his hands as they walked, a man Ben didn't recognize walking between them, a hoodie obscuring his face. Nate listened to Aki, but his reactions were limited to the occasional nod. *He might look like normal—but I bet things are far from normal inside.* Aki abruptly waved goodbye to the other two, ducking inside the small corner shop.

Ben realized George was watching him. He stepped back from the window. "We're not good for each other. We mutually exacerbate each other's weak points."

"Come again?"

"Basically, I put him into a really dangerous situation and he got hurt. You can imagine how he feels about that. I refuse to endanger him again." Ben picked up his chalk.

"Nate's pretty good at endangering himself without your help." George grabbed her courier bag, pulling out her crossbow. "Shit."

Ben had a moment of foreboding as he hurried back to the window. A van emblazoned with loud, clown-themed graffiti had pulled up, and the man they'd encountered at the junkyard had jumped out, along with four other men. They were headed straight for Nate. "No! The wolves—they were supposed to be coming after us."

"Evidently they didn't get that memo." George loaded her crossbow and Ben helped her heft the window upright.

The Juggawolves were proving Wisner's opinion of them accurate. After a cursory demand for surrender, they waded in, fists swinging. Nate met them, easily throwing the first, only for two more to jump him. The remaining two men circled the man in the hoodie, who mirrored their prowl perfectly.

Ben stared. *No ordinary human moves like that…*

George swore as the two men made a dive for their prey. "Can't get a straight line of fire!"

"Hold off the crossbow unless they transform," Ben said.

"But—"

"Nate's got this."

Nate stood, shaking one of the two men in the process. Ignoring the remaining man clinging to his neck, he blocked a punch thrown at him and waded into the fight. He bodily tackled the man from the junkyard, and as his companion turned to see what had happened, the hooded man kicked his legs out from under him. Nate dislodged the man trying frantically to strangle him, and all five Juggawolves were laid out on the pavement.

"No shit!" George whistled. "When did he learn to do that?"

Ben smiled faintly, keeping his eyes on the street below. Instinct told him that this wasn't over yet.

Nate made a comment to the hooded man, gesturing toward the apartment door. The man shook his head, looking toward the shop that Aki had entered. As they hesitated, one of the five men rolled onto his stomach. He was large in every sense of the word, dressed in ragged jeans and the same black T-shirt as the rest of his pack. He snarled as he pushed himself onto his knees. He raised his voice in an ear-splitting howl.

"They're insane." Ben stared down at the street. "Transforming here?"

The hooded man darted forward, grabbing the man by his collar and shaking him, but the call had been made. The men staggered onto all fours, gathering their strength to transform. The air was thick with their howls.

"Are they mad? Transforming in broad daylight—the entire city will come down on them!"

"Exactly what Wisner wants. He's probably waiting for the callout so he can swoop in and 'fix' everything." Ben ground his teeth. There was nothing anyone could do to halt a werewolf transformation—

But Nate's not anyone. Ben sucked in a deep breath. He ran to his bedroom, scrambling out the window, onto the fire escape. He scanned the plants, grabbing the one that looked the most vine like. *This has got to work!* Ben dashed back, not letting himself think about what would happen if it didn't.

Nate and the hooded man had backed up onto the steps of the apartment as the smirking pack leader got to his feet. Around him, the men's bodies contorted, starting to expand in ways that no human body was meant to.

"Shit, shit, shit." George had her crossbow raised. "What do we do?"

"Trust Nate." Ben leaned out the window, the morning glory in his hands. "Look out below!" he yelled, letting go of the pot.

The pack leader jumped as the plant hit the pavement. He looked up with a faint sneer. "You missed!"

Nate looked up at Ben. His eyes widened, and he looked back to the morning glory sitting on the pavement.

Ben leaned against the window sill, his fingers gripping the ledge. He held his breath, watching as the men continued to transform. Had he been in time?

"You motherfuckers think you're tough," the pack leader said, folding his arms as he watched the first of the werewolves scramble to his feet. "Just wait till you meet the real Juggawolves. No holding back now."

The man with the hoodie snarled as he approached him. "Are you out of your mind? This is a public street—anyone could get hurt!" There was an authority to his voice, despite his nondescript appearance. Ben had a sudden idea of who the man in the hoodie was.

"You should have thought of that before you challenged the motherfucking Juggawolves." The pack leader extended a hand, ordering his wolves to attack.

They leapt—and were instantly tangled by the mass of morning glory that exploded out of nowhere. The first wolf yelped as he fell, the vine swarming over him. Adding insult to injury, dark-blue flowers unfolded as the plant covered him completely.

The wolves whined, drawing back. They snapped their teeth as they sized up the threat. It didn't take long for them to work out the cause. The three wolves growled as they prowled around Nate, sizing up their attack.

"I've never seen anything like that." George's words startled Ben. He'd entirely forgotten she was there. "Your boy's just full of surprises."

Ben swallowed. "Let's get down there before the situation can get even more out of control." Fortunately, they already had the armory open. He scanned the supplies, grabbing a set of leather muzzles. "Come on."

"Is that a werewolf muzzle?" George grabbed the rope from the box and followed suit. "Your old man was really something."

"Dad was a hoarder. Never threw out anything that might come in useful one day." No time for the elevator. Ben ran down the stairs. *Please let us be in time.*

He dashed past a frightened resident, sheltering in the stairwell, and ran across the lobby, making his way through the door.

He couldn't see Nate at all. He was entirely obscured by the furry bodies of the three wolves who had clambered on top of him, the morning glory vines latching onto them. As Ben watched, one of the wolves was thrown free.

Ben dashed toward the wolf. Before it could pull itself to its feet, he'd scrambled onto its back, looping the muzzle across its jaw.

Snarling viciously, the wolf shook his body. Ben looped his arms around the wolf's body, hanging on for dear life as the wolf fought to throw him. He growled, summoning the vampire. "Surrender. You cannot win."

He felt the wolf's body tense underneath him and then start to tremble. *Fear?* Ben let threat color his voice as he growled low.

The wolf slowly, carefully, lay its body down. As Ben stood, he rolled over, exposing his throat.

Ben smiled. "Smart dog." He looked around.

George was reloading her crossbow. The fired bolt pinned the pack leader to the wall by his jacket. One of the remaining wolves was rapidly disappearing beneath the morning glory vines, and the other—

Ben stared.

The man in the hoodie stared the remaining wolf down. He was unarmed and had made no move to fight. But from the way the wolf's hackles were raised, his tawny eyes were a weapon all of their own. As Ben watched, the wolf faltered, lowering his gaze.

But Grant wasn't done with him. "Into the van," he ordered. "All of you." There was a crisp note of authority in his voice, and Ben wasn't surprised that the muzzled wolf instantly rolled to his feet. He followed the other wolf into the van. Nate followed, with one vine-wrapped wolf under each arm. He slammed the van door shut after the last.

Only the pack leader was left. He managed to tug the crossbow bolt loose, freeing himself from the wall, and snarled, showing his teeth. "You've made a serious mistake. You're gonna regret picking a fight with us—"

"Have you any idea what you've done? Ordered a wolf attack in a public space." Grant bristled with fury. If he'd been in wolf form, every hackle would have been raised. "You're setting every wolf in this country back decades!"

The man snarled. "Just following orders. Wisner's got a plan for this city—a plan that's going to put an end to sorry punks like you causing trouble for the rest of us. You act real high and mighty, but you're the one whose tail should be between his legs. Wisner's going to make an example out of you—"

"And you." Ben strode over to join the conversation. "You've been played."

"Who do you think you are?" The man's nostrils flared. "You—you're the creep who smells like a vampire! I do not take kindly to anyone trespassing on my pack's property—"

"Well, listen up because we have something you're going to like even less." George kept her crossbow leveled at him. "After your wolf locked me in the kennel—which is an offense and I'm in half a mind to press charges, by the way—we stuck around. And man, did we get an earful."

"Your man was too quick to assume that we'd left," Ben confirmed. "We heard Wisner talking to his subordinates. He sent you after me and George to intimidate us, hoping that you'd create a public disturbance—which he would take the credit for suppressing."

The man blanched. "You're lying. Don't piss me off! Wisner's solid. He wouldn't—"

"He's done it to me," Grant said. "His own pack. What makes you think he wouldn't do it to yours?"

"Wisner wants a scapegoat. Someone he can use to make himself look good—to justify the power he's about to grab," Ben continued. "If he can't get it from recapturing Grant, you're a good second best."

The pack leader hesitated. "I don't believe you," he said, but he didn't sound convincing.

"Whether you believe us or not, you're in big trouble. Listen."

A siren split the air.

"Department Seven!" The pack leader turned back to them with a snarl, taking a threatening step toward him. "The Juggawolves aren't going down for this."

"Don't be stupid," George said matter-of-factly. "You were seen transforming in a public location. Best thing you can do is turn yourselves in."

The man sneered. "We don't show throat to no government stooge!"

"Then you'll be charged with resisting arrest and threatening the police as well as public endangerment," Grant was matter of fact. "Playing into Wisner's hands."

The man hesitated, but the siren getting closer decided him. "What do I do?"

"Turn yourselves in," Ben said. "Tell them everything. That Wisner ordered you here, that he ordered you to tell him if the missing werewolf tried to use your pound—show him that he's not going to get away with manipulating your pack."

The man snarled. "No one tells us what to do." He shouldered his way past Ben and climbed into the driver's seat of the van. "You ain't heard the last of us," he yelled through the open window as the van made a U-turn and careened wildly down the street.

"Back!" Aki darted across the road. "You would not believe the wait—" He came to a halt, noticing the torn clothing and vines littering the street. "What the hell did I miss?"

Ben fought the urge to laugh. "That is a very good question."

Chapter Eighteen

"I DON'T KNOW how Ben's done it, but the police are leaving." Nate leaned out the window, watching the patrol car and the animal control vehicle go down the street.

"Probably unleashed his personality on them." Aki sat on the sofa of their apartment's living room, drumming his heels against the floor. "It's going to be our turn next."

Nate frowned at him. "That's not a bad thing. Ben's got a much better idea of what to do in this kind of situation than any of us."

"And if he doesn't, I'm sure the hunter with him has a few ideas." Aki scowled at the door. "We're not turning Grant over to them."

Nate raised an eyebrow. This was an abrupt reversal from Aki's attitude earlier—not that he wanted to point that out. "We don't know what George or Ben plan to do. And they did rescue me and Grant from the...Juggawolves."

Aki winced. "How do you manage to get yourself targeted by the single most embarrassing wolf pack in the entire city? I left you alone for what, five minutes!"

"You being there wouldn't have made any difference." Nate paused. "Was that one of your...moments?"

"An intuition?" Aki worried at his lip. "Maybe. At the time, I just thought that coffee sounded like a really good idea." He leaned over to the coffee table where he'd deposited the cups. "We're in luck," he reported, snagging one cup. "Still warm."

Nate swallowed. His stomach was jittery enough without the caffeine. He and Ben hadn't exchanged more than a dozen words downstairs before Ben had ordered them to get Grant upstairs and out of sight. That was enough. It felt like the clouds had parted, letting the sun shine down on Nate for the first time in days. And now, his stomach rolled in equal parts trepidation and excitement. "I'm not really thirsty."

"I am." The door opened and George sauntered into the apartment. "Mind if I?"

Nate gulped. "Help yourself." He hadn't expected George and Ben to arrive so soon.

Ben scanned the hallway before closing the door behind him. "We took the elevator to my apartment and then walked down the stairs. I'm pretty sure we weren't observed. You?"

Nate closed the window, pulling the curtain shut. "We took the stairs like you said." He tugged the hem of his T-shirt.

Aki stood, crossing his arms over his chest and staring at Ben. "Just so you know, Grant's here because we invited him. So don't think you can tell us what to do about him."

If Ben was surprised, he didn't show it. "Noted. Though I have to remind you that I am the landlord of this building and have a responsibility to protect the safety of all tenants." He leaned back against the door.

Aki's eyes flashed. "What about Nate's safety when you—"

"Not the time," Nate said loudly. Ben had stiffened and his skin drained of what little color he had. *He hasn't forgiven himself—or me. And he won't, either.* "We're here to talk about Grant, not me."

"And as the reason that you're all in a lot of trouble, I'm ready to answer any questions you have." Grant had opened the bathroom door without any of them noticing. He wore a T-shirt and jeans of Nate's and had a towel around his shoulders. He'd shaved his beard into order, revealing a lean face with sharp angles and an alert air. "I owe you an explanation."

Aki shot Ben and George a hostile look, as if he thought they might interrupt him. "We're very interested in what you have to say." He waved Grant toward one of the two armchairs.

"Fascinated." George dropped into the remaining armchair happily.

Ben shot a look at the empty space on the sofa beside Aki, and then at the bean bag, before deciding to remain standing. "I think we've worked out most of it. There's more to the story than the papers are telling, isn't there?" His tone was rueful, and Nate felt something inside him ease. The situation was tense, but Ben was taking it in stride. That had to be a good sign.

He sank onto the sofa. "Is Wisner really your stepdad?"

Grant's mouth twisted and he nodded. "I'm from California, originally. Dad was the leader of our pack in LA. It wasn't a good place to be a werewolf. There was a history of turf wars between packs, the competition for land mixed up with gang rivalries. Dad tried to leave it behind, and he moved Mom and me to Anaheim, only to get killed in a revenge attack. Wisner was the specialist in werewolves brought in to advise the Orange County police on how to handle the resulting fights. He spent a lot of time with Mom and eventually asked her to marry him. He promised her that we'd both be safe, and—well, you can't blame Mom for wanting that. He was a widower with three pups of his own, so she decided she could trust him. They were married within the year, and we moved to New Camden with him."

Grant looked down. His hands were long and lean like the rest of him, and they rested on his knees as he talked. "At first it wasn't so bad. Wisner was a lot stricter than my dad, and I quickly learned not to offer my opinion. But after I hit puberty, transformed for the first time…things just got worse and worse. Wisner's pack was bigger, and he was busier than ever. The decision-making process became more and more arbitrary, until in the end, he was the one making all the calls about pack business. If anyone questioned him, he took it as a personal attack."

"Has he been challenged?" Ben stepped forward to lean against the back of George's chair.

"He challenges others. Goads them into a position where they have no choice and then devastates them." Grant's fingers curled into fists. "He's been alpha for decades and is still a strong man. He's got more clout than any other wolf in this city, and he knows it. All the same, I think he's scared."

"Scared?" Nate knew he sounded startled, but he didn't care. "Wisner?"

Grant nodded. "He's getting older and he knows it. Once his strength goes, he won't be able to dominate the pack like he did, so he's obsessed with power. Securing more of it, proving his own… He's forced more and more packs to join us, painting a picture of a New Camden ruled by werewolves. At the same time, his rules started becoming increasingly strict. No one but his team was allowed to leave the housing compound without telling him where they're going. Single wolves needed permission to leave. I wasn't allowed after-school activities—and then I wasn't allowed to see friends. Disobedience resulted in physical punishment—"

"He beat you?" Aki sounded horrified.

Grant's tawny eyes rested on Aki. He'd been matter-of-fact throughout his recital, but Aki's reaction flustered him. "Not just me. It was accepted. Wolves—werewolves—pride ourselves on being closer to nature than others. That comes with an emphasis against suppressing instinctual reactions. It doesn't always work well."

Aki swallowed but didn't say anything. After a moment, Grant continued his explanation.

Nate slipped onto the sofa beside Aki, bumping him with his elbow so that he knew Nate was there. Aki didn't turn to look at him, but he leaned back so that Nate was supporting him.

Upset. And who can blame him? Grant's story raised a lot of questions.

"As I got older, I felt more and more like I was being targeted specifically. Things my stepbrothers did with impunity, I was punished for—and continually humiliated in front of the entire pack. The compound felt suffocating. I made plans to escape. Wisner paid my stepbrothers' entire way through law school, but when I said I wanted to go to college, it was as if I was challenging everything the pack stood for. I'd been expecting it, and I'd managed to secure a scholarship. I didn't need Wisner's permission to go to school. The scholarship included accommodation. I had moved out, made arrangements for the full moon. For three glorious weeks, I was free, living life on my own. Then the day before the full moon, Wisner's squad showed up to drag me back." Grant's hands flexed, wanting to curl into fists. "I was locked inside for a week. Made to show throat to the entire pack. You—don't know what that does to a wolf."

Grant didn't meet their eyes. His cheeks burned. "It's devastating. I was absolutely shattered. Wisner sent me back to school three weeks later, knowing I'd missed assignments and confident that he'd ruined my chances of a second scholarship. But I had friends. My roommate, Vazul, and my study partner, Charlotte. I was so low when I got back to school that I broke down and told them everything. And they wanted to help. While I concentrated on getting my grades back up, they researched my options. We found out that Wisner had warned all the hotels in New Camden against taking me."

Nate stared at Grant. He couldn't imagine that situation—finding every door shut before you reached it. *That's a lie. I don't have to imagine what it's like to be cut off without another word...* The difference was that Grant hadn't let it rattle him.

Nate looked up. George's gaze was fixed on Grant, but Ben—Nate felt a jolt of awareness shoot through his body—Ben was looking at him. His eyes widened as they met Nate's and he turned aside—but not before Nate had seen a flash of emotion in them.

It's not that Ben doesn't feel. It's that his feelings go deep. What was it that Ben hadn't wanted Nate to see? Nate let his gaze linger over Ben.

He leaned against the back of George's chair, his posture casual, but there was an inner tension that couldn't be suppressed. His long fingers were clasped together, as if it took effort to keep them from moving. Outwardly, his expression was calm, but Nate was pretty sure that Ben was furious—as furious as Aki, seated beside him. He placed a hand on Aki's shoulder.

"What did you do?" Aki asked.

Grant's eyes softened as they rested on him before quickly darting away. "For a long time, there wasn't much we could do. Asking about the hotels brought Char and Vaz to Wisner's knowledge. He had us watched and then lodged trumped up charges against them with Department Seven." For the first time, Grant smiled. "That was supposed to scare them off. Not bring us together. And it introduced me to the first non-pack werewolf I'd spoken to in years."

"Kenzies." Nate grinned. "She's great."

Grant's gaze alighted on him and he smiled faintly. "We didn't see eye to eye on everything. And that in itself was a revelation. In Wisner's pack, the single males were kept apart from the women and me—well I was more isolated than anyone else, being on the lowest rung of the pack hierarchy. I haven't talked to my mom in over a year, but I know that the restrictions on what they can do are even tougher. Mom was an interior designer in California, but she had to give that up when we moved here. Kenzies had a career outside her pack, and she worked alongside nonwolves. And she told me how she'd emancipated herself from her birth pack and joined her current one. That got me thinking I could do the same." Grant winced, pausing to run his hand through his hair. "I don't know how he found out about it, but he knew that I was planning to file for independence as soon as I had a suitable place to spend the full moon. I came home from lectures one day, and the compound was shut against me. I thought I'd just been forgotten at first, so I went to Vazul's to crash. And he told me that Department Seven had already been by to ask if he knew where I was, that Wisner had launched a runaway charge."

"What a dick." George leaned back.

Grant was startled into laughter. "Yeah. We didn't have time to plan or to find a place—everyone in the city was looking for me. Luckily, Vazul and Charlotte had been working on something."

"The dog collar!" Nate straightened. "Those runes—"

"Were a transformation spell," Ben finished. "No wonder you didn't want us looking closely at them."

Grant squirmed. "The city was looking for a wolf. Not a stray dog. And if the magic was inherent in the object, it would be harder to detect. I smelled different as a dog to a human or a wolf, so it seemed foolproof."

"You've spent the last three weeks living as a dog?" George shook her head. "Seriously?"

"I didn't have a choice. Wisner had gone to the pounds directly, and I knew that he would continue to watch Char and Vazul. I didn't want to risk bringing anyone else into it. I was afraid of what Wisner might do."

"So that had occurred to you." Aki folded his arms.

Grant winced. "Yeah. I should have kept my distance, but...weeks without talking to anyone had taken a toll on me. I was lonely, and you and Nate... I guess I felt drawn to you."

"Wolves may be social creatures, but that doesn't give you the right to take advantage of Nate and Aki's hospitality on false pretenses." Ben's voice was stern. As unhappy about this as Aki was?

Still looking out for me. Nate fumbled for words to let Ben know that it was cool, that he and Aki could handle themselves.

"I know." Grant's admission took him by surprise. There was a note of sorrow in his voice, but his expression was clear as he turned to face his inadvertent hosts. "I'm not proud of my behavior. I told myself that if I thought I'd get you in trouble, I'd leave—but then I heard you talking about the attack at the club you work at. You were already involved. I was horrified. In that short time, I'd—well, I'd come to think of you as friends." Grant dropped his gaze. "I told myself I was staying to keep an eye on the two of you, but if I'm honest, I think—I just wasn't strong enough to make myself leave. I—" His eyes flickered up to rest on Aki and then immediately looked away. "Well, that's my explanation, such as it is. I know it doesn't excuse my actions. I'll leave—"

Nate felt Aki's body tense beside him. "Leave?" Aki's mouth snapped shut, and he shrugged as everyone looked at him. "Where would you go?"

"Department Seven." Grant glanced around the room. "Charlotte got me the paperwork for my application for independence. I've got everything except for the secure location for the full moon. But Department Seven has cells. If I time it right, Wisner won't have time to drag me out of there and the courts will count it."

"Department Seven's not got a lot of power where Wisner is concerned." Aki shot Nate a look. "At Century, remember? The wolf didn't even get charged."

"It's a risk I have to take," Grant said. "The full moon's almost here. I have no other options, not unless I want to risk transforming in an insecure place—and that would be a disaster. Even in the worst case scenario, if Wisner takes me back to the compound before the full moon, my paperwork will be in as proof I wanted to do this legally, so Char and Vaz can continue the fight on my behalf."

While Wisner put his stepson through another round of punishment? Nate felt sick. They couldn't let that happen. "You just need a secure place to wait out the full moon, and you're legal?"

"Essentially. It's a bit more complicated than that." Grant scratched his neck.

Nate stood. "Aki, can I have a word?"

AKI FOLLOWED NATE into his room without a word. He waited until Nate shut the door behind them to speak. "You want to let Grant crash here for the full moon."

"It's just one night."

"And one werewolf. It's not going to be like taking care of the dog. Werewolves go nuts at the full moon. It'll make what happened with those clowns outside look like obedience training."

"I know. But I can handle a wolf—and Grant—well, the guy needs a break."

Aki sucked in a breath. "And you really think we should give it to him?"

Nate sat down on the edge of the bed. "I've made a lot of dumb decisions. Maybe I don't condone what Grant did, but I can understand it. Not that I'm saying it's okay for anyone to hurt you or that you shouldn't be mad—"

Aki smiled faintly. "I liked him. Really, really liked him. Should have known the situation was too good to be true."

Nate patted his shoulder. "Nobody's perfect. Grant can't help being a werewolf."

"Yeah, but—I feel like I'm setting myself up for a fall." Aki hunched his shoulders, looking at his knees. He kicked the side of the bed with his heel. "He's still—he's trying not to say anything, but he's still interested in me, Nate. I can tell. And I don't know how I feel about that. I'm afraid that—the more time I spend with him, the more I'm going to want to forgive him."

"And that's a bad thing?"

"Yeah." Aki snorted. "I do not want to end up making your level of bad decisions."

"No fear of that."

Nate's head whipped up. "Ben!"

To his dismay, Ben was shutting Nate's bedroom door behind him. "Nate's logic is unique. And even if it wasn't, your ability should be able to counter it."

"Do you mind?" Aki glared at him. "This is a private conversation between myself and Nate."

"I don't want to interrupt," Ben said. "But there's some information that I thought you should know." He leaned back against the door. "To provide a safe place for a werewolf to be contained during the full moon, the room has to satisfy a Department Seven or Registry agent that certain safety conditions are met."

Aki gripped the edge of the bed. "Such as?"

"A secure door, ideally of steel or some other metal, that locks from the outside. A room without windows, or else a window so small that the wolf could not leap from it."

Nate's heart sank. "We can't organize a door like that in a day—and both our rooms have windows."

Aki's shoulders sank in defeat. "My room's six stories up. So what if there's a window? If he jumped from that, he'd die. No way he'd endanger anyone but himself."

"But it wouldn't satisfy the Registry, and if he doesn't do that, Grant's proved nothing." Ben's tone was matter-of-fact, but Nate thought there was something behind it. Gone was the hesitation of earlier. Instead of fidgeting, Ben's hands rested by his side. His eyes dwelled with concealed sympathy on Aki.

"You've got a plan."

Ben glanced at Nate, clearly startled. After a moment, he smiled, ruefully. "I do." He turned back to Aki. "My father was a senior ARX employee, who worked closely with ARX's inner circle of night-investigators."

"Vampires," Nate translated.

Again, Ben shot him a look. "He converted the walk-in closet in the spare bedroom to a secure room where a vampire could wait out the day in safety. There are no windows, and the door is reinforced with steel."

Nate stood. "You're kidding. How did I not know about it?"

"Normal people don't outfit their apartments with rooms designed for vampires." Ben ran his hand through his short hair and pulled a wry face. "I was trying to impress you with my ordinariness—" Aki smothered a laugh. Ben ducked his head. "I didn't realize what a losing battle that was."

Nate glared at his friend. "Have you told Grant about this room?"

Ben shook his head. "I'm making the offer to you. You know him better than I do, and it's your call." He hesitated. "There's something else you should know."

"We're all ears." Aki waited.

This time, Ben frowned at him. "It's personal to Nate," he said.

Aki made no attempt to move. "You barged in here on a conversation that was personal to me and Nate."

"Don't be like that." Nate scratched the back of his neck. He could feel Aki's eyes boring into him. "Whatever you have to say, you can tell both of us. Aki's going to hear about it later anyway."

Ben hesitated. "All right. You know Wisner's a councilor. He's also New Camden's head of security. His brainchild is the Final Register, the solution to all of New Camden's supernatural problems. The idea is that in a situation like the necromancer, his name could be entered on the Final Register, and from then on, he exists only to himself. He can't interact with or harm anyone else, meaning he is no longer a threat to anyone. The problem is that for the Final Register to be a successful deterrent, it has to be seen in action. So Wisner's on the hunt for a suitable candidate." Ben's eyes fixed on Nate.

Nate felt the gaze like a weight pressing down on him. "You're telling me that could be me? I haven't done anything."

"If you help Grant, you'll be aiding an illegal supernatural," Ben warned. "Yes, I know how unfair that is—but that is how Wisner will argue it. And you're already a Class Three Unknown, with involvement in two Department Seven investigations. Wisner can use that against you—and get you put on his Final Register."

Nate swallowed. He felt the echo of his premonition again. *Ben's not here. He's not anywhere. You'll never see him again.* "How do you know this?"

Ben's mouth was thin. "The work I've been doing on my own application. Let's just say that Wisner is very adept at working the Registry."

"So all the problems you've been having—"

"We've got bigger issues here than Ben's questionable humanity." Aki said abruptly. "You're basically saying that if we choose to help Grant, we could be in major trouble."

Ben nodded. "I had to make sure you were aware of the risk."

"It's a risk I'm willing to take," Nate said. "We go with your decision, Aki."

"You're sure? I mean—" Aki rubbed his arm. "Worst that could happen to me is that I lose my fortune-telling license. You—Class Three Unknown already sucks. This Final Register sounds serious."

Ben continued to watch him. "You should think carefully about this."

"I already have." Nate drew a deep breath. "Helping people—it's really important to me. I've ignored it for too long. I'm not going to ignore it any more. And Grant—if we help him stand up to his stepdad, we weaken Wisner's hold on New Camden. That's good for everyone." He raised his eyes to Ben's. "You're not going to talk me out of this."

Instead of the frown he was expecting, Ben smiled. "I don't want to. I just wanted to make sure you had all the facts."

Nate felt the pressure in his chest ease. "Really?"

Ben nodded. "I think you're right about Grant—and Wisner. Me..." He looked down abruptly. "I was so focused on proving my humanity that I ignored how much I enjoyed supernatural investigations. While George and I were investigating Grant's disappearance, I felt alive—for the first time since we...parted." He drew a quick breath. "I was trying to live safely, isolating myself from any danger. But you—you remind me that being human is about caring for others and that means taking risks. Whatever you decide, you have my support."

Nate felt his cheeks heat. He looked down, trying to keep his broad smile off his face, but knew he was unsuccessful. *He means that?* No, he knew Ben too well to think he'd make a statement like that without meaning it. "Sounds like we're in agreement. Aki?"

"As if I'm really going to be the one to rain on this parade." Aki slid off the bed. "I'll let Grant know the good news." At the doorway, he turned around, waving a finger at both of them. "Just so you know, this had better be for keeps. I cannot deal with this constant roller-coaster ride of making up and breaking up."

"Aki—" Nate was too late. Aki was out the door before he could reach him. Nate turned to Ben. "Sorry about that. I know there's no way..." He stopped.

Ben's smile was sad. "That's my line. I mean, after what happened, it seems ludicrous to pretend that we could go back to how we were."

"That's not happening," Nate agreed. "But that's because I've changed. Not my feelings—me." He took a deep breath. "I thought I knew what being strong was. Turns out, I was playing a part. Trying to impress you—by ignoring that I need to care for people. I got carried away—but that's not going to happen again."

Ben smiled thinly. "I discovered that holding myself apart from the supernatural didn't help me find out who I was. I still don't know who I am—but I know that I don't want to be someone who stands on the sidelines while his friends risk everything to help those around them." He took a deep breath. "You and me—we complement each other in weird ways. I can't accidentally kill you if I lose control of the vampire. And the vampire—there's no interest in feeding from people at all now."

Nate forced himself to breathe. He wasn't sure where Ben was going with this. "You can't be sure that will last."

"No," Ben agreed. "But I'm starting to wonder if what I thought was a weakness is actually a strength." He shook his head. "I'm going about this all wrong. What I want to say is that you've got really good instincts for helping people. I've got the knowledge of the supernatural. It strikes me that we could do a lot of good together. We could make New Camden safer and fairer for supernaturals."

It was more than he'd ever expected. More than Nate knew he had any right to hope for. But he stepped forward, standing right in front of Ben. "And us?"

Ben colored. "I'm not stupid enough to think there could be an us. I know what I did was unforgivable—"

"You've been fighting the vampire in secret for a really long time," Nate said. "A constant fight like that, you can't possibly hope to win. So it makes sense that when the vampire broke through, you didn't have the strength to resist him."

"Nate—"

"Let me finish." Nate put his hand on Ben's cheek, turning his face up so that Ben's eyes couldn't escape his. "We're stronger together. You keep me focused and put things in perspective. Me—if you leaned on me when you needed, maybe—"

"Maybe I can find the strength to contain the vampire?" Ben stared at Nate. "You can't possibly mean that." His eyes searched Nate's as if seeking confirmation of the doubt he knew must be there. And then he didn't see it.

"The worst has happened," Nate said. "And I'm still here. And I still have feelings for you. You?"

Ben leaned his head against Nate's chest. He breathed in deeply, his hands settling around Nate's waist. "I didn't think there was any chance you could feel anything for me but disgust, and I was too scared to see repulsion in your eyes. I still—you're still everything to me, Nate."

Nate ran his fingers through Ben's hair. "We have been through the worst. If we can survive that... What are you afraid of?"

Ben sighed. "When you put it like that—" He raised his face to Nate's, his eyes closed.

The kiss was hesitant, gentle. After the first meeting, Nate shut his eyes, content to let their bodies speak for them.

Ben was hesitant in a way that Nate found heartbreaking, but he seemed to draw strength from his explorations. He brushed his mouth against Nate's, as if expecting to be pushed away. It was Nate who deepened the kiss, keeping it gentle as he caught Ben's lip between his own and held it.

He could feel the tremor in Ben's breathing and extended his other arm around his body to pull him tight. He felt Ben tense, felt the exact moment he chose to surrender, felt his mouth part to draw Nate in.

Nate rested his forehead against Ben's, feeling a warmth he hadn't imagined he'd feel again. "I guess that settles that."

Ben snorted, but he smiled. "That settles that."

Nate knew they didn't have time to waste, but it was almost more than he could do to raise his head and drop his arms from Ben. "We'd better go."

Ben nodded. "We have a lot of work ahead of us." But as he turned toward the door, his hand sought Nate's automatically.

Nate swallowed. From Ben, that was a major admission of need. As they walked into the living room, Grant getting to his feet to greet them, Nate felt a renewed determination. Against all expectations, Ben had trusted him again—and he was not going to let him get hurt.

Chapter Nineteen

BEN MADE A slow, counterclockwise circuit of his apartment, scattering salt as he did. It was the final stage in a lengthy spell-casting. His shoulders ached from crouching to write runes in chalk on every possible entrance into the apartment, and he balanced a flaming candle in the hand holding the bag of salt. It was a precarious situation. His wrist hurt, but if he tried to adjust his grip, he risked burning himself. *Just one more room to go.* He pushed open the door to his father's study.

The bookcase stood open, revealing the concealed steel door and the room behind it. Aki and Nate were cleaning out the safe room.

"Go easy on the air freshener!" Nate stopped scrubbing the floor to try to wave away a vanilla-scented cloud. "Some of us have to breathe, you know."

"It's so musty." Aki frowned, looking around the enclosed space. "I'm sure that can't be healthy."

"There's a ventilator grid above your heads," Ben said. "I'll make sure to have the air circulating, so everything's fresh for Grant." He paused to remember where he was in the ritual and began his slow circle of the study.

Nate sat back on his heels to watch. "Better forget about vampires then, Aki. They all smell like that."

Aki frowned, reaching for a broom. "Has Hunter stayed here?"

"He has. As a matter of fact, the room was built for him." Ben caught the glance Aki sent him. "My father worked with him on a lot of investigations. They ended up using our apartment as a meeting point to review evidence."

"About Hunter," Aki said with a casualness that fooled no one. "You don't happen to know if he's single or anything, do you?"

"He's way out of your league." Nate stood, eying the finished floor with distinct satisfaction. "Forget about him. Grant cleaned up really nicely."

Ben glanced at Nate and then winced as wax dripped onto his wrist. He hastily righted the candle. *That's what I get for listening in! It's none of my business if Nate thinks Grant is attractive—*

Aki chewed his lip. "I guess."

"You were all about his good looks at first. What did you call him?" Nate took a step back as Aki used the broom to clear up the inevitable spiderwebs on the ceiling. "A chiseled god?"

"We've seen him pee, Nate. I mean, even leaving out everything else, that there is a potential deal breaker—"

Ben froze.

"He was a dog at the time."

"It still counts. Also, licking his own balls—"

The doorbell rang twice in rapid succession.

Thank god. Ben blew out the candle, putting the bag of salt down on his father's desk. "I'll get it."

The doorbell rang twice more as Ben made his way to it. He was not entirely surprised to open the door on Gunn, leaning against the bell. "What's the matter? Ran out of underlings to bully?"

Gunn bared his teeth in greeting. "We've had a very interesting report of your activity. What's this I hear about wild dogs fighting in the street outside your apartment?" His eyes raked over the apartment, lingering on George and the collection of knives she was polishing at the table, before looking at the fresh rune marks and scattered salt. "Smells of magic. You picked an interesting day to redo your runes."

Ben came to a quick decision. "You'd better come inside."

"Don't mind if I do." Gunn swaggered through the door. "What links this sudden surge of activity with a very interesting altercation between what sounds to me like a wolf pack known to the authorities, and a complaint by Councilor Wisner of a man seeking entrance to his compound?"

"Don't act like you don't know." Ben folded his arms. "I said I'd find the missing wolf—and I have."

"What?" Nate's exclamation was startled. "Were you—"

"Planning to turn Grant over to the authorities this entire time?" Aki's hands were formed into fists and he took a step toward Ben. "I can't believe you—"

"Calm down." Grant's barked order sent silence over the entire apartment. Aki slowed to a halt, and even Gunn paused to size him up. "Let Ben speak. We haven't heard him out yet."

Deep within, the vampire snarled. *The pup thinks he can give orders in my own apartment? He will find out how mistaken he is!*

Aware of the vampire, Ben found it easier to separate its thoughts from his own. He took a moment to thrust back the instinctive need to assert himself. "I agreed to find the wolf. I never agreed to turn him over. As a matter of fact, I've invited Grant to stay here." Ben waited until Gunn's attention had returned to him. "According to the Auckland protocol, a werewolf has the right at any stage to request emancipation from his pack, providing that he can prove that he is of age and has the means to do so without endangering anyone. I can provide Grant with those means—"

"No can do, Benny. With the full moon so close and rumors of a fight between transformed wolves in a public place, the mayor's announced a state of emergency. The city wants this pup in custody."

"As soon as you arrest him, Wisner's going to take him back to the compound."

"Boo-hoo. You know better than to take me for some bleeding heart. This pup has been giving my entire department a headache for the last three weeks, and I've had his loathsome stepfather breathing down my neck the whole time. Even if I cared, what could I do?"

"Wisner's broken the law," Ben said. "He's launched a deliberate campaign of intimidation against New Camden's hotel owners, scaring them out of giving Grant shelter. That exceeds his authority both as councilor and pack leader."

"I'm not feeling it. He's already claimed special privileges in order to bring the pup to heel. Claims he has knowledge about Grant the rest of us don't."

"Withholding information from Department Seven," Ben said. "Deliberately undermining the department's authority in the process."

Gunn's eyes glittered. "What do you think will happen if I fail to show up with the pup? Especially once it's known I had him in my grasp. I'll be sacked instantly—and Kenzies will be out tonight for the full moon. There's no one to lead the department."

"Tell the council you're satisfied with Grant's arrangements for the full moon."

"I've got my paperwork here," Grant said. "All I'm lacking is the security check."

Gunn studied him a long moment. "Let's see it then." Grant held out the papers, and Gunn snatched them. He raised an eyebrow as he thumbed through them. "You've been sitting on this application awhile."

Grant held himself still with difficulty. His nostrils flared—evidently he was finding Gunn's pernicious odor a challenge. "It's kind of hard to file paperwork in a timely manner when your stepfather has wolves stationed outside the Registry office to stop you."

Gunn's eyes glittered. "That a fact?"

"You can verify it easily," Ben said. "I bet Wisner's sudden concern for the safety of the Registry dates from Grant's decision to go after independence."

Gunn shook his head. "If I'm going to stick my neck out for this pup, I want more. At the moment, it's just your word against his, kid. Wisner's got an entire city behind him."

"You know Wisner," Nate said. "You've got to know that there's been something underhanded about this entire thing. I was there at Department Seven. I saw the way he refused to answer questions or even give you the basic information to do your job."

"We don't suspect Wisner's trying to discredit your department," George spoke for the first time. "We know he wants to destroy it. Replace it with his own werewolves obedient to him."

Gunn tilted his head as he weighed George. "That's a very serious allegation to make."

"So is kidnapping." George glanced at Ben.

He nodded. There was nothing to lose now by telling Gunn the entire story. "George and I teamed up to investigate the missing werewolf. We found a lot more than we were expecting."

George took over the story, detailing her visit to the pound and subsequent imprisonment. "And before you ask, no, I was not acting threatening in any way. I just asked the guy if anyone matching Grant's description had asked about spending the full moon there, and he said, possibly. Did I want to come out to the kennel to check?"

"And locked you in?" Gunn's eyes narrowed. "How does this tie to Wisner?"

George grinned at him. "Guess who the owner of the kennel called to report once I was safely locked up? And guess who came to see who'd been snooping around the pounds in person?"

"Wisner?"

"And two of his posse. Ben can confirm—he arrived shortly before they did to let me out."

Ben was aware that Nate was staring at him. He winced, shooting Nate an apologetic look. *I was going to tell you!* "We hid and were able to overhear their conversation. Wisner identified my scent and sent the kennel owner and his pack off to threaten me."

"The cause of the disturbance downstairs?" Gunn's eyes narrowed. "Hold it right there. I'm calling Kenzies up to hear this."

Gunn dragged each of them in turn into the kitchen to give their version of the story, leaving his subordinate in the room to make sure they weren't collaborating.

Ben watched the clock, trying to stay as still as possible. *Time is wasting. We need to get on with our preparations.* He was conscious that the passing time was only one cause for his unease. Grant prowled the room, obviously on edge. He tried to keep as far as possible from the other wolf. For her part, Kenzies sat on Ben's sofa, discussing the difficulties of finding heavy-duty boots in sizes for women with George, with an appearance of placid calm, but every time Grant whirled around, she tensed, her eyes following him across the apartment.

Nate bent over the back of Ben's chair to talk to him. "Were you going to tell me about Wisner threatening you?"

"It wasn't a secret. I told you part of it when we faced off with the Juggawolves." It was a relief to focus on Nate rather than the tense atmosphere of the room. "I'm certain that when the wolves arrived here, it was me they were expecting to find, not Grant." He bit his lip. "I was rather surprised about that myself."

Nate ducked his head. "We didn't know he was the wolf when we adopted him. We thought he was a stray dog. We only worked it out last night."

"And what happened when you did work it out?"

Nate winced. "We were pretty upset. Aki, especially. We threw him out. In the morning—I guess we had second thoughts. After all, we've all seen how Wisner treats people."

"He doesn't deserve to be pack leader." Kenzies lip curled. "Leading by fear is a fast way to create a monster."

"If Wisner succeeds, he's going to put pressure on every wolf in the city to join him or face supernatural restrictions," Grant said. "There's no way—"

"I'll be allowed to keep working at Department Seven?" Kenzies nodded. "I've got no illusions about what Wisner has planned. But I have a responsibility to keep the city safe. As long as I've got this job, that's what I'm going to do."

Ben considered Kenzies. The woman was no fool. "Grant's clearly no threat. You don't really believe you have to protect the city against him, do you?"

Kenzies snorted. "It's less Grant, more the situation. The city's at powder keg levels of tension. If that goes off—you saw the fallout of the necromancer attacks. The city's vampire population saw a chance to cut loose and did."

"It's not Grant you're afraid of, but Wisner's wolves?" Nate straightened.

"And Wisner's pull. He's got a lot of influence with the mayor." Kenzies's eyes hardened. "He's been gunning for Department Seven for a while now. If he decides to come down on us over this—well, it might not just be me losing my job."

Ben felt Nate tense behind him. He squeezed his hand. "You okay?"

Nate took the invitation to lean in. "I remember New Camden during the necromancer attacks. It looked like a cyclone had hit it. Everyone was afraid—and I was responsible. I don't—we can't let that happen again."

The kitchen door slammed open, making everyone flinch. Gunn sauntered out, hands in his pockets. He was followed by Aki, the last to be interviewed. "Stories check out. Kenzies?"

Kenzies stood. "Let's see your safe room."

Kenzies was thorough. She tested the door from the inside and out. "Room meets standard," she said crisply. "If you had more time, I'd get the walls padded and soundproofed. Makes such a difference."

Gunn scrawled his untidy signature on Grant's paperwork. "We had to go by the Registry anyway. We can file this at the same time."

Ben breathed out. If anyone was waiting to block Grant's application, they wouldn't be expecting Gunn to have it.

"All my decades of hard work for this city and here I am, reduced to playing filing clerk for a rogue werewolf and Benny of all people." Gunn snarled half-heartedly.

Ben raised an eyebrow. "You know we're grateful. But you don't want to hear us say so."

"God, no." Gunn shuddered. "Keep your gratitude firmly to yourselves."

"What my superior officer is trying to say," Kenzies said, "is that once we file these, Wisner's going to know where you are. He's going to come down on you like a ton of bricks—and there may be little we can do to help."

Gunn gave her a look of dislike. "You take this on your own risk."

"We understand," Grant said. "And we're prepared to take the consequences."

"Your funeral." Gunn smiled. "Isn't that a nice thought?"

THE KNOCK AT the door was authoritative and demanding. Ben halted, in the midst of an incantation. *Far too soon.*

He glanced up, meeting the worried glances of Charlotte and Vazul. Grant had phoned his friends to let them know what had happened and warned them of possible consequences from Wisner's pack, and they'd come over to help get the apartment prepared for a werewolf attack. "Wisner."

Charlotte glanced at the clock. "We don't have to let him in, do we?"

"If we refuse, he might be able to lodge a claim of obstruction." Vazul had a thick volume of the laws regarding supernaturals in front of him. "At this exact moment, he is still Grant's alpha."

The knock repeated. It was every bit as demanding.

"Better get this over with." Ben set down his candle carefully and made his way to the door.

Wisner stood there, fully dressed in a crisp business suit. The two men with him were similarly attired, and shared their father's blond hair and tawny eyes. Clearly his sons.

Ben, braced for one wolf, found it took an effort to bear the stares of all three. "Can I help you?"

The younger of the three men snarled. "Don't act like you don't know why we're here."

"Ronald," Wisner said. There was only a faint hint of censure in his tone, but the wolf flushed and stepped back. Wisner didn't take his eyes off Ben. "Would this be your apartment? That's not terribly wise. Harboring a known fugitive is not likely to impress the committee."

"On the contrary," Ben said. "I'm helping a fellow citizen pursue legal means of emancipation—legal means that you are obstructing." It took an effort to hold his ground as an expression of fury flickered over Wisner's face. *The wolf is close to the surface.* The full moon was only hours away. Civilized Councilor Wisner was rapidly becoming even more dangerous.

"You have no idea what you're doing," Wisner ground out. "And frankly, I don't care to enlighten you. I'm here to see my stepson."

"He doesn't want to see you." Charlotte looked as startled by her outburst as everyone else. She yelped as Wisner transferred his venomous gaze to her.

His angry son snarled. "Don't disrespect the pack leader, you—"

Vazul gathered his breath. "With all due respect, Wisner is not our pack leader."

"I'm a civilian," Ben stated firmly. "This is my private property. I'm entirely within my rights to refuse entry. If you attempt to remove Grant against his will, you'll be trespassing—"

"Grant!" Wisner barked, drowning out Ben's words. "Show yourself!"

"Here."

Ben's heart sank. He turned to see Grant, Aki looking on anxiously behind him, in the study doorway.

But while everyone else looked dismayed, Grant looked determined. "I know why you're here, and it's not going to work. I'm not coming back."

"My dear boy. You're not yourself—you've allowed this last month to blow everything out of proportion. Consider your actions." Wisner's voice took on an overly soothing tone. "You've cut yourself off from the pack who raised you, and taken up with strangers—none of whom have any experience in meeting a full moon. I know we don't always see eye to eye, but I have your best interests at heart. Believe me, wolves need wolves—especially at the full moon. You don't want to risk hurting someone—or losing your mind."

"Mind?" Aki repeated. "What do you mean—"

Wisner's expression took on concern. "Grant didn't tell you? That was very remiss of him. It so happens that the full moon is an incredibly stressful time for a werewolf. At any other time of the month, the wolf is tempered by the human. However, on the night of the full moon, the change is irresistible and complete. There is no human remaining. We are wolf—all wolf. And wolves need the society of other wolves." He smiled, and there was a distinctly predator-like note to his smile. "It is only one night, but spending it in an unknown place, surrounded by unknown sounds and smells, is torture to the wolf. Without the presence of others of its kind, the wolf had been known to injure itself in its attempts to free itself, working itself up into a frenzy that leaves its human self fatally injured, or worse—their mind shattered and broken." Wisner spread his hands wide. "Grant will tell you I'm not exaggerating."

Grant narrowed his eyes. "There are cases on record of wolves not surviving the full moon alone."

Wisner looked from Ben to Charlotte and Vazul, his arms spread in an expansive gesture. "Why subject him to that risk? If you consider yourselves Grant's friends, then it is in your interests, as well as ours, that Grant return to his pack."

"No longer my pack," Grant said shortly. "Going back would mean surrounding myself with hostile influences. You—" He glanced to Aki standing behind him, then looked back at Charlotte and Vazul. "—you are my pack now."

He's not just saying that. Ben frowned. If Grant succeeded in freeing himself from his stepfather's control and set up a new pack, one that didn't discriminate against nonwolves...

"Them?" Ronald began to laugh. "Don't fool yourself. Do you know how many wolves we have? There's no way—"

Wisner held up a hand, silencing him. He didn't take his eyes off Grant. "You persist in this foolishness? Even knowing that you risk your very life?"

Grant glared back. "I know what I risk going back. And I consider my chances of survival better on the outside."

"You dare—" The son that had been silent up until then made a lunge for him, his teeth bared. As he barreled through the doorway, he collided with the runes. The barrier was invisible, but they all heard the impact.

"Mickey!" Wisner's snarl was vicious.

"Don't blame him," Ben said. "I told you that an attempt to take Grant from this apartment by force would be considered trespassing. My wards guard against that."

The look Wisner turned on him made Ben very glad that they'd just redone the wards. It was with a visible effort that the councilor regained control of himself, turning back to Grant. "Grant. Look me in the eyes. Tell me that this is truly your choice."

Grant took a step forward. He raised his gaze to his stepfather's. "You won't change my mind."

Wisner's mouth flickered into something that looked like victory. "You know I only want what is best for my pack."

It wasn't silent. As the moments stretched out, every movement seemed astonishingly loud. His hand locked around the door handle, Ben could only watch the contest of wills unfolding right before his nose. The atmosphere seemed to crackle with pressure. The inner vampire stirred, urging him to hiss and fight for his territory.

And if it's bad for me, it must be even worse for Grant. Ben couldn't raise his head to look at him. He had bowed his head, unable to resist the inevitable pressure, but he could see Grant's bare feet shift on the wooden living room floor. All Wisner's attention was focused on him, the wolf's natural power augmented by the presence of his own sons, both powerful wolves approaching their prime. Their combined weight was too much for Grant to resist indefinitely. He took a hesitant step toward the door—

Aki gasped. It was an involuntary sound that broke the spell. Grant's head jerked up and back to look at him, and Charlotte raised a hand to her temples. Vazul shook his head as though dazed, and Ben discovered he could move again. And Grant—

After a long look at Aki, Grant turned back to his stepfather. "I'm staying here."

Wisner ground his fists together. His fury was naked on his face for the first time. "Insolent pup! You will pay for your defiance!"

There's more than the full moon at play here. Ben looked around for something that might make a suitable weapon against a werewolf.

"Pay for my existence you mean." Anger flashed through Grant's eyes, and he faced his stepfather without fear. "You've begrudged me every moment of my life as a member of your pack, but you can't stand the thought of me being free. You want to contain me. But I'm not going to be a pawn in your power play. I'm my own wolf, Wisner. Get used to it."

Wisner strode angrily toward him, and Ben had a moment's panic. The man was larger than Grant and had all the cunning of an old wolf. But Wisner suddenly jerked away and stumbled, his hand coming up to his face. It took Aki's startled laugh for Ben to realize what had happened. Wisner had collided with the defensive barrier created by his wards.

Grant's hand on Ben's shoulder made him start. "As you can see, my security needs are met. My friends will not let me become a threat to the public."

Wisner growled, his eyes settling on Ben. "Think twice about where you put your faith. Not everyone you have trusted deserves it."

Ben folded his arms. The vampire surged within him. In his apartment, Ben had full rights—and the magic to back them up. "It's getting late, Councilor Wisner. I suggest you think about getting home yourselves. You don't want to risk getting caught out by the full moon."

Wisner leaned on his son's arm, getting himself back on his feet. "You're making a very big mistake." He was back on sure ground now, his eyes settling on Charlotte and Vazul, and frowning at Aki, before returning to Ben. "I came straight from a meeting of the City Council. A vote of no-confidence in Department Seven's ability to handle the situation was made and a state of emergency declared. You can expect no help from Gunn and his lackeys. Your only option is to surrender Grant to me now, before you find yourselves in serious trouble."

"You've tried intimidating us before," Vazul said, his voice bored. "You're wasting your time. You know what our answer will be."

"You are all fools," Wisner said. "I look forward to the moment that you realize just what a mistake you've made." He turned aside, his sons immediately falling into formation behind him. "Until tonight, Grant."

Ben shut the door with more force than he'd intended. The noise made him wince. He turned back to his friends. "So—"

"Tonight?" Aki said at once. "But he'll be a werewolf tonight. There's no way he can leave his safe room—is there?"

"And without Department Seven, who is going to stop him?" Grant turned to Aki. "I told you to stay out of sight with the others. Why didn't you listen?"

Aki folded his arms. "You can't tell me what to do."

"It's for your own good! My stepdad's got something planned. I'm sure he has." Grant looked around the room. "You're all putting yourselves at risk for me," he said. "I'm grateful—but I also don't want you guys to endanger yourselves for me. If you need to get out of here. I won't hold it against you—"

Vazul snorted. "Grant, we've been waiting for this moment."

Charlotte nodded, tucking her hair out of her face. "I'm the last to condone violence. My coven's practice specifically prohibits it. But this— A stand has to be made. For all of us."

Grant was unable to meet their eyes. "You don't know what this means—"

A tug at Ben's elbow brought his attention to Aki standing beside him. Aki glared at him. "Your wards able to stand up against a pack of werewolves?"

Ben nodded. "Wisner doesn't have the legal right to make Grant leave, and magically it's my apartment, and my wards. He can't break them through sheer force."

Aki hesitated, watching Grant hug Charlotte. His hands fluttered to a halt, curling into fists. "You're sure about that?"

Aki had no problems letting Ben know that he was unimpressed or angry, but Ben couldn't remember seeing Aki uncertain before. "What's the problem?"

"I hate to say it," Aki said. "But I've got a really bad feeling about your wards."

"Can you—" Ben's phone rang. He tugged it out of his pocket, intending to turn it off, when the name on the caller display stopped him. *Diya?* "One moment." He walked into the kitchen. "This is a really bad time, Diya."

"You're telling me. What on earth did you think you were doing—sheltering a known fugitive?"

Ben winced. He couldn't blame Diya for being upset. "Grant's a great guy and thoroughly undeserving of the grudge that Wisner has against him. And once he passes the full moon and is able to appear in public without Wisner being legally allowed to drag him back to the pack compound, he'll be able to give his side of the story. Just wait until tomorrow—"

"We don't have until tomorrow. Wisner's called a hearing on your status for right now."

The kitchen swayed around him. Ben slid into the nearest kitchen chair.

"Ben? Speak to me—this is too important to hang up on! Ben!"

"I'm here." Ben shut his eyes. He felt sick. His stomach twisted and his skin felt clammy. His mind replayed Wisner's satisfaction, his thinly veiled threats making a horrible kind of sense. "This is his revenge."

"There's still time to stop it. He has to wait for the mayor and Hartman to arrive. I'm on my way to pick you up now. Wisner's not expecting you to make it here in time to defend yourself. There's still a chance that we can win this."

The kitchen door opened. Nate looked in on him, his expression creased with concern as he took in Ben. He put the spider fern he was holding down on the kitchen table, pulling the door shut behind him.

If I leave—they'll be on their own against Wisner. Ben swallowed. "What if I don't show up?"

"Then you'll be sentenced in absentia. Wisner will be able to paint your no-show as a further sign of contempt—"

"Okay. I'll come." Ben ended the call.

"Going somewhere?" Nate's voice was incredulous. "Now? From what Aki says, it was only your wards keeping Wisner from dragging Grant out of the apartment."

Ben winced. "I—have to go. It's the hearing for my application."

"Now? During a state of emergency?" There was a dawning comprehension in Nate's eyes. "This isn't any ordinary hearing is it?"

"I didn't want to tell you, but things are really serious. Wisner's involved and he's using me helping Grant as proof that I'm dangerous. If I don't show up for this hearing, well—he can pretty much do what he likes and I can't stop him."

"Shit." Nate's hand rested on Ben's shoulder. "You should have said. If I'd known, there's no way—"

Nate's hand felt warm, despite the clamminess of Ben's skin. He put his hand over it, discovering that its warmth eased something of the sick feeling he felt. "And that's precisely why I didn't tell you. I'm not letting Wisner push me around—and neither should Grant."

"It'd be like him to have something dirty planned." Nate picked up his jacket. "I'm coming with you—"

Ben took a deep breath. "No. You're not." He looked up, meeting the hurt and worry in Nate's eyes. "Grant needs you here. Wisner doesn't know about you—he doesn't know what you're capable of, so he doesn't have a plan for you. You can help Grant—and Grant's really going to need your help."

Nate's shoulders sagged. "And you don't. Is that it?"

Ben didn't think he'd ever felt more for Nate than that moment. "There's nothing I want more than to take you up on your offer. Trust me. But Grant needs you more." He stroked Nate's arm, his fingers lingering over Nate's.

Nate turned his hand up, capturing Ben's fingers within his own. He looked at Ben, his hazel eyes capturing Ben's gaze. "You promise me you're not just saying that—staying here is truly what you want me to do?"

Ben nodded. "You—you said you pushed yourself, trying to prove yourself to me. Now it's my turn to show you what I'm capable of." A car's horn sounded in the street below. "That's probably my ride."

Nate didn't let go of his hands. "You remember my premonition. The feeling I had that I wasn't going to see you again. It's back. And it's really strong. Ben—" Nate's arms folded around him and he was pulled into a hug. "We only just put things right between us."

Ben swallowed. He shut his eyes, sealing in his mind how Nate smelled, the feeling of his chest moving against Ben's. "I still have to go."

Nate's fingers tightened around him. "Even if it means you might not come back?"

"If I go, I have a chance. If I stay, I have none." Ben took a deep breath. "My case is—complicated. There's a good chance that I'm not going to win this. And if that happens, I need someone on the outside to fight for me." He placed his hand on Nate's cheek. "I need you, Nate."

Nate let go of him. "There's more to this than you've told me."

Ben nodded. "My case worker is Diya Patel. If I'm not back by tonight, look her up. She'll explain everything."

He stepped out into the living room. Grant looked up, an obvious question in his eyes, and George and Charlotte paused their discussion of a spell. "You're going out? Now?"

"I don't have a choice," Ben said. "Wisner's pulling strings at the Registry. I have to defend my classification." He looked around at his companions. "There's the possibility that he's going to try something similar with the rest of you. Be ready for anything."

"We'll come with you—" Grant started.

"You're safe only so long as you're within my apartment," Ben said. "You're staying put, Grant." He looked at Nate. "I'm trusting you to hold the fort here."

Nate nodded. He didn't look happy, but the gaze that met Ben's was determined. "You can count on me."

Ben felt some pressure in his chest ease. "I do." It was the truth.

"YOU'RE FAR TOO calm." Diya gripped the steering wheel, glaring at the red light in front of them. "You must grasp the seriousness of the situation."

"I do. If we can't convince Wisner's committee, I'm looking at the Final Register." Ben rested his hands on his lap. "We've done everything we can to prepare."

The light changed, and Diya's car surged forward. "I really don't like this situation. Calling the case so suddenly—he's got something up his sleeve."

"Hoping that we wouldn't have time to complete our documentation," Ben said. "He doesn't realize how efficient you are."

Diya winced. "Even with Department Seven's clearance, I'm worried. Here." She pulled up outside the Registry. "You go straight in. I'll park and join you."

The men on guard outside the Registry straightened as Ben approached, snarling as they recognized him. "You—"

"Have an appointment." Ben smiled tightly. "I believe Councilor Wisner is expecting me." He was past them and down the corridor before they could stop him.

The first man made a grab after him, but his companion stopped him. "So what if he goes in? It's not going to help his case any."

Probably accurate. Ben took a deep breath and retraced his steps to the hearing room. *Still, I can't think like that. If I give up, then there is nothing stopping Wisner from succeeding.*

The wooden doors to the hearing room swung open silently at Ben's touch. He stepped into the room to find Wisner holding forth to the mayor.

"Understand that he failed to meet with his appointed counselor, in addition to an appointment made by his own advocate with a legal representative. In those circumstances, I don't think we can count on Hawick showing himself. In fact, given his obvious disrespect toward authority, I think we should continue without any further delay—"

"I'm here," Ben announced. "I'm sorry if I'm late. I heard about the change in my hearing time from my advocate. If there was a message sent to me, I didn't get it."

Wisner's eyes flashed, but he didn't comment.

The mayor looked up sharply. "Take the stand, Hawick. Wait till you're addressed." She looked to the empty seat to her side. "Hartman's not here."

"My aide is trying to reach him. I've also had a car sent to his residence and one to his office. We'll find him. In the meantime, we can't allow legalities to delay us. The city's security is at stake, your honor. With Department Seven gone, we need to make a strong statement to supernatural miscreants. We need to show them that we will not allow them to hold the safety of our citizens hostage to their own whims."

Ben laid his palms against the wooden lectern. The smooth polished wood, steady beneath his skin, made him think of Nate's strength. "I protest. I have done my best to provide the documentation the Committee requested of me. Getting declared safe by ARX is hardly threatening anyone—"

"ARX cleared you?" The mayor looked up sharply.

Ben held up his folder of papers. "I've also got my Department Seven report and a psychiatric assessment."

"Bring me that." The mayor waited as one of the Registry staff, another wolf, snatched the folder from Ben and, after a glance at Wisner, placed it before her. She thumbed through the papers, frowning. "Hawick's telling the truth. ARX seems to have done a very thorough investigation—"

"Of course ARX would clear him. He has history with ARX—" Wisner's growl was checked by the glance the mayor gave him.

"ARX is the last organization to let personal bias sway their decisions," Ben said quickly. "And they're at pains to disassociate themselves from anything to do with the necromancer incident. If there was even the slightest hint of something untoward in my interview and tests, they'd have taken full advantage of it to distance themselves from me. The fact that they haven't—"

"Is significant." The mayor leaned back. "Why did you miss these appointments?"

"I was sick."

"Can you prove that?"

Ben winced. "No."

Wisner grinned in triumph, before bending to the mayor, adopting a conversational tone. "Even if we give Hawick the benefit of the doubt, you can't get around the fact that he is hiding a known fugitive in his apartment. I visited him myself. I saw the rogue werewolf there in his living room. And I have witnesses to prove it."

The mayor's head jerked up. "The rogue werewolf?"

Ben gripped the edge of the lectern. "As far as I'm aware, there are no criminal charges laid against Grant. He is within his rights to leave his pack—a fact that his stepfather seems very anxious to overlook."

The mayor looked at Wisner. "You failed to mention that the missing werewolf is your stepson."

"I treat him as I treat any other member of the pack. Our familial status doesn't earn him any special treatment." Wisner tugged at his collar. "I saw no reason that the investigation should be hampered by any possible concerns about loyalty to myself."

"So the fact that Grant is also an alpha wolf and becoming increasingly more confident, while you know yourself to be declining in power, has nothing to do with your persecution of him?"

Wisner snarled. "Silence!"

"I give the orders." The mayor's voice rang out sharply. "Councilor, get control of yourself."

For a moment, Ben thought Wisner was too far gone to obey. His face was flushed with anger and he stared at Ben, his fury naked in his eyes. With an effort, he contorted his face into a smile and sat down.

The mayor turned back to Ben. "Continue, Mr. Hawick."

Ben took a deep breath. "This is Grant's second attempt to leave his pack. The first time, he was dragged back to Wisner's compound from his new residence and imprisoned for weeks. This time, he has been driven into hiding by an organized campaign by Wisner's pack, ensuring that no hotel or pound would offer him shelter. Grant was prevented from lodging his appeal for independence by the wolves stationed around the Registry—wolves loyal to his stepfather and who had a vested interest in having him recaptured. He's committed no crime and has made every effort to legally free himself from his pack—all of which is his right to do."

Wisner smirked. "Do you have any proof to back up these outrageous claims?"

"Grant's application was filed with the Registry," Ben said.

"An application filed after he was discovered is hardly proof—"

"Both of them." Ben continued. "Grant's application was lodged last year at the start of the university year. That's how you found out about his plans, wasn't it, Councilor? Through your position on this board."

The mayor raised her head. "You did seem awfully astonished. Hartman remarked on it at the time."

"Of course, I was astonished. You don't know the boy like I do." Wisner stood. "As pack leader, I have to take personal responsibility for the actions of all of my pack. And Grant is simply too reckless to strike out on his own. Besides, it is not my stepson's application we're reviewing here, but yours, Mr. Hawick." He turned to the mayor. "Hawick once again demonstrates that he feels perfectly justified taking the safety of the city into his own hands. He is willful, disobedient, and thoroughly misguided. In fact, I wouldn't be surprised if it was his influence that was behind Grant's rebellion."

The mayor frowned. "You haven't proved that he poses a threat to the city."

"A threat! What do you call the current crisis if not a threat? We have hunters converging on a private residence—an apartment building Hawick owns—in pursuit of my stepson, and the only organization ready to deal with supernatural threats disbanded. We need decisive action, or we'll see a repeat of the necromancer riots. The Final Register is the only way to prevent widespread panic."

The mayor didn't move. Her hesitation was clear.

Wisner glanced at the clock. "We don't have much time. It's going to be full moon soon. And once night falls, there will be nothing preventing the rogue werewolf from laying waste to the city. You need to instigate a citywide curfew." He looked down at the mayor, and his lip curled. "Your predecessor hesitated and lost control of the situation. You can't afford to make the same mistake."

The mayor stood. "You'll find me equal to any emergency, Wisner," she snapped.

Ben realized, with a lurch, that she walked toward the library. He hopped down the lectern steps. "Don't the three members of the committee need to reach a unanimous agreement to put a name on the Register?"

The werewolf nearest him grabbed him before he could follow.

Wisner turned back. "Not in a state of emergency," he said. "In the current circumstances, the decision is in the mayor's hands."

The mayor stepped forward to the book placed on the desk. "Mr. Bennet Hawick, you have failed to convince the committee that you do not pose a threat to the safety of New Camden's citizens. You have been found guilty of plotting to destroy public peace and conniving against the institutions governing this city. For this reason, you are hereby entered into the Final Register."

With every movement of her pen, Ben felt the air press down on him. "But this is absurd! I've done nothing—except not be a vampire!"

There was a sudden rush of wind. The mayor started back as the pages of the book rippled and then the book slammed shut. The wind surged around the room, rushing through the open door. Ben heard the thundering of hundreds of pages turning at once.

"Bennet Hawick," the mayor shouted to be heard over the rising sound, "you exist only to yourself."

Chapter Twenty

"THE NUMBER YOU have dialed is not in use." The electronic voice said with bland efficiency. "Please check the number you wish to dial and try again."

Nate looked down at his phone. The number was entered into his contacts but the name was blank.

"Who are you calling?" George raised her crossbow, testing her line of sight from the living room window.

"Good question." Nate hesitated and then dropped his phone into his pocket. "I know I had someone in mind, but now—" He shook his head. "My mind's blank."

"Gunn?" Aki suggested. "Maybe he'd have a clue what to do now we've got every hunter in New Camden camped on our doorstep."

"How did they even find us?" Nate placed a hand on Aki's shoulder, looking down at the street below.

The hunters weren't even trying to be discreet. They were blocking the road, standing with arms crossed and their weapons clearly visible in the center of the footpath and on the road. Others had taken up sniper positions on the roofs of the surrounding buildings. Passing pedestrians did their best to give them a wide berth, but those unlucky enough to look as though they might want to enter the apartment building were subject to an intense interrogation.

"Wisner. Naturally." Grant stood in the doorway of the safe room. "He doesn't care if civilians get caught in the cross fire. It'll be just one more thing he can use to justify him seizing power."

"Stay where you are," Nate said immediately. They'd discovered the presence of the hunters outside when Grant had stepped too close to a window. The building's wards had prevented the bolt from breaking the glass, but they'd all been given a fright.

Grant raised his hands in a gesture of frustration. "I hate this. Standing by while other people are in danger, knowing it's my fault but not being able to do anything."

"There's a difference between 'your fault' and what's going on here," Vazul's voice drifted in from the other room. "And it's a pretty big difference."

Grant turned to speak to Vazul and as he did, the building seemed to sway. Grant stumbled, clutching the doorframe. Aki stumbled, grabbing Nate's arm to steady himself. George's crossbow swung wildly and she swore, just managing to keep her feet.

"What was that? An earthquake?"

"We don't get earthquakes," Aki said. "Pretty much every variety of supernatural disaster, sure, but not earthquakes."

Charlotte came dashing into the room. "Something's happened to the runes."

Grant's head whipped up. "The defensive runes?"

Nate couldn't blame Grant for his alarm. The runes were all that was keeping the hunters out of the building. "Get into the safe room now. It's the best place for you."

"And let you fight my battle for me?" Grant clenched his fists. "This isn't your fight!"

"Please, Grant?" Charlotte wrung her hands. "You've been struggling on your own long enough. Now, it's time to share the fight."

"Turning tail while my friends risk their necks? No way." Grant didn't budge. "You're putting your lives on the line for me. I have to prove that I'm worthy of the risk you're taking—"

"For fuck's sake!" Aki marched up to Grant, jabbing him in the chest with his finger. "Do not even start! These people are worried enough without you adding some more needless dramatics to the mix! You're going to go into the box where you're safe, and we can protect you more easily, and you're going to stay there, concentrating on keeping your sanity intact. You can make it up to us—after the full moon. Got that?" It was not actually a question.

Grant tensed. His nostrils flared as he breathed in, his eyes narrowed at Aki. His body shook, a low growl escaping him.

Werewolf, Nate reminded himself. *Full moon is super close.* Even he knew that werewolves were much more dangerous around the full moon than at any other time. He saw George raise her crossbow out of the corner of his eye and edged toward Grant so that he was ready to tackle him should Aki seem threatened.

Abruptly, Grant sagged. "You—are right. It is difficult for me to do nothing, but it seems that is all I can do." He looked up, his clear eyes resting on each of them in turn. "I won't forget this. And I give you my word that I will do all I can to make sure you do not regret this." His voice had a mellow note that seemed to swell, giving his words a larger-than-life air. "This is not my fight. It's our fight."

If Nate hadn't been so worried, he'd have been impressed.

Grant stepped into the safe room, and Nate and George stepped forward to lock and bolt the door. They heard Grant pulling the bolts on his side shut as they closed the bookcase, hiding the door entirely from view.

"There." George slapped the bookcase. "No one would ever suspect there's a room hidden behind there."

"But they'll know Grant is in here. They've been watching the apartment—they'll know he hasn't left." Charlotte twisted her hands. "If only we knew what had happened to the wards!"

Nate looked out the window. So far, it didn't seem as if the hunters had noticed that the wards were down. "Can't you redo them?"

Vazul snorted. "Obviously, you've never studied magic. Proper runes would take hours. That's time we don't have."

Nate walked into the living room. The only thing they could do now was to barricade themselves in. He ran his hand down the surface of the Norwegian pine table. It was strong, solid wood. It would make a secure barricade—

"Nate." Aki was at his heels. "I have an idea you're going to hate, but you need to hear me out."

Nate let his hand rest on the table. "What's up?"

"It was what Charlotte said just now. The hunters aren't going to leave unless they see Grant go—and the longer they stay here, the greater the chances of someone getting hurt. The police aren't doing anything. It's up to us." Aki took a deep breath. "George. What's going to happen if the hunters see Grant leave this building?"

George leaned in the doorway. "They're going to go after him, of course. He's one hell of a payload."

"But they're not going to see Grant go anywhere," Vazul said stiffly. "He is going to stay in that room—"

"But the hunters don't know that, right?" Aki scowled at them. "You've still got the collar you used to make him look like a dog, right? Could you do that again? Only, to make me look—"

"Like Grant," Nate finished. "No way, Aki!"

George whistled. "Seriously?"

Aki folded his arms. "I don't know why you're all so surprised. It's a great idea. And I'm totally equipped to pull it off."

"But Aki, you're—" Nate hesitated. How to phrase this?

Vazul had no compunctions about hurting Aki's feelings. "You're short, unarmed, and about as threatening as a limp rag."

"I'm taller than you," Aki shot back at once. "And at least I'm fit. I can run—"

"Running's not going to do you much good when you've got twenty odd crossbows leveled at your back," George said slowly. She was watching Aki with a thoughtful expression, almost like she was taking his suggestion seriously.

"That's where my talent comes in."

"Talent?" Charlotte clutched her hands together.

"He's got hunches," Nate said flatly. "Aki, that doesn't count!"

"Foresight, and for your information, it does too!" Aki took a deep breath. "You've only seen me in...standby mode. But this would be different. This time, I'd be using my ability."

"This is a terrible idea," Nate said. "Aki, are you looking at me? Terrible. Think about this. I am telling you it's a bad idea."

"But if instead of Grant in trouble, it was—" Aki paused, frowning. "It was—" Suddenly, his expression cleared, and he darted to the side.

"Aki—ow!"

A wooden practice sword bounced off Nate's funny bone. He spun around to glare at George. "What was that for?"

She smiled sweetly at him. "Testing Aki's reflexes. They check out." She eyed his hand, clutching his throbbing arm. "Yours don't."

"So don't even think about using the 'I'm less breakable so I should do this' argument," Aki finished. "I'm doing this."

Nate shot George a sour look. "Charlotte and Vazul haven't said it's possible."

Charlotte shot Vazul a look. "It is," she admitted hesitantly. "But—"

"It's for Grant," Vazul said. "Let's do this."

Vazul hadn't struck Nate as any more charitable than Aki—then again, he wasn't recklessly endangering himself for someone he professed to dislike. *There's something odd about this.* Nate glanced over at Aki, his arms crossed as he watched Charlotte hunt through

Grant's duffel bag for the collar. Aki looked serious, his expression set. *He's really going to do this.* Nate felt a moment's panic. He couldn't lose Aki too!

Too?

Again, there was that feeling of something just out of reach—

"Move it." Vazul urged him away from the table. "Genius needs space to work."

Charlotte worked out the spell, consulting a runic dictionary she carried in her shoulder bag.

Vazul cast the runes, thoroughly enjoying himself in the process. "For best results, this should be heated in a blacksmith's forge and hammered out beneath the light of a full moon," he said. "And then the runes carved while the metal is still working. In the circumstances, you're lucky you have me around."

He held the collar beneath his hands. It glowed a molten orange, waves of heat radiating outward from him.

"You're going to cool that down, right?" Aki tugged nervously at his neck. "I don't want to be branded."

"Nate!" George slid out of her watching place at the window. "The hunters have figured it out. They've made their way inside."

"Right." Nate took a deep breath. With one chair under each arm and another in his hands, he waded out into the hallway by the elevator. He planted the two chairs down, one after the other, in front of the elevator and stretched out his hands. *Grow.*

The power came readily. Just like it had when he'd shown—someone—important. Someone who'd stood at the windowsill of the bedroom of the apartment he was now protecting—

There was a cracking sound as the chairs expanded, drawing Nate's attention back to the branches protruding from the chairs. They expanded outward, spreading out into branches of their own. Distantly, Nate heard the elevator button chime below, as the hunters made their way toward the top floor. *Faster!* Nate urged the growing trees onward.

"Hey, Nate, you need a—holy crap!" George stopped in the open doorway to stare. "Did you just make an entire forest in here?"

Nate glanced over his shoulder at her, as the branches continued to twine and intertwine around the space. "What do you think?"

"Fire hazard," George said. "But considering that they're stuck up here, we'll just have to hope they're more into self-preservation than hunters usually are."

The chiming elevator door put an end to their conversation. The branches were so thick that Nate couldn't see the hunters, but he could hear their shouts as they discovered the barrier between themselves and the door.

"Inside." George nudged him toward the door.

Nate carefully lifted the Norwegian wood table against the door, George watching.

"I like a guy who is good in an emergency," she said. "You sure you don't want to join forces, Nate? I'd look after you. Forty-sixty split on profits—and I don't make that offer to just anyone."

Nate straightened up, putting a hand against the table to make sure that it would stay put. "George—this is going to sound like a weird question, but what are we doing here?"

"Saving Grant?"

Nate nodded. "I know me and Aki met him at the park. But you—" He considered her with a frown. "How did you get in on this?"

George snorted. "Doubting my hunting skills? Thirty-five-sixty-five then. I'm a professional."

"I'm serious, George. I didn't call you in on this."

George opened her mouth and paused. "I—huh." She stared at Nate. "I know one of Wisner's goons seriously pissed me off. Locking me in a kennel. I don't quite remember how I got out—but I know that Wisner's going to regret setting his wolves on this hunter."

"Can you two finish your conversation later?" Vazul's voice was pitched at an even more grating level than usual. "Aki is ready to go."

Nate looked up and stared. "Shit. Aki?"

Grant folded his arms across his chest. If it wasn't for the fact that he wore Aki's hot-pink running shorts and T-shirt, and was tapping the toe of his sneaker against the floor as Aki did while waiting for Nate to catch up to him, Nate would have thought Grant had gotten out of the safe room. Even knowing what he knew, he couldn't believe what he saw.

Grant rolled his eyes. "Who did you think it was? Seriously, Nate. You were here when I outlined my plan."

"Yeah, but—this is really unreal." Nate put his hand on Aki's shoulder. "You're sure you want to do this?"

Grant glared at him. "I have put more thought into this than you have any of your ridiculous decisions, so don't even start, Nate."

"Yeah, but—" Nate glanced at their companions. Vazul and Charlotte were pantomiming tidying up their tools, while George made no secret of the fact that she was watching the two of them argue. "In here." He pulled Aki into the master bedroom.

"We don't have time to waste," Grant—*Aki*—protested. "The hunters—"

"Are going to be fully occupied hacking their way through my forest," Nate said. "This is important." He frowned at Aki. "You're not—I mean—"

"Am I doing this out of an attempt to impress Grant?" It was strange seeing Aki's thin, ironic smile on Grant's face. "I can see why you'd think that. My track record isn't doing me any favors here. But, you have to believe me. Dating Grant is about the last thing I want to do."

Nate stared down at him. He could read Aki pretty well—but his current appearance was throwing him off. "Then why?"

Aki picked at the sleeve of his T-shirt. "I don't know. I've been trying to work it out myself. All I can tell you is that supporting Grant—it feels right. You know—he's got something I haven't seen in someone before."

"Something?"

Aki shook his head. "I don't mean that sexually—or even physically. It's like—well, look at us. Charlotte's a magical pacifist, George an unapologetic supernatural hunter. Vazul's got all the attitudes of a supernatural supremacist, and you're the most humble guy I know. And me—I am the last person to do anything for the common good. But Grant's got us working together against Wisner. I don't think anyone else could do what he's done."

Nate turned to look at the closed bedroom door. Now that he thought about it, the fact that such a disparate group had even come together at all was kind of incredible. "Grant's definitely got something. Leadership, maybe?"

"Whatever it is, it's enough to stop Wisner for good," Aki said. "And that's why I'm doing this, Nate. Because if I hadn't had you there to spot me, there would have been nothing to stop that werewolf wiping the floor with me. And I'm selfish, but I'm not selfish enough to let someone else take that fall."

Nate put his hand on Aki's shoulder. "I get it. I wish—you didn't have to do this, but—"

Aki elbowed him. "You're just mad I'm stealing your self-sacrificial thunder."

There was a knock at the door, and George pushed it open. "It's about time we made tracks."

Nate quirked an eyebrow at George. "You're going too?"

She grinned at him. "You missed this part of the discussion setting up your forest. I'm going to provide backup should Aki need it."

"You realize you can't claim the bounty if it's not Grant you capture?"

"Details." George grinned. "Well, Aki?"

Aki swung himself up and over the windowsill. "Jesus, Nate. You realize that people are going to want to use this fire escape—"

"You're going to be really glad I moved my plants out here in a minute." Nate caught Aki into a brief hug. "Be careful. If anything happens, don't be brave, be safe—"

"Don't worry." Aki slapped him on the arm. "I'm not that far gone that I'm going to pull a Nate." He jogged down the fire escape.

Nate became aware that George was watching him. "What?"

"Don't I get a hug?"

She was joking, but Nate felt a sudden ache. He pulled George into a quick hug. "Take care of him—and you."

George breathed in appreciatively. "Forty-sixty, Nate. Remember that." She made her way after Aki, and Nate heard the fire escape rattle with the sound of their footsteps.

Just in time. There was a rhythmic banging from the front door, each crash making the apartment shudder. Nate winced. He felt the moment the door gave way, and the table was heaved aside. A moment later, the hunters were in the apartment.

Nate heard Charlotte's panicked yelp. He moved toward the door, only for it to be flung open.

"Hands where I can see them!" A burly hunter raised a crossbow at Nate. "Well, well—if it isn't our friend from the park."

Nate gritted his teeth. It was one of the pair that had interfered with them picking up rubbish. He raised his hands above his head. "You're wasting your time. The werewolf's not here."

"Yeah. Like we believe that." The hunter scanned the room, his gaze falling on the open window. His eyes widened. "Calvin! In here!"

His partner appeared. "No sign of him in any of the—shit." He'd also noticed the open window. "Fire escape?"

"Check it out."

Nate kept his face impassive as Calvin leaned out the window.

"I can hear someone on it—Damnit! It's him!" Calvin jumped out the window. "Come on!"

His partner followed suit. The sounds of their boots thundering down the fire escape caught the attention of the other hunters. Most followed them, but a few scattered for the stairs and elevator. In a matter of minutes, the apartment was empty.

"Charlotte? Vazul?"

"In here!" Charlotte had taken shelter beneath the kitchen table. She held Nate's arm, trembling as he helped her to her feet. "Are they—?"

"Gone." Nate helped her into a seat. "I'm going to look for Vazul."

He found Vazul sprawled in the study. He had a bleeding nose and swayed when Nate got him on his feet. "Hunters—ha! Common thugs is more like it—barging into private property—who is going to pay for this damage, I ask you?"

Nate looked around the study with a sense of hopelessness. The boxes were knocked over, their contents scattered, and the desk had been tipped in an effort to discover anyone hiding behind it. He looked at the bookcase.

Vazul smirked and shook his head. "No one gave it a second glance."

Nate breathed out.

Vazul limped into the kitchen in search of the first aid kit, and Nate followed suit. "Vazul—this isn't your apartment, is it?"

"Of course not. I live with my grandparents—an arrangement that is beneficial to both of us and not indicative in any way of an inability to keep an apartment of my own. I simply prefer to remain close to my own people."

"Your people being?"

"I don't share that information." Vazul stalked into the kitchen.

Nate decided to let it go. He looked around. The dining room, usually so dignified, was a complete mess. The table was badly damaged, and the furniture kicked about. A thin haze of smoke hung about the room. One of the hunters had announced his presence with a smoke bomb.

Nate opened the windows, drawing back the curtains. The late-afternoon sun fell on his face. Nate stood a moment, savoring it, letting it restore the energy he'd expended. He tried not to think of Aki and George, making their way across the city, but he couldn't suppress his worry. *I should be out there. If I hadn't promised—*

Nate raised his head slowly. His reflection stared back. "I made a promise." *To stay with Grant—I made it here in this apartment.* But who had he promised?

Grant was the obvious person—but somehow Nate didn't think it was him. He shook his head, but the feeling stayed. There was something wrong. Something even bigger than the fact that Aki and George had every hunter in New Camden in hot pursuit, while Nate waited in safety in the apartment, gearing for a fight against something none of them had any clue about.

But what is it? Nate took a deep breath, turning back to the apartment. He didn't know what was giving him the nagging feeling of something missing...but if it was in the apartment, he was going to find it.

"CONGRATULATIONS. YOU HAVE succeeded in tidying the apartment, only for the next lot of hunters to come along and thoroughly mess it up." Vazul had taken an aspirin and gone to lie down in the master bedroom. He'd emerged, with the twilight shadows, to sneer as Nate finished sweeping up the dirt tracked in by the hunter's boots.

"I had to do something." Nate hunched his shoulders miserably. Cleaning the apartment hadn't helped. It had only made him more aware of how out of his depth he was. He didn't know what he was doing there or what he hoped to achieve. He only knew that Grant needed his help, and Nate had promised to aid him.

"We've both been busy." Charlotte knelt by the doorway. "Aki and George's diversion bought us time. I've been able to redo the wards on the front door." She paused, resting her hand on the doorway. "Whoever did the runes before me did an excellent job. Their markings were so clear, I only had to trace them. And the salt—" She frowned. "It must have been done today. But I don't remember—"

"Remember?" Nate held his breath.

"I must have helped. I remember looking for candles for—but who was it?"

Nate swallowed back a rush of eagerness. "Someone you know was here, but you can't put a name or a face to them?"

Charlotte stared at him. Her eyes were alarmed. "You, too? I don't like this—"

Outside the open door, the elevator bells chimed. Charlotte hastily stood, while Vazul and Nate straightened, bracing themselves to meet this new challenge.

"Well, now." The voice was male and brisk, with an unmistakable note of authority. "You'd be Charlotte Everett? Superintendent Jacobs, New Camden police." Jacobs was accompanied by a clatter of feet indicating backup.

Charlotte swallowed. "I am."

"Meaning that Vazul Lascar shouldn't be too far away."

Vazul saw Nate step toward the door and shook his head. He pointed to the kitchen. "You're still an unknown," he whispered. "Stay out of sight." He drew himself up and marched himself over to the doorway. "Here I am. And I demand to know the meaning of this intrusion."

Nate leaned against the kitchen door. His fists clenched. *Again, I'm just standing by while other people put themselves in trouble. It's not right!* For a moment, he had a startled moment of clarity. *This is what Grant's been feeling this entire time.*

"I've got a warrant for both of your arrests." Jacobs sounded perfectly polite, but there was a hint of steel in his voice. He would play nice only as long as they did.

"On what charges, may I ask?" Vazul's sneer made Nate wince. He longed to go out there and attempt to defuse the situation.

"The illicit use of magic in order to obstruct the location of a known fugitive—"

Vazul scoffed. "What proof do you have?"

"An associate of yours, an Akihiro Fujino, is already in police custody." Jacobs sounded grim. "We know all about the collar—and that Fujino did not have the magical skills to produce it unaided. You're coming with us—"

"Slow down," a familiar voice drawled. "Give them the chance to turn themselves in."

Gunn! Nate felt a sense of relief.

"What makes you think we want to turn ourselves in?" Vazul did not share Nate's elation at seeing the Department Seven officer. "For that matter, what are you doing here? I thought you were disbanded."

"I may be freelance now, but I still take an interest in these things." Gunn sounded less bothered by the dissolution of everything he'd worked to achieve than Nate had imagined possible. "And I'm interested in seeing that you two get your rights. You go with Jacobs here willingly, and he can't charge you with resisting arrest, assaulting officers, or any of those things that make such an unpleasant impression on judges."

Gunn might sound calm, but Jacobs had the tone of someone who'd had more than they could stand of Gunn's company. "Your opinion was not asked for or wanted. Now, Everett, Lascar, you have the right—"

"We surrender. Or whatever it is you want us to do," Charlotte said.

Vazul gave an impatient bark. "I wish to lodge a formal complaint at the brevity of the investigations, but fine. I will also submit to this indignity."

The snap of the handcuffs locking shut echoed through the empty apartment. Nate hoped that it wasn't audible in Grant's room. He could only imagine what the man felt about now.

"I will be availing myself of legal counsel at the first opportunity," Vazul continued. "And if there is even the slightest irregularity in your treatment of me—"

"Get them downtown," Jacobs ordered. "At once."

The scent of tobacco wafted through the air. "You're overdoing it. Those two kids are licensed magical practitioners, and there are doubts about the validity of the alarm put out on the werewolf."

"Fuck off, Gunn. We no longer have to listen to you."

"But you can't ignore what I'm saying. After all, you know I'm right— and do you really want to piss off the Magic-Users Guild? Imagine the outcry. Two promising young magic-users singled out for discrimination enforced by New Camden's own police department—"

"Shut it, Gunn. Or we'll shut your mouth for you." There was a creak of floorboards as the officer approached the front door.

"You don't have a search warrant," Gunn said immediately.

"Got to check that the apartment is secure. Can't just leave it here to be burgled."

My cue. Nate stepped out of the kitchen. "Thanks, but we've got that covered."

Jacobs looked up in evident surprise. "Who are you?"

Gunn grinned. "Don't worry. Nate is known to the department. He's got a good reason for being in this apartment."

"Such as?"

Gunn paused. "He's...a friend of the owner."

Friend of the owner? Nate frowned. That was only half the story.

"We're going to need more than that." Jacobs studied Nate closely. He was a short man with an alert look, younger than Nate had guessed from his voice and manner. "Is the owner here?"

Nate shook his head. "No. But—"

Jacobs snorted. "Then I think the circumstances warrant a search." He stepped toward the door, only to be met by an invisible barrier. "What the hell?"

"Huh." Gunn made his way to the door. He placed his hand on the invisible barrier. "Protective wards."

"That witch." Jacobs snarled, speaking into his radio. "Get Everett back up here."

"You're wasting your time," Gunn said. "She can't undo these from the outside."

"But aren't they her work?"

"She was working on an overlay. Right, Nate?"

Unsure what was going on, Nate nodded. "Right. She said that she traced over runes that had been left here before."

"Give us the full story." Jacobs barked.

"I'm not a magic-user," Nate warned. "But midafternoon, soon after the hunters turned up, the building shuddered. Charlotte said that the wards had failed. After—" Nate hesitated, casting a look at the officer. "After Aki left, Charlotte repaired the wards."

"These are tied, not to the caster, but the presence of the apartment's owner," Gunn said. "Interesting. I think it's worth looking up who that owner might be."

Jacobs, who already had his phone out, gave the former Department Seven officer a glare and walked toward the elevator. He made the call and stood, watching Nate and Gunn as he waited for the results.

Nate glanced at Gunn. He looked just as he always did. "I'm sorry about Department Seven."

Gunn snorted. "You'd be one of the few."

"Then phone them at their place of residence!" Jacobs ended the call. "Trouble?" Gunn asked.

Jacobs marched over to them. "If you're involved in this, Gunn—"

"It's not my fault if the mayor's curfew meant that you can't get hold of a representative to tell you who owns this apartment." Gunn grinned. "But I'll tell you one thing. In magical spells, possession is not nine-tenths of the law. For those runes to be active, Nate's either got the right to be in the apartment, or the actual owner is still on the premises and—by implication—approves of Nate's presence."

"And if you're worried about burglars, then the runes are going to keep them out." Nate wasn't clear about what was going on, but he understood that much.

Jacobs narrowed his eyes at Gunn. "I know you. I know you're up to something."

"Maybe I'm no longer an officer of the law," Gunn said. "But I know more about supernatural law than you do. You don't believe me, you can look it up." He dug into the pocket of his gunner jacket, digging out an immensely filthy wallet. "Here." He extracted a muddied business card. "Magic-Users Guild. Ask about the laws governing defense runes when you find out what constitutes a breach of the magic-users license."

Jacobs snarled, refusing the card. "I don't need to double-check. Wisner made it perfectly clear—"

"Is Wisner's word your only reference? 'Cause he doesn't exactly have an unbiased interest in this whole debacle." Gunn raised his cigarette to his lips. "Look it up, unless you want to see your department go the way of mine."

Jacobs frowned. He snatched the card and marched for the elevator. "Stay here," he barked to the two officers remaining with him. "Anyone enters or leaves this apartment, I want to know about it."

Gunn's smile was supremely satisfied. He turned to look at Nate. "Going to invite me in?"

Had Gunn's eyes always been so dark? Nate realized he was staring. "Uh. Sure. Come on in."

Gunn slammed the door on the watching officers. "Desperation tactics. Wisner's running out of time. Trying to isolate the pup, make him as exposed as possible for whatever he's still got up his sleeve."

"And you're here to help?" Nate rummaged in the kitchen for a saucer and set it down in front of Gunn. "Here."

Gunn ignored the impromptu ash tray, flicking ash over the floor. "Expected you to be causing mischief out in the city somewhere. Didn't expect you'd have the common sense to stick around and keep your head down."

Nate squirmed. He felt like he didn't deserve the compliment—if compliment was what it was. "Gunn. Do you know who this apartment belongs to?"

Gunn gave him a flat look. "Why the hell are you asking me?"

Nate shrugged. "It just seems...weird. Here I am in this place, and I know it—it seems familiar. But I can't remember why I know it. Like that picture." He pointed to the screen print of the pier hung above the dining table. "I know I've seen it before. I know where it came from. But the context—the who—is missing."

Gunn sauntered over to inspect the painting. "Sloppy," he said. "And they call this art? I could do a better job."

Nate frowned. "I'm serious, Gunn."

Gunn glanced at him. "You want to worry about something, worry about that." He pointed to the window. The sun was sinking below the horizon. "Only a few hours now before the moon rises and your friend's battle really begins." Gunn straightened up, losing his habitual slouch. "He's here, of course?"

"In the safe room."

"Good. We'll leave him there. Show me what we've got to work with by way of defenses."

As Nate showed Gunn around the apartment, detailing the events of the afternoon, a suspicion began to grow—a suspicion that was confirmed as Gunn took a pistol from a holster. He leaned against the wall beside the window that George had occupied as a vantage point, checking that the pistol was loaded.

"You're here to defend Grant."

Gunn snorted. "I'm not here for the pleasure of your company. I don't do socializing, Nate."

"No—" Nate hesitated. It was just one more strange thing in an afternoon of surprises. "What is it about Grant that he's got you, me, *Aki* of all people, ready to defend him? You put your department on the line, Aki could have been seriously hurt—" Nate came to an abrupt halt. "He's not—"

"Fujino's fine." Gunn snorted contemptuously. "Led the hunters on a merry chase and then surrendered willingly to police. There was almost a brawl over who was going to claim the bounty on him. I tell you, there are some very unhappy hunters in New Camden tonight."

"But he's safe?"

"Yeah. Behind bars is probably the best place to be with Wisner on the prowl." Gunn looked over the streets, his posture suggesting that he was preparing himself for a long vigil. "Your pup better appreciate everything we're doing."

And that was it, wasn't it? It all came back to Wisner's word against Grant's. Nate caught his breath. "Hey, Gunn? How do you tell if a wolf is a leader?"

"An alpha you mean?" Gunn shot Nate a quick, appreciative glance. "You know, I think you're on to something. It would explain a lot. He say anything to you?"

Nate shook his head. "It's a feeling I've got. There's got to be a reason why we're so ready to help, even ignoring how terrible Wisner is."

"Alpha wolves are known to inspire intense loyalty in their pack of followers," Gunn allowed. "But that only applies to werewolves. This kid—it wouldn't surprise me if he was something special."

THEY KNEW THE exact moment the full moon rose. An anguished wail from the locked safe room made Nate jump to his feet, catching his arm on the desk he was sitting on.

Gunn simply went still, turning his attention to the bookcase behind which the door was still concealed. "Don't even think about it, Nate. You can't do anything to help and remaining in there is the safest place for him."

Nate had taken the step toward the room without thinking. "Are you sure? He sounds so—" He flinched. The wail was repeated, this time with a sound that sounded far too much like snapping bone.

"I know so." Gunn's voice remained hard, even as the wail turned into an abrupt whimper. "It hurts a wolf to transform at any time, but the full moon is always worse because it's against their will. The only thing we can do is let Grant get on with it. At least, that's what Kenzies says."

Nate took a deep breath, pulling himself back up onto the desk. Kenzies was nothing if not a trustworthy source on werewolves. "Where is she tonight?"

"Where do you think? Holed up with the rest of her pack in their version of this safe room."

"She's not—inside Wisner's compound?"

Gunn shook his head. "Nah. Give her more credit than that, Nate. Her pack is different. All she-wolves, and they've banded together to protect their independence. They've got a warehouse downtown somewhere that they've kitted out for situations like this."

Nate breathed out. He was pretty sure that Kenzies had a plan to resist Wisner's attempts to bring all the werewolves in New Camden under his jurisdiction, but having that confirmed felt good. Another cracking sound, and a howl that sounded definitely inhuman put an end to his confidence. "You're sure—"

"Trust me. We have to wait."

It was one of the worst experiences of Nate's life to date—including his own death. The change seemed to go on for hours of agonizing waiting. Nate was convinced that each whimper he heard would be the last sound Grant made. Even worse was when the whimper changed to growls and finally a full-fledged howl.

"Told you." Gunn had lit a fresh cigarette. "Now all we got to worry about is him getting out of there."

The sound of a full-sized werewolf body hitting the wall indicated that this was no idle remark. Crash after crash indicated that Grant had no intention of remaining locked in the room.

"He's going to hurt himself if he keeps this up." Nate's fingers clenched the edge of the desk he sat on. "We have to do something."

"Only thing we can do is wait it out," Gunn said. "For crying out loud, Nate. I shouldn't have to keep repeating myself."

"I know. But—" Nate bit his lip. Was this why he'd had to promise? Whoever had chosen him to remain knew how hard it would be to stand by while Grant fought to free himself from his prison.

"We've got two missions tonight. Stopping him from getting out and attacking anyone, and making sure that Wisner doesn't get to him."

"But with the full moon, Wisner's out of time." Nate looked through the study to where Gunn leaned against the living room window. "He's not allowed to leave his safe room. No wolf is."

Gunn looked up then back at the street.

Nate felt cold. "You think he's going to come here?"

"He's got no other option. Not if he wants to ensure Grant's challenge fails—and he has tried everything else. My gut says that he wont' give up now. And my gut's never wrong."

Nate cast a look toward the bookcase, shuddering with the force of Grant's latest attack. *This—this is only the start.*

It was about two hours later that Gunn's instincts were proven correct. A high-pitched wail split the night air.

Nate groggily sat up. Grant had ceased his fight to free himself, and Nate had fallen into a doze. "A siren? What's happened?"

Gunn cast him a contemptuous look. "Listen carefully, Nate."

Frowning, Nate walked across the study to join Gunn at the window. The siren wail repeated itself, and as it did, Nate realized that it was made up, not of one source, but of many. The noise rose and fell like a wave, leaving him cold. "Wolves."

"Tens, possibly hundreds of them," Gunn reported. "Wisner's pulling out all the stops. Here they come."

It was an impressive sight. Shadows flickered across the street, the wolves appearing out of the spaces between buildings, before finally massing in the street in front of the apartment building. Their eyes glowed as they looked up. Nate flinched. "Can they see us?"

"Who knows? One thing I'm sure of—they know exactly where Grant is." Gunn ground out his cigarette on the windowsill and cocked his gun.

Nate stared down at the gathering of wolves. It was hard to tell exactly how many there were. They seemed to melt together as one mass in the shadows, only their glowing eyes, catching the street lamps, separating them. "But this is all kinds of illegal! Where are the police?"

"Cowering behind their badges and praying that everyone's obeying the curfew." Gunn's lip curled. "They're not authorized to deal with this kind of situation."

"But this means—" Nate stared down. "No one's going to stop them?" Now he saw Wisner's purpose in disbanding Department Seven. He was in charge of New Camden's security, and there was no one to stop him and his wolves from doing as they liked.

"There's us."

Nate stared at Gunn's back. For the first time since he'd first met Gunn, the man sounded—upbeat. No. Positively happy. "You're serious? No—stupid question. You are."

Gunn grinned. His expression was wolfish. "I'm not hampered by any 'departmental regulations.' I got nothing to lose, and Wisner risks everything." He looked down at the street of wolves with satisfaction. "Finally, we got a level playing field."

There's only two of us. And— Nate did some quick mental calculations. Even divided by two, the glowing eyes came to a lot of wolves.

A movement went through the crowd of wolves. They melted aside, clearing a path for a tan-colored wolf, larger than those surrounding it, and flanked by two almost identical tan wolves. It made its way to the center of a pool of lamplight before it raised its muzzle to look up at the apartment, baring its teeth.

"Wisner." Nate caught his breath.

"So he finally makes his entrance." Gunn watched. "What is he waiting for?"

Wisner didn't so much as glance at the wolves surrounding him. In his werewolf form, he was even more supremely assured of himself than as a human. He raised his voice in a powerful howl. Unlike the siren call from earlier, this one had a penetrating note that had Nate raising his hands to his ears. Immediately the call was taken up from inside the apartment. Grant snarled, battering the door in a renewed attempt to break free.

"Fuck." As Nate stared, a book was dislodged from the shelf. "He's not supposed to be able to do that."

"That was a challenge." Gunn leaned against the glass of the window. "He knows we're not going to let Grant answer that. So what—"

Wisner raised his head, repeating the chilling howl. Immediately it was taken up by his sons, and in the next breath, all the surrounding wolves.

Nate clapped his hands to his ears. It wasn't the volume, though that was bad enough. It was the sound itself. It was like being face-to-face suddenly with something primal and out of control, something he knew instinctively to fear. "What are they doing?"

"They're going to drive the kid mad." Gunn glanced at the window and then decided against it. He pulled the curtains shut. "Is there anything in here that can muffle the sound?"

Nate helped him check the windows were secure and the curtains pulled. He helped Gunn stack all the mattresses they could find against the bookshelf blocking the safe room entrance. "You're sure about this?"

"The full moon is a difficult time for wolves even in less fraught circumstances." Gunn beckoned Nate out the study door and shut it behind them. "Wisner knows this, knows that Grant, a young wolf facing his first solo moon is especially vulnerable. He's deliberately antagonizing the wolf inside, playing on its fears of being trapped and hunted."

Nate glanced over his shoulder. "You know that?"

Gunn's snarl was unexpectedly vicious. "I can feel it. And I tell you, Nate, it's dangerously close to working."

Nate froze. Gunn had displayed teeth that were savage, too close to the wolf's for his peace of mind. *Lemur. He feeds on negative emotion—*

"We have to put a stop to the noise downstairs as soon as possible." Gunn flung open the doors of the apartment. "Or—"

"Hold it right there!" The two police officers stationed on the doorstep raised their weapons.

"I'm putting an end to the wolves downstairs," Gunn said.

"We're under orders," said the first police officer. He was blond, with sweaty hands, and he kept readjusting his grip on his gun. "We know you've got the rogue werewolf in there. You've got to let him out."

"Are you crazy?" Nate's explosion earned him the attention of both cops. He found himself on the receiving end of both barrels. "If you heard him, then you know what kind of a state he's in."

"You don't want an upset werewolf loose, especially not in close quarters like this," Gunn agreed. "You'll be dead before you've had the chance to radio a report."

The second officer gave her colleague a worried glance. "The superintendent said it's the only chance to get the wolves downstairs to disperse. The city's in a full state of emergency. The army's not going to get here in time—"

"I'll talk to him." Gunn snatched the radio. "Jacobs. You're out of your mind."

Nate hovered in the doorway, unsure of what he should do. The officers had lowered their guns, but the woman kept an eye on him as her partner monitored Gunn. Nate winced as the howl drifted up from downstairs, seemingly even louder than before. *Every moment we waste here is another moment that Grant goes through hell—*

He stopped.

An acorn rested in the center of the foyer, shiny beneath the overhead light. Nate knelt to pick it up discovering that it was warm in his hand. *It wasn't here earlier. I cleaned up the leftover wood, I would have seen it...* So where had it come from? *And why does it remind me of something?*

Jacobs's voice was distorted by the radio but still audible. "Wisner left instructions for this situation. Should the wolves form a group and take to the streets like this, we are to avoid provoking a confrontation at any cost. The only way to do that is to give the wolves what they want— the rogue werewolf—so they can deal with him their way."

Gunn's vicious snarl made them all jump. "You spineless cretin! So you're going to turn over the kid to save your own pathetic hide! I can't blame you for throwing a wolf under the bus, but I thought you'd draw the line at sacrificing your own officers!"

The two cops exchanged a startled look.

Nate turned the acorn over in his hand. The situation was dire, but somehow he felt comforted. The acorn was no coincidence. *It was put there for me to find. By someone who knows what it means to me.* And that—even more than the reminder of Nate's own strength—gave him resolution.

"Wake up and smell the wolf piss. These wolves didn't unlock themselves from their cages. This is not a spur of the moment outbreak by werewolves pushed to the limits of their endurance. Wisner had this planned. This is the city's head of security demonstrating how little he thinks of the rules handed down to protect everyone."

"But even if that's true, what do you want me to do? If we don't do something, those wolves are going to hurt someone. Listen to them!"

The wolves had lost their synchronicity. They still howled, but it was now a discordant series of howls that followed one after another in an endless loop, made worse because of how unpredictable it was.

Nate's hand tightened around the acorn. "Hey, Gunn? What would happen if someone were to challenge Wisner now?"

Gunn snapped his head around to stare at Nate. "I don't have to dignify that with a response, do I? That's suicide."

"Yeah, but would Wisner accept?"

"He couldn't do anything but. With his pack, hell, every wolf in New Camden watching?" Gunn narrowed his eyes at Nate. "The idea is ludicrous."

"And if I win?"

"You're not going to win." Gunn raised his hands as if he wanted to physically shake Nate but was prevented by the presence of the two cops. "I appreciate an idiotic endeavor as much as the next guy—"

"But if I did win? Could I make Wisner call the wolves off?"

Gunn narrowed his eyes. "It'd be chaos. You'd have destroyed the wolves' hierarchy. It'd be every wolf for himself—" He glanced down at the radio. "The perfect opportunity for the cops to step in and establish order."

The radio crackled. "I don't condone this. Who is this idiot, Gunn? What does he think he's going to do?"

"Challenge Wisner. And I'm doing it whether you condone me or not." Nate's heart thudded in his chest, but it was the steady beat of certainty. The way when a difficult decision falls into place and the path forward is clear. "I win—he loses control over the wolves. That's all that matters."

The radio gave an outraged squawk, and Gunn casually silenced it, tossing it back to the nearest police officer. "The last time you fought a wolf, you got your ass handed to you," he said. "Or did you hit your head so hard, you forgot?"

"I did all right," Nate said. "And this time I know what I'm in for. Wisner doesn't." He looked Gunn dead in the eyes. "I know I can do this."

Gunn snorted. "I can never resist a stupid idea and overwhelming odds. All right, Nate. You talked me into it." He glanced at the two officers. "Monitor the situation from up here, but don't interfere in the fight, even if things look bad for Nate. Any interference from an outside party and the challenge is void—and we lose any protection we've got."

The police officers exchanged a glance. "You really think this will work?" the woman said. "It sounds really unlikely to me."

Nate slipped the acorn into his pocket. "Full moon. Anything can happen."

Chapter Twenty-One

THE INTERIOR OF the elevator was completely silent. Gunn leaned against one side. Nate stood stiffly in the center, his hand on the acorn within his pocket.

Ben had long since given up on trying to get either of them to notice him. His body ached, and he was exhausted. It had been a long walk back across the city to the apartment, and he'd suffered in the altercation between the hunters and his friends. Being effectively invisible was no defense against being trampled, charged, or bumped. Ben wanted nothing more than to collapse and let the nature of his new reality crash down on him.

But I can't. Ben took a deep breath as the elevator opened on the ground floor. *Nate needs me.* Even if he couldn't see Ben or hear him or even feel his presence, he was not letting Nate face Wisner alone.

"Werewolves are about as strong as a grizzly," Gunn said casually. "And an alpha even stronger than that. If he pins you, that's it—game over."

Nate, halfway across the lobby, glanced back. "A pep talk? Gunn, you shouldn't."

"But it's the bite you've really got to worry about." Gunn swaggered after him. "A werewolf's bite is considered lethal. If you don't die outright, it's ten to one your first full moon will kill you."

Nate snorted. "That's assuming I get infected. And I'm pretty sure that I don't work that way."

"Here's hoping you're right." Gunn had no business sounding so pleased with himself.

Ben shot him a glare and then darted ahead to make it out the door with Nate. Existing only to yourself meant that he was vulnerable to things like closed doors. The buttons on his phone refused to register his touch. And any marks he left on surfaces disappeared instantly. The acorn had been the only thing to work. Ben was sure there was a clue there—if only he had time to understand it.

And they were out of time.

Nate walked to the edge of the steps, looking down at the crowd of wolves in front of them. Ben stood at his side. Even knowing the wolves couldn't see him, it was an alarming sight. The wolves' eyes glowed eerily, reflecting not the streetlights, but their own wildness. The full moon hung in the air above them, impossibly large and threatening.

The last wolf trailed off as Nate's presence registered slowly through the crowd. The silence was almost more alarming than their howls. No wild animals should stand so quietly. Was there still something human left within them? Or was this a sign of the near-absolute control that Wisner held over them?

The large tan wolf that was Wisner stepped forward. Ben felt Nate tense and automatically put a hand on his arm. "You've got this." Even if Nate couldn't hear him, the words made Ben feel better. He raised his jaw, staring hard at Wisner, projecting his own confidence as loudly as he could. He couldn't interact with the world, but maybe, just maybe, he could still be felt.

I have to believe that. If I don't—

Ben wasn't going to let himself think of the alternative.

Wisner barked an inquiry. One son growled, and the sound was quickly taken up by the rest of the wolves. Ben watched the wolves nearest to him move, clearly eager to leap. They snapped their teeth, creeping forward into the glow of the streetlight, their eyes fixed on Nate.

Ben felt Nate shift beside him and could imagine his misgivings. Somewhere among the crowd was the wolf who'd attacked them at Century.

"Yeah, tell someone who cares." A wolf got too close and Gunn flicked his cigarette ash at him, before making his way to join Nate on the steps. "Wisner. Not showing much regard for the rules now."

Wisner's snarl spoke volumes. It was deliberate and nuanced, far more articulate than Ben would have ever believed possible for a transformed werewolf. It said, as plainly as if Wisner had spoken the words, that Wisner was himself far above the necessity of rending Gunn limb from limb personally, but he would be delighted to order his underlings to destroy him.

Gunn grinned. "You don't say. I got an offer for you. I'm not one for making deals with anyone holding my city hostage, but the kid here is young and foolish, and well, they got to learn at some point. He wants—" and Gunn's voice was suddenly loud, projected to be heard across the entire scene "—to challenge you, Wisner."

Wisner's bark was sharp and savage. It sounded like a laugh.

Nate clenched his fists. "I'm serious."

"Let me do the talking," Gunn said. "I speak the universal language of fear. And if Wisner looks at you, make sure you look him in the eyes and don't flinch." He resumed his loud tones. "Wolf to man. First to fail to rise loses the match."

Wisner yawned, displaying an abundance of sharp teeth. The surrounding wolves edged closer.

"If you lose, you agree to cease your pursuit of the pup," Gunn said. "But if you win, we'll let you have him."

Wisner cocked an ear. He immediately laid his ears flat against his head, thinking, but Gunn had been heard and understood by the surrounding wolves. They began to bark, baying for Grant's blood.

Gunn grinned. "Well, Wisner? What's it going to be? Don't tell me you're afraid of a foolhardy pup."

Wisner's gaze fell on Nate.

Nate's eyes widened. Ben saw him move as if to step back, but only just stop himself in time.

Wisner's mouth fell open. He looked over his shoulder and barked once more. The baying wolves fell silent. Wisner began to walk in a circle, the wolves drawing back before him, forming an empty space in the center of the road.

"First not to get up, right?" Nate took a deep breath.

"Make sure you get up." Gunn said. "Once you're down and you stay down—there's not going to be much I can do."

Nate stared at Wisner. "Here goes everything." He walked into the ring.

Ben followed, but the moment he reached the bottom of the stairs, the wolves closed in, forming a barrier between himself and Nate. They hung back from the combatants, hissing and snarling, constantly in motion.

Ben struggled to keep his feet. *This is deliberate. Scare tactics.* The wolves didn't know Nate if they thought that was going to intimidate him.

Intimidate—or distract? Ben saw Nate take a deep breath, steeling himself for the fight—and his concentration waver as a wolf broke the barrier. "Nate! Look—"

Wisner leaped. The wolf barreled at Nate, landing with his full weight. Nate hit the concrete surface of the road with a crash that sounded like felled timber. Wisner rolled to his feet and turned to see Nate stagger to his knees. Wisner growled low in his throat.

"Why the surprise? You knew he wasn't human." Gunn flashed his teeth in a wolfish grin. "Nate's only doing what is natural to him as you're doing what's natural to the wolf. Surely you're not afraid?"

"Don't encourage him," Nate said. He flexed his fist, the ivy spilling down his arm moving with the gesture. "You're supposed to be on my side—"

"Heads up!" Gunn barked too late. Wisner had made his leap.

Nate went down under the full weight of the wolf again, but Wisner didn't have it all his own way. He was engulfed in vine, and for a second, Ben lost sight of the combatants as the bodies of the wolves jostling each other for a better view threatened to crush him.

"Move!" Ben shoved the nearest wolf with both hands. He didn't succeed in budging it, but the wolf's ears flattened against the back of its head, and it snapped at its neighbor.

It—felt me? Ben stared. *But that would mean—*

Wolves couldn't read. So were the werewolves not governed by the Register...?

Only one way to find out. Ben ran his hand up the back of the nearest wolf, deliberately going against the smooth weft of its hair, leaving fur spiked up behind him. The results were immediate. The wolf snapped its jaws and lunged at the wolf nearest it.

This wolf was already on edge from the situation. He dived at his attacker, and the two went down in a tangle of furry limbs and snapping jaws, the surrounding wolves darting back to avoid being drawn into the fracas.

Ben was knocked down in the rush. He curled up, awaiting a chance to draw himself up in safety.

A slow growl made every hair on his body rise. Ben looked up directly into Wisner's tawny eyes. The alpha wolf kept his gaze locked on the scrapping wolves as he continued his menacing rumble. Behind him, Ben heard the two wolves whimper as they sank to the ground. That was a clear warning against any more fights.

Ben swallowed. In his chest, he could feel the vampire rising and fought the urge to hiss at Wisner. *Not now! I have to hold him back—*

Hold back?

Wisner, seemingly satisfied that his subordinates were going to behave themselves, turned his attention back to Nate. He feinted one way and then leaped, obviously intending to bring him crashing down again. This time, Nate was ready for him. He met Wisner full on, grunting as he threw the wolf back.

"That's the ticket!" Gunn called from the steps.

One of Wisner's sons barked and instantly the air was full with the sound of the wolves, their determined volley of barks drowning out any other sound.

Wisner rolled to his feet in one fluid motion, circling Nate. Nate kept his eyes on him, braced for his next move.

Ben lay still on the concrete. His mind was racing. *No one can see me, feel me—the vampire's not a threat to anyone! And I might help Nate—*

Nate had the strength, but he lacked the fighter's instinct that would tell him when to go for the kill. Wisner had no such problem.

Ben stared at the werewolf's parted jaw and swallowed. *The vampire's not a threat to anyone. For the first time, I don't have to worry about what happens if I lose control.* He shut his eyes.

It was not hard to find the vampire. Surrounded by the snarling wolves, there was an undercurrent of predatory instinct that Ben reached for. He sat up, swiping his tongue across his bruised lip, and felt a note of hunger. *That's it!* Ben focused on the hunger, let it become a need.

These wolves have strayed far from their home. The vampire's thoughts came readily. Ben swiped his tongue over his teeth and discovered the fangs. *Do they know how lost they are?* The vampire stalked over to a wolf, staring him right in his golden eyes.

The wolf did not seem to see him, but he knew something was there. His hackles raised and he backed away into the wolf behind him, setting off a chain reaction of startled wolves. The vampire bared his fangs. *They know to fear me still!* And he did not need to hide. He could show his fangs openly and did not need to disguise his hunger or his strength—

Wisner's warning bark brought the vampire's attention back to the combatants. They stood, locked in a stare down in the center of the road. Both of them were breathing heavily, Nate bleeding from a new wound on his other arm, Wisner tangled in ivy and holding one leg stiffly. They glared at each other, the battle now a contest of wills.

An uneven battle. Now that the vampire was attuned to it, he could feel the presence of the surrounding wolves pressing down on them like a weight. Wisner's natural strength as an alpha wolf was bolstered by the presence of his followers, the sheer number of them making his natural command almost irresistible. Nate had great natural reserves of strength, but this—

This might be more than he can handle.

Ben's alarm mingled with the vampire's proprietary instinct. He snarled, stalking across the ring. Wisner crouched, his eyes locked on Nate.

The vampire thrust his face right up to the wolf's and snarled. He let all the venom he'd been holding back, all the frustration and fear come to the surface, using it with the deliberate knowledge of an apex predator. He brought all the hunger of the vampire into his threat, pitching it at animal level, predator to predator. *You can't see me, can you, wolf? But you know I'm here. You know I'm close.* The vampire crowed in triumph. *You know you can't stop me—*

Wisner whimpered. He took a step back before he caught himself, his gaze jerking up in alarm.

It was a moment's weakness—but the moment was all Nate needed. He lunged forward. Wisner's paws scraped across the surface of the road as he scrabbled for purchase and found none. He turned on Nate, snapping his mighty jaws, but he was too late. Nate heaved him up bodily and slammed him into the concrete. As Wisner struggled to rise, Nate grabbed him by his rear leg, sending him flying across the street. Wolves scattered to get out of the way as Wisner slid to a halt. Nate strode over to him, but the wolf made no attempt to get to his feet.

"The deal was first to fail to get up." Gunn's voice made the vampire start. He'd almost forgotten the presence of the *lemur*, and he bared his teeth in a perfunctory growl. "Well, Wisner?"

It didn't seem as if the wolf even heard him. Its eyes were tightly clenched. As Nate stood over it, he whined again, rolling onto his back. His forepaws raised, Wisner lay on his back in surrender.

Showing throat? The vampire crowed in delighted understanding. *The wolf admits he has lost!*

It took a moment for the surrounding wolves to understand what had happened. They stared at Nate, staring down at Wisner, absently wiping his bleeding arm. "I win, right?"

That was the cue for chaos. Wisner's sons leapt forward, making for Nate. They probably had some idea of avenging their father by destroying Nate. But the damage was done. With Wisner's defeat went Wisner's control over the vast body of gathered wolves.

Shaking himself, a massive gray wolf jumped toward Wisner. Killing him would ensure the wolf's place at the top of New Camden's lupine hierarchy. But the gray wolf wasn't alone in his ambitions. A brown wolf, with a speckled coat, jumped in front of him, teeth bared and hackles raised. Behind the brown wolf, his pack members assembled themselves for a fight. The gray wolf raised his voice, calling his pack to his side.

The vampire dodged under a leaping wolf. He made his way through the mass of furry bodies, heading toward where he'd last seen Nate—

"Not on my watch." The words were spoken, but the vampire felt as much as heard them. They were the screech of nails on a blackboard, the inescapable certainty of a nightmare. *"Badge or no badge, this is my city—and you're about to learn why."*

The wolves froze, hackles raised, as they turned to make sense of this new threat. Ben looked up to the steps.

Something Gunn-shaped stood there. There was something not right about it, a movement that didn't fit the body, a sense of something too big for the form that contained it. *"But if we're done playing nice, then I'm going to let loose. This is your only warning."* The Gunn-shaped thing took a jerky, uneven step down toward the road.

The smart wolves darted for the shadows. The foolish ones held their ground, snarling as they watched the thing approach.

The vampire hissed. The wolves gave him a wide berth, but he was too preoccupied to notice. All his attention was fixed on this newest threat—a threat he was only beginning to guess at. *So this is a lemur?*

"In a way, I got you to thank for this, Wisner. You got it wrong. Department Seven didn't make me what I am. Department Seven was meant to control me. Without it"—the thing bared teeth, but it wasn't the jagged, broken edges that alarmed, it was the cavernous space behind them, gaping, empty, *hungry*—*"I get to come out and play. Isn't that nice?"*

Wisner, flanked by his sons, got to his feet with an effort. He bared his teeth, but it was reflexive. His sons held their ground, but their eyes rolled wildly.

Afraid. The vampire was suddenly worried. *That's like blood to a lemur—*

Without any warning, the thing that had Gunn's shape let itself fall. As the person part of it slid to the ground, only the *lemur* remained. A rapidly expanding shadow that rushed toward them—

With a whimper, the first line of wolves turned and fled. Their fear communicated and soon the street was a mass of fleeing wolves, fighting and climbing over each other in their effort to escape. The vampire made a dive for the alleyway, but he was clipped by a leaping wolf, and a second wolf knocked him to the ground. As he struggled to rise, the third wolf collided with him, and he went down hard. There was a sudden sharp pain in his head, and his vision blurred.

Ben tried to rise and couldn't. He lay in the alley, hearing the howls of the terrified wolves and the awful screech of their pursuer, a thousand nightmares let loose at once. The *lemur* left fear in its wake, and Ben swallowed back the sudden knowledge that he would die in the alley with no one to know or care or even find him. *I'm lost—*

The distant shrill of sirens was the last thing he heard.

THE SUNLIGHT WAS persistent. Ben lay still, knowing instinctively that to move was to hurt, but eventually the light grew too much. He opened his eyes.

It was much, much too bright. Ben winced, shutting his eyes. But the strangeness of what he'd seen registered. Throwing a hand up between himself and the sun, Ben ignored the twinge of pain in his arm, and looked up at the buildings above him. He recognized them at once, but it took him a moment to realize what was so odd about his apartment building and the neighboring building. He was lying on his back in the alley, looking up at them.

Cautiously and very slowly, Ben levered himself into a sitting position. In addition to the numerous aches, his body felt stiff and bruised from lying on stone. *Have I been here all night?* Ben looked out at the street.

There were a few police cars parked by the side of the road. Their presence was something of a surprise, and Ben stared at them, until he realized why. *Police! That means the wolves—but why so few cars?* Using the wall to help him, he stood.

The road was reopened to traffic. Ben gave it a troubled glance as he climbed the steps to the entranceway. Was that a good sign or bad? It was good that the city was returned to normal, but if Wisner had succeeded in brushing last night's events under the carpet...

We could be in even bigger trouble. Ben frowned as he stood in front of the automatic doors.

His reflection frowned back at him. He looked thoroughly disreputable, his clothes torn and a cut he didn't even remember across his cheek. There were large shadows around his eyes, and a generous amount of dust.

Ben smiled tiredly at himself. *A shower—no, a bath,* he promised himself. *And then bed. Actual bed, not some alley.* The automatic door was taking a really long time to work so he waved his hand in front of the sensor. *And then something to eat.* For the first time since returning to life, he actually recognized hunger unprompted.

The doors still refused to open. Ben stepped back and repositioned himself in front of the sensor. "Come on."

He glared up at the camera—and felt a chill come over him.

Bennet Hawick, you exist only to yourself.

Ben sagged against the door. *How could I forget?* This was his life now—not living—existing.

A car pulled up in the street. Ben heard it without any interest. The enormity of his future seemed to occur to him for the first time, and he swallowed, fighting back a sense of panic. *What do I do?*

"Come on, Nate. You can daydream later."

Ben's head whipped up. *Nate?*

Aki was already halfway up the stairs, hands on his hips as he waited for his companions to leave the taxi they'd arrived in. Charlotte slid out of the back seat, while Vazul paid the driver. And Nate—

Nate stood beside the taxi, watching Vazul pay, with a slight frown.

"Earth to Nate! Hello?" Aki jumped back down to the base of the stairs. "What are you even thinking about?"

Nate turned to Aki. He had a Band-Aid on his chin, and one arm was resting in a loose sling. He looked tired, but there was a quiet satisfaction to him. "I was just thinking I seem to have taken an awful lot of taxis lately."

Ben caught his breath.

Even knowing it was hopeless, he couldn't look away from Nate. He watched him climb the stairs, one hand resting on Aki's shoulder. In a minute he would look up.

I should move. It would be too painful—the moment when Nate looked through him and didn't see him—but Ben couldn't force his limbs to obey him. *Please, Nate—see me!*

"I don't know what you're talking about," Aki said. "We can't afford taxis, remember? We're broke."

They were almost on top of him. The automatic door parted behind him. They were close enough now that Ben could reach out and touch him—and he did.

"Nate." He clutched at Nate's arm, but it was like there was an invisible barrier between them. Ben felt himself cut off from Nate's warmth. He didn't even see a flicker of awareness in Nate's eyes. "*Nate.*" His voice sounded hoarse, cracked and broken. "I'm right here—see me! You've got to—"

Nate walked past without even glancing in his direction. Ben was bumped to one side. He stepped back numbly as Charlotte and Vazul followed Nate and Aki into the building. Nate hadn't seen him. Nate couldn't see him.

Nate's premonition. Ben fought back a shaky sob. *You weren't there, and I was never going to see you again.* "I'm still here!"

No one reacted to his words. Ben turned to see Vazul join the others in the elevator. If he was fast, he might still be able to join him. But as Ben stepped forward, the automatic door slid shut.

Ben placed his hand on the cool surface of the glass. *This—this is my life now.*

GRANT WAS THE center of an excited crowd of greetings. He beamed widely, accepting the congratulations of his friends. Charlotte had thrown her arms around him in a hug, while the rest of them all tried to give him their news at once.

Vazul managed to drown out everyone else through pure volume. "The charges against you were dismissed. The council passed a no-confidence vote in your stepfather and they'll be laying charges of fear-mongering and abuse of power once he's well enough to leave the hospital."

"Hospital?" George wandered out of the kitchen, holding a pot of coffee. "I didn't hear that. You really went to town on him, Nate?"

"It wasn't me," Nate protested.

Vazul nodded. "Some kind of nervous break. Members of his pack are coming forward saying Wisner had been obsessed with you and with gaining power for some time. Whatever happened last night was just the icing on the cake. He couldn't face the fact he'd been defeated and just...collapsed."

Nate cast a worried look at the street outside and said nothing.

Ben, watching the conversation from the fire escape, smiled faintly. He didn't blame Nate for being nervous. The memory of the *lemur* was still fresh. Ben shuddered. The vampire's predator instincts should have shielded him from the *lemur's* attack, but instead, he'd been caught up in it like any of the wolves. *Not a good sign.* How long had Gunn been sitting on that particular power? Had he used it before? *There was a riot—just before Department Seven was formed.* Ben frowned. He'd have to look it up the next time he was at the university library—

He caught himself too late. *No libraries. No looking things up.* What was the use when you were unable to turn pages yourself?

He was just grateful no one had shut the door of the master bedroom. If they had, he wouldn't be able to see anything of the group gathered in the living room at all. *Although I'm not sure seeing is really a good thing.* This was as close as he could get to his friends, but it was still unbearably distant, a bittersweet reminder of what he couldn't have. He watched George slap Nate on the arm and laugh and felt an ache.

"I talked to Kenzies about you." Charlotte was excited to share her news, and her voice carried as far as the fire escape. "She said that without Wisner's opposition, there was no reason to suppose your application for independence wouldn't be granted. You've just got to pass an interview demonstrating you're still of sound mind and produce a permanent address."

"I know. She and Gunn dropped by earlier to check on me." Grant turned to Aki and Nate, an uncharacteristically shy smile on his face. "Aki, Nate. I was wondering if I could stay with you—and do it properly this time."

Nate looked up but whatever he was about to say was cut off by Aki. "We have a two-room apartment. And both rooms are taken."

"The sofa—"

Aki folded his arms across his chest. "I have plans for the sofa."

"You can share my RV," George offered. "I've got an air mattress. Play your cards right, I might even let you have a blanket."

Vazul snorted. "You do know there is no longer a bounty on him, hunter?"

As George turned to defend her motives, Ben looked away. Nate was safe. Grant had survived and was now almost assured of his freedom. *I have plenty of things to be grateful for. I knew the risks...* The thought trailed off. Knowing the risks did not make reality any easier to bear.

A noise behind him made him turn. Nate raised the window, looking out over the fire escape. His gaze flickered over Ben without making even the slightest difference to his frown.

I should go. Ben wrapped his arms around himself. He'd quickly realized nothing hurt as much as Nate's obliviousness to his presence— but at the same time, he couldn't bear to give up what slight contact he had.

Did I really choose to avoid him? Ben winced, thinking back on his choices. *For all my reasons, it came down to one thing. I didn't trust him.*

He swallowed. "I should have said this earlier." His voice had lost some of its hoarseness, but it still sounded far too weak for Ben's liking. "Now you can't even hear me. But I have to say it—whether you hear it or not—it's the truth." He looked up. "I didn't take your premonition seriously. I didn't take a lot of your concerns seriously. I should have trusted your instinct, and I didn't. It took me a long time to realize that your way of doing things wasn't my way, but I could trust you to be there for me—and I do." His voice wavered, and Ben made it fierce. "I'm trusting you to look after yourself. You've got to be all right, Nate. You've got to—" He swallowed. "I love you, Nate. I wasn't brave enough to say it when you could hear me, and now you'll never know, but—I love you."

The fire escape didn't creak as Ben stood. He carefully avoided looking back at Nate, knowing it would be too painful. Instead, he would find somewhere quiet to think, come up with a plan—

"What are you doing in here?" Aki's voice drifted down the fire escape after him. "Seriously, Nate. We should be celebrating."

Nate sighed. "Do you have the feeling that something—no. Someone—is missing?"

Ben stumbled to a halt, clutching the rail to keep his balance. He looked back at Nate, standing in the window, looking over his shoulder at his friends.

"Someone?" Aki sounded skeptical.

"I'm thinking back over everything that's happened. It's like putting together a jigsaw puzzle with a missing piece."

Aki laughed. "Since when do we do jigsaw puzzles?"

"No." Grant's voice was quiet, but commanding. Everyone stilled to listen. "I think Nate's right. There's something— I keep getting this feeling like there's someone else here, just out of reach, but when I turn to look, there's nothing there."

"A ghost? You know, our apartment is supposed to be haunted—"

"This isn't a ghost," Grant said with certainty.

Nate turned his back to the window. "It's not a ghost," he agreed. "I don't know what's going on... But I know I have to find out. I know it's important."

Ben caught his breath. Nate held the acorn in his hand. *The Register was written for people. I can't make them see me—but the wolves could sense me. They're not people. Plants aren't people—is that why I could move the acorn? And why Nate—remembers something?*

For the first time since the mayor had entered his name into the Final Register, Ben felt a spike of warmth. "I said I trusted you, Nate—and you can trust me too. I'm not giving up. *We're* not giving up."

About the Author

Gillian St. Kevern is the author of the Deep Magic series, the Thorns and Fangs series, the For the Love of Christmas series, and standalone novels, The Biggest Scoop and The Wing Commander's Curse. Gillian currently lives in her native New Zealand, but spent eleven years in Japan and has visited over twenty different countries. Her writing is a celebration of the weird and wonderful people she encounters on her travels.

As a chronic traveller, Gillian is more interested in journeys than endings, with characters that grow and change, becoming empowered to achieve their happy ending. She's not afraid to let her characters make mistakes or take the story in an unexpected direction. Her stories cross genres, time-periods and continents, taking readers along for an unforgettable ride.

Email: gillian.stkevern@gmail.com

Website: www.gillianstkevern.com

Mailing list: www.gillianstkevern.com/newsletter-sign-up.html

Facebook: www.facebook.com/gillian.stkevern

Twitter: @GillianStKevern

Pinterest: www.pinterest.com/gillianstkevern

Other books by this author

For the Love of Christmas!
The Ugliest Sweater
Ibiza on Ice
The Charity Shop Rejects—Live in Concert

Thorns and Fangs
Thorns and Fangs
Uprooted
Dead Wrong (coming February 2018)

Coming Soon from Gillian St. Kevern

Dead Wrong

Chapter One

THE AFTERNOON HAD all the gloom of a funeral. The concrete pavement and the drab external walls of the surrounding buildings extended to the gray sky above. Nate and Aki stood in silence in the alley beside their apartment building and contemplated the dead.

Nate, six feet tall, had to bow his head to look down at them. "You're sure it's not, I don't know, some kind of vampire cat?" He winced. The question sounded even worse out in the open.

Aki looked up at Nate, his hazel eyes flat. "You're kidding me. Have you ever heard of a vampire cat?"

Nate made a helpless gesture toward the bodies. "Look at them." There were two desiccated rats and, nearby, a shriveled up bird. "Animals don't eat like this." He turned the nearest rat over, noticing what looked like a puncture wound. He crouched to get a closer look.

"Maybe they were sick. Rats are riddled with disease, and pigeons are not any better—don't touch them!" Aki made a disgusted noise. "Ugh. Keep your gross, infected hands away from me."

Nate set the rat down and turned his head, giving Aki a speculative look.

Aki stepped backward. "Touch me and I promise I will dump you."

Nate snorted, turning his attention back to the dead animals. "You can't dump me. We're not dating."

"I can friend dump you—and I will."

"I co-signed the lease. You're stuck with me."

"I'm pretty sure Grant can find me a legal loophole involving pestilence." Aki stuck his hands in the pockets of his plaid trousers. He drummed one foot against the pavement, the movement making his keychain rattle. "Come on. Let's go."

Nate stood slowly, still looking down at the animals. "There's got to be some kind of explanation for this. Maybe we should call Department Seven?"

"They'd laugh in your face. This isn't even a case for animal control." Aki heaved a theatrically loud sigh. "If you're that desperate for excitement, ask George to take you hunting. She'd jump at the chance."

Nate frowned at Aki. "I'm not desperate for excitement."

Aki raised an eyebrow. "Aren't you? This is the longest we've gone without any supernatural mishaps since you got mixed up with the necromancer, and for the last month, you've been glancing over your shoulder, listening to sounds that aren't there, and watching the news for anything paranormal. If that's not desperation, I don't know what is."

Nate shivered. How to explain to Aki that for the last month, he'd had the constant suspicion that there was something there, just on the edge of his awareness? "I'm not desperate."

"Then why are we hanging out in a shadowy alley, acting like revenant bait?"

Nate blanched. Revenants were the most basic form of the undead, recently deceased with a taste for blood and no thought beyond acquiring it. Nate had been closer than he wanted to hungry revenants. "Bait implies I want to find one. I don't."

"Then can we please leave before one finds us—"

Something crunched in the shadows beyond the dumpster.

Nate's breath froze in his throat. He didn't dare turn his head to see what Aki was doing, concentrating all his attention on the shadows.

He heard a second crunch, as if something shifted on the stones beyond the dumpster. Nate stepped toward it.

"Don't." Aki grabbed his arm. "Please, Nate. This is a seriously bad idea."

"Stay here." Nate disentangled himself. "Get ready to call Department Seven."

"And after that, I'll call the funeral home." Aki had his phone in hand. "I'm having them put 'I told him not to do it' on your gravestone."

"Quiet." Nate knew a revenant couldn't kill him. At least he was pretty sure he was safe. His experience with the necromancer had woken Nate's own supernatural side. Being part plant could be inconvenient at times, but it did mean that he was impervious to things that were fatal to ordinary humans. But being a card-carrying psychic wouldn't protect Aki from becoming monster chow. Nate edged his way around the dumpster carefully. If it was a revenant, he'd have to act fast to stop it preying on Aki.

Nate rounded the corner.

Nothing there? The newspaper was spread out as if someone had been sleeping rough—never a good idea in New Camden, the city with the largest monster population in the world—and it crackled under foot. Was the sound just the wind rustling through its pages? Nate turned to leave and caught a dull glow out of the corner of his eyes. He grinned. "Aki, come and look at this."

"Is it more dead animals? Because I can pass."

Nate crouched down. "Here, kitty. I'm not going to hurt you."

"A cat?" Aki snorted, and Nate heard his footsteps on the stone behind him. "All that over nothing."

Nate clicked his fingers. "Come on."

The cat watched him balefully. She stretched, displaying her claws, before taking a step into the light. She flicked her tail, watching Nate out of her one good eye. Her left eye was milky white, with the lines of an old scar above and below. She was skinny, her fur bare in patches, and her tail was crooked. Part of one ear was missing, looking like a tattered flag on a pirate ship, with her prominent ribs the hull.

"Whoa. That's the ugliest cat I've ever seen."

"She can't help that. Poor thing. Who knows how long she's been living out here?"

Aki smacked Nate's hand away from the cat. "Stop risking animal diseases! Look at it. Probably crawling with fleas!"

"It's just an old stray cat."

Aki scoffed. "I was wrong. That's definitely some variety of hell beast."

Nate clicked his fingers, succeeding in drawing the cat closer to him. "You're so mean. Just because she's been on the losing end of a few fights..."

"More than a few. It's probably got every disease in the book."

Nate extended his hand, and the cat cautiously sniffed it. "I think she likes me."

Aki leaned against the dumpster to watch. "Haven't you learned anything from the disaster that was you adopting the last stray?"

Nate looked up. "The last stray turned out to be Grant, who we saved from his evil stepdad, getting you a boyfriend in the process."

"We're not dating," Aki said immediately. "If you're so stuck on Grant, ask him out yourself. I don't want him."

Nate smiled to himself, stretching out his hand to the cat's tattered ears. She hissed, and before Nate could react, sunk her teeth into his hand. He jerked his hand back. "Ow!"

"Ha! Told you!"

Nate sat back on his heels, nursing his hand. "Are you grinning?"

"It's called *schadenfreude.*" Aki nudged Nate with the toe of his sneaker. "And you deserved it."

Nate looked back down, but at his exclamation, the cat had darted back into the shadows. She squeezed into the narrow gap between the dumpsters. All he could see of her was the gleam of her dead eye. "You're a bad best friend."

Aki just shrugged. "You should have checked the fine print. It's too late now. You're stuck with me."

Nate stood, dusting off his hands on his jeans. "Maybe Grant will find me a legal loophole."

Aki elbowed him. "Not allowed. It's 'best friends forever.' Not best friends until Aki hurts my feelings."

Nate draped his arm over Aki's shoulders. "Since when is BFF legally binding?"

"Well it is. So it's a good thing I plan on keeping you around." He leaned comfortably against Nate's side. "That's your cue to say there's no one you would rather be stuck with."

Nate paused, guiltily conscious something wasn't right. There was something—someone—missing.

"Nate?"

Nate realized he'd stopped walking.

Aki was watching him with an expression of concern on his face. "I was only joking."

Nate grinned. He leaned over, tapping Aki on his shoulder. "Got you."

"You!" Aki demonstrated his feelings of friendship by trying to kick him.

THEY WERE STILL bickering when they arrived at the apartment.

Nate paused to fish in his pocket for the key." Grant's nice and obviously into you."

Aki jiggled impatiently. "I liked him better as a dog."

Nate paused, key in hand, to stare at him. "You didn't like him as a dog. In fact, you complained constantly."

"Just open the damn door."

"I'm just saying"—Nate unlocked the door and pushed it open—"that there are a lot of inconsistencies in your story—"

"Surprise!"

Nate's mouth dropped open. Grant stood in the center of their apartment, a smug grin on his face. The werewolf looked relaxed and happy, a big change from their first meeting. While he still looked like a shave wouldn't go amiss, his gaunt face no longer looked starved and his eyes sparkled.

He wasn't alone. Charlotte and Vazul, Nate's friends from supernatural counseling, held up a sign. The difference between angular Charlotte's height and stocky Vazul's lack made it lopsided. Despite the angle, the message was clear: Thirty-one days since Nate started a supernatural event.

Nate looked from the banner to his friends, taking in the decorations strung across the apartment walls. "What's all this?"

George grinned at him from the kitchen doorway. The supernatural hunter was dressed for fun, with dangly earrings and a bright-orange shade of lipstick. She'd ditched her usual headscarf, her curls trimmed to uniform length. If Nate hadn't known where to look, he wouldn't have noticed the damage done by the demonic attack George had only narrowly survived. "You've gone an entire month without a near-death experience. I say you're slacking, but I was outvoted. These wimps consider that an accomplishment."

"Wow. I don't know what to say." Now that the surprise had worn off, Nate saw a lot of effort had gone into the party. Food was laid out on the coffee table—three pizza boxes, a selection of what looked like cakes, a salad, and cupcakes with delicate icing that looked suspiciously like Mandy's handiwork. Nate jerked his head up and saw her standing behind Charlotte and Vazul, nervously picking at her sleeve. "Mandy—Bea?"

Mandy smiled tentatively, but Beatrice just raised her glass in an ironic toast. "Aki told us about it. We agreed it was an occasion worth celebrating."

"I hope that's okay." Mandy bit her lip. "I mean, it's been a while."

"Of course it's okay." Nate closed the distance between them to give her a hug. He breathed in the familiar scent of her jasmine perfume. "It's great to see you." How long had it been? Not since... Not since he'd come out as supernatural. Nate paused. Mandy had made her views on the supernatural clear.

But Mandy squeezed him tightly with obvious relief. "I'm glad."

Nate grinned as he released her. "Wait. If Aki invited you—" He turned his head to stare at his friend.

Aki smirked at him. "Like taking candy from a baby. You've got no idea how many times this week you walked in on us planning this and had no idea."

"Given that we're talking about Nate, I am not surprised." Vazul always sounded superior, but now he was infuriatingly pleased with himself. "Going thirty-one days without incident is more of an accomplishment than I thought."

"Was that what you were doing?" Aki had seemed unusually keen on his coursework, but Nate had put that down to the fact that Grant was brushing up on his study.

Grant cleared his throat. Immediately the group felt silent, all faces turning toward him. "I think it's time to come clean. Aki?"

Aki slouched on the arm of one of the apartment's two armchairs. "As fun as teasing Nate is, his ability to keep himself out of trouble for an unprecedented thirty-one days—"

"Hey!" Nate protested.

"Was only a front." Aki stuck out his tongue. "The real reason you're all here is because Grant's got some news."

Every head turned back to Grant. He grinned. "My application to live independently of my pack has been approved. I'm a free wolf."

Charlotte squealed, dropping the sign as she clapped. "Grant, I'm so happy!"

"Took their time," Vazul grumbled leaning the sign against the wall. "I suppose your old pack contested it?"

Grant nodded grimly. "Naturally. They argued that if anything, the extreme circumstances around my first Full Moon proved I was a hazard. The judge wasn't having any of it. He pointed out the extreme events were the result of my stepfather's machinations, and I had shown considerable self-restraint in the face of overwhelming opposition." His grin displayed very sharp teeth. "They slunk out of the courtroom with their tails between their legs."

"You didn't tell us you had your hearing!" Charlotte stared at him with astonishment. "We would have come to support you."

"And risk your final exams?" Grant shook his head. "No. You'd already done so much for me. I couldn't ask any more."

"Congratulations, Grant." Nate held out his hand. "No one deserves this more than you do."

Grant looked at him, light flashing in his tawny eyes. Then it was gone, and he squeezed Nate's hand. "Thank you. This wouldn't have been possible without you."

Nate ducked his head. "At least my tendency for starting supernatural events is good for something."

"Oh god." Aki groaned. "Don't encourage him!"

"We need a toast." George cracked open the wine bottle and Charlotte hastily grabbed glasses. "Gather round."

Grant was perfectly at home as the center of attention. He thanked everyone, even Mandy and Bea who gave their congratulations awkwardly, before planting himself in Aki's chair.

Charlotte immediately sat opposite. "Now that you've got your independence, what are you going to do?"

"He's going to legalize chasing cars." Aki, still perched on the chair's arm, looked sleek and satisfied, like a well-fed cat.

Grant shot him a look, before turning back to Charlotte. "I'm going back to law school. Now, more than ever, it's important for the supernatural community to have a voice in the legal system." His arm settled around Aki's waist, and Aki gravitated slightly toward him. "My experiences of the last month have shown me just how open to exploitation the current laws surrounding werewolves are. I'm sure there are more cases like mine right here in New Camden."

"One step at a time." Aki nudged him with his elbow. "Before you change the world, you have to pass your bar exam. And while you may be able to take on werewolves, you've yet to prove yourself against *lawyers*."

And he expects anyone to believe he's not interested in Grant. Nate shook his head and sipped his drink. From the wine's quality, it was clearly Beatrice's contribution to the party. He made his way to where she leaned against the wall. "Thanks for coming," he said quietly. "How did Aki manage to drag you into this?"

Beatrice cast him an amused sideways glance. "We invited ourselves. We've been listening to Aki complain about the freeloading werewolf in the flat above for the last month, and well, it's a rare man, werewolf or otherwise, who can hold his attention an entire month."

Nate suppressed his snort of laughter with difficulty. "Now that you've seen him, what do you think?"

Beatrice studied Grant as if she was appraising him for a photo shoot. "Interesting. Very handsome—but with Aki, that goes without saying."

Nate bit his lip. Aki's taste in men was not always so discerning.

Beatrice continued. "He's got something else. I don't know how to put my finger on it... But it's there. I'm not interested at all in men, but I can't deny it. Whatever it is."

Nate studied Grant afresh. Was that Grant's natural charisma, or the latent power of an alpha werewolf?

"He's very good-looking," Mandy agreed. "But he's not the only reason we're here." She looked at Nate. Her copious eyeshadow highlighted the bright blue of her eyes, while her dark lashes made her naturally blonde hair seem even lighter. "You're a very hard man to track down recently."

Nate squirmed. That hadn't been entirely accidental. His memory of exactly what Mandy had done to get him into trouble with Department Seven was fuzzy, but her tearful apology had not been enough. Now that time had passed, he was pleased to see an old friend. "Yeah, well... I've been putting in daytime shifts."

Beatrice took her eyes off Grant to consider Nate. "There's a rumor going round you're looking to leave Century."

Century was the nightclub where Nate and Aki worked—not that nightclub came anywhere close to describing the club. Yes, it had a bar and music and events. The dance floor was nearly always busy, and when it wasn't, it was only because it was too packed for people to dance. But people didn't come to Century to dance.

They came for Century's reputation and for its staff. The club was notorious as New Camden's most well-known brothel, but it was its respectability, not its vice that attracted. Century dressed its staff in designer clothes, gave them protection and a hefty price tag, and encouraged them to employ their charm and their power of veto in equal amounts. The result was a club with an atmosphere unique in New Camden. Mandy and Beatrice were among those attracted by the club's promise of spice and safety, and they'd quickly gravitated to Nate.

Nate was skilled at putting people at ease, and it hadn't taken long for him and Mandy to discover they were both small-town graduates trying to find their feet in the big city. They had enjoyed a low-key flirtation that had continued over months of drink orders and endured Beatrice's pointed remarks. Now?

I've missed Mandy. But the same way as I've missed Bea. Nate frowned. Mandy was lovely, generous, and sweet. More importantly, she got things that only someone who grew up in the country got. *It's great to see her again, but that's as far as it goes.* Nate realized with a guilty start that Beatrice waited for his answer. "Yeah. It's going to be weird not working at Century, but I think it's time."

Mandy tilted her head. "How come?"

Nate shrugged. In many ways, Century was the best thing to have happened to him. How to put into words the nebulous feeling that was behind him giving it up? "I'm not feeling the job anymore."

Beatrice and Mandy exchanged a glance. It was only a second, but it was layered with so much feminine significance that Nate, shameless to a fault, had to fight a blush.

"Did you meet someone special?" Beatrice asked.

It was strange. The answer was no. You didn't meet someone special enough to quit Century over and forget them—but Nate almost thought that there was. "Nah. I think I just reached the point where I want something more from my relationships, and I'm not going to find that while working at Century."

He expected one or both of them to pounce on that, but Beatrice simply nodded, sipping her drink. "Aki's not happy about it."

Nate winced. "No." Not happy was an understatement, and probably behind Aki's recent insistence on emphasizing the importance of their friendship at any given opportunity. "I was hoping Grant living so close to us would be a distraction, but it hasn't worked like that."

"Give Grant time." Mandy looked around. "Who are your other friends?"

"That's George with the pizza." Nate nodded toward her. "She's a supernatural hunter. We met when—" Shit. Nate couldn't tell Mandy that George had been investigating his brother as a suspect in her hunting partner's murder. "She was on a hiking vacation."

Beatrice raised an eyebrow. "Hiking?"

"I met Vazul and Charlotte at my counseling sessions." Nate didn't want to get into this any more than he wanted to get into George investigating him, but at least no one had died during their counseling sessions. "As a newly awoken supernatural, I have to do them."

"Makes sense." Mandy looked curiously at the others. "Are they...newly awoken, too?"

She was taking this way better than Nate expected. "Uh, no, actually. Charlotte's a witch and—" Nate paused. Vazul refused to say what he was.

"A witch?" Mandy brightened, sharing an eager glance with Beatrice.

"Not like a bad witch," Nate said hastily. "She's —" He paused. Mandy seemed interested, not alarmed.

"Would she mind if we asked her about it?" Beatrice asked.

"I don't think so." Nate looked across the room, where Charlotte stood, holding a vegan brownie and looking as though she wasn't quite sure what to do with herself. He caught her eye and beckoned her to join them. "Charlotte, these are my friends Bea and Mandy. They're interested in witchcraft."

"It's not what you think it is," Charlotte said immediately. "Most harmful spells are outlawed. Witchcraft today mostly concentrates on self-improvement. Like yoga, except without the yoga."

"Without the yoga?" Beatrice put her drink down and turned, giving Charlotte her full attention. "Tell me more."

Charlotte looked from Mandy to Beatrice. "Are you interested in practicing?"

Mandy nodded. "We might be. From what I've read, it sounds fascinating."

"Wait." Nate couldn't keep the incredulous note out of his voice. "You've read about witchcraft?"

"An example you could follow." Charlotte frowned at Nate. "You have the makings of a natural witch, if you would only apply yourself."

Nate ignored her, speaking to Mandy. "I didn't think this was something you would want to learn about."

Mandy looked at her feet. "Since learning about you, I had to rethink a lot of my assumptions about the supernatural. I want to learn more. Beatrice and I took a basic spellcraft course at night school."

"Yeah?" Nate grinned. "That's really cool."

Mandy smiled, tucking her hair out of her face. "Well..."

"I was actually thinking of forming a coven," Charlotte said hesitantly, "if you were interested."

The feeling bypassed Nate's nerves and went straight to his fight or flight reflex. *Danger,* it said. *Close and drawing closer. Inescapable.*

Nate's head jerked up. He scanned the room, looking for the source of the threat. In New Camden, danger was never far away. Even daylight was no promise of safety. Vampires were the most well-known of New Camden's population of monsters, but there were many more who hunted during the day.

Instead, he saw Grant laughing at one of Aki's jokes, Vazul busily explaining that whatever Aki had just said was an impossibility and George rolling her eyes as she grabbed another slice of meat lovers. Nate stared. *Am I dreaming?* The feeling was vivid, clinging to him with the same clammy grip as a nightmare. His heart still raced. But not a single one of his friends reacted.

Nate swallowed. Charlotte was an experienced witch. As a werewolf, Grant's reflexes extended beyond the natural world. If anything sinister lurked in the apartment, he would know. Vazul... Nate couldn't speak for his senses, but he was a good ally to have in a fight. And Aki... Nate watched him closely. Aki had the ability to see the future. Foresight was hard to tie down, but it gave him a sixth sense for threats. If there was any danger around, Aki would be the first to know.

Aki leaned forward, helping himself to a slice of pizza. "I'm just saying the sign could have been thirty days since Grant did laundry and have had just the same impact."

Aki couldn't talk. He had only once done the laundry since he and Nate moved in together. But it wasn't his chronic untidiness that troubled Nate.

If there was anything to sense, Aki should have sensed it. Nate looked around the room, from Charlotte, deep in conversation with Beatrice and Mandy, to Grant, trying to steal Aki's pizza, to George, picking up the argument with Vazul. His friends' lack of reaction said it all.

Nate felt sick. *I'm the only one who feels this?*

NATE LEANED AGAINST his bedroom door with a sigh. Excusing himself from the party without seeming suspicious had been a challenge, but finally he was alone. He took a deep breath. The sense of menace was muted but still there.

I know it's nothing. Ruthlessly, Nate faced the feeling with the knowledge that it was only imagination. *You've got to be a proper Fortune Teller to have precognitions! Someone—people are always telling me that!* He took another breath, this time letting it out slowly. *You're over this.*

By the third slow exhale, some of the feeling of imminent menace had gone. Nate dropped backward onto his bed with a sigh. *Why now? I'm not allergic to parties. I like everyone here. There's no reason for me to be anxious.* He stretched out his hands, absently stroking the quilt Ma had sent in her last care package.

He encountered something cold and smooth. Nate knew what it was even before his fingers closed around the acorn. It hadn't been there when he'd made his bed that morning. *Another one.* He turned it over in his hand, admiring its warm grain. *Just when I needed it... Is that deliberate?*

It had to be deliberate. Acorns didn't appear out of thin air. Aki had insisted that Nate start locking his window at night, but the acorns kept coming. *Someone's behind this.* The thought gave Nate a warm feeling. *Someone's telling me something.*

The door opened. Nate sat up, instinctively hiding the acorn within his fist. "Aki?"

Aki shut the door behind him and leaned on it. He took a moment to eye Nate. Unlike Nate, he was dressed for a party. Nate considered Aki's bright plaid pants, chunky leather belt and boots. *That should have been a major clue.* Aki was dressed to impress, not for a casual coffee with his roommate.

"Are you okay?"

"Me?" Nate licked his lip. Had Aki noticed his reaction?

Aki rolled his eyes. "I'm not talking to your jungle." He gave Nate's collection of plants a glare and then took a step toward him, plunking himself down on the bed next to Nate. "You know the sign was just a joke, right? The only reason we did it because we thought you'd find it funny."

"Because it was." Nate nudged him. "If a bit exaggerated. Still, it was for a good cause."

Aki looked at his nails. "I suppose Grant barely qualifies as a good cause."

"Careful. Werewolves have really good hearing. What if he hears you?"

"I hope he does." Aki glanced at Nate. "So if you're not nursing a sense of injustice, what are you doing in here when you could be making eyes at Mandy?"

It was the perfect opportunity to tell Aki about his feeling. Nate rolled the acorn around his palm as he drew a deep breath. The difficulty was putting it into words—

Aki's eyes dropped to Nate's hand and he froze. "Another one?"

Nate stiffened. "I found it just now. It was on my bed."

"This is getting seriously creepy." Aki stood, tossing Nate's pillows aside as he searched for any further acorns.

"They're just acorns."

"For now. See if you feel this way when it's a disembodied ear." Aki tossed a pillow at Nate and continued his search in Nate's wardrobe.

"An ear?"

"It could be any body part. I don't think serial killers really care."

"It's not a serial killer, Aki."

Aki spun around. "How else do you explain it then? No normal person would spend a month leaving acorns in our apartment!"

"We don't know it's someone," Nate protested.

"They're not getting in here on their own." Aki waved a hand toward Nate's window. "We've both been careful to lock the apartment when we go out. Neither of us are leaving windows open. But this keeps happening!"

"It's no big deal."

"Bypassing a locked door to get into a room is a big deal!" Aki waved his hand toward the door. "Look. One of our friends has to know something that could help us figure this out. Let's ask."

Nate's fingers tightened around the acorn. The idea of sharing something so personal with the group repelled him. "No." The vehemence in his tone startled him.

It startled Aki. He stared at Nate, a faint red tinge spreading across his cheeks.

The doorbell rang.

Thank god for latecomers. Nate nodded toward the door. "Shouldn't you get that?"

Aki shook his head, refusing to be diverted. "They can handle it. Like they'd handle this weirdo if you'd just say something!"

"I don't want to say something."

Aki folded his arms across his chest. "If you don't, I will. This can't keep happening."

There was a knock at Nate's door. "Nate, Aki? Mind if I come in?" Grant's voice had an unusually strained note.

Aki and Nate shared a glance and turned as one to the door. "What's up?"

Grant opened the door. "You've got a visitor, Nate."

"We didn't ask anyone else," Aki started.

Grant stepped out of the doorway. "He insists."

Nate stood, sliding the acorn into his pocket. He stepped into the living room.

The party was not just dead. It had an obituary to prove it. Mandy and Beatrice had retreated into the kitchen, and Vazul looked as if he wished he didn't have too much pride to follow them. Charlotte was doing a very poor job of pretending not to gag on the vaguely sulfurous smell that clung to the air, stifling all the energy in the room. George, never daunted by anything, looked uncomfortable.

The only person, in fact, who looked at home was Gunn, his head tilted as he studied the discarded banner. "Cute," he pronounced. "If wildly inaccurate."

"Gunn?" Nate felt a sense of relief entirely at odds with Gunn's entire existence. Not only was the Department Seven officer's presence a sign that something was seriously wrong, but the man was a *lemur*, a supernatural being Nate didn't fully understand but knew equaled bad news. Despite his better knowledge, he grinned. "What are you doing here?"

Gunn jerked his head toward the sign. "You're going to need to change that."

"What do you mean? I haven't done anything."

"Shows what you know." Gunn bared teeth that were yellowed, jagged, and feral. "You're coming with me, Nate. I got a crime scene that has your name all over it."

Chapter Two

NATE GRIPPED THE side of his seat. His life flashed before his eyes, a fact that had nothing to do with Gunn's summons and everything to do with his driving.

The *lemur* drove like he did everything else, turning a blind eye to the rules when it suited him, or flagrantly pushing them as far as he could. He dived into New Camden's crowded roads with characteristic recklessness. In a good car, Gunn's risk-taking would have been less hair-raising, but the car took Gunn's philosophy of inflicting misery as widely as possible to new lows. Not only was it old, with gears that gasped alarmingly when forced to accelerate, but it seemed to have adopted its owner's carefree approach to little things like signals. It stank of putrefaction and cigarette ash. Nate would not have been surprised to learn someone had died in it.

Gunn charged through a red light, causing a compact sedan to screech to a halt. He hurtled round the corner to a barrage of screeching brakes and horns. "Women drivers."

Nate dared to take his eyes off the road. "Aren't you supposed to use a siren when you're in a hurry?"

"Where's the fun in that?"

Nate bit his lip. "The party was Aki's idea of a joke. I'm not bored or anything, so if this is on my behalf, you don't need to."

Gunn turned his head to grin at Nate. "Don't like my driving?"

"I'm surprised you're driving at all. I didn't think they had cars in your time."

Gunn snorted. "Your education is sadly lacking. I was driving when all you needed for a license was proof you owned the car."

"I'm no longer surprised." Nate shut his eyes.

A few minutes later, after hearing nothing but the screech of tires and the abuse of the other drivers, it occurred to Nate that this was unusual. Gunn was infamous for his terrible interpersonal skills, and Nate was a captive audience. He should be gleefully fanning Nate's fears, not sitting in silence. "You're weirdly quiet. What happened?"

"Don't want to spoil the witness by giving you ideas," Gunn said.

"You've never cared about that before." Nate hesitated. "Is something wrong?" He winced. "Wronger than usual, I mean."

Gunn growled. "Don't push it, Nate."

"What? I'm just saying. You're normally a lot more abrasive."

"I figured I'd go easy on you." Gunn's mouth soured. "After all, the last time you saw me, I wasn't exactly myself."

Nate stared at him. "What do you mean?"

"Jesus, Nate, do I have to spell it out?" Gunn threw his hands up. The car, with no one steering it, lurched dramatically. "You saw the *lemur*."

Nate shivered. A month later, the feeling of sheer terror enfolding him was still very near. He remembered the gaping mouth of the...thing...as it stretched out, all hunger and death. He'd dropped his gaze in the hopes that not looking at it would make it less, but not being able to see it gave its approach the horrible certainty of a nightmare—a living nightmare he couldn't escape. All around him, the werewolves had whined, rolling eyes and baring teeth until their nerves failed them, and they turned and fled. Some had been too petrified to move, and stood shivering, their eyes fixed on the thing as it drew nearer.

And then it had moved beyond them, leaving Nate gasping for breath, surrounded by the werewolves—transformed back into naked men and happy to see the police officers there to arrest them.

"Yeah. I did." He hesitated and then decided that with Gunn's driving, this was hardly going to make things worse. He slapped the officer on his arm. "And I'm pretty sure the *lemur* saved my life."

Gunn snorted. "You've got the worst self-preservation instincts of anyone I know, and that's really saying something." He leaned over, fiddling with the car radio. "How do you feel about jazz, Nate?"

"Hate it."

"Perfect." Gunn cranked the volume up. "Jazz it is."

OLD CEMETERY WAS the most famous of New Camden's many cemeteries. It dated back to when New Camden's settlers innocently looked forward to a prosperous future, untroubled by the knowledge of the supernatural already present among them. Its dead were housed in elegant marble crypts with the expectation they would stay there. Stone angels placed their hands together in attitudes of solemnity, something of their silence extending to the police officer stationed at the wrought-iron gates. He caught sight of Gunn and flinched, snapping to attention as if stung.

"Sir! The—"

"I know the place." Gunn waved the officer aside. "Like old times, isn't it Nate? Can't think of the last time I was here. Oh wait. Yes, I can. You locked me in a crypt."

He should have known Gunn wasn't over that. Nate hunched his shoulders, concentrating on the path. Twilight had been and gone, and the night gave the cemetery even more gravitas. "It seemed like a good idea at the time."

"A good idea. I don't know what happens inside that pretty head of yours, Nathaniel, but it bears no resemblance to thought—" Gunn stopped suddenly.

Nate barely avoided stumbling into his back. He looked over Gunn's shoulders to the path ahead. They were in one of the more modern areas of the cemetery, where marble had been replaced by quartz and crypts and statues by plain slabs. The wrought-iron lamp posts illuminated an orange tent set up over a grave and uniformed officers milling around outside. Nate caught sight of the stocky figure of Kenzies, Gunn's long-suffering deputy among them. She stood next to another woman in the Department Seven uniform. "There's Kenzies." Nate felt some of his tension ease. Kenzies did not share Gunn's attitude to their work.

Gunn's nostrils flared. He stalked over to the tent, fury evident in every line of his wiry body. "What are *you* doing here?"

Nate gave the Department Seven officer a second glance. She looked just as startled by Gunn's appearance as the others, turning a pale face toward them. Her blonde hair was streaked with gray. Nate would have put her around forty. She looked ordinary, far too ordinary for Department Seven, and Nate frowned, wondering what on earth this mild-looking woman had done to rouse Gunn's ire.

It was then he became aware of the smell of leaves in autumn, and like the brush of a cobweb, the consciousness of a presence that made his skin leap. *Vampire.*

A figure with his back to them turned. Nate saw that what he'd taken for a uniform jacket was actually a navy peacoat. "Evening, Isaiah." Hunter's dark eyes glittered with amusement, and his sultry drawl made his use of Gunn's name sound affectionate, rather than the calculated provocation it was. "You took your time."

Gunn growled. "Kenzies, I gave you orders to boot any spectators."

"ARX was just as involved as Nate in this case." Kenzies bore Gunn's anger with stoic indifference. "Hunter has a right to be here, and we could benefit from his insight."

Gunn grit his teeth. "If you called him in—"

"Give us some credit." Hunter casually rearranged his scarf. Two of the female officers and one of the men slowed what they were doing to watch him smooth his scarf and lift his shoulder-length hair free of it. "ARX has monitored this graveyard ever since the incident. I knew as soon as I woke tonight. I have a right to be here."

"Go about your work," Gunn snapped at the staring officers. He glared at Kenzies. "And I suppose you've been passing the time instead of scouting the scene."

Kenzies smiled at him. "I knew you'd prefer that someone kept a close eye on Hunter."

Gunn dug in his habitual bomber jacket for a cigarette. "A close eye, she says." He turned his glare back onto Hunter. "No flirting with my staff."

Hunter shrugged. "We were merely making polite conversation. I'm aware that 'polite' isn't in your vocabulary, but you might want to try it some time."

"Catch more flies with honey, you mean?" Gunn scowled. "I'll pass."

"There're no flies on your staff," Hunter said. "I haven't even been allowed to view the corpse yet. And I did ask, very nicely." He turned his gaze on Nate, his eyes lingering. "Hello, Nathan. You look well."

Nate gulped. Even with the warning he'd been given, Hunter's gaze was still a shock. It didn't matter how much time he spent in the vampire's presence, it was still hard to think of anything beyond the man's physical presence when he was there. Nate deliberately ran through a list of Hunter's flaws—callous indifference to taking advantage of others to get his own ends, manipulative, questionably honest, way too charming for anyone's good, tried to kill him—and still he found himself breathless. "Hunter. I didn't expect to see you." The effort of speaking made his voice sound gruff, and Nate winced. He summoned the calmness of an oak to meet the vampire. "What's going on?"

Hunter raised an eyebrow in surprise and opened his mouth, but Gunn cut him off. "I want Nate to see the scene without any preconceptions. Kenzies?"

"Nothing's been touched," she reported. "The crime scene photographers have been in, but no one else."

Nate looked toward the tent with trepidation. "I'm no expert on investigations. I don't know what you expect me to do here."

The third member of the Department Seven staff cleared her throat. "If he isn't an expert...?"

"Right. Forgot you'd missed the fun." Gunn waved his cigarette toward Nate. "Nathan Granger. Pretty much single-handedly kept the city's police forces occupied while you were off relaxing."

"Hospital isn't exactly what I'd call R and R." The woman's eyes settled on Nate with undisguised interest. "Well, well. I've heard some interesting things about you. Helen Tremaine."

Nate returned her handshake. "I was trying to help." He turned to Kenzies. "I still have no idea what you want me to do."

Kenzies beckoned him to follow her and started toward the tent. "We'd like your opinion on the scene."

Nate followed slowly. "I know nothing about forensics. I don't even watch *CSI*."

Tremaine snorted. "That's a mark in your favor."

"Just give us your honest impressions," Kenzies assured him. "We've got experts for the rest of it."

If they have experts, why are they wasting their time with me at all? Nate was uneasily conscious of the curious glances of the white-coated forensics officers standing around waiting. What did they think of this all? Did they know who—what—Nate was?

Kenzies held the tent flap aside and ushered Nate in. Immediately, he was assailed with a familiar scent. The metallic tang of blood was underlain with a potpourri-like smell of herbs that even the smoke couldn't muffle. Nate felt a cold hand settle on his skin, the rain that fell the night he died running again down his neck. He knew what he would see before he raised his eyes to the gravestone. "No!"

The man sprawled like a puppet with its strings cut. He was shirtless, with jagged red lines carved into his bare chest. With the smooth gray slab of the grave beneath him, he looked like some bizarre entree served at a horrifying feast.

Nate looked helplessly at Kenzies. "He was supposed to stay dead. To be gone for good!"

Kenzies's eyes softened, but her voice remained crisply matter of fact. "Who are you referring to, Nate?"

"The necromancer. Peter de Silver." Nate looked down at the man and immediately wished he hadn't. "You have to see it. Who else worked like this?"

"You're the only person living who saw de Silver's work." Gunn's voice was right behind him and made Nate jump. He turned to see that Gunn and Hunter had both joined him in the tent, watching him closely. "Well, his unofficial work at least." He sneered at Hunter.

The vampire ignored him. "I, too, had the chance to observe his handiwork," he said. "I agree with Nate. This is too much to be coincidence, especially given the location."

The location? Nate knew that asking would do him no favors. Gunn operated on a need-to-know basis, especially in front of Hunter with whom he shared an acrimonious history. Instead, he took a hesitant step toward the body. He looked at the name on the headstone. "In memoriam, Austin Hawick," he read aloud. "This wasn't on the job description." He frowned. "Hawick." The name sounded familiar. Intimately familiar. So why was it coming up blank?

"Former ARX employee," Gunn said. "On whose grave the first of the necromancer's victims was discovered."

"Brook." The memory came back to Nate with a guilty start. Brook had been murdered because of his association with Hunter, an association Nate had briefly shared.

"I'm starting to wonder if old Hawick was the virtuous staff member you took him for. I mean, once is bad enough, but to have two guys murdered on your grave..."

"Austin was a stalwart opponent of black magic, the last person to encourage a necromancer," Hunter said promptly. "I'm entirely at a loss as to why the necromancer would fixate on him at all, unless he was jealous of Austin's position within my household. But even that doesn't make sense. Austin died a year before he made his bid for power."

The necromancer. Nate watched Hunter closely. Odd that he would call him what he was known to the public rather than by his name. When he'd worked for ARX, he'd been 'Peter.' Or was the name too bitter a reminder? After all, Peter had been an integral part of Hunter's staff.

"There's a lot I don't understand," Tremaine said quietly. "I was reading the case files on the way over here. One of you censored it?"

"I wish," Kenzies said promptly. "It's hard enough getting Gunn to fill out reports at all. I've given up attempting to moderate his language. If I had time to go through them—"

Tremaine shook his head. "Not like that. If you read through the notes, there are large chunks of text missing." She held out a manila file.

"Missing text?" Hunter sounded interested.

Gunn glared at him. "You've seen what you're here to see. Scram."

"Perhaps I can offer my assistance. I was heavily involved in the case, as you might remember."

Kenzies skimmed through the file. "Strange. It seems as though any reference to one particular person has been erased."

"Not just that, but anything that might give us a clue as to what their relationship was to the case is gone with it." Tremaine looked hopefully at Kenzies. "You don't remember?"

"I should," Kenzies said. "I don't." She held the file out to Gunn, snapping his fingers for the document.

Gunn's lips moved as he read over the report. His scowl deepened. "Who was the last person to read this?"

"I'll have to check the records back at the Department," Tremaine started.

Nate edged closer to the corpse. Now that the initial horror had worn off, a new one had taken its place. Was this death following the pattern that Peter had established? Hunter had a particular type when it came to men, and Nate had been very lucky not to end up dead like Brook. He had to know. Could this have been him?

The man's hair was a light brown, very different from Nate's short black hair. He was older, with a heavily lined face, and deep purple bags around his eyes. At first glance, Nate had taken him as toned, but looking closer, he could see that the man was merely extremely thin—

The man's eyes jerked open.

Nate's mouth moved, but he couldn't speak. He could only stare, caught by the dangerous glitter in the eyes that should not be working at all.

The man's mouth stretched wide, baring wickedly sharp teeth in a smile that promised violence. He raised himself from the stone, his movements at odds with his body. Little things like pain from twisted muscles or balance didn't mean much to a revenant. They registered only one thing: insatiable hunger. The man growled and leaped.

Run! The thought came much too late for Nate, trapped by the awful certainty of death. He stumbled backward.

Thunder boomed suddenly, unexpectedly. The corpse swayed. A hole appeared in his chest, driving him backward. There was another crack of thunder, and he dropped to his knees. A rough hand jerked Nate away from him, and a storm of gunfire broke out. Nate saw the man twitch and spasm in a gross parody of life and finally fall.

"God."

Kenzies kept her gun leveled at the body. "Hurt, Nate?"

It took Nate a startled second to grasp her meaning. He looked down at himself, registering for the first time that the hand on his arm was Hunter's, and that the vampire was positioned in front of him. "No. Just...shaken."

Gunn lowered his pistol and approached the corpse. "Where were you standing, Nate? Here?" He crouched. "Looks like you were right, Tremaine. A deliberate trap."

"And you let me spring it?" Nate couldn't keep the dismay out of his voice.

"No one else could. We figured knowing who the trap was aimed at would tell us a lot about who set it." Gunn looked down at the body with a frown. "If it helps, Hunter was going to be our next attempt."

"Your manner is charming as ever." Hunter dusted himself off. "Though, I hate to admit your method is not without result."

Nate wrapped his arms around himself. "What do you mean?"

"It's obvious, isn't it?" The tent was thick with the smell of gunpowder, but Gunn still lit a cigarette. "I imagine there's a few people in New Camden who would like to take a shot at you, but only one with the knowledge to rig up a revenant to attack you—and only you."

Nate had felt sick before. Now he felt nauseated. "Peter's back."

Gunn took a long drag on the cigarette. "Back, and it looks like he's out for revenge." He grinned. "It's been far too quiet around here."

CENTURY WAS PACKED. Nate squeezed through the foyer after Gunn. The crowd was so thick that the Department Seven officer, who'd made the unusual decision to change into uniform for the visit, did not raise any eyebrows, any more than Nate did, dressed down in his battered T-shirt and jeans.

When they reached the staff-only staircase, Gunn stopped Nate. "I'd like to talk to your boss alone. Wait here."

"Sure." Nate did not object to the chance to gather his thoughts. He loitered in the stairwell, listening to the music pumped through Century's speakers with a feeling of dislocation. The beat was fast, with an accelerating baseline that spoke directly to the pulse. In any other circumstance, that would have Nate on the dance floor in an instant. Now, dancing was the last thing on his mind.

Nate clenched his fists. *Another guy dead because of me.*

He couldn't stop thinking about the dead man. He had a worn face, the kind acquired through a mortgage, a partner, and kids. He must have family somewhere, people who missed him. Perhaps right now his family was learning that he wouldn't be coming home ever again.

And he was dead, just to set a trap for Nate. *It's my fault—just like Peter's death was my fault.* Nate winced, but he couldn't escape the thought. He leaned back against the wall of the staircase, wrapping his arms around himself. He had a sick feeling in the pit of his stomach. *I didn't know my magic would kill him!* It was the first time he had used his powers on purpose. They were still new. Even now, Nate was unsure what exactly had happened.

I took control of Peter's necromancy, turned it into plants... Nate frowned. That much was clear. In trying to control Nate, Peter had inadvertently linked them, allowing Nate access to the workings of his spells. *But I went too far. Somehow, I turned Peter into a plant—*

"Nate!" Aki barreled into him. "You should have told me you were here! I've been so worried!"

Nate squirmed. He'd hoped to avoid notice by sticking to the staff-only areas. Clothes aside, he felt ill at ease at the club. With everything he'd seen, the idea that other people were having fun, enjoying life, was too much to take. "I sent you a text. Told you I was okay."

"You don't get attacked by a revenant and be okay!" Aki released Nate from his chokehold and stepped back, eyeing him critically. "I know you. You might not be hurt, but there's no way you're not shaken."

Aki knew him well. Sometimes too well. "I'll be fine. I'm just not in a social mood."

Aki snorted. "Reassuring your best friend that you're not going to do something stupid isn't socializing. It's a necessity." He eyed Nate. "Please tell me you don't feel sorry for that thing."

"He was a person until tonight." Nate bit his lip.

"Nate!" Aki stomped his foot. "This is what gets you into trouble! You have to stop feeling sorry for monsters and concentrate on taking care of yourself!"

"This is different. The guy that got killed, it was a trap aimed at me. I can't just shrug it off and say it's none of my business."

Aki narrowed his eyes. "Can't you? Because I can—"

An electronic buzzing sound interrupted him.

They both looked down at Nate's wristband. The sleek black band was standard issue for Century staff, but the technology contained within the seemingly benign device was anything but ordinary. The wristband contained a credit-card reader, GPS system, heart-rate monitor, emergency alarm, and other features designed to keep Century's workers safe. It also contained the in-house messaging system currently being employed.

"Denise wants to see me." It was rare that Denise demanding his presence in her office was a relief. She was notoriously strict when it came to the safety of her workers. There was no way she would take the news of Nate's evening well. But compared to Aki, obviously worried...

Aki narrowed his eyes. "I think it's a really dumb idea," he said. "Seriously stupid and you shouldn't even consider it. But why listen to me? I am only your best friend. Stupid me, for wanting you to take care of yourself!" He flounced off, heading for the club and within seconds was lost from sight among the club-goers crowding the dance floor.

Nate stared after him. He had no idea what Aki was referring to, only that his friend was genuinely worried. He remembered his feeling of that afternoon, and a shiver crept down his shoulders. Maybe Aki's right. Maybe I should stay out of it.

Too late for that, the feeling whispered. Nate remembered the dead man's eyes fixing on him. He began to climb the stairs.

Nate had spent so much time in Denise's office that he found his way automatically. He knocked and pushed the door open. "I'm here."

"Take a seat, Nate." Denise stood at her desk, dressed in the pastel-green suit that was her trademark. She folded her arms across her ample chest as she subjected Nate to an intense examination, very similar to the one he'd just received from Aki. "Gunn has just informed me why you missed the start of your shift. You are not hurt in any way?"

Nate shook his head. "Shaken, but fine."

The first time Nate had met Gunn, he'd been sprawled insolently across Denise's sofa. Now, he sat up straight, his hands resting on his knees. "Nate's safety was never in question. Three Department Seven officers including myself were ready in the event he was threatened."

But sharing that info would have spoiled the witness? Nate looked to Denise for permission to sit and at her nod helped himself to an armchair. "It's not that the revenant tried to attack to me that I mind. It's that it happened at all." Nate hesitated. The necromancer's reign of terror over New Camden had claimed many victims—among them Denise. Broaching the subject was the last thing he wanted to do, but how could they avoid it? "If Peter is back, more people are going to die."

Denise's expression sharpened, like a string pulled tight. "We were told the necromancer was dead."

"Unfortunately, death is not as permanent as it once was." Gunn's eyes flickered over Denise speculatively, but he clearly decided against saying anything. "Especially to a someone who specializes in death like a necromancer. It was always a possibility that Peter left behind some means of resurrection. If that's the case, he just had to wait for some fool to trigger it."

Nate stared at Gunn. Denise did not like talking about her death. As a *lemur*, Gunn must sense that. *A prime chance to get under her skin...and he's ignoring it?* Nate looked from Gunn to Denise, conscious that something was off.

If Denise noticed Gunn's restraint, she clearly wasn't impressed by it. "Do you know for a fact that is what happened?"

"No. And that's why we need Nate." Gunn nodded to Nate. "I asked Denise if I can hire you."

Nate froze. He liked Gunn just fine—usually—but this was more than he was prepared for. *I didn't think Gunn liked me like that—liked anyone like that!* The *lemur* gave the impression of being more interested in women. "I, uh...have to think about it."

"Of course Nate needs time to consider." Denise sat on the edge of her desk. "Assisting Department Seven is a serious undertaking. You can't guarantee his safety."

"Maybe not," Gunn conceded. "But he'll be safer with us than he'll be on his own—and your clientele will be safer if Nate's not here." He leaned forward across the coffee table. "If Peter is back and he's targeting Nate, where is he going to go to find him? He knows where Nate works. On the other hand, with Nate assisting us, we can track him down, contain him, and neutralize him much faster than we could otherwise."

Oh, thank God. For a terrified minute, Nate had thought Gunn wanted him for his sexual skills. "What do you mean, assisting Department Seven?"

Gunn smirked at him. "We'll make you a special officer. You'll come with me and Kenzies as we look into this. We need your knowledge and your powers."

Nate looked at his feet. "It's my powers that started this." He bit his lip. "That's why Peter's targeting me, isn't it? Because I killed him."

"Best thing you ever did." Gunn patted his jacket, searching for a cigarette case before remembering where he was. He sat up, trying to pass the gesture off as nothing. "You also tracked him down when the entire city couldn't find him anywhere. It's my hunch that you're the key to this—and maybe you'd cause less trouble if you were in on our plans." He grinned at Nate's discomfort. "Just a thought."

Nate flushed. His attempts to help never worked out how he intended them. "I wouldn't have to have a gun or anything?" As a country kid, Nate knew how to shoot. But the idea of carrying a gun in a city made him seriously uncomfortable.

Gunn shook his head. "No gun, and you would always be accompanied by one of my team. Keeping you safe, the city safe, and trying my patience less."

Gunn has patience? "I don't know. I mean, there's my work here to think about." Nate was indentured to Century. He couldn't see safety-conscious Denise agreeing to the plan.

"Officer Gunn has considered the financial side of things." Denise's tone was cool, giving no hint of what she thought.

Nate looked suspiciously at Gunn. "And?" It was highly likely that Gunn, considering the financial strain that being co-opted by Department Seven would put on Nate, would be even keener to use him.

"The city is willing to foot the bill." Gunn slouched back against the back of the sofa, resting his battered boots on the coffee table. "Can't afford your full rate, of course. But in the circumstances Denise was willing to make us a deal." Gunn suddenly collected himself, sitting up with a speed that would have been comical if he wasn't one of the more terrifying people that Nate knew.

"You approve of this, Denise?"

His boss's gaze rested on him. "If it's what you want to do, then yes. But only if it's what you want to do."

Nate stared at the floor. He wasn't an investigator. He had been completely lost at the crime scene. Yes, he wanted to help people, but his track record in that area was not great. *This is only the start. There are going to be more deaths. I can't get involved.*

But I can't ignore this either. Gunn had come to him for help—and Gunn didn't ask for help from anyone. That meant that he truly believed they needed him. Nate raised his head. "Okay. I'll do it."

Gunn got to his feet. "Good man. I knew—" His phone buzzed. Gunn glanced down at it and his expression darkened. "I have to take this."

It wasn't until Gunn left the room that Nate realized a large part of the tension he felt was the officer's presence. He breathed out. *What have I gotten myself into?*

"Agreements made in the presence of a supernatural with power are not legally binding." Looking up, Nate saw Denise watching him closely. "If you have second thoughts, I'll tell Gunn you are unavailable."

It was tempting, but Nate shook his head. "No. If there is a chance I can stop Peter before anyone else gets hurt, I have to take it."

Denise pursed her lips. Her vivid red lipstick was too close a reminder of her bloody death for Nate's comfort, but Denise refused to let death change her. "Just remember that you're important too, Nate. You're not responsible for the necromancer."

Nate ducked his head. He couldn't look Denise in the eye. "I'll remember." He glanced at the door. "I'd better find Gunn."

Gunn paced the corridor, listening intently to the person on the other side of the phone call. "Yeah. Yeah. I got it. Put all units on full alert and inform the mayor. I'll be there as soon as I can." He hung up as Nate approached. "Ready to roll?"

Nate nodded. "Didn't you say we needed to stop by the department first?"

"No time." Gunn strode down the hall toward the stairway, forcing Nate to jog after him. "Welcome to the life of a Department Seven officer. No rest for the wicked—or anyone else."

"Something's happened." A feeling of dread settled over Nate's chest. "Another death?"

"Not yet—but something tells me it's only a matter of time." Gunn took the stairs two at a time. "Someone's only gone and robbed the Registry."

Nate scrambled to keep up. "You mean the place where all the records of New Camden's supernatural are kept? Why would anyone want to do that?"

Outside in the street, Gunn paused to fix a siren to the roof of his beat-up car. "I can think of a dozen reasons. None of them good."

Also Available from NineStar Press

Connect with NineStar Press

www.ninestarpress.com

www.facebook.com/ninestarpress

www.facebook.com/groups/NineStarNiche

www.twitter.com/ninestarpress

www.tumblr.com/blog/ninestarpress